I PLAY THE DRUMS IN A BAND CALLED *OKAY*

'Litt can sure as hell write' *Irish Times*

'Of all the films and books about being in a band, Toby's book is the most accurate and true to life, not necessarily the japes and hi-jinx that go on but the emotions and politics that exist between the ifferent band members. I thought it was a beautiful book, touching, subtle and very funny' Matthew Priest, Dodgy

'Well-written and deftly constructed' *Q*

's like he's been hiding under the beds in hotel rooms, in the corner rehearsal rooms, in the toilets in bars, in the darkest corners of our ninds, listening all the time. Spooky! Spinal Snap not Spinal Tap!' Peter Hook, New Order

'A measured, fully fleshed examination of what it means to be in a rock group' *Scotland on Sunday*

'Litt's crisp writing and sardonic wit make this a treat' *Elle*

'Unexpectedly profound and moving' *Sunday Herald*

Toby Litt was born in 1968. He grew up in Ampthill, Bedfordshire. A graduate of Malcolm Bradbury's Creative Writing MA at the University of East Anglia, he is the author of two books of short stories: *Adventures in Capitalism* and *Exhibitionism*, and eight novels: *Beatniks, Corpsing, deadkidsongs, Finding Myself, Ghost Story, Hospital, I play the drums in a band called okay* and *Journey into Space*. He edited Henry James's last novel, *The Outcry* for Penguin Modern Classics. He was also the co-editor, with Ali Smith, of the British Council/Picador *New Writing 13* anthology. He is a Granta Best of Young British Novelist. His website can be found at www.tobylitt.com

I play the drums in a band called *okay*

TOBY LITT ·

PENGUIN BOOKS

PENGUIN BOOKS

Published by the Penguin Group
Penguin Books Ltd, 80 Strand, London WC2R ORL, England
Penguin Group (USA) Inc., 375 Hudson Street, New York, New York 10014, USA
Penguin Group (Canada), 90 Eglinton Avenue East, Suite 700, Toronto, Ontario, Canada M4P 2Y3
(a division of Pearson Penguin Canada Inc.)
Penguin Ireland, 25 St Stephen's Green, Dublin 2, Ireland
(a division of Penguin Books Ltd)
Penguin Group (Australia), 250 Camberwell Road, Camberwell, Victoria 3124, Australia
(a division of Pearson Australia Group Pty Ltd)
Penguin Books India Pvt Ltd, 11 Community Centre, Panchsheel Park, New Delhi – 110 017, India
Penguin Group (NZ), 67 Apollo Drive, Rosedale, North Shore 0632, New Zealand
(a division of Pearson New Zealand Ltd)
Penguin Books (South Africa) (Pty) Ltd, 24 Sturdee Avenue, Rosebank, Johannesburg 2196, South Africa

Penguin Books Ltd, Registered Offices: 80 Strand, London WC2R ORL, England

www.penguin.com

First published by Hamish Hamilton 2008
Published in Penguin Books 2009

1

Typeset by Rowland Phototypesetting Ltd, Bury St Edmunds, Suffolk
Printed in Great Britain by Clays Ltd, St Ives plc

A CIP catalogue record for this book is available from the British Library

ISBN: 978-0-141-01792-1

www.greenpenguin.co.uk

For Henry and George

Acknowledgements

The author would like to thank Adam Warner, real-life Canadian drummer and God-hating Buddhist; Tony O'Neill, expert on the virgin of Guadeloupe; Richard Thomas, where vox meets roll; Matt Thorne, for the new sounds; Julian Grenier, for the old sounds.

All the band members of Senator, Eratnos 5, The Rotanes, Space Band, Platinum Demon, The Psychic Arabs, Squadron is Pill, Mujaki, Benzoin Silica, The Unhip, Click, Innocent People, Heat the Feet, Obviously Five Believers, The John Wesley Harding Band.

Also, Levon & John, Keith & Ringo, Mo & Karen, Charlie & Clem, Linn & Roland, Philly Joe & Bill, DJ & Elvin. Boom-tssk!

Versions of these episodes have appeared in the following places: 'Dog #1' (as 'Tourbusting') in *New Writing 8*, Vintage, and (as 'tourbusting1') in *Exhibitionism*, Hamish Hamilton, 2002, along with 'Lindsay' (as 'tourbusting2') in *Exhibitionism*, Hamish Hamilton, 2002; 'Roots' (as 'tourbusting3') in *Talk of the Town, Independent*; 'LA' (as 'tourbusting4') in *The Stinging Fly*; 'Yoyo' (as 'tourbusting5') in *Ambit* and *Inculte* (French); 'Lydia' (as 'tourbusting6') in *Stand*; '333' (as Girl333') in *3:AM – London, New York, Paris*, Social Disease, 2007, and *VLNA* (Slovak); 'Forest' (as 'Tree/Forest') in *Hype Magazine* (Czech). Thanks to all the editors.

And I remembered something you once told me
And I'll be damned if it did not come true
Twenty thousand roads I went down, down, down
And they all led me straight back home to you.

Gram Parsons,
'The Return of the Grievous Angel'

'Wouldn't the coolest thing now be to be Japanese, eh?'

We are in Rotterdam Europe lost in thick fog together.

'A bridge over a river next to a church. Haven't we walked past this once before?'

That's me, name of Clap, dissecting the bridge-river-church interface. With me, Nippo-theorizing, is Syph.

We are from Canada. We are in a band called *okay*, lower case, italics. We are on our second European tour.

'I mean, think about it. We can't match those copycats for hipness. No way. You see, Clap, we've completely forgotten how to be ourselves. But *they* know how. They know that it's about *choosing* who you want to be, not being destined to be anyone in particular. And they are better at choosing than we ever were.'

'Can we sit down for a minute?' I say. 'I'm not feeling too great.'

'When the Japanese are punks, they are the greatest punks ever; when they are rockabillies, not even Elvis can touch them.'

Twenty days in.

This is it – we have reached the point of self-annihilation. So much of what comprises who one is has been left behind. Jackson Browne found a phrase for it, Running On Empty. In this non-state you can go for two days without having a single real thought. *How did I get here?* – that is the thought that most intrudes. The non-thought is always – *next, next, next*. Next gig. Next girl. Next goodbye. Aspects of it I do sincerely appreciate – I love the sense of left-behindness. You never use a bar of hotel soap more than once – if at all. (And if you're really sensible, you carry your own with you: so that's not a very good example.) But if you don't like something – a magazine containing a bad review, a tape that's gone fucked in your Walkman – you just drop it. Within seconds, it is miles away. Another country. (As the lyrics to my favourite of our songs go: 'I've reached out in the dark to touch/Things a thousand miles away.') Similarly, if you freak out some girl and she has hysterics at you, she's two towns behind before her slap even hits your face. You become impervious to pain – of a non-serious sort. Self-harm becomes a bit of a game. (Not that *okay* are great ones for stage-diving. It's not part of our image.) You eat nothing but shit. You look like a piece of shit. And you talk shit a hundred per cent of the time.

Twenty days to go.

'You see them,' Syph continues to talk shit, 'walking around downtown – children dressed like souvenir teddy-bears – groups of girls with their heads close together and their hands over their mouths – couples holding hands, each so cool you can't decide between them – serious young men buying huge stacks of CDs – salarymen, who break into a sweat as they move from the pavement to the road – senior citizens in beige and fawn golfing clothing.'

I am the drummer. Syph is the lead vocalist. We have a bassist, Mono. We have a rhythm guitarist, Crab.

Our mothers did not call us by these names – though Syph's is starting to. None of us knows if she knows what it means.

'Do you remember when we were on tour in Tokyo?'

'I feel bad. I'm sitting down. You can keep walking.'

I sit down on a low concrete wall with black railings stuck in it looking out across a street of cobblestones and grey-green walls.

'Like, no-one gives blow-jobs like the Japanese. It's the kind of thing they probably have instruction manuals about that are a thousand years old. Like the Karma Sutra.'

'The *Kama Sutra* is Indian.'

I stand up, lean over the railings and puke into the hedge.

'They do ancient things with their tongues and with the roofs of their mouths.'

I hear a whining sound.

'Did you fart?' I ask.

Syph looks shocked. He can't remember.

'I don't think so,' he says. 'Was it in tune?'

I lean back over the railings and look beyond the hedge. I see a paw, an ear – black and white.

I turn back to Syph. I say: 'I think I just puked on someone's dog.'

'Are they Japanese?' he says, and does ancient things with his tongue.

'What are we going to do?' I ask.

'We need to score.'

Syph is right – we smoked the last of the grass before the border. Syph is superstitious about carrying grass over international divides. He says it has to do with Paul McCartney. But he is quite happy about having speed in his pocket while making passport control. Which means that, until we score some dope in each new city, he is unbearable. And because he is likely to speed his way into getting arrested, I always go with him to try and track something down. If we are lucky, there's someone from the local fan club to help us connect. But *okay* aren't very big in Rotterdam, as we are finding out.

'I'm going to have a look at it.'

'Whatever,' says Syph, and plucks his Marlboros from his suit pocket.

Members of *okay* wear suits at all times. We play gigs in suits and we play hockey in suits. It's part of our image.

Our music is slow and formal with lyrics about love and guilt. We also sing about the sea.

We sound like the Velvet Underground on quarter-speed.

Climbing over the railings feels surprisingly easy. I haven't eaten anything in two days. Maybe I am getting the better of gravity.

I fall into the hedge, branches digging into my legs through my suit.

With a flip of my arms I roll off onto a patch of grass.

'Are you okay?' says Syph.

'Dollar,' I reply, keeping very still.

Whenever one of us uses the name of our band in a context not relating specifically to our band, that person is required to put a dollar in the stash-pot. It is a band rule.

'You didn't break your back?'

'I'm fine,' I say. I haven't opened my eyes yet. I don't feel any pain in my body.

Then a warm wetness crosses my nose and I smell a bad smell. I open my eyes into the face of the dog.

'Hi,' I say.

It continues licking.

I'm not sure if the bad smell is the smell of the dog's breath or the smell of my puke, which runs all down the dog's back.

I roll away.

The dog tries to follow me, to carry on licking, but it is tied to the railings by its lead.

'You've gone all quiet,' says Syph, then laughs. 'Is the dog Japanese?'

'Throw me your smokes and your lighter,' I say.

He throws them. I light up. I throw them back.

'Shit,' he says. 'That almost went down the drain.'

'Sorry,' I say.

I lie on my side on the lawn in Rotterdam Europe looking at the dog.

It is a mongrel, black and white. It doesn't look like anything much. Except thin. It looks kind of bony and shaky. Like Syph.

To this day, he's never been able to find a pair of pants that stay up. His mother used to make him wear suspenders or dungarees. For a while his nickname was Huck.

The girls always loved him. Still do.

Some nights I get seconds and some nights thirds and

maybe once a tour I'll settle for fourths. But Syph always gets firsts.

We drummers have our own distinct kind of girls. They are enthusiastic long before you are successful and loyal long after you're shit.

Drummer-girls tend to have long hair and large breasts and bring their own contraceptives and leave when asked.

Lead-singer-girls, from what I've seen and heard of them, are model-like and neurotic and bring drugs and want to do really weird sex-things on you so that you never forget them.

Some nights Syph doesn't even get laid, because none of the girls in that town comes up to his high standards. But that is rare. Syph's standards vary from town to town. Sometimes he ends up with Little Miss Rancid-and-a-half. (And I end up with her mutant grandmother.)

'It's a nice dog,' I say.

I look down at myself. There are a couple of muddy paw prints on my shirt. There is a bit of puke on my lapel.

'I think it's homeless.'

'Hey!' I hear Syph shout. 'Hey! Yeah!'

'Yeah?' I say.

'Come over here, I wanna talk to you. Yeah, come on. Yeah. Hi, I'm Steve.'

It was a girl. It wasn't hard to tell.

'What's your name?'

There is a giggle.

'I'm Inge.'

'Would you like a cigarette, Inge?'

'I have to go.'

'Hey, Syph!' I shout. 'Ask her if she knows whose dog this is?'

'Who is there?' Inge asks.

She was *so* beautiful. I just knew it was going to break my heart all over again to watch Syph closing his hotel door behind them as they walked in, smiling.

'That's my drummer,' said Syph. 'He's found a dog.'

Inge says, 'A dog?'

'Yeah,' says Syph. 'Woof-woof.'

Usually the beautiful ones laugh at Syph's less funny jokes. And the more beautiful they are, the more they laugh. And the sooner that door closes behind them.

I decide to stand up.

'Do you happen to know where we might chance upon some blow?' Syph is now doing his comic Englishman.

When I get to my feet I find myself standing face to face with an angel called Inge, with only a vomit-covered hedge separating us. Inge is very slim with short-cropped white-blonde hair. Her eyes are dream-blue. And oh her skin . . .

'I'm Inge,' she says.

Syph rises to stand slim-hipped beside her.

'I'm Brian,' I say, hating my name totally.

'Where is the dog?' she asks.

'It's down here.' I point. 'Is this a garden or something?'

'I think it is a park,' Inge says. 'I will come round.'

Without turning towards Syph she starts off.

When she gets a few paces away Syph looks at me and mouths: *mine.*

I shake my head.

'Musical differences,' I say. This is the threat anyone in the band always makes when they take something so seriously that they are prepared to break up the band over it.

'I saw her first,' says Syph. 'You wouldn't even have said hi.'

'If it hadn't've been for the dog, she'd've walked off.'

'I tell you, if she goes for me I'm having her.'

Inge has found a way into the park.

'Hello,' she says, and holds out her hand to be shaken. 'Brian.'

She has an angel's ankles.

'Hi,' I say.

We shake.

Then she turns her attention seriously to the dog, address-

8

ing it in Dutch or whatever language they speak in Rotterdam. She can't fail to notice the puke, but she doesn't seem to associate it with me. I reach in my pocket and take out some gum to chew, to get rid of the smell.

Syph climbs up on the railings, jumps the hedge and joins us.

'What does he say?' I ask. 'Does he belong to anyone? Are they coming back?'

Inge says, 'I think he was left because they want him not.'

'Sometimes they have addresses on their collar,' says Syph.

Inge says, 'There is no address.'

Inge stands up.

'What were you going to do?' she asks.

I look at Syph. Inge's eyes follow mine.

'Well,' he says, 'we are actually going to score some blow. Do you know where we could find some?'

Inge turns back to me – a little shrug, eyes rolling to the heavens-where-she-belongs.

'I was going to wait here to see if his owner came back. Then I was going to try and find a police station.'

And please can I kiss you?

'Give me your handkerchiefs,' she says.

Members of *okay* have handkerchiefs in the breast pockets of our suits at all time. It's part of our image.

'We must clean the dog.'

I hand over part of my image quite happily. Syph is flirting with the idea of refusing and of using his refusing as a way of flirting.

'Give it her,' I say.

Inge cleans most of my puke off the black and white dog with our handkerchiefs.

'You want them again?' she asks.

Syph says, 'Nope.'

I say, 'Yep.'

Inge hands them back, and I wrap them in the handkerchief I always keep in my side pocket for real use.

'I will take you to the police station,' Inge says.

Syph looks at me with *no way* in his eyes.

'But we have to be somewhere else,' he says. 'Don't we?'

'I'll come with you,' I say.

Inge kneels down and unties the dog's lead from the branch of the hedge.

'But we need to score,' says Syph.

'See you back at the hotel,' I say.

Inge looks inquiringly at both of us.

'Come on, boy,' I say to the dog.

Inge speaks to it in the Rotterdam language.

We walk off, leaving Syph behind.

Outside the park gates we turn left into the fog.

'You are drummer in a group?' Inge asks.

I am stunned. She's been paying more attention to Syph than she's let on. She really doesn't like him.

'Yeah. We're on tour. We're playing tonight at some club.' As I am halfway through the line, I go on with it anyway. 'Would you like to come?'

'Maybe,' she says. 'The police station is very close here.'

I hear footsteps running behind us in the fog. I don't need to look. Things have been going too well. It is Syph.

'I thought I'd lost you guys,' he says.

Inge leads us up to a doorway and into the police station.

Inge tells the policeman the story in the Rotterdam language. He then asks us to confirm a few details in English. It seems like Inge's left out any mention of the puke. I am glad of that.

We give them the name and address of our hotel.

Inge gives them her address and telephone number.

Inge and I say goodbye to the dog and watch the policeman take it off down a long white corridor.

On the foggy street outside the police station, Inge says, 'What is the name of your band?'

'It's *okay*,' I say. 'Spelt o-k-a-y.' And just so she knows, I tell her the name of the club we're playing at.

'Do you know where we can score?' whispers Syph.

Inge looks at him pitifully.

'Come on,' she says, and leads us off round the corner.

Unexpectedly, she stops, reaches into her rucksack and brings out a clingfilm-wrapped chunk of dope. She breaks off a corner and hands it to Syph.

'God,' he says. 'The woman of my dreams.'

Inge turns to me.

'You are a kind person,' she says, and kisses me on the cheek. 'Good-bye.'

I watch as she walks off into the fog.

Syph doesn't even look. He is sniffing the dope.

'This is really good shit,' he says. 'Let's get back to the hotel.'

That evening the lighting set-up means that I am unable to see anything of the audience – it is just a sheet of white light which applauds whenever we finish a song.

Our set-list goes: 'Thousand', 'Blissfully', 'Jane-Jane', 'Motherhood', 'Sea-Song #4', 'Hush-hate-hum', 'Walls', 'Queen Victoria', 'Long Cold Lines', 'With Strings', 'Gustav Klimt' and 'Work'. We encore with 'Sea-Song #1' and our cover of 'Marquee Moon'.

Syph dedicates one song to a girl we met today. Thanks. For services rendered.

At the end of the encores, I walk straight up to the mic and say, 'Inge, if you're here, I'll see you in the bar.'

Two Inges show up, neither of which is the right one.

Back in the dressing-room there is a drummer-girl but I brush her off.

'I'm going for a walk,' I say.

'What?' says Mono.

'A walk?' says Crab.

'See you back at the hotel,' I say.

'Maybe,' says Syph, who has one girl sitting in his lap and one opening him a beer.

For an hour or so, I wander about trying to find my way back to the park. But the fog has gotten even thicker and everywhere looks even more the same.

I stop a cab and tell the guy to take me back to the hotel.

Inge is sitting in the lobby with the black and white dog at her feet. As I walk up the dog I puked on recognizes me and starts to strain on its lead.

'You didn't come to the gig,' I say.

'I was there,' she says. 'I left.'

'I asked you to meet me in the bar. Didn't you hear?'

'I thought you would get another girl. I wanted to see. I came to wait here.'

'What, you were testing me?'

'I don't know,' she says, smiling. 'Maybe.'

'Hi,' I say to the dog.

Someone has obviously given it a bath. And love. He licks the salty spaces between my fingers, looking up at me with wet eyes.

'Brian meet Brian,' says Inge.

'They let you keep it?' I ask.

'I went back and told them that the story we said before was a lie. I told them that I lived with you and that you didn't want the dog, so that you made me give it to them. I told them that we had split up and that I wanted my dog back. They didn't want the problem of a dog. They gave it to me without question.'

'Do you have a boyfriend?' I ask.

'No,' she says. 'I have a dog called Brian.'

I am very close to saying woof-woof.

Just then, Syph and his two girls, both Japanese, plus Mono, Crab and their girls, plus several other girls and a couple of boys come through the hotel doors.

'Great dope,' Syph says to Inge as he walks up.

His girls are already getting jealous. They touch him even more.

'Musical differences,' I say to the whole band. 'I'm afraid to say.'

'Nice doggie,' says Mono.

'Irreconcilable musical differences.'

'Really?' asks Crab.

'You have dope?' asks one of Mono's girls.

'Yes,' I say. 'I think so.'

Syph says, 'No way.'

'Yoko,' says Crab.

I smile at Inge and she smiles back.

'Let's go,' Inge says.

And I say, 'Okay.'

That last bit didn't really happen. It's just how I daydreamed it the following afternoon on the tourbus. Cologne was next. Then Munich. Then Berlin. Nineteen days to go. What really happened was that I went back to the hotel, alone, only to find Inge not there. No sign of that dog, either. Then I went for a walk, to try and find the park or the police station. But I couldn't. I got lost again in the fog. Then I stopped a cab and told the guy to take me back to the hotel. That detail was true. Syph and the others were there in the bar with a group of girls. None of them was Japanese. But one of them I saw straight off was a drummer-girl. I think she had long hair and large breasts and brought her own contraceptives and left when asked. It's just, you meet so many and remember so few.

LINDSAY

I'd like to tell you about Lindsay, now, if you'd like to hear.

(I think I mentioned her yesterday or the day before, when we were in that bar, in, you know – that one with the ... yeah, right. Wild, huh?)

I knew Lindsay all the way through high school, but we never really dated. I have my suspicions that we kissed, once, maybe – I can't remember where or when. And I can't think why. I didn't even like her then, and she was in love with – well, I'll tell you that later.

(This isn't for the profile, you understand. This is just, like, between you and me. Because I *like* you.)

Anyway, I can't remember the first time we met, either. Though it was probably in a corridor somewhere. You always meet the most important people in your life in corridors or on stairs. Never in rooms. Don't you think that's weird? And we would've not even – whoa, let's try that again. We didn't shake hands. We just, I guess, shrugged and said *hi*.

Just saying that to you now makes me think I can see it all over again: Lindsay pulling the hair out of her eyes with a half-curled finger. But that's way too convenient to be a real memory, isn't it?

(Can I borrow another cigarette? I always fucking forget to buy them when we pit-stop.)

Anyway, we were just starting to form the band that later went on to make history as *okay*.

(Thanks.)

Only later did we get our famous nicknames. I wasn't yet Clap: I was just plain Brian. And Lindsay was just plain Lindsay – and Lindsay, really, was always just *plain*. She looked unfortunately like Carole King or Laura Nyro. One of those great women songwriters who you just love, and really try hard to find attractive, but just can't. Nina Simone, even. Where you love them with your eyes closed and them singing, but you can't even bear to have their poster on your wall.

We used to rehearse over in this shack that used to be attached to a church. But the church was gone. Someone bought it – the whole thing – and moved it to another town. It was made of corrugated iron.

And I heard, where they moved it to, they put it inside *another* church. And they called it something like 'the heart of the Lord'. Because the new church didn't feel like it had any o' dat ol'-time religion in it: so they drove down the road, stopped off and bought some. Seriously.

One of the walls of this shack was wood, the rest were iron. Sometimes, if you got the feedback going just right and loud enough, you could make the whole thing shake like it was going to fall down on top of you.

Lindsay was our first fan. Also, I suppose, our first groupie – though I think only two of us actually slept with her.

(I'll let you figure out who.)

When we were just banging away, sounding really trashy, she would sit there behind one of the amps – nodding her head like we were the Velvets or something. In the beginning, Lindsay was really important to us – really encouraging. When we were down, she'd say, 'Hey, you were really getting somewhere today.' In fact, she could hear things in us that we couldn't hear ourselves. She heard *through* us. I think, back then, she heard everything we've ever done since – right up to the break-ups and beyond.

I know a lot of people have come along claiming to have discovered us. But it's Lindsay really that was the first. If you asked the others, if you asked Syph, he probably wouldn't even remember her. She's exactly the kind of thing he was always trying to forget.

What makes me feel really guilty is that we kind of dumped her early on. Like a girlfriend who's becoming an embarrassment. We had to. There was a reason. Banging away at our practice sessions in that iron shack, we were actually getting to be quite good. But no-one knew it, and when we told people, they wouldn't believe it. In school we were actually known as 'the band that Lindsay hangs out with'. You see, association with Lindsay was making us out to look like losers. The logic went something like this: the girls thought, *They must be really sad and unsexy if Lindsay's the only girl who hangs out with them*; the boys thought, *Why go and see them play, there's no-one there but Lindsay to pick up?* And so Syph dumped her for us, on our behalf. He found some lame excuse, like she'd been stealing patch cables or something, and he balled her out and threw her out and that was that.

Almost immediately, a better class of girl started to come around. In other words, getting rid of Lindsay *worked*. It helped give us a start. When we played, the girls came. And when the girls came, the boys came. They all liked the music.

I remember the first time we played to over fifty people, and that was like a big deal for us back then – Lindsay was there, standing at the back, crying: all through the gig, crying. She tried to speak to Syph afterwards, but he just blew past her – blew her off. I stopped and talked for a while.

'You're doing really well,' she said. 'You sound really tight. You're going to make it.'

And we did, in a sort of way. We weren't the Beatles or anything. But we started to get the opening slots. We could headline locally. Play anywhere we liked, locally.

Next thing we knew, we had the deal, cut the record and started to go off on tours. We went to Great Britain first of all. Support slot. Before we'd even toured properly at home. I've always liked Great Britain. My mother came from there. My grandmother still lives there. This music paper, the *NME*, gave us a really good review for one of our singles. 'Sea-Song #1' I think it was. And lots of people turned up for this gig at the Marquee Club. Like that Television song, 'Marquee Moon'.

But you know all that shit already. I'm going to try to stay focused on Lindsay from now on.

We were away for about two months. Did Holland, gateway to Europe, and then Belgium, Germany and Spain – or maybe not Spain. Italy. When we got back, we went into the studio to record. That was the second album. The shack had long ago been knocked down, and the 'good old days' were knocked down with it. We started to get really serious about things like The Snare Sound – which is when you know it's starting to go a little wrong. Honestly, no-one cares about The Snare Sound. Or like, one per cent of people do – the ones that listen on hi-fis that cost more than they get paid in a year.

So, Lindsay wasn't around to hook up with. I only saw her again by accident. She was working in the library – behind the counter, checking out books. I went in there to get something by August Strindberg, who this English music journalist told me I'd, you know, *empathize* with.

(That was how come we wrote the song 'August'. It wasn't the month, it was the gloomiest fucking playwright that ever stuck a pair of cripples on-stage and made them hate each other. But I guess you know that already. Done your research all the way, haven't you?)

I didn't recognize her at first. She was wearing these bottle-thick glasses. Her hair was done up in bobbie pins. Not fancy ones with butterflies on or anything. Just plain brown slides. And her hair was the same old Carole King Jewfro – you know, thick, really thick. And the slides just couldn't cope. They kept pinging out onto the books.

I stood looking at her from behind one of those turnaround things they stack paperbacks on. The sight of her made me want to cry, really. I mean, she had never looked anything like good. But it was as if she were trying *really* hard to look shitty. And nature was giving her more than all the help she'd need.

Here we come to the second thing that makes me feel

guilty: I didn't speak to her that time. I found a back way out, so I didn't have to walk past the counter again.

I was feeling bad the whole way home. I couldn't stop thinking about it. What if she'd seen me? What if she knew I'd decided not to go up and talk to her? She'd think I was playing the big star.

(But then, what the fuck – I was going into a library! We hadn't made any money then. None at all. Top Ten album, and *no money*. Believe it.)

All the band met up that night in a pizza place, and we were surrounded by really good-looking women. Syph was playing the local hero. Really, he was such a *knob*. Dropping names of people he'd seen, like, for five seconds crashing the Executive Lounge at some airport. Like he'd jammed with them all night in the studio. And I couldn't stop thinking about Lindsay.

So, anyway, the next day I go round to the library. And on the way I even buy her a bunch of flowers. I don't know why. I wanted to say sorry for not talking to her the day before. But I also didn't want her to know that I hadn't talked to her the day before. So I realized I couldn't give her the flowers. So I hid them behind a fence before I got there.

(Went back to pick them up later, and they'd gone. Some fucker had seen them and stolen them. To give to his poor disabled mother, I hope. (Isn't it weird the things you remember?))

I'm rambling, I know. It's the JD talking. What was I saying?

(The library – right. The library.)

It was a big yellow building. Made out of concrete. But somehow yellow. '70s yellow – like California sunshine going down on the hood of a gold Chevrolet. She was in the exact same place, and I pretended just to notice her when I went up to get the Strindberg book out. It was black and had about four plays in. One of them was *Ghost Sonata*, the play the journalist had namechecked. Lindsay was so delighted to see me, it made me feel even worse about the day before. We agreed to go for coffee, after she got off.

(I can remember *so* many girls working behind counters who, before the band made it, I'd wanted to ask when they got off. But it never worked out – if I did ask, they never said *around six thirty*. And now, when it didn't matter at all, when it meant something completely different, it was the easiest thing in the world.)

I turned up back at the library. I told her I'd gone home, but I'd just gone and sat in the park and read that weird fucking play. I was so nervous I could hardly read. I don't know why. I have no idea. I mean, this was Lindsay – Lindsay who looked like Carole King: I didn't find her at all attractive. I couldn't remember having talked to her that much, even when we were rehearsing in the shack.

She came down the concrete stairs in the sunlight. My hands were shaking, like a half-hour after a great show – adrenalin. I was glad to see she hadn't done anything with her hair or her appearance generally. That would have suggested she had *hope* – which would have broken my heart. I didn't want her to have any hope as far as me and loving her was concerned.

(Does that sound cruel? I meant it to sound kind. I felt really ... compassionate towards her. God, that sounds even worse, doesn't it?)

She noticed the shaking in my hands.

'Caffeine,' I said.

'Yeah,' she said. 'I know. It's terrible. Shall we go get some more?'

We went and sat there, in one of the booths in the coffee shop. It was an old high-school hang. A few of the students knew who I was, and looked at me, but this was before anyone started coming up for autographs.

Lindsay said, 'I was surprised to see you getting that out.' She meant the Strindberg.

I explained about the journalist.

'That's very studious of you,' she said. 'It's not exactly rockstar behaviour.'

I flashed back to Syph, bumping past and cutting her at that first big gig.

'Well,' I said, 'I'm not exactly a star. I'm a drummer. Drummers are never stars.'

'Except Ringo,' Lindsay said.

As I laughed, even though it was a bit lame, I realized how much I *liked* Lindsay.

Liking isn't meant to be a particularly strong emotion: the whole liking vibe is meant to be pretty mild. But sometimes, you know, you can just be overwhelmed with how much you like someone. And at that moment I *liked* Lindsay more than I've ever liked anyone. I wanted everything to go well for her. Her job. Her life. Love.

We talked about Strindberg for a while. She'd read him, and knew a lot more about him than I'd managed to pick up in the previous four hours. Then she started to ask about what life in the band was like. I told her. I told her the old stories, but I tried to put some truth back into them. I didn't exaggerate as much as usual. I really wanted to give her some idea of what it was like, although I wasn't sure if that would make her feel bad about not being there with us. She wanted to hear, I think. I wasn't just torturing her. Thinking back, I should probably have insisted on asking her more questions. Because this coffee date – which wasn't a date – set up our relationship for what was going to be the rest of it. She would ask; I would answer.

My liking-buzz started to wear off. Lindsay's breath smelt a little, and she had a slightly annoying way of dropping her jaw and going *Wow* whenever I said anything even remotely starry. I tried to keep liking her as hard and as much as I had when she told the joke, but it just didn't work. It was easier to concentrate on telling her the stories that she wanted to hear. We talked till late. I kissed her on the cheek when we said good-bye. Even half-hugged her.

I'd like to say something like *As she turned away from me, smiling, I thought, Maybe there's just a chance* –

That would be a lie. I had a girlfriend. I *thought* I loved her.

I saw Lindsay a couple more times, before we went off on tour again.

And that was how we fell into the rhythm. I'd be gone like five, six months. When I came back round, older, tireder, more famous, richer – having had huge amounts more sex (I decided pretty soon I didn't really love that old girlfriend of mine) – I would go to the library. Lindsay would be there. It seemed like from one tour to the next, she didn't move from the Books Out counter. Her hair never got longer or changed.

In all the madness that goes on, she was the thing I clung to. I would be getting loaded in some Tokyo strip bar, and I'd be thinking about Lindsay stamping books. She was my *O Canada*.

Whenever I heard Joni or Carole or Laura, and I had tapes of theirs for the bus, I thought of Lindsay. I often wished she were more beautiful, so I could make her into my poster-girl – put her up on the wall in my head.

Sometimes, when I made it home, I'd even go to the library intending to start something with her: her goodness was so much more important than all the sluts on the road who just want to say they've banged someone in the band.

But when I saw her, standing like she always did, where she always did, I knew it wasn't meant to be.

We became like old people in our habits. We'd go out for coffee, and try and sit in the usual booth. We'd order the same thing. At some point, I'd get that same *whoosh* of power-liking. (Power-liking, I like that.) Then it would fade away. She'd ask me questions; I'd tell her what she wanted to hear. Sometimes, I sounded to myself like Syph – Thurston Moore this, Michael Stipe that. Lindsay was my hometown reality check. She was the valve on the decompression chamber.

So, one time, when I got back from a whole six-month deal

– touring the fifth album (the live one) – it destroyed me to find she wasn't there.

I mean, I was half-destroyed just by her not being at the Books Out counter. I'd always believed there were worn places in the lino where she used to stand. Another librarian was in her place. A boy. He knew who I was. When I tried to ask him where Lindsay was, he was like, 'You know *Lindsay*?'

'Yeah,' I said. 'Where is she?'

I knew he was going to ask me for my autograph. He just had the *look*.

'You don't know about Lindsay.'

'What about her?' I said.

'She left.'

'Left where?'

'Left town, I guess.'

'Left to go where?'

'I'm not sure. I can ask.'

'Ask,' I said.

He hesitated.

'*Then* you can have my autograph,' I said.

He went off. I heard him say *asshole*. Perhaps he *hadn't* wanted the autograph.

When he came back he said, 'They don't know.'

'Let me talk to them,' I said. 'It's very important that I find out where she is.'

Because, you see, in all those times we'd gone for coffee, I'd never got her number or found out where she lived. She was always at the library. I didn't need her address.

The librarian-boy goes and gets the head librarian, Miss Watts, who was like this figure of myth from my childhood. She used to be as tall as New York City. (Crab had nicknamed one of his amps Miss Watts.)

'How are you, Brian?' she asks.

We chat for long enough for it to seem polite, then I ask about Lindsay.

Pretty soon it becomes clear that Miss Watts really *doesn't* know where Lindsay went. Reading between the lines, it sounds like Lindsay especially didn't want Miss Watts to know where she was going.

I was able to get Lindsay's home address out of her.

Miss Watts asked for my autograph, for her daughter.

When I dropped by Lindsay's old place, it was an apartment block. After pressing all the buzzers, someone let me in. The elevator had piss in one corner. Her number was 44. No-one was in.

I left a note with my number.

No-one rang.

All that time I was away on tour, Lindsay wasn't behind the counter in the library. She was living in an apartment block where people pissed in the elevator.

And that's Lindsay for you. That's all I know.

I hope she's happy, wherever she is. Whatever she's doing.

When I think of her these days, though, she isn't in the library. She's back behind the amps, reading some philosophy book. She looks younger, and better than she ever really did – like your memory of Carole King when you're trying to be kind in your mind about what she looks like.

Hey, on second thoughts, maybe you could put something about her in the profile.

Just a line at the end.

'Lindsay, if you're out there, call.'

Something like that.

Or maybe not.

(Hey, forget it. You know. Forget. It.)

Friends make jokes about you being famous, to let you know that's what you've become, and that it's starting to worry them – as it should.

I never thought we were *that* big a deal, until we paid our third visit to England.

First time over had just been us supporting a band called John Craven, who split shortly afterwards. Their fans hated us, and we only had about five of our own – and those were too poor or shy to travel from gig to gig.

Second time was better. We headlined, and sold out half the midsize venues we were booked to play. There was a TV on the bus. At least a hundred of the fans I met claimed they'd seen us on the first tour.

But the third time (just promotion, no gigs), we had girls waiting for us at the airport. It wasn't Beatlemania, but it was a little freaky. Our last single had gone Top Twenty there – on the back of that video with the ghosts in it. After which, most of our interviews seemed to be with British magazines – not all of them music ones. Style entered our lives, along with, for a brief while, stylists.

After this, we rapidly became blasé. Fame gets old fast. England was our first taste, though.

We were driven from the airport to our hotel in downtown London, which our efficient British PA informed us was where all the best bands stayed. We asked who, and when she named them they all sucked but were huge. It wasn't a great omen.

Some of the same girls from the airport had rushed here, too. They wanted Syph and Syph, of course, wanted them right back. He stood in the lobby for about half an hour, chatting them up – as if *You, follow me, now* wouldn't have done the business.

In the meantime, I went up to my room (alone), had a shower (alone), ignored the complete lack of timid knocks on the door and came back down –

– just in time to see Syph put something in the hands of one of the girls. She was the most beautiful – long glossy-black hair and big eyes done in kohl that a year from now, six months even, she'd be sneering at. She was young, too – too young: sixteen or seventeen.

As I walked up to Syph, she started off towards the elevator. She turned and waved, shyly but knowingly, when she got in. I was surprised Syph didn't just follow her. I knew where she was going; I thought I knew what would happen when she got there.

'No!' said Crab, to something else.

'I'm sorry,' said the PA, who was small, Asian, tough and dressed in tight black.

'What's up?' asked Syph.

'We have to get on a fucking train . . .' said Crab.

'There's a TV show,' said the PA. 'It shoots tomorrow morning in Manchester. They've just confirmed.'

'*Morning*,' said Mono, like he'd say *death*.

'So we'll go tomorrow,' Syph said.

'It starts at seven,' said the PA. 'I know you wouldn't want to miss it. It is broadcast nationwide. Five chart places, at least.'

'Shit,' said Mono.

'We'll do it,' said Crab, who later in the junket, thanks to much more of this puppyishness, was granted the privilege of one night in the PA's room. (He never said what happened. Nothing, we think – either that, or some very heavy SM.)

'But –' said Syph. 'But I –' He made a gesture that included the whole of the lobby and, by implication, the whole of London.

'There's a very nice hotel we've booked you into there,' the PA said. 'And I'm sure there will be girls.'

'Well, honey,' said Syph, despicably rock'n'roll, 'if you put it like that.'

Two minutes later – this is the way things were starting to happen for us – we were in a limo on the way to the station.

I didn't want to mention the beautiful black-haired girl in front of everyone. Not because I didn't want to embarrass Syph but because I didn't want to give him the chance to embarrass me back – by being not at all embarrassed, by treating it as if it was nothing.

I waited until we were in the lobby of the Manchester hotel – which, as the PA had promised, and Crab was confirming back to her, was very nice.

'Can I have a word?' I asked.

Syph, thinking I meant drugs, came across. 'That girl you left behind,' I said. 'You will call her, won't you?'

'Yeah, yeah,' Syph said. 'Sure.'

'As soon as you get up to your room.'

'Definitely.' But his eyes were around the lobby and over by the elevators and anywhere else that girls might be.

I knew *he* wouldn't call, so I did. I went upstairs to my room and, after taking my London room-key out of my pocket, dialled the number on the dangling metal triangle. (It had been an old-fashioned hotel.)

The desk clerk I'd seen through the revolving doors two hours earlier answered, still on shift. I explained who I was – he said he knew.

'Can you put me through to –' And I gave Syph's check-in alias: Thomas Jerome Newton. (Long story.)

The phone rang about ten times before the young woman picked up.

'Hello,' she said. Her voice was very English, pure and doorbell-like.

Again, I explained who I was. My accent convinced her, I think.

'Where's Syph?' she asked.

'We're in Manchester,' I said, expecting upset. 'We're doing a show. So Syph won't be back today.'

'Oh,' she said.

'I think,' I said, carefully, 'well, that you should go home. You can meet him again when he's back in London.'

'But he'll be back in the next few days, won't he?'

I tried to reason with her. As she spoke, I listened to the sound of the London hotel room. She didn't seem to have the TV on, the acoustic wasn't that of the bathroom.

'Go home,' I said, then hung up, went to bed.

We did the show in Manchester – and were told immediately after that we'd been booked for another in Scotland. 'Really important market,' said the PA. 'They buy lots of records up there.' We left without even changing.

It was only in the Glasgow dressing-room, afterwards, that I spoke to Syph. 'Did you call the girl?'

'What girl?'

'The one in London – in the hotel.'

'Oh, yeah. I called her.'

'No, you didn't. I did. When I called, she was still waiting for you.'

'I did – I called her.'

'When?' I asked.

'After you, obviously.'

'And she was still there?'

'Well, she answered.'

'I told her to go home – she was still in your room.'

'Have we still got rooms in London?' asked Crab.

'Cool,' said Mono.

'We couldn't cancel them,' said the PA. 'The hotel wouldn't allow us. Don't worry. The record company's paying.'

'We should call her now,' I said.

'Why?' said Syph. 'She won't still be there.'

I asked the PA if she could call the London hotel for us on her cellphone. She did, then handed it to me. Again, I asked to be put through to Syph's room, memorably number 333.

'Hello,' said the girl.

I handed the phone over to Syph, thumb on the holes where the sound goes in.

'Tell her to leave,' I said.

Syph took the phone and immediately started to chat the girl up again. He walked over to the corner of the room and I thought to myself, *Try trusting him, for once. Let him gently persuade her home with promises of future sex.*

'We're going to Paris now,' announced the PA. 'This is really building well.'

'Not back to London?' Mono asked.

'Maybe tomorrow,' the PA said.

'Anything you want,' said Crab.

When Syph handed the cellphone back to me, it was off.

'You did tell her to leave, right?'

'She's gone,' he said. 'History.'

I pulled up the last-dialled number and pressed Connect. The desk clerk put me through to 333.

'Hello,' said the girl.

I hung up.

Syph knew from my face what I was about to say. 'She didn't *want* to leave,' he said. 'She wanted to wait for me.'

'Didn't you tell her there wasn't any point?'

'What can I say, dude, she seems to think there is.'

He pulled the cellphone away from me and handed it back to the PA.

'Car outside for *okay*,' said a production assistant, head round the dressing-room door.

'Everybody out!' shouted the PA, who had already learnt that direct orders were the only way to move us.

We shuffled off.

In the limo, I borrowed the PA's cell again, called the hotel again, got 333.

'Hello,' said the girl.

'Go home,' I said.

'Oh,' she said, 'I thought it was him. He just called.'

29

It was time to be cruel. 'He called because I *made* him call.'

'No, he called because he wanted to speak to me.'

'Did he ask you to leave the room?'

'. . .'

'Did he?'

'He said he might not be back for a few days.'

'But did he ask you to leave?'

'Not exactly,' she said.

'He's not going to be back until at least the day after tomorrow. Surely you have better things to be doing with your time than sitting in an empty hotel room.'

'I don't.'

'You must.'

'I want to be here. It's his room.'

'It's not his room. He's never even been in it.'

'It *is* his room. They booked it for him therefore it's his room.' She wasn't stupid, this one.

'He may never come back,' I said.

'I'll take the chance,' she said and – really, she did – hung up.

Over the next few days, we went from Paris back to Scotland, Scotland to Liverpool, Leeds, somewhere even more industrial-looking, then back to Manchester. We even passed through London, doing three radio interviews back-to-back. But we didn't return to the first hotel. A plane to Brussels. A train to the Hague. Occasionally, I would call – by now I'd got hold of a functioning cellphone for myself ('Hello,' the girl said), but as soon as she heard it was me and not Syph, she would hang up. I tried to get him to speak to her again but he was totally stubborn. 'If she wants to stay, she wants to stay.' He had other girls, he had other concerns. In the end, I gave up. I'd thought about speaking to the desk clerk and asking him to have the girl thrown out, but I knew there was a big chance she'd just end up waiting for Syph on the sidewalk outside the hotel. However neglected she was, at least in room 333 she was safe. I thought about all the meals she must have ordered – all the TV she must have watched. Just like us. The whole thing was so immensely sad that we could probably have written a pretty good song about it.

The girl in room 333 – She's waiting for me – Patiently – Eternally. Or maybe not that good.

We went back to Paris. Then to Barcelona and I don't know where else. I gave up keeping track. And then and then and then. Our original schedule was forgotten as more and more important markets demanded our physical presence. We did the single a hundred times – playing live when we could, otherwise miming. Finally, we returned to London and to the hotel.

Syph wanted to go up alone but I made it absolutely clear that I was coming with him. I needed to see this girl – to try and talk to her.

Syph had no key. That was what I'd seen him put in her hand, back in the hotel lobby, ten days and twenty thousand miles ago. So we just went up to the room, unannounced, and knocked.

She answered the door – her face all delight – not a flinch of resentment, not until she caught sight of me over Syph's shoulder. 'You,' she said. 'Why don't you fuck off and leave us alone?'

For a second, I couldn't be bothered, then I changed my mind (maybe my heart) and *could.*

Pushing past them, I entered the room. The curtains were drawn. The bed was made. The TV was off. It looked like hotel rooms do when you first walk into them. There was no bad smell.

I could hear the girl saying to Syph, 'I waited for you.' And him replying, 'I'm glad you did.'

I went and opened the mini-bar. It was full. Perhaps it had been restocked. Perhaps the bed had been remade.

'I didn't drink anything,' the girl said to me, bitterly. 'Only tap water. I didn't eat anything, either.'

'You didn't?' said Syph – even he was shocked.

'Well,' she said, 'I had a couple of chocolate bars in my bag. But I didn't eat anything of yours.'

On the desk, beside the lamp, was a bowl containing complimentary packs of peanuts, potato chips.

The girl looked beyond-ghost: inch-thin arms and panda eyes.

I walked out – all the way out of the hotel. I walked until I found a wall I could retch and weep against. After that I just walked.

By then, they were probably fucking.

YOYO

Yoyo from the fanclub website (hi Yoyo!) has been nagging me very nicely for over a year to put something on paper (hotel stationery – the best & most romantic) about the very, very, very beginnings of *okay*.

I think she wants to hear about when we were young, innocent, idealistic – stuff like that.

And after all the bad shit that's gone down, especially recently with Syph (although I'm glad to say he's getting better – with relapses – thanks for all the cards & emails), I thought it might not be a bad time to remember when we started out – remember it, I mean, whiles I still can.

I wish I could describe it better. Success of the sort we've endured isn't too good for clear recollection. Here's what I have.

Young, innocent, idealistic – one, two and three – I wish I could be sure we ever were. Rather than the four ego-monsters we've become.

But it's very hard to remember what it felt like to unload my second drumkit (the first was a kiddie Christmas set I knocked to hell by age twelve) from my cousin's van and carry it, piece by piece, up the stairs and into Crab's room.

Of course, *then* he wasn't called Crab. He probably would have known what crabs were, in theory. But he was yet to have his first visit to the white-walled clinic above the doll and puppetry store. *Young*, we were definitely that: fifteen years old when we started rehearsing seriously.

I think, now, that you probably play the drums differently if you've had to carry them to wherever yourself. It's such a fucking huge labour to move the things that, when you set them down, you want to make them speak in a particularly special way. Maybe that's hippie-thought, I don't know. Perhaps it's just that, having to bear the burden of them, you really want to punish them for being such a painful instrument – painful to transport, not to play – playing them was never less than a joy. Particularly when we got to somewhere (not my parents' house) where I could bash the shit out of them.

And that's what our first rehearsal room was, Crab's sock-and-crotch-smelling attic. But *okay* truly started in another room – a room about ten feet by twelve that Mono had found, somehow. It was just out back of a store selling spare parts for motorcycles. The owner, T-Bone, could care about the noise. He was so deaf from tuning engines that I don't think he even heard us.

Musicians will yammer on for ever and ever about chemistry – almost as much as they'll bitch about not getting paid enough. But the truth of it is, or was, from the first occasion the four of us played together, we sounded like a true band.

We'd all done stuff before – played with other kids in other styles: prog, pop, punk.

okay, which didn't have the name yet – which wasn't to be *okay* for over a year – *okay* really and truly started (have I already said this?) the moment Syph opened his mouth to sing over the slow-roaring noise Crab, Mono and I were making.

Innocent? – innocent I don't know about.

Right from rehearsal one, along with the pleasure in knowing we *worked*, there was a kind of resentment. (I'm sorry, Yoyo – sure you were hoping for band-of-brothers, but this is the dirty truth.) We knew that we were tied together. Anything about another band member that annoyed you now was, because we sounded so damn good, going to be paining you for years to come.

We didn't doubt our success. That, too, makes us sound uninnocent. We were aware of the standard of bands our age, and we knew that we were far better than all of them. Syph had somehow managed to find a way of performing without being embarrassing. A true front-man. And though I wouldn't want to sit down and read the lyrics to our first few songs as poetry, they too were far from laughable. Quite unlike the guy who wrote them, who was an absolute knob from the get-go. Really, Yoyo – he was, is, and please God will be for a long time yet. If he weren't, he'd just be some guy. And Syph was never some guy.

To backtrack even further:

Our first meeting. I've told this too often in interviews. I know when I say about Syph dropping out of a tree in front of us, it's probably a story I made up years ago and now believe is true. But I do believe it's true.

Me, Crab and Mono were out walking around the neighbourhood. I think we were discussing how much Rush sucked or whether Leonard Cohen really banged Janis Joplin in the Chelsea Hotel (*innocent?*) – perpetual topics. And Syph, who had just moved in round the block, fell all the way down from quite a tall branch.

He landed on his ass, and made a huge wailing screech of a cry as his ankle twisted.

You can check with the others, but the first word I remember hearing him say was *motherfucker.*

We ran over to him and picked him up. All of us hoped he'd broken his leg – in those days, a trip to hospital counted as excitement. But he felt it up and down and said it wasn't too bad, it didn't feel broken. We asked where he lived and then helped him hop home.

The way Syph tells it, I know, is slightly different. He says he'd been sneaking around the new neighbourhood for several days and had caught us practising. He liked what he heard, wanted to meet us. (Mono was singing back then – and anyone could have told you we needed someone better, or more confident.)

When Syph asked his mom, she just said (like moms do,

seeing no difficulties), 'Why don't you go over and introduce yourself?' But this wasn't enough for Syph. He wanted to impress by making a big entrance.

I don't know how long he'd been waiting up that tree for us to come past.

So, according to Syph, he didn't fall, he jumped. Also, according to Syph's revised version, his ankle wasn't twisted at all. But I was there – I saw him land awkwardly, I saw the ankle swell up, and I saw the look on his mom's face when she answered the door.

We were invited in, rewarded with milk and cookies. A bigger reward was Syph's mom, who immediately went in at number one of our collective crush chart. She only seemed about ten years older than us – slim, quick, flirty and hip. And *divorced*.

To begin with, at least two of us were much more concerned with getting to talk to her than with Syph's injury.

He was charismatic, I suppose – that immediately made us want to ignore him. To punish him for having something we knew we'd never have. Skinniness helped. But he had cute eyes and, from the way we lusted after his mom, we could be certain girls lusted after him.

He took his sneaker off, and his foot ballooned (I swear it did). But his mom checked for breaks, too, and found none – so we were able to go up to his room. He was under orders to put his foot on a pillow on the bed. We helped set him up, whilst looking around, impressed, definitely. He had cool stuff. Rare posters of the right bands. Plus there was a guitar, acoustic: a Guild – a serious guitar.

'Can you play anything?' asked Crab.

Syph showed he definitely could, even lying on his back.

'And I write songs.'

Without being asked, he started in – no embarrassment, instead, that thing which has always been his greatest gift: shamelessness.

The song . . . put it this way, it didn't make the first album. But it did make the first gig. It was called 'Celibacy', and was about moving away from where he'd grown up. (For the first year I knew him, *all* his songs seemed to be about that. He missed the north, the snow.) We tried our hardest not to be impressed, but started smiling at the strange changes in the bridge. There was strong implied harmony, too.

'We're a band,' said Mono.

'Would you like to join?' asked Crab, without even calling us into a pow-wow. There was no point – whether he'd plotted it or not, Syph had just sung his way into our lives.

What was the last of the one, two and three? *Idealistic*, yes. This is hard. There is an idealism of whores, I'd say. They're all sentimentalists, if only in their weepy love for cash. Our motives were always mixed, and we tried to be honest about that – with one another and also in our songs. Money was quite important. Fame was very important. Music was sometimes more important than fame and sometimes less important than money. We liked the way we sounded and we wanted other people to like it, too – as many people as possible. Stadiums.

Of course, in our heads, we competed with the biggest, with The Beatles. That's the thing of being in a band, especially a bass, drums, lead, rhythm combo. We thought we could do something similar, although the great breakthroughs (even then we sensed) had already been made.

There was another thing, too, a fascination. I'd known Crab for five years and Mono for eight. A large part of the thing about wanting success was wanting it for yourself, but there was also the fascination of doing it with your friends, seeing it happen to them and, through them, feeling it happen to yourself.

That's where Syph was a difficulty. He came in as an outsider and stayed as a permanent latecomer. *okay* needed him but it didn't always want him. We played together but, after the tree-climbing-falling, we only played music – with Mono and Crab, I'd played *played* played. We had sandpit history.

Syph brought the excitement. Without him, we'd be – I don't even want to think what we'd be. Certainly, we wouldn't be being asked by charming Japanese fans (hi Yoyo!) to reminisce about fifteen–twenty years ago.

What else do I remember? One thing, above all, from after that first rehearsal. It's not really to do with music – at least not directly.

We arranged to meet again the next weekend and start practising for real. Everyone swapped phone numbers, and we were very band-y – no hugs but lots of smiles and yeahs and hummings of riffs as we packed up.

Middle of that week, I'm walking down the street in the centre of town. Coming towards me I see just the most beautiful girl in our school, Katie Proudhon (Catty Proudhorn, as she inevitably got called), and with her? alongside her? – to my young, innocent, idealistic astonishment: Syph.

Years of experience have now taught me that, to him, this kind of company is nitrogen. He breathes it in without noticing, without metabolizing it. To me, it's oxygen. Most of the time, I'm gasping.

So they come towards me, and I put on a scared smile and I think how great it will be to speak to such a lovely girl. Even if, and I accept this completely (almost completely) (alright, I work really hard to accept it) – even if she walks away with Syph and is his girlfriend and wife for ever.

And Syph sees me. I see him see me. (He denies this now. Ask. He *denies*.) Syph sees my smile, and he steers Katie Proudhon round me.

He *steers* her.

As if I'm *dog mess* on the *sidewalk*.

'Hi,' I say, to their together-backs.

I'm astonished, *mortified*. But like the jerk I am, I say, 'Hi.'

And, still steering her, Syph says – and he doesn't look round and he certainly doesn't *stop* – Syph says, 'Hi.'

Motherfucker.

After recording, releasing and touring the live album, we – the four band members – sat down in a skanky diner and decided what *okay* needed was change, radical change.

Enough of hotel rooms, enough of road-food, enough of contempt-fucking – what all of us required was a zone of long hibernation.

And so, we did what we hadn't done since the very beginning: loaded our own equipment into the Big Van, and drove –

(Alright, we took two roadies, Shed and Monkey Boy, but they were almost band members anyhow. Don't tell them that, though.)

– drove East.

One reason we could do this was, for once, we were all single. Syph never kept a girlfriend for more than a week, and that was only if we were doing a six-night residency – in NYC, say. Crab split up with Kerrie three weeks into the live-album tour, after they'd been seeing each other for a year. (The band record at that point, a year of solid faithfulness.) Mono had been divorced two years, and was still living out his depraved version of *la vida*. And me, Clap, you probably know a little too much about me already: homeless: hopeless: helpless.

It was *okay*'s intention to reconnect with 'the country' (meaning Canada). Not an original idea, but –

– basically, no band can do anything that hasn't already been done by the four great archetypal bands: The Beatles, The Band, The Velvets, The Stooges. These bands did every variation upon every move a band can make.

We drove our van cross-country to Northern Ontario,

looking for our own homegrown version of Dylan and the Band's Big Pink. We took our time, secret-gigging on the way.

I think when we first got there – and one of us is still there – we thought we'd found it. (I won't say where *there* is – don't want to spoil it for the old chap.) On the very edge of a flat stretch of the most beautiful water you have ever seen, a three-storey house with an alpine-sloped roof and a huge basement.

The owners had two of our CDs, and were Dylan aficionados – they didn't take much persuading to move out. Money, also, was involved.

Town was about two miles back along the track. It had a population of 350 – shaped like a T, with a long main drag and a couple of churches off to left and right built on less expensive land. The stores were old-fashioned, and not chains. Junk food was available, however. We wouldn't have stopped there otherwise.

Town was the colour of asphalt and blackish wood – what gave it colour was the sky and the trees against the sky. Its yearly cycle was a round of dulling to gray and brightening to green. We caught it at the start of the end of spring, if that makes sense.

For the first few days, life in the house was perfect. Monkey Boy had found a supplier of decent weed. We relaxed and I – I'm not sure about the others – started to hanker after some good ol' unplugged music-making.

Syph posed around – *getting inspired*, he said it was. This meant having female photographers come and take his picture up against trees in forest groves. He spoke to some music journalists, too. Probably telling them about the great new material we were hard at work on.

Mono went fishing. He is terrible at it, and whenever any of the rest of us went along with him, we always caught more, but he loved it.

Crab installed himself at the far end of the roughest local

bar, put on his *eat shit* face and prepared himself for greaser homage.

The roadies were down in the basement, setting up the equipment – a modest sixteen-track mixing desk, etc., etc.

In the afternoons, we could hear them banging around: they weren't a bad rhythm section, and Monkey Boy could sing in his own sweet way. He had often soundchecked when our lead singer was otherwise engaged.

After he ran out of photographers, Syph set himself up on the barstool next to Crab – who hadn't received any homage, greasy or not. Syph was different, though. Within about a half-hour, the crush (female) was such he had to move the party back into a booth. Crab followed him, and together they began to make artistic arrangements out of their empty bottles – much to the amusement of the five or six local girls who fit round the table, too. One whiff of Syph, that's all they needed. I don't know what it is he sends out – weasel, skunk, buck or coon; it works.

I joined Mono by the lakeside.

You can see where the split was starting to develop.

Two weeks in, and we hadn't spent a single hour down the basement. The roadies had it all ready to roll – drumheads tuned, strings shiny-new. We still heard them, trying the equipment out in a variety of styles: gospel, country, blue-grass, funk. Whenever we were ready, they were ready. Syph had been generous: both Monkey Boy and Shed would get to engineer whatever we laid down – credited, with royalties.

This was roundabout when Syph fell in love. A strange phenomenon, never before been known to have occurred. Mainly we knew this was serious because to the woman in question (definitely a woman, not a girl) Syph made no protestations. *I love you* with a wink and a grin, was one of his best lines. He could conduct an entire seduction, saying nothing else. Apart, maybe, from *Hey, what's your name?*

The woman was called Major. Half Native Canadian, Sitka tribe, born in Alaska, brought here by her mother (after the divorce and the attempted murder), working the cosmetics counter in the town's only pharmacy – Syph saw her come into the bar the third Saturday night.

I was there too, and I would like to say I saw in her what Syph saw. The rest of the band, plus roadies, were also there.

Up until this point, this epoch, our table had been doing its pale cowardly impression of Led Zep's dominion over the Whisky-a-Go-Go, *circa* 1972. There were empty bottles of JD on the table, of which we were all secretly keeping a count. Apart from Crab.

Mono had been monologuing about fishing techniques, and I was distressed to find myself fascinated – hooked.

'Look at her,' said Syph. He had his arms round two local girls, but they could tell straightaway they'd lost him. He was a lunar module, they were just booster rockets.

The band must've heard something in Syph's voice, because we all looked over.

Major had entered the bar on her own, so she wasn't hard to spot.

'Mmm,' yummy-yummed Crab. '*Beefcake*, eh?'

Syph slapped him. 'Don't ever speak like that about the woman I love.'

We thought he was joking. We mocked him, pretending he meant it, and in this way found out he did.

I'll never know how it happened. The moment she walked through the door, Syph turned from hound dog to lap dog. (He was never not going to be canine, but he had in a second gone from a leg-rutter into a heel-worshipper.) I've never known a thing like it: she *transfigured* him.

'Well, go and speak to her, then,' said Crab, assuming this was the role Syph wanted him to play.

'I can't,' said Syph – he seemed paralysed by the idea, and delighted by his paralysis. It was years – put it another way, I don't think he'd *ever* felt at a disadvantage, sexually, when faced with another human being. Major scared him, as well she should. She was taller than him, broader than him, and probably stronger than him. She looked like an Olympic swimmer, a specialist at the butterfly. Syph had never gone for the Amazonian type before, not that I'd seen. The rapid destruction of the most delicate beauty, that had always been his speciality. But with Major, he must surely have felt himself to be the potentially delicate one.

'*Talk* to her,' I said to him, about an hour later. He had become boring with out-loud longing.

'I *can't*,' he whined.

Mono got frustrated with not knowing, and went and asked the barman who she was – the barman gave him the basics: the pharmacy, the cosmetics counter.

Next time Major went up to get drinks, the barman told her about Mono asking who she was. I saw him nod in our table's direction. Major followed his eyebeam, picked out Mono, thought she caught his eye, smiled. But he was staring right through her, describing to me the joys of nightfishing.

After she came in, Major sat down as part of a large group of women, many of them familiar from the stores in town. Most of them were ten years older than us, sturdy of leg, and none of them gave any sign of knowing who we were – although we knew word had gotten round within about a day of our arrival.

Major took another trip to the john, passing right by our table. Syph's eyes followed her, like puppies chasing a butterfly.

'Talk to her,' Mono said.

'I can't,' Syph said.

This time he seemed genuinely tortured by his paralysis.

Early the next morning, we left the bar – Syph not even taking one of the local girls back with him to his room.

Mono, Crab and I traded glances – they were humorous but also anxious. What if it were true? Would we have lost the old Syph? – the one upon whom we could blame all our own lapses? the one who made the worst of our behaviour seem mild?

Another consideration was whether Syph would start maybe writing songs.

As we went to bed, I got the answer – an acoustic guitar starting to plang-plang down in the kitchen.

Next day, we found Syph in the studio with Monkey Boy. They had been up all night, and had laid down rough mixes of four tracks.

After breakfast, Syph played them back to us. The first was called '*Coup de Fou*'. It was clear almost from note one that this was 'a solo project'. Drums, bass, guitar – it was all there already. We weren't needed.

That afternoon Syph took a ghetto blaster down to the cosmetics counter.

From what we later heard, Syph walked up to Major's counter, slammed the monster boombox down and pressed Play. His first heartbreaker kicked in. 'You make me feel like a baby, baby.'

A female customer almost immediately came up and shouted a question about combination skin. Major tried to answer, couldn't be heard, so pressed the eject button on the boombox. She then spent ten minutes in close discussion of the virtues of various foundations.

Syph, defeated, took up his tape-recorded declaration of love and walked. He'd had refusals before, of course – girls who seriously *did* love their boyfriends, girls who loved God. But it was at least a decade since he'd been ignored.

He hiked the long way back to the house, went down in the basement and immediately set to work on another two tracks.

'You didn't talk to her?' asked Crab.

'Couldn't,' said Syph. 'Just couldn't.'

*

Mono and I went fishing, though I was getting bored. I tried to talk to him about the Major-situation, but he replied by questioning whether he was using the correct ground bait.

A little later, Mono said the sight of that flat expanse in front of him, rippling under the wind, made him feel true calm. It had the opposite effect on me: I wanted to throw stones into it.

The fact there would never be real waves on such a stretch began to make me weirdly fearful. I wanted the sea; I wanted to surf. (I've never surfed before, but now I got a mad craving.)

I handed back the rod Mono had lent me. 'I'm going for a walk,' I said.

'Yes, you are,' he replied, Buddha-like.

Frustrated, I went for a long hike along the forest trails on my own – and found it far more satisfying than fishing: the birds, the insects, the whole natural vibe, man.

From then on, Mono went fishing on his own. This he did at increasingly unrock'n'roll hours of the day – early morning, after sleeping eight full hours.

Syph didn't dare risk another failure. He spent the week hard at work in the studio, writing and recording an album's worth of devotional material. Monkey Boy and Shed split shifts to keep up with him – the other band members were still surplus to requirements. I bought some decent backpacking boots and went for more long hikes. Mono got to bed early, so that he could be down by the lakeside well before dawn.

About this time, Friday of the fourth week, it came clear that *another* album had already been recorded in the basement. During the first couple of weeks, the roadies had put together their own set of fourteen tracks. Now, it seemed, Syph had made late-night promises to start up a record label in order to release it. Mono wasn't concerned but Crab and I thought this could be the end of the band. We confronted Syph. He told us, no, it was just something he needed to do. The label would be called Major Record Label.

Saturday morning, Syph had a plan. He drove over to the bar we'd been frequenting, spoke to the manager. The roadies spent the rest of the day shuttling equipment and sound-checking. Without even asking, Syph had set up a gig for us. Crab and I refused to play, so Monkey Boy, Shed and Mono took the stage. They were pretty good, not as good as *okay* but okay.

Syph spent the whole evening looking out for Major. The gig was entirely for her benefit. He was going to do a solo acoustic set of all the songs he'd written her. But she never showed.

Mono turned in early, wanting like most days to get up before the dawn and fish.

Syph, distraught, by the end of the set was getting drunk. I enjoy plinky-plinky on-the-edge burnout music – Neil Young's *Needle*, Big Star's third. Syph was going for something like the same effect. I felt sorry for him.

The bar cleared, as a result.

Syph had a long maudlin talk with the barman, then went off to make a fool of himself for the third time.

We later heard he'd persuaded the barman to give him Major's address, and had gone round to serenade her.

Turns out, she wasn't at home – was somewhere else entirely. In fact, I may as well tell you now, she was camping out by the lake, wanting to get up before dawn and fish. (I *know*.)

Come morning, she and Mono picked roughly the same pitch, and when it became clear nothing was biting, they said hello and had breakfast together. Then she went into work.

Mono kept quiet about it that afternoon, whilst playing bass on some new Syph tracks. He had ditched the gentle acoustic style, and was off into the angry clatter. As drummer, I was now his main man – and I was glad to be.

We laid down three pretty good tracks, keeping going till 2 a.m. Mono again went off early, the better to fish in the morning.

Whilst we slept, Mono's luck changed – he and Major had a dream morning of bites, hookings, tugs, nettings.

Thinking little of it, they came in their joy to show us their catch. The house was very quiet. None of us was up, except Syph, who still hadn't gone to bed.

Mono and Major walked in, a line of fish hung between them, and Syph *knew*.

Before Mono knew, before Major knew, Syph *knew* that they were one another's final destination.

He also knew, I think, that it meant the band was over – in the original form. No-one was ever going to persuade Mono away from this place again. The wide stillness of the lake, the careful speech, the values, the fish – he was at home. We wouldn't be a living-in-eachother's-pockets gang any more.

Mono introduced Syph to Major, and Syph started crying.

Major excused herself and, when she had gone, Syph tried to punch Mono – he missed, and Mono calmly retaliated. With a single jab to the gut, he laid him down gently, like a baby into a cot, leaving his beautiful face undamaged.

'Now why did you want to do that?' Mono asked.

'Go away,' said Syph, deathbed-scene style.

Mono went after Major – and they realized what was going on about halfway to town. They didn't come back to the house, carried on going to hers.

When we got up later, Syph was bent over at the kitchen table. He explained the situation.

Bless Syph, bless what he was before he was in the band, and bless what he's now returning to.

He took the whole thing as 'educational'. The anger was gone. He'd already written two gorgeous songs of leaving.

We rehearsed them, recorded them, one take each, no Mono, and he left before Major came off shift at the cosmetics counter. He took with him the tapes of his own album and the roadies'. Both were released.

You've probably heard theirs, *Mountain Men*, big hit, Grammies and all; Syph's – *Hook, Line and Sinker* – is a little harder to find, but worth finding.

LYDIA

Just like the song says, I fall in love too easily.

I wish I could stop myself, but I can't, it's a function of me being alive, of me being me.

There was that girl in Rotterdam, Amsterdam? Rotterdam, Inge her name, who is still there or thereabouts – in my heart.

I've fallen in love three times today already, and I haven't even gone for lunch yet. There'll be another *then*, guaranteed: all waitresses, I fall in love with.

I really shouldn't be allowed out the house: it hurts too much. There are so many alternate lives I could be leading, in the parallel universes of these women's arms.

I want to live with one of the English ones, a rich girl if not an actual princess, in a castle her family has owned for five hundred or a thousand years. (I wonder, does it make any difference, five hundred or a thousand? To the plumbing, probably. Not to the girl.) I'd like there to be at least one warm room, for wintering in. I think of these details.

But sometimes, girls fall in love with me, too.

Yes, there are groupies, but that's not exactly what I mean. What I mean is, they fall in love with me in a way that's disturbingly like the way I fall in love with them. Hopelessly, in other words – immediately, stupidly and in a way designed to ensure maximum loss of dignity. And this is what I'd like to tell you about, because it's different.

I was in England, perhaps following my yen for an aristocratic beauty but more likely because *okay* had finished a month's promotion in Europe (*Underlings*, the B-sides and rarities collection) and I couldn't face getting on another airplane. It's amazing how some deeply scary turbulence over Portugal impacted on the life of Lydia I-Won't-Include-Her-Real-Surname. Chaos theory in reverse: a thunderstorm above Lisbon brushes dust off the butterfly's wing that Lydia definitely was.

We met cute, in the bar of the hotel *okay*'s new management had booked me into.

I was sitting there on my own – such a beautiful thing, that; unhassled and away from the other guys in the band. No publicist. No questions to answer. Nothing I had to do *that* minute, that evening, *that* week. Time without a schedule was a different thing, chewier.

So, I was sitting there in a big velvet booth with a neat double vodka in front of me, nicely iced, trying to decide whether or not any of my friends in London were really my friends – and if they were, whether that made me want to contact them more or less. There are occasions on which what you most want to see are vague and largely facetious acquaintances. Cocaine-friends – or 'mates', as they call them in the UK, with the implication that some form of mating has gone on, among all the matiness. And then again, sometimes what you need is a friend so old and true that you can be ugly and selfish and generally a 'twit' – all the while knowing you'll be forgiven, eventually.

I was leaning towards wanting a genuine Canadian grownup-with-them person when I saw Lydia and Lydia saw me.

And I *knew*, just as I've known (of myself) in the past. Oh, I knew so many things – I knew about her months of cool, drizzling endurance, about the sunbursts of searing, flame-yellow hope – I too had lived beneath that emotional sky. I knew of transient and hopefully-permanent relationships. And I knew that this was one that could go a certain distance but which would never make it to the end, or anywhere close. I also knew, above all, that she knew who I was. Her glance showed sweet recognition.

She was there with a female 'mate' – later, they told me they had been to a 'naff' rom-com and didn't want the night to end in disappointment. Her friend came with hope, too – a hump of hope. They were fellow hunchbacks – carrying round that great useless lump of optimistic stuff on their backs: deformed by it – aching in every bone to be relieved of it – hating and growing it like an angry zit rather than a romantic burden.

She whispered to her friend and her friend whispered back. I had seen these head movements before, seen them on all five continents – the dip, twist, jerk and shake. Like defunct dance-crazes. There is a rhythm to it. Finally it comes down to shake and nod, shake and not. Reluctance and encouragement. No and *yes*.

Yes usually wins. The smaller the town, the more exciting yes seems. But even in capital cities, yes has an edge.

Do it, yes.

I was expecting both of them to come over, but Lydia was braver and more foolhardy than I'd given her credit for.

The walk across, as I felt it for her, was very wearying. I tried to help by not staring at her approach.

'Excuse me,' she said, the traditional opening. 'I'm sorry to bother you, but ...' I hated it that this was an unoriginal experience for me – in fact, a screamingly tedious one. 'But are you ...'

'Hello,' I said. 'Yes, I'm –'

'Aren't you that gardener from television?'

She had heard my accent, and realized her mistake. 'I'm sorry – I didn't –'

But I was the more horribly shocked. Not that I'd been so wrong – that my knowing had been disproved. Not *that*, and not that she didn't know who I was: drummer with a mid-rank Canadian indie band. No, what shocked me was that I'd felt the whole of this encounter from her side. There was a very wounding quality about Lydia, right from the start.

'No, it's okay. Why don't you –' I said.

I was in her embarrassment with her, beneath her sky as it blushed into excuse and anecdote. Go into reverse, she thought. Reverse gear. Get back to the bar. Drink up and leave. Or leave the drinks and go. Laugh about it in the taxi home – or the bus. They looked like maybe they used buses.

'It's just, you look like him. A bit.'

'A gardener?'

'He's famous.'

'Well, that's something at least. Would he be here?'

She looked back at her friend. And this time I wasn't so sure what her face would be saying: *Join me*, *Rescue me* or *Don't you dare leave me*.

The friend, good friend, got down off her barstool and walked across the room. She walked very carefully, so as not to upstage Lydia – her skirt was shorter than Lydia's, and her legs longer. But she was walking towards me as a famous gardener, not as a semi-famous-in-some-circles-and-countries musician.

'It isn't him,' Lydia said, when her friend got close.

'No, I'm only me,' I said. What surprised me most about this situation was that, despite these two young women being neither my friends nor my acquaintances, I was quite enjoying it – being misrecognized for someone else public. It took some of the pressure.

'Oh,' said the friend, 'we thought you were –'

'You must like him a lot,' I said. 'What kind of gardens does he make?'

They looked at one another, each hoping the other would answer. I liked that they weren't too drunk, hardly at all. I liked, also, that they seemed to be trying to answer seriously, informatively.

'Very "architectural",' said the friend. 'He uses metal quite a lot.'

I decided to flirt. 'You think I look like a famous gardener of metal?'

'From over there you did,' said the friend. I was worried she would take over. I could feel Lydia mentally exiting from the evening.

Reader, I pitied her. (That's an allusion to Charlotte Brontë's *Jane Eyre*, Miss Ullshawn – see, I didn't forget *every*-

thing from fifth grade. I think my English is pretty good, for a fail student.)

I introduced myself – looking all the while at Lydia – and, to end the confusion stage of things, explained who I was and what I did and why I was there. Then, unthreateningly as I could, asked, 'Why don't you sit down?'

'Sure,' she said, suddenly confident. Again, I was pained – this was the flood-of-liking moment. For me, it goes both ways at the same time: I like her; she likes me! Two waves crashing into one another and whoosh.

The friend was a little more hesitant. I think I had disrupted their girls-together evening. But as the friend was aware of Lydia's singleness and her hope and the fact I might, despite not being off the 'telly', be someone worth having met – as the friend was a kind sort, she sat down too.

I had shifted round the booth so they weren't flanking me pimp-style; Lydia was closest, the friend opposite.

There was a moment, a definite moment.

Then the friend introduced herself, taking over again, briefly. And then Lydia, quietly, brought her name out. She was far shyer about it than, later on, about stepping out of her dress. This, I empathized with: by that point you are committed – it's in the tentativeness that torture lurks.

We talked – for over an hour, while the lovely waitress brought us drinks which I insisted went on my room bill and which they tried to give me money for. When I promised that my management, and not me, would really foot the bill, they quit. Both understood the joy of drinking on someone else's tab: alcohol tastes lighter – like the air above vodka.

I felt I knew what was going to happen, and switched to singles – so as to be ready for it. Not for sex but for explanations, more talk and deeper. Tonight was neither for London friends nor acquaintances; tonight was for a complete stranger who, fittingly strangely, felt as known as myself.

I looked at Lydia and, by slow steps, worked it out. So many of *okay*'s songs are about wrong romances. But in all pop and most rock there's a basic belief in the true love, the soul-mate, the long-awaited other. And I'd done so much waiting. And Lydia had, too. And now we'd found one another. But not in the way we should have done. She was attractive. I could say, *she had a beautiful figure* but that would be senti-mental: she had a very sympathetic face and beautiful breasts – truly gorgeous and loveable. But the bits in between, the supporting bits, weren't model-like. They were sketchy and touching. Her legs, when I saw all of them, were comic in some way – not advertisement legs; friend legs, sister legs. Her legs made me want to cry almost as much as her breasts made me want to cuddle, nuzzle, semi-suffocate. But I knew it would feel wrong – wrong for both of us, eventually, though with her lessness of experience it might take her a year to realize. I'm sure she knew a lot about heartbreak, for want of a non-country'n'western word, but she certainly didn't know as much as me about strangers in hotel bars, strangers in hotel bathrooms. (Very few people do.)

We talked about their lives. Lydia worked in arts adminis-tration, her friend in telecommunications. They felt mildly glamorous to be in my company – though the fact I'd arranged it so they weren't sitting either side of me made it feel both less glamorous and less sleazy.

'Okay,' said the friend, just after twelve. 'It's now or never for the bus.'

Well, I'd been right about that, at least.

I didn't avoid the moment's eye-contact that was the necessary next. Lydia understood: 'I think I might stay a little longer.'

I said nothing. I didn't need to. I felt weak with Lydia's brave achievement – her liking hurt me. Mmm, and her love. It was important to be deeply kind to this young woman. I wanted to treat her like I wanted women to treat me, women I loved. What I wanted was not to be politely put off – I wanted them to let me have the pleasure and catharsis of a fuck.

Yes, we would talk for another hour – more soulfully, even sobering up a little. Yes, I would invite her up to my room – just so she could see what the suites looked like in a 'posh' place like this. Yes, I would maintain the guided-tour pretence for a couple of minutes after we got upstairs: I wouldn't jump and hump her. Yes, I would seduce her by using her name just as I would want a woman I loved to use mine – to speak it as if it were a name to be spoken many times more, in together-future.

I found the making love difficult, having seen Lydia's legs. Once the idea of sisterliness entered the room, it was very hard to dissipate. I tried for a while to get off on it, but eventually decided to focus on her face and her breasts. It sounds horrible and sexist. (I'm not ripping her body to bits.) But they were exquisite – and they were exquisite because they were truly *hers*, not just voluptuous add-ons that didn't fit with her personality.

(This isn't going the way I meant it to.)

Making love, note, not having sex: my lump-o'-hope wanted me to try – I knew it wouldn't work, and it didn't. This wasn't a woman I'd ever love as I'd loved the ones who didn't care for me or let me near them.

Afterwards, she went to sleep very soundly.

As I lifted my arm from behind her head, she woke up a little but I kissed and whispered her back to sleep.

Then I got dressed.

I wasn't able to pack everything, but I took my passport, a few clothes and a book for the flight. If she wanted to steal something of mine, I didn't mind: as I looked round the dim room for the last time (it was still only three thirty in the morning), I wondered what it was she might take. Everything? Might she rip my clothes up in anger at being abandoned? Not Lydia. Nothing – would she want nothing? I hoped not. I tried to inventory what I saw.

When I left, I left no note. I kissed the air silently above her head, said *I don't love you. I'm sorry* and walked out of the room.

I was lucky with the taxi and made it to London Heathrow in under an hour. Lucky, too, with the airline – ticket on the first flight out. I could have flown business class, but didn't: I felt a little emotionally tough and wanted my travel to reflect that.

I was sure I'd done the right thing. I only hoped that, next time I met her and it didn't work, my so-long-awaited would leave me as absolutely.

MODEL

One night, in my hotel room, in Paris, in the middle of everything, I had a long conversation with a model who was, incidentally, very attractive and, inevitably (or else she wouldn't have been there), very stoned.

She told me all about it: being beautiful. I don't think she meant to. Her nature didn't include lectures – nothing conventionally didactic, though educational. Truancy was written all over her, misspelt. But recently written. She was a good girl trying not to be.

I was thirty-five then, and the naked body of an eighteen-year-old model made me think first of all of death – my own and death in the abstract. After that, I could usually bring it round again to desire. Some nights, though, and those were becoming more frequent, sadness won. Sadness, from time to time, was all there was.

I should probably accentuate the positive. At least, given my position (middle of a modest drum-stack – out-of-shot and out-of-focus for 90–95 per cent of the videos – one quote per all-band interview – millionaire) – given my ignominious and by-proxy glamour, I still occasionally got access to the bodies of eighteen-year-old models.

It would be dishonest not to note there was a downside to this, too. Along with access to their bodies came an open invitation to enter their minds – and that, as I hope you can imagine, was a corner of Hell that Virgil somehow neglected to show Dante. Probably thought he couldn't take it.

Her name, that night, was Barbra, spelt like and in tribute to Streisand.

She was best known for a lingerie campaign in Europe – which had picked her up the tabloid nickname of Bra-Bra and, more cruelly but less frequently, Baps.

Like I said, and probably don't need to say again but will, Barbra was beautiful. But, in the flesh, there was something not exactly off-putting but quite *taming* about her.

Which was why she ended up, at 2 a.m. Central European Time, with me and not with Syph.

I've heard one reason Marilyn Monroe looked so radiant on-screen was that her face was covered – cheeks, nose, everything – with a very fine pelt of white hairs. This is why she remained peachy, right up through *The Misfits* and *Something's Got to Give.*

It was also why quite a few men, confronted with the real Norma Jean, and not the celluloid goddess, found her more than a little grotesque.

Of course, this didn't *stop* them from doing what they were going to do: sexually punish her for being sexual. In fact, it probably added to the viciousness of their attacks.

Poor Norma.

Poor Barbra.

I'm not saying Barbra was at all fuzzy-like-a-peach. But there was a definite teddy-bear quality to her, close up. She would prefer a cuddle, and she looked like she needed it. Anything else brought thoughts of soft-toy violation – and if that's your thing ... It isn't mine.

Barbra called out to be treated with kindness. And so, without sounding too knight-on-steed, I rescued her from the end of the evening.

I should, perhaps, mention the evening. Just to give you some context: after-show party in Parisian warehouse (yes, they do have such things in such places). Our French fans are some of our most loyal (read crazed) and attentive (read obsessive). There's a noticeable difference between gigs there and, say, Belgium. The Belgians come to rock, the French to think about the existential nature of what it would be to rock – or some shit like that. So, we were on a mild high, a slightly frustrated we-didn't-break-on-through buzz.

'I can't even *look* at people,' said Barbra. 'I can't look at *men.*

If I look at them, they look back and they see me and then it's like the whole eye-contact *catastrophe*. They think I'm interested in them and come over and try and chat me up – when I wasn't looking at them for *that* at all. I don't even *dare* to look at men I find really attractive. I just go and stand as far away from them as I can, sometimes in another fucking *building*, and I think about what it would be like if they *did* come to find me. It's lonely. I'm shy – no-one understands. And I *want* to look at people. I'm *interested*, you know. I want to see what they're *like* – what they look like, what they are doing. I think I'd like to be some kind of *artist*, or maybe a photographer. Then I could hide behind the camera and no-one would fucking see *me*.'

Fucking – the word *fucking* – really didn't suit her, but she'd picked it up as a habit, probably around the same time as those other habits, puking and cocaine. Fourteen, maybe fifteen, maybe younger – I was getting out-of-date. Anticipating forty.

And I'm going to cut out some of the Valley Girl *like*s and *you know*s and *really*s – she used lots but, *you know*, you don't *like really* need them. Barbra was from Washington State, upstate, but sounded like she was from everywhere. Secretly, she was Canadian, she just didn't know it – had a wide-open and snowy soul.

'It's lonely,' she said.

I won't interrupt much more, but she used the word *lonely* almost as much as *like, you know* and *really*.

'It's so fucking lonely. I mean, like I said, I'm interested in people. How am I going to learn anything about the world if I get *attacked* every time I look at it? Someone said to me this morning, at the shoot – they wanted me to be more, what was the word? *Aristoscrat* – he wanted me to be more aristocrat. It was the photographer. *Really*, he just wanted me to lift my chin a little higher. Like that. Anyway, I'm getting lost, this is good shit, *aristoscrat*, hah! This famous fucking photographer said to me, "Beauty is distance." He said it like he was a phisollopher – I mean, a phillo-soffa, a pheelosofr, philosofpher. "Beauty is distance." And he let that hang for a few moments, while everyone listened to him and I stood there freezing in the Summer Line. And then he said, looking at me with a strange look, "That's why we all want to get close to it." And everyone clapped, stylists, everyone, like he'd said something really intelligent and *true*. And what I really hate is that I think probably he *did* – but I'm sure he stole it off of someone *genuine*, a real deep thinker from the past.'

Line of coke.

'I'm beautiful. I wouldn't be here if I wasn't. And people are always trying to get closer and closer until they're all over you and up *inside* you. Did I tell you that people touch me up *all* the time? Not just men. *Women* will stand so I can feel their *nipples* against my *arm*. It's fucking *true*! What's *that* about? These aren't *lesbians* – not all of them. I'm not charismatic, I know that. It's not *real* talent. Not like you guys. That's why it's lonely. Because I know I *have* it and I know it will *go* and so I better *enjoy* it while it lasts, like *everyone* is always *telling* me, usually because they want to *bang* me, but having it makes you sort of *not* able to enjoy it. Do you understand? It's easier for them to think they would enjoy it if they had it than for me to enjoy it being me and having it. You're cute. No, you *are*. Believe me – you may not think so, but I see your inner cuteness. I have x-ray vision and superkinetic powers, and you are a cutie.'

Line of coke.

'I want to touch you,' I say, guiltily. 'I'm not that different.'

'At least you fucking ask,' Barbra says. 'To some of them, I'm just a piece of *meat*. People talk about me all the time as if I wasn't there. "Her hair's looking a bit *frizzy* today." "Can we do something about the *bags* under her eyes?" "I really don't think she has the right *look* for this *campaign*." "God, is that *cellulite*?" And they're always moving me around, putting me in this position or *that* stupid fucking position, not asking, and sticking fucking pins in me. I really should be a doll. In

French they call us *mannequins*. I learnt that today. See, I'm interested. Anyway, this photographer who said about beauty – after we're done, he invites me to his apartment. His *Paris* apartment, I should say, he has one in New York and one in *Miami*, too. I thought he was gay enough for me to be *safe* with him. Some of the others came, too – his assistant. And when we got there, he got out *another* camera, a little *digital* one this time, and he told me *to take my clothes off* like we were still working. I said, "Why?" and he said he did this with all the girls he used. He said he liked a *record* of them. And I thought about saying why didn't he just use some of the shots from the shoot. Shots from the shoot – hah! Pretty funny. But I didn't say that because I was a bit scared of him. And he says, "Come on, you're *wasting* my *time*." So I ask who else has done it, and he takes me into his bedroom – big view of the Eiffel Tower – and pulls out this drawer and there's a book inside it, like a photograph album, and when I open it I see *everyone* – all the models going back, like, ten–fifteen years. But they're not just *standing* posing, like for the record, like he says. He's got them all on their hands and knees looking back over their right shoulder, like *this*.'

And she shows me. And I'm dismayed not to be more dismayed.

'And not just that, but they have their fingers in their – you know – in a really porny way. Spreading it apart so you can see all of it. And this is the record, because when he turns the page I can see he's blown up this part of the photograph for all of them. And underneath, in tiny tiny neat writing, he's written their *name* and a *date*. He turns the page – more models – he turns the page – more clitorises. "You see," he says, "it's an *art project*. And I want *you* to be part of it." So, anyway . . . Do you have some *Coke*, please?'

At first, confusingly, I think she doesn't mean soda, but it turns out she does.

I open the mini-bar and then offer her a choice of five different kinds. She goes, as I knew she would, for fat *Coke*.

'So what happened?' I ask, as I pop it and hand it over.

'I *did* it,' she says. 'He's an important photographer – and it's not the *worst* thing I've ever done. But I don't want to fucking talk about that fucked-up ... Let's talk about you. What's it like being in a band? You guys really *rock*, you know.'

And I give her the speech – one of the speeches (I think I have about five by now), which I playlist randomly and occasionally remix, cutting from one to the other. I give Barbra the gentle version, the I-don't-want-to-ruin-your-illusions vamp. She doesn't seem to have many illusions left, except about herself.

When we return to *that* subject, she talks for ten minutes or so about clothes. She has theories – what the designers are doing wrong, what women really want. I nod and ask her to explain more. Then she says, 'When I was ten, I used to be a real tomboy. I was climbing trees and fighting with my brother – some of the time even beating up on him. We lived in the country and I didn't know a *thing* about anything. I'd never even *seen* a fashion magazine. My mother didn't buy them. The first model I saw was on a poster when my daddy took me into town to get the truck fixed. It was up in the office of the mechanic, behind his desk. She was a blonde and was covered in something that looked like a fishing net, orange string in diamonds. Of course, it didn't cover her very well. She had brown nipples and they were stiff. You couldn't see anything else, which was lucky or I'd have screamed. I didn't scream, I just said, "Look, Daddy, she's got no clothes on." And he said "Who?" and I said "Her" and he said, "No, I don't think you'd call that clothes" and the mechanic, I remember he laughed at that. I was a little brat, so I kept on asking. "Is she cold?" I said. Which made the mechanic laugh again, but Daddy didn't. He was more serious. "It looks like she's on a beach," he said, "so she's probably quite warm." And the mechanic said, "She's *hot*." And my father laughed, but not really. I didn't understand what was going on – they were laughing about something I didn't know. It annoyed me. I turned to the mechanic and straight out asked, "Is she your sister?" And he laughs fit to burst. He laughs so he can't speak. "It's not his sister," says my father. Oh, I was so obnoxious. I say, "Then why does he have a picture of her there?" And the mechanic says, "She's not my sister. Boy, I wish she was. Sure would have made bathtime a whole lot more fun." And my daddy says, "We'll be back in two hours. You'll have it fixed by then?" And the mechanic looks at me and says, "You're a very pretty little girl." I can't remember any more than that. I think we went to a diner and had burgers. Or to the movies. The next thing I do remember, we were in the truck driving home. "Why did he laugh?" I say. And my daddy knows who I mean. He doesn't answer. "Did I say something funny?" I want to know. "No, honey," he says, "the man was just laughing at something else." "So was she really his sister?" I ask, and he says, "Did she look like his sister?" "No," I say, "he was ugly and she was pretty." "He's a mechanic," says my father, "and she's a model." I thought about this for a couple of minutes as we drove. And I can't remember this, but my father swears it's true – after a couple of minutes I said, "Daddy, I don't want to be a mechanic." That's the family joke, that I said, "I don't want to be a mechanic."'

'I'm sure you'd make a very good mechanic,' I say, mechanically.

'Perhaps I should've,' she says. 'I never wanted to be a model, either. It just happened. But, after I finish, I want to do something useful. I want to have a *skill* that people want. I can be *original*. If I took photographs, people would see how *I* see things – they wouldn't be looking *at* me. I could show them how they look through my eyes. *All* of them. The *mechanics* and everyone.'

She starts to cry. And it is such a sad moment. And the saddest thing is, I've heard it all before. A hundred times, at least. Heard it all.

Every.
Single.
Like.
Fucking.
Word.

ELVIS

I have never been any good at endings. In relationships, I always hang on long past the points of viability, dignity, sanity, forcing my girlfriends – eventually – into full-on dump mode. That way I end up getting custody of a few delicately bejewelled regrets whilst they have to accommodate the buffalo guilt.

Here, though, for once, I am going to tell a story that is all endings. A true story, though not a good one.

The first ending was of the band. Some fool at a record company thought Syph capable of a solo career – I mean, a *successful* solo career. Not the long day's journey into nightmares on wax that is Syph's speciality when disconnected from his life-support system (a.k.a. us).

There was money involved. Too much of it, Syph insisted, at the this-is-something-I've-just-got-to-do meeting – far too much to turn down.

I knew from the looks they gave me that Crab and Mono knew how this would end. (Those guys are much better at endings than me.) They could script the humiliation, the apologies, the grovelling, the reunion. All it meant, in practice, was a year's holiday – at least, if we didn't plan on doing anything else.

I hadn't even started thinking about what I might want to do with myself when the second ending came along: my father died.

There was a message on my machine to phone home – from Betty, a friend of my mother. So I assumed whatever had happened had happened to my mother. I called, and Betty told me.

My house is only a couple of blocks from my parents'. I don't know why – I have a perfectly decent car, or two, or three – but I got on my bike and ripped round. It was probably the fastest way. I could cut across lawns and through back alleys. Head down. Sprinting.

Didn't matter how fast I rode to the rescue, I was still too late to save my father –

– save him from his heart.

He was an active man. He lived a healthy life and, if you believe the cereal boxes, it should have been a long one.

When I got home, he was still on the toilet. That's where he died. He was half resting back on the cistern, half sideways on the wall.

My mother was too calm. At first I thought it was because she didn't really care. I became angry with he : I wanted some hysteria – if she wasn't going to provide it, 1 was. Only later did I understand she was in shock. That's why she had her friend, who was round for coffee when it happened – had Betty call me and not call the paramedics.

Dad hadn't locked the door. It was the en-suite of my parents' bedroom, so there was no danger of Betty coming in. A sports magazine lay in the bathtub, wet. The toilet roll had unspooled until it was touching the floor. Perhaps one of his arms hit it, when he flailed around, made it spin. These are the details.

Together, all three of us, we lifted him off the toilet and into the bedroom. I was wearing tracksuit bottoms, T-shirt, sneakers, no socks. He was going stiff. We didn't have to wipe him – the piece of crap which killed him was still inside, and would be for all eternity.

My mother pulled his pants up while we held him above the bed. Betty closed his eyes, like it was something she'd done before – though later she confessed it was a TV-learnt skill. I stood uselessly, thinking about Elvis.

That was what I'd have to tell the band – that my daddy went like the King: on the john, straining.

It's not very rock'n'roll, that's what I thought. *Even if Elvis did it, it's still not very rock'n'roll.*

My father, I'd like to say, having stripped off all his dignity just now, was a wonderful and dignified and unrock'n'roll man. But although he wanted me to be educated and have a career like his (law), he didn't kvetch about it. He understood me and he understood what I was trying to do – even when that was telling him to go fuck himself.

I never used those exact words. I'm glad about that.

He said he liked our music. And, truly, I think he did. Some of it – the quieter songs.

When I checked the browser on his computer, the last few sites he'd looked at were all to do with us. He had also been ordering bulbs for the garden. Since he took retirement, that was where he'd spent most of his time.

The funeral was arranged very quickly. Betty had another friend, Clara, whose husband had died three months before, and Clara gave me and my mother a list of telephone numbers, some handy hints about where to buy a coffin and totally unexpected amounts of love.

My father was buried after a service in the church he had regularly attended since boyhood. Crab and Mono were there – Syph turned up, ten minutes late.

There's something drastically sad about middle-aged rock stars in mourning. The jewellery picked up on tour, the bangles and beads and earrings – it's all wrong, unnecessary. Wearing black was nothing new for us. We should have worn white, like John and Yoko in the 'Imagine' film.

With a lot of persuading, the band didn't re-form to play one of our melancholy songs. How could I drum grief? Grief isn't played in 4/4 time. I spoke, slowly and audibly, even for the partially deaf. I kept the in-church music to Bach, Schubert and Mozart.

There were a few fans waiting, when we got outside, and I was proud of them for not asking for autographs.

Afterwards, everyone came back to our house. They stayed for a while, we talked, we ate, then they left.

That was the worst moment. It was me and my mother

and my father's death and the rest of our lives without him, hers more than mine – I'd expected to have to mourn them; for her, it had been a fifty-fifty chance. Theirs had been a great marriage. She was sixty-one years old. He had been her third boyfriend. Fifty-fifty, and she had been the one to lose.

Although I wanted to junk them, the words *This isn't very rock'n'roll* kept sounding in my head.

I moved back in, just to be there – back into my old basement room. I played records, tapes. I played comfort music. Something was missing – not just my father. Something in me.

It is hard to be involved with and dependent upon youth, after a certain age. The young have yet to learn mercy – well, most of them. I got some really sweet cards and emails. They, too, made me think about what I might be missing. I remembered that girl Barbra, the model. I remembered what she had said about wanting a *skill*. I wanted a skill, too. She'd thought I had one – Barbra thought that bashing skins and watching Syph's skinny ass every night counted as a skill. I knew it didn't. Grief needs a tune. Grief quite likes a lot of voices raised in pitch-perfect lamentation. But grief isn't thump-thump-thump-thump, boom-tssk boom-tssk boom-tssk boom-tssk.

That's what I was thinking, during those first few weeks.

My mother lost weight, and she was never big. I worried that she might become frail and so tried to trick her into eating. But she was thinner in every way. Without her husband, who I suddenly saw quite clearly as that, there was less reason for her to take up space.

I kept very quiet. Didn't touch my sticks. Didn't drink, smoke, hardly spoke.

Then my thoughts went flip-flop. Grief, now I had spent some time there, was in fact very like thump-thump-thump-thump. There was a real eloquence to the repetitious stupidity of it.

I got on a train of thought, and I rode and I rode and I rode.

To Africa.

It was my mother asked me to leave. I would have stayed as long as she wanted. Longer. A month in, she said she appreciated what I had done but it would be better if we both got on with our lives. 'Stop wallowing,' she said, 'we're very privileged to be able to wallow. Most people can't afford it.'

I told her I didn't want to go – I didn't have anything to do. She told me I should find something. She told me in the same way she'd told me, on rainy pre-teen days, that I had no inner resources.

It was true. I had no plural, only a singular: drumming.

The train of thought took me through some fairly desolate ghost towns.

One night, I went to see Skullfukk, a local deathmetal band, and thought I'd found the answer. The Answer. They were *so* loud. Their drummer was a total monster. Skullfukk's noise left no space in the universe for anything but itself. And the noise was either all grief or all not-grief – I couldn't tell which.

In the bar afterwards, I found the drummer and tried to explain how profound what they were doing was – how moving I found it that he could drum that way, so defiant of death, so brave. He was coming from a very different place – and where he was going to, accompanied by a little drummer-girl, was even more different.

Then the train stopped off at a gay club. I don't even know how I wound up inside. I think I was just walking past and heard the siren thump-thump sounding. Paid my entrance, got looked up and down, down, then stood in a basement full of men who'd put a lot more effort into themselves than I ever had. I wanted to persuade myself I didn't feel as uncomfortable as I did. I bought a drink and, when I was offered, a couple of pills, too.

I wasn't offered anything else. They all knew I was hopelessly straight.

One really kind man listened to my whole tale of woe. He couldn't hear very well, over the thump-thump. I didn't want him to.

I explained about my mother, telling me to leave home. 'Mine did, too,' he said. We had a moment of connection, and I thought of sleeping with him just out of gratitude.

Our music, *okay*'s, has never had much of a gay following. That night, I could understand why. It, our sound, is full where it should be empty and empty where it should be full. Our melancholic euphoria just doesn't suit these lives of euphoric melancholy.

I told everybody I could grab that I loved them and they either thought it was the drugs, which wasn't untrue, or were wiser still – this sweaty, out-of-shape man with the tight grip would never, in any sense of the word, be gay.

I *so* wanted to be.

I looked at the men kissing and grabbing ass and felt truly proud of them. It made me cry. They were the national anthem for a country I had only just discovered. We were noble compatriots in the Democratic Republic of Thump-Thump.

The kind man put me in a taxi-cab and blew a kiss through the open window. 'Take good care of yourself,' he said, and meant it.

My last thought-train experience happened to me when I was completely on my own. I call it the Music Room, but it only amounts to a couple of drumkits, a stereo and a guitar I can't get much out of.

It was a week, maybe, after the night of the gay.

I'd just gotten off the phone with my mother and gone downstairs, nothing in my mind.

When I picked up the sticks, they felt comfortable – and the snare was crisp when I tightened the skin.

I played.

I played everything.

I played like a drum machine. I played like a monster deathmetal drummer. I played half of our set. I played 4/4. I kept on and on playing it – boom-tssk boom-tssk – for about an hour. I sweated, gasped, spat and near pissed myself. I tranced out.

And then it happened.

I stopped playing, went upstairs, phoned our management, got them to book me on the next flight to Africa.

'Where?' they asked.

'Africa,' I said.

'Which country, exactly?'

'Anywhere,' I said. 'I don't care.'

'What are you going to do there?'

I refused to say. It would sound corny – drummer finds World Music. Stewart Copeland. Mickey Hart. That wasn't what it was about.

'South Africa,' I said.

With relief, they hung up.

Three hours later and I was on my way to the airport. They had someone from the record company meet me at the other end. To her, finally, sworn to silence, I confessed what I was after.

Her name was Dorothy. I thought about the gays back in the club. I was a friend of Dorothy, too.

She was the blackest person I'd ever met. And she had the whitest teeth. It sounds a racist stereotype, but it was true.

I wondered if the record company had her in this job deliberately – so visitors got what they expected, or hoped for: an African-looking African.

'Can you take me somewhere?' I asked.

'If that's what you want,' she said.

okay are even less popular with South Africans than with gays. I'd been surprised even to discover we had a record company there. A few sad souls in gated compounds, American exiles – our market.

We took a taxi down dusty airport-environs highways to smaller roads and then to tracks. I saw black people walking with burdens. I tried to smell the Africa-smell everyone mentions.

Dorothy called her funky aunt. Her aunt knew some musicians. The musicians would be glad of an excuse for a party. Simple as that.

I could tell Dorothy was humouring me – it was her job but, also, I genuinely annoyed and amused her. Should I tell her about my father? I decided not to. Perhaps the management had already informed her I was Handle With Care.

When we got to the house, it disappointed me. I think I'd wanted something made out of corrugated iron, no drains. The garden was a neat square of greenish lawn.

Dorothy's aunt sat me down in the shade of a tree and gave me a beer. She was wearing jungle print.

I am so profoundly embarrassed about what happened over the next few hours that I don't really want to put it on record. (Shouldn't have started then, should you?) This was just the latest of the endings – there have been many more since, but none so awkward. Almost with my first sip of beer, I realized I'd made a mistake. It wasn't that I shouldn't be there – being there was fine, despite Dorothy's pained and painful smile. Fine, fine, fine. There was a lot that was colonial and horrible about my motives for coming. What the fuck did I expect? *Roots?* To reconnect with the spirit of the drum? To jam into the night with master musicians? Still fine. No, my being there wouldn't have been a problem – if only I could truly have *been there.* That's the thing Africa requires of you: *presence.* Although I'd come at the right time, after my father died, I was still too early: my body was there but my whatever, my thump-thump, wasn't. It was a terrible mistake. I thought I'd been following an instinct, and it turned out to have been the most cerebral, calculating, contrived of motives. I was such a fucking honky.

The musicians came, one by one. They set up and played,

beautifully. Effortless slithering rhythms that are a lifetime's achievement, transcendently twangling melodies – all I'd wanted and expected. Everyone apart from me was present. Not in a soulful way. They were just at an impromptu party.

Dorothy explained who I was, and the musicians insisted I join in. They gave me a drum.

Which was when I started crying.

I didn't stop until I was back on the plane – it was the same plane, I checked with the air-hostess, the same air-hostess.

I felt so *ashamed*. I'd tried to *use* Africa. Like deodorant. Or disinfectant.

Halfway through the flight, the world began to look better. The ocean was blue beneath us. I'd seen it from a thousand planes. I was reassured. It, Africa, had worked – worked by failing to work. The embarrassment of it was good for me. I had needed *exactly* that: to go somewhere completely wrong and then to run away, to be welcomed and to feel excluded, to try to do what I really do and to find that it isn't what I do at all – that it's never been what I do. My truth is my absence from myself, my isn't-ism.

For the next nine months, until the call came through from Syph, I did *nothing* but watch TV.

'I want – man, this is so difficult – I've been such a hosehead – I wanna get the band back together.'

For nine months, I watched TV seriously, passionately, with absolute devotion.

As an ending, from the outside, it doesn't look very happy – but, strangely, it was.

FOREST

If the *Tree* album had been a big hit, I'm sure we wouldn't have split.

It's a shame – going into the studio, we had some good songs.

I'll admit, there was also obvious filler, which wouldn't have happened earlier in our career. E, A and Bm, chunka, chunka, twelve bars of the stuff. Don't leave me, baby-ooooh.

But we were trying to get out of that studio before there was a murder – i.e., before one of us killed Syph.

That was the second set of sessions, the second studio.

The first studio had been in Geneva Switzerland. Brutalist concrete exterior. State-of-the-art mixing desk. Floor-to-ceiling window overlooking the lake. Nice nibbles always around. Very bad choice.

There were no distractions, so we made our own, resurrecting old feuds, animating new ones.

Once upon a back in the day, we might have appreciated the magnificent view – might even have looked at it, now and again. But we recorded (like we always record) mostly late at night, so what we saw was not an expanse of subtle water but our dysfunctional life-size selves in a huge black mirror.

There was a strip of lake-edge lights, around head height, which meant that none of the others could make eye-contact except directly. Sitting where I was, low down on the drum stool, I caught all the flicking searches they made for one another. We played towards the unseen, behind-glass water, as if it was our audience – pretty good metaphor, when you think about it.

After we taped versions of the songs we'd brought, we wrote no new ones. We tried jamming, but it was all about

77

animosity – fucking up the other guy's groove before he'd had a chance to get into it.

What we needed was Syph to get his heart broken – to think he'd gotten his heart broken. Not too seriously. That would incapacitate him. We needed some yearning, some *saudade*. Then he would write lyrics for Instrumentals $\#_1$, $\#_2$, $\#_3$ for 'Slightly Wonky Song', for 'Hooping Coffin' and for 'Stray Bridge and Maybe-Outro'. But he'd convinced himself he was so happy for ever.

Her name, and I hurt myself by remembering it, was Forest. Only child of some serious California hippies, she followed her name wherever it took her. She said those very words, when we met her, 'I follow my name wherever it takes me.' We laughed, she didn't, Syph didn't.

Hello, new feud.

Forest wasn't shitting us, though. She had followed it. First off, aged about fifteen, she became convinced she had to be both deep and dark. So she took drugs, to help with deep, and most of all heroin, to ensure dark.

Second, in her twenties, she got badly lost within herself. The polite way of putting it was 'periods of hospitalization' – friends (she still had a couple, and they leeched onto us) elaborated: 'Oh, she'd started to bite children.'

'Where?'

'Wherever she could get to. Mostly ears. Lobes. She nearly chewed a couple of those off, before they locked her away.'

Thirdly, she did silence. For two and a half years, she said not a word. This coincided with being mental. If a tree falls in the eponymous, does anyone hear it? Well, Forest seemed to be listening.

In the middle of it all, somehow, this complete loon got hold of a cigarette lighter and, predictably enough, if anyone had been following the name-logic, tried to set herself on fire.

She started with her toes, which I never saw but which Mono swears were still black.

Luckily, one of the other patients told on her – and was believed. Imagine that: if they'd thought, 'Napoleon's just hallucinating, *again*.'

Then, amazingly, showing a forest's powers of regrowth after decimation, she returned to the world – green, springlike, smelling strongly of damp earth, ready to circle back round to deep dark drugs.

Syph picked her up and for some secret reason of his own refused to put her down. I don't even know where they met, some S&M club somewhere. He'd been hanging out a lot in San Francisco. All the times we'd wanted him to settle, and then when he does it's with a woman who makes Nico look like a fitness instructor. (*Instructor* not *instructress*.) I can only think that Forest's hopelessness was what did it for him.

(By the way, if you ask him, I'm sure he won't be able to remember any of these little details. When she wanted, Forest was still pretty good at extended silences. I, fool that I am, tried to befriend her – and so her friends befriended me. In return for my company, they became selectively indiscreet. I feared, even then, the things they didn't say. What Syph knew from Forest was the myth – *I follow my name, wherever it leads*.)

Syph wasn't built for monogamy, so they did three- and foursomes. These were surprisingly difficult to arrange, given Syph's past history – but this was fucking (non-fucking?) Switzerland. I'm sure there were orgies where whole mountain villages took part, after christenings – we just hadn't been invited. Perhaps it was Forest who put the other girls off – those ear-biting stories got around. I'm not saying who spread them.

Crab and Mono tolerated her. Mono had brought Major over, so they fished the lake whenever they could. But whether in a boat or not, Major took no crap from anyone, and Forest, she could see, was fundamentally founded upon crap. This, too, caused problems in the studio.

Just because someone can *hold* a tambourine doesn't mean

they can *play* it. Just because you're *fucking* someone doesn't mean you should give them a *tambourine to hold.*

Syph even kept the assistant engineer behind one early morning and laid down some of Forest on backing vocals. It sounded like an operatic cow yodelling in a mineshaft, after falling down the mineshaft. To try to save things, the engineer had put on enough echo to satisfy even the Seven Dwarfs.

Hi-*ho*!

When the engineer guiltily and reluctantly played us the tape the next morning, Syph nodded along as if the presence of a cow-yodel in our mixes was quite usual.

The argument began, nothing strange in that, but Syph insisted early on, 'If that track goes, I go.'

Then he left, with Forest.

He *left* but he didn't *go*.

We all knew the difference. Industry lawyers had explained it to us on numerous occasions, at our own expense. Vast.

For a couple of days – yes, we started working while it was still daylight – for a day or three, we added overdubs. Cow-yodel track was left untouched, though we did listen back to it with Forest faded out. True to historical precedent, the best song on the album was the one we were in the process of majorly fucking up.

Me being me, I thought we could sort it out. Get Syph to listen to the song without Forest in the room. Ask him his honest opinion. Suggest we do two mixes. He and Forest had been inseparable for a month, but I didn't let that deter. I got the engineer, who had somehow kept his job, to rip me a copy – then I took a limo to Syph's house.

He was staying separately from the rest of us. They had checked out of the large, new and admittedly soulless corporate tower-hotel on the first night. He needed something a bit more *funky*, he said. Later I heard that it was Forest who craved funk, and so got them thrown out by urinating on the lobby couches. Not one couch, several.

What they'd found was a two-room cottage with a steep roof and a garden of thick mud.

The driver who most evenings brought Syph across to the studio was able to drop me there.

Europe, I love you. Why don't you love me back? Why do you always make me suffer?

The tinfoil covering the windows was a not-good-thing. The last time I'd seen this was during the so-called Thin White Duke breakdown. Since then, Syph had been if not *clean* then only mildly grubby.

I knocked on the door. There was a bell, an actual bell, but the rope had been pulled off the clapper – I saw it lying in the snow.

Did I say this all happened during early winter?

Knock, knock harder, and still no response. Knock once more, then, deep breath, try the door. It opens – in I go, to face whatever.

Or nothing.

The room was without furniture. But there was a huge fireplace. I looked in the other room, also empty, then came back to see if the ashes were still hot. Fallen out onto the floor was a chair leg. A couple of charred CDs, too. Syph and Forest must have moved on when they'd burnt everything there was to burn.

I tried the neighbours. All they gave me was grief. In French. Did I know those terrible people? Had I ever heard of the law? Of decency?

Back to the hotel.

At the three-quarter-band meeting I called, we voted not to search for Syph.

The decision-making process went like this:

Me: I think he might be in genuine danger . . .

Crab: Fuck him.

Mono: Yeah, fuck him.

Me: Fine.

I set off to search for Syph as soon as the others left.

When I say *set off*, I didn't actually leave the room. These days, the best way to find someone, or something, is to ask a few thousand strangers to help.

At first, I ghosted through the fansites, looking for sightings. News that we were recording a new album had been officially announced – after being widely leaked. It had taken Yoyo (hi Yoyo!) about three hours to track us down to Switzerland. Her contacts at Canadian airports are *astonishing*. Two Swiss fans helped her identify the studio, our hotel and were even able to give her a rundown of our bar tabs that evening. All this was up there for the world to see dot com.

I'd hoped one of the true faithful had been hanging around outside Syph's lovenest. No.

I was sure they'd have been spotted in whatever new hotel they were trashing. No.

I used my lurking identity, posted the question, sat back to wait.

No.

No-one had seen Syph or Forest for forty-eight hours. The fans knew of Forest. Many were infuriated by her. Many, particularly our monosyllabic or entirely giggly fifteen-year-old Japanese girlfans, believed Syph was, by rights, *theirs*. They had constructed elaborate shrines of on-line hate to Forest. Some were hilarious. Some were terrifying. I learnt things about her I didn't need, just then, to know. When I said *genuine danger* to the other guys, I thought I'd been exaggerating; I hadn't.

I wondered whether or not Syph had burnt their passports along with everything else in the room.

Trying Yoyo's approach, I called the airport – tried a couple of Syph's favourite airlines. They were so tight-lipped it was hard to get them to admit they even knew what a plane was. I slammed the phone down.

Then I thought.

Thought like a detective.

Addicts.

Therefore.

Drugs.

Therefore.

Dealer.

How many could there be in Geneva?

So, off I went to buy heroin.

I thought I was thinking like a private dick but really I was just thinking like a dick.

In the first bar I went to, I was arrested.

I've stayed in hotels that were less amenable than that Swiss jail cell: so clean, so well designed, and with a great echo. Even Forest's cow-yodel would have sounded bearable in there.

My phonecall brought record-company lawyers down, and I was bailed within six hours. They told me I'd have to leave the country, probably the next day.

Back in my hotel room, feeling a real idiot, having fucked the whole investigation (and whatever was left of the recording sessions) up completely, the phonecalls started. *I heard you had some problems*, they said. *I can help.*

Getting arrested had been an act of detective genius – now every dealer in the country knew I was looking to connect.

Few of them were informed enough to know I'd been in town a month already. If I hadn't scored before, I'd either have kicked or died.

I asked each of them whether they'd sold to Syph or Forest – and on number five I got lucky.

Yes, they'd purchased this and that from him. No, he wasn't going to divulge on the phone exactly what. No, he hadn't encountered them in a couple of days. Yes, he was sure he'd have heard if they'd gone looking somewhere else. Yes, he'd used a gofer. No, he couldn't put me in touch. No, not for anything would he put me in touch. Yes, for X amount he would put me in touch.

The gofer came.

The phrase 'pissholes in snow' almost covers it – but piss with lots of blood in it.

Otherwise, he was pale, thin, quiet, obviously close to dying.

He was also a blessèd angel sent from God – sent to collect Syph and Forest from their house and drive them to the airport. They had no bags to carry but, starstruck, he saw them onto a flight for –

– Stuttgart.

(Germany has always been one of my favourite countries.)

Stuttgart? What was there? A few minutes on my computer told me. I was so *dumb*. I should have followed the name-logic. Forest was taking Syph to herself.

Notorious junkie that I was, I had to fly out of Switzerland – disgraced, never to return – the next morning. Mono and Crab knew I'd been looking for Syph. I'd never scored drugs myself: it was one of the reasons I'd hung out with them – right from cigarettes up. Me getting busted was the funniest thing they'd *ever* heard. In Switzerland already!

I told them about Stuttgart, the Black Forest. Get it, guys? Forest? They said they might follow, if I found a. Syph, b. two decent songs and c. a small and unostentatious recording studio. Oh, and I had to get rid of that fucking talentless bitch, too.

It took two weeks. I don't know if you know this but the Black Forest is big. The fansites were no help – Syph and Forest had gone underground. Our management refused me access to his credit-card records. I let my instinct guide me – my instinct for Syph's instinct for the sordid. I looked for black-eyed underage girls crying in the darkest corners of bars. And when I found them, I talked to the barmen, the boys at the bar and, finally, the girls themselves. One of them, number fifteen or sixteen, had heard something from a friend of a friend. A story. A bad story. Her English was good. In the taxi over, she told me she liked our music. Some youth cultures interpret what we do as Goth or Emo. Which is distressing but not un-understandable. The friend was amazed it was *really* me. 'Is it really you?' she kept asking. She would have done *anything* for me, and was clearly *dying* to, but I just asked to speak to the next friend. The one with the story. I was touched by the sight of friend two's bedroom: dolls which had been blonde subjected to re-dyes and dressing up in homemade vamp outfits; posters of bands half my age on the wall; an autograph book with the names of all their teachers in it – no-one famous before me. Her parents were out for the evening. The friend phoned the next friend (friend three) and the next friend came straight round. Perhaps she had been boasting about Syph, perhaps she hadn't really met him, but, no, there were lots of bracelets on her wrists to cover the bruising. More than that, her eyes were a decade older than those of her friends. (Please, not heroin. Not that.)

'Do you know where they are?'

Her English wasn't as good as friend one or two. Friend two translated. Friend two would do *anything*. Because, unlike, friend three, she hadn't already had to do it.

'She knows somewhere they were, yesterday.'

'Can she take me?'

'She can take everyone. We also will come.'

Another taxi. The longer we spent together, the more fanlike the three girls became. Friend three noticeably less so than the other two. She'd brushed up against the object of their awe – brushed and been bruised. I didn't ask directly what had been done to her. Her nails were black and bitten. I wondered, *If I had a daughter, would she be a Goth?* Thank God I didn't, if Syph hadn't fucked her, it would have been all her friends and most of their moms.

We tried one bar. They weren't there. The taxi driver almost refused to take us to the next place we wanted to go. Money persuaded. The girls told him I was famous. His eyes in the mirror looked me over, thinking: *famous kiddy-fucker.*

I was no longer doing this for the album. (When you say we didn't put enough effort in, Mr Music Critic, did you ever think of *this*?) I certainly wasn't doing it for Syph. Over those two weeks in the forest, I'd had enough time to think about what I'd say to him when I tracked him to his lair. No, I was doing it because I had decided it should be done; as a detective, I wanted to solve the case.

They weren't at the next bar, and the barman said he didn't know where they had been staying, but the owner overheard our conversation, said *hi*. He really was a fan. His bar was odd – Goth but in a very German way. (They should be experts at Goth, shouldn't they?) Lots of antlers and assorted wildlife-heads. Then a TV screen showing American sports. And paintings of stormy mountains.

In return for a promise that one day we'd play a concert on his pool-table of a stage, the bar-owner said he'd take me to Syph. I tried to ditch the three little gothlets but they insisted on coming.

We got in the owner's SUV. He told me stories of small-town excess. I laughed when I had to. He wouldn't tell me where we were going, but he *would* tell me that he wouldn't tell me where we were going, and also that he wouldn't tell me why he wouldn't tell me. That was the best joke of all. As far as he was concerned. And that was all that mattered. As far as he was concerned.

We arrived.

They were living in a treehouse. That was the punchline. My arm was punched. A treehouse, yes!

The owner's drug dealer had one at the bottom of his garden – for him, not his kids. In fact, to get *away* from his kids. A treehouse, the dealer told me, equipped with electric heating, sound system, widescreen TV, satellite, phone, bathroom. There was no tinfoil in the windows. Then I realized how dark it was, beneath the branches of so many trees.

'Go up,' said the owner.

'Yes, go,' said the dealer.

Girls one and two looked excited, three showed signs of fear. I thanked them all.

Climbed the ladder, lifted the trapdoor, pulled myself up into the room, looked around.

There were blankets on the bed, a fleshy spiral lump of pale white in the middle of them.

It was Syph, foetal, sobbing.

I said, 'I quit,' and it felt good – *I quit.*

'She's gone,' he said.

'I've had enough,' I said.

'She's left me,' he said.

'This is the end,' I said. 'I'm not coming back.'

'Didn't you hear me?' he said. 'She said she couldn't stand me any more. I disgusted her. I was so corrupt, so impure.'

A head came up through the floor.

'Please go away,' I said.

The trapdoor dropped.

'I need her,' Syph said.

'That's your problem.'

'She took her stuff this morning. She was gone before I woke up. I love her.'

'She was a total bitch. You're much better without her.'

'I love her.'

'Look at you.'

'She was . . .'

'She sang like a cow,' I said. 'And you wanted that on our album.'

'She was beautiful.'

'Goodbye, Syph,' I said and turned to go.

'You have to help me,' he said. 'You have to help me find her.'

So I did.

(I *know.*)

With a little help from the Baden-Württemberg police, and a man out collecting firewood.

Forest had handcuffed herself to a tree. Hypothermia. The

keys were found stuck into an apple, kicked out of reach. Not that she'd tried to reach them — forensics told us that. No, Forest just sat still and waited. I wonder if she sang to herself. I wonder if she liked the sound of her own voice.

The interrogator asked me where I thought she'd got hold of the cuffs. *That* made me laugh.

Home in Canada again, at the second studio, we mixed the album. We left Forest's vocals on the best song, 'So Holy', made it a Track One Side A, finished the rest of the good songs, added some filler, put it out, got slaughtered by critics worldwide, split, re-formed.

I play the drums.

FANS

They gave us an award, the fuckers.

No, I better be exact: we were offered the chance to accept a lifetime achievement award on not-quite-live-because-someone-might-swear Canadian TV, and we accepted *without hesitation*.

Not without discussion. *That* went like this –

Syph (manic): Fuck, yeah.

Mono (imitating): Aye aye, Captain.

Crab (slurred): Yessir.

Me (blah): Hey, shouldn't we at least talk this thing through?

Syph: We just did.

What it meant was, we stayed in an over-luxurious Toronto hotel, were driven to an atmosphereless air-hangar, sound-checked, were driven back to the hotel, hung around, showered, got dressed up, were driven back to the air-hangar, hung around backstage exchanging friendly greetings with members of the rock'n'pop community for whom we once expressed nothing but contempt, went out to watch the show begin, drank our table dry in competition with the adjoining tables, won (thanks to Crab), were mentioned, applauded, praised ludicrously by two talentless no-wits, watched a montage of our greatest misjudgments, were applauded again but *louder*, strolled to the stage through a crossfire of eat-shit glances and I'll-call-you gestures, made it to the microphone stand and said –

I know I wasn't the only band member to give thought to the question of what we really *had* achieved in our lifetime, so far. I was merely the only one of us to become radically depressed over the answers I came up with.

When we started out, we wanted to make a record. Our dreams still had the oil-slick sheen of vinyl. Simple. Make a record – prove everybody wrong. See, it's been worth all the sacrifices.

Well, there weren't *that* many sacrifices. The main one, respectability in our parents' eyes, only applied to Mono and me. Syph's funky mother even packed him a lunchbox before waving him off down the road he's been following ever since. The lunchbox contained some very powerful weed.

Crab's father was never sober enough to take a stance one way or the other, or, in fact, any stance but monged out on the couch of rancid. His greatest moment of clarity came the first time we appeared on TV. He thought Crab had been fucking with his video-player, about the only sacred object in his house, so he crawled over, picked it up with both hands and rammed it straight through our screen images – electrocuting himself.

Not seriously but not hilariously, either. He had a minor stroke two days later, which the doctors told Crab was completely unconnected.

The loss of control in his right side meant Crab Senior had to change his beer-can hand but not a whole lot else.

He stopped off on the way back from hospital and bought a new TV. Video-players, he's never trusted again.

So, what was our achievement there? Performing our first single on a local chatshow (you've never heard of it) or part-killing one of our parents? (Though Crab's father is still alive and mine isn't.)

There has always been collateral damage. So much so that *collateral* is clearly bullshit. *Necessary* damage, *required*, *essential*, *without which* . . .

I have a terrible ringing in my ears. Tinnitus. It's a minor thing, I know, but it never goes away. Have I told you about this before? The only time I really forget about it is when we're playing music – or I'm listening to something else. Rock, mostly, I can still hear it over classical. It's like someone has leant a guitar up against a still-on amp, right in my head. But feedback would at least change, warp, tie itself into a knot of a note. ('I Feel Fine' by The Beatles.) This is the sound of a television after the channel goes dead and before they put a continuity announcement up. A *beep* with an infinite number of *e*'s. The *b* was way back when. I'll know I'm dead when I reach that *p*.

'First off,' says Syph, lifting the award to head height, 'we'd like to thank our record company – everyone at Colombia – you've worked so hard, over the years . . .'

We suck corporate cock. That's what Syph's saying, and not even in code. We take it and we lovingly suck it.

As usual, we're letting Syph be our spokesperson. Always a mistake but no-one else wants to do it, and he'd throw such a tantrum if they did.

I am standing far back from the podium – any further and I'd be in our dressing-room toilet. At the end, I'll probably do the usual drummer-thing and lean too close to the microphone, boom out a word that sounds like *Hanks* and try to exit stage left without, please, falling on my ass.

When we started, we had principles. It was almost a manifesto: Never say what we were doing was rock'n'roll. Treat the people who liked our music with respect, as the intelligent and sensitive individuals they had shown themselves to be (by liking our music). Put halfway-decent songs on the B-sides. Split the publishing equally four ways. Don't exploit women as sex-objects in the videos – and try as hard as possible to exploit them as sex-objects on all other occasions. (Oh, that last bit was Syph's contribution.) What else? No guitar solos, drum solos. No lighters-aloft moments. No cocaine, no heroin.

Then we went on tour, and what happened to all mid-way successful bands happened to us. It's such a cliché, listening to some group who put out a delicate and well-arranged first album start talking about how the songs really only came alive 'in a live context' after they took it on tour and rambling on about how the second album was all about 'catching some of what this band's really about – which is the live show' and how that meant it was really important to keep a 'live vibe' in the studio and how they can't wait to get out there again and play these songs 'live'. All of which means turn the motherfucker up to eleven and rock the fuck out!!! And that's what happened to us on tour.

Gradually. Not the first time out. Our second album was still pretty un-rock. But after three or four years, we began to realize the *Why?* – the *Why?* of Mick Jagger's minstrel show, of Roger Daltry's wire-act, of Robert Plant's silk trousers.

Why?

It fucking works – makes a good night great, a great night transcendent, and a bad night survivable.

So, we ditched our trademark suits. Syph's posing became more extreme. Crab's solo grew four bars every other night – and had bastard offspring. The lightshow stopped being monochrome and became just a touch heavy metal. We haven't stooped to dry-ice, not yet.

'And we'd like to send a big thank-you out to our management team – Tony, Jordan, you guys – you really bring it on home, man – you're the best . . .'

We are pretentious no-lifes. It doesn't matter that Tony and Jordan, or whoever is managing us that month, despite being utterly unscrupulous, achieve the almost impossible task of keeping us idle enough to write and record songs. It doesn't matter that Cindy, their assistant, never gets mentioned but does at least 70 per cent of the real work. It doesn't matter that Clarissa and Maggie, who do publicity and marketing, are the truest friends this band has ever had. The fact that we're even able to use the words 'management team' puts us in that group of abysmal sell-outs who shift (not make) product (not music).

'And last, and most important, we'd like to thank the fans . . .'

We do have fans, and it is entirely correct that we thank them – also, that we blame them, hate them, fear them, feel infinite contempt for them.

If it weren't for the fans, we wouldn't have a reason to keep on keeping on. We do, some of us, quite literally owe them our lives.

Crab was married for a while to the woman who runs the Canadian branch of our Appreciation Society – named back when we thought it was patronizing to call fans fans.

Mono was introduced to Jesus by Shirley from Lubbock, Texas. Thankfully, he excused himself and went and hid in the spiritual bathroom a short while afterwards. But Jesus, thanks to Shirley, straightened him out at a difficult time.

And at least three female fans have saved Syph from overdosing.

The best fan-related story/worst fucking nightmare took place in Moscow Russia.

We'd just finished a gig and were relaxing, each in his different way, in the dressing-room.

The venue was an old theatre. Syph was sitting in front of one of those mirrors surrounded by bulbs. He also was surrounded by a bright halo of dyed-blonde heads.

Into the middle of this walks Irina. Very confidently, she pushes a couple of lanky, high-cheekboned beauties aside and says, 'I hov drogs. Gokaine. Yeroin. The byeast.'

Syph, whose eyes have been wandering, and not over the fans' bodies, says, 'Well, what are we waiting for, baby, let's go!'

I think about following them. The ease with which Irina gained entrance to the dressing-room is suspicious. She's no looker, not in comparison. Short, muscular, savage mouse-brown bob, shiny black boots. And usually there's five minutes whining-pleading with security – promises according to the old contract of no head, no backstage pass. As far as I can see, Irina's just waved straight in. Perhaps it's the drugs. Perhaps they are the best.

I think a second time about following them. But then I opt for an early night, alone if possible. I made a mistake in Sweden, the week before, and I'm still regretting her.

'Later,' says Syph, halfway out the door.

What happened after this has been stuck together from various sources, mostly deeply unreliable.

Syph's version, for what it's worth, runs thus:

'How was I to know something was wrong? She says she has drugs. She does. We go to the toilets in the theatre and do a couple of fine lines. Whammo. But the heroin, she says, is at her apartment. So the limo takes us there and, you know me, I waste no time. Next thing, I wake up in hospital. Only it's more like a prison. I feel like shit and I'm in a cell with a locked door. There's mould on the walls. I think I hear rats in the corridor outside. Someone tells me afterwards it used to be a KGB mental hospital. Now, I've been in a lot of fucked-up places . . .'

At which point, he'll lose the plot and start telling you about the English castle which still had a fully operational torture chamber or the brothel in Greenland where you could fuck a strapped-down bear. But we've got most of what we need from him. If pressed, he'll add two further details.

'I didn't really think anything much at the time, but outside the girl's apartment an ambulance was parked. I wondered who was ill. And when we go upstairs, two men are in there playing some faaassst game with shooting on her computer. I don't even ask who they are – or why they're wearing white coats.'

The first we knew about it, three that morning, the management get a phonecall saying Syph has been taken into a very exclusive private hospital – after overdosing on heroin. The hospital, in fact, is so exclusive that some clients have objected to the high fees charged for their world-class life-saving work. Syph is recovering well and is perfectly safe, but will remain under doctor's supervision until the sum of Z has been paid.

(Z, to put it in proportion, was our gross takings on gigs in Moscow and St Petersburg, plus Vilnius, Tallinn and Riga.)

Tony and Jordan stall, ask for a number. The hospital administrator (Irina, I think) says she'll call back in the morning.

Jordan calls the promoter who is handling the Russian tour. 'Ah,' he says, or words to this effect, 'so they're still trying that old scheme.' He doesn't want to talk on the phone. He will come to the hotel.

Tony wakes me, Crab and Mono. We join them in their suite. Boy, are we pissed.

When the promoter arrives, he is nothing but business. There are two options, which he proceeds to lay out. First, pay the ransom – that's what it is, a ransom. Second, let him (the promoter) hire a small army of former KGB operatives, supply them with weapons of choice, pay a few people off to find out where Syph's being held, storm the place. With surprising calm, he then mentions the upsides to the courses of action. With the first, we're guaranteed to get Syph back. The promoter had dealt with these people before (naming no big names) and believes them to be trustworthy. With the second, we'll be greeted with a lot of respect if we ever come back to town. Then he gives the downsides. First option costs probably twice as much as the second (killing is cheap) and, quite frankly, isn't the Moscow way of doing things. He would much prefer it if we could sort this out with the maximum number of people getting hurt. Second option could leave us with a dead lead-singer, thirty years each in a Siberian jail and the Russian mafia after us and our loved ones for the rest of our (short) lives.

When the management say, after due consultation (a series of nods around the room), that we'll go for option the first, our promoter does something very odd: he pulls out his phone, speed-dials a number, says, 'Da,' and then smiles very broadly.

Yes.

That old scheme.

Syph, two hours after the financial arrangements have been concluded, which takes a day and a half, is delivered safely to the hotel lobby.

As a farewell gift, Irina has injected him with a full dose of the premium Afghan brown she used in the sting.

Before she did this, though, we eventually find out, she has him sign copies of *all* our albums, singles and even some majorly obscure bootlegs.

Irina is a true fan, you see.

'So, thanks for supporting us all these years,' Syph says. 'We love you. We couldn't do it without you.'

I step up to the microphone, lean in too close, boom out a word that sounds like *Hanks* and exit stage left.

BEADS

Rock'n'roll is dead.

Thank God.

But God is dead, too.

Thank Whatever.

Whatever is whatever.

Everything, as someone once sang, is everything.

But nothing is never nothing.

I'd given up – I'd given up not *everything* (I can't quit breathing; eating I've tried and failed), but *everything I can*. And on top of that, as much as I could, I'd given up caring about having given up. No longer did I live my life, my life lived me – and it was more of a lifestyle, to be honest. We were mid-way through an American tour, with only two weeks' holiday afterwards before we had to go to Europe and Asia. I was doing unspeakable things in rarely thought of States of the Union. And, looking ahead, I feared for the integrity of 22nd London, 23rd Cardiff, 24th Glasgow, 25th Belfast, 27th Dublin ... I feared for myself because I hadn't managed to give myself up: I still cared about the fact that it was just conceivable someone might possibly care about me – and, in my tourbusting state, I would probably have thousand-yard-stared right through them. Lost – but not enough – in America, I spent a lot of time with Syph. (Words of doom.) I didn't try to rival him, that would have been suicidal, but I did do my best to *accompany* him. For the first time in quite a while, I stopped saying *no*. One or two afternoons, as we emerged into the lobby or climbed onto the bus, I was the one to be lauded for my squalour of the early morning hours, for outrages committed. I even sunk so low, back then, that I earned the affectionate respect of the roadcrew.

In the middle of the beginning of the end of all this, I met a Buddhist monk in San Francisco.

Religious types are particularly skilled at gaining access to dressing-rooms of all sorts – more adept, even, than slutty High School girls. Many a rock star has found himself down on his knees before a visitor saying 'OH GOD PLEASE FORGIVE ME FOR THE SINFUL LIFE I HAVE BEEN LEADING.' (An unusual situation for rock stars, who are much more used to having visitors on their knees in front of them – for contrary purposes, though the kneelers may also say 'Oh God,' occasionally.)

It was before the show. The monk had a bright saffron robe, a nice smile and wanted to give me some beads.

That was it.

He didn't have a speech to give me. I'm not even sure if he spoke English, though he may have been fluent in six languages for all I know. He may have been live-and-direct from the Potala, Lhasa, Tibet.

After handing me the beads, he pray-bowed like they do, smiled once more, nodded as if something had been understood between us and then left.

I put the beads down somewhere and went back to what I'd been doing, which was long, narrow and snow-white. All around my brain.

We got the gig over with.

I forgot about the monk's visit and gift until the next morning when I found the beads on my bedside table.

There was only one rational explanation: the girl I'd been with the night before had picked them up from the dressing-room, had maybe worn them or kept them in a pocket (but she had very few pockets, as I recall) and then, when she was about to leave, had felt guilty about taking them, so put them where I'd find them.

This made me feel guilty, about the beads and about her. She'd been a nicer girl, I now saw, than I'd taken her for. I hadn't appreciated that, and was getting old-style Clap-

feelings of regret. Annoyed, I left the beads where they were.

It took less than twenty-four hours for them to catch up with me again. The hotel we'd been staying in was monstrously efficient – and it was their policy to FedEx everything a VIP guest left in their room (everything including suspiciously might-be-valuable items in the trash) either to that guest's home address or, as in my case, their next hotel. A gold-leafed shirtbox was sitting waiting for me on the counterpane – inside, the two unused condoms, a copy of *Wire* magazine and the reincarnated beads.

I did not take this as a sign – I was *resolute* in *not* taking this as a sign. A sign was not what I needed, right that moment. The minibar, however, was.

Soundcheck, hotel, gig, hotel.

We had a rest day the following day. I had a choice of fishing with Mono or drinking with Crab or drugging with Syph. I followed my heart – it wanted to beat as pointlessly fast as possible.

We were staying every night in another one, another link, in a chain of hotels. I knew that if I left the beads here, including in the trash, they would follow me to the next room, the next city.

But there was always a chance, my decelerating heart told me at 3 a.m., that they wouldn't.

So began the secret game of a week. Day one, I left the beads under the pillow. Day two, in the safe. Days three, four and five behind the bed, beneath the bed and between the bed and the mattress. Day six, under a pile of bloody tissues in the bathroom bin. Day seven, in the cistern.

HOTELS 7 – ME 0.

Or maybe that should be BEADS 9.

I found out, later on, that it was part of our management's deal with the chain that our rooms be subjected to an FBI-style search every time we left. I'm not sure if this was the direct cause, but we'd once been forced to cancel a show because Syph wasn't able to find his lucky guitar pick. His paranoia had gotten to the point where he believed, if he didn't play with it, he would forget all the words to all the songs in his solo acoustic set.

At the time, though, because I didn't know this, I put the beads' pursuit of me down to a bizarre combination of the supernatural and the corporate. And so I decided to have one final go, a real good one, at getting rid of the little danglers – I threw them out the window of the tourbus, the toilet window.

They almost killed a 6' 4" biker – hit him full in the mirror-shaded visor. He turned his big old Triumph around and went back to collect the evidence, always knowing we in the bus weren't going fast enough to get away. It was a lonely stretch of freeway in East Texas. I'd tried to ditch the beads in the driest, dustiest part of the desert. Once he'd found the projectile, the biker got back on his silver machine and in about two minutes pulled up alongside us, made some easy-to-interpret gestures, flagged us down.

'I should sue you,' he said. 'I'm going to sue you.' Sue was a lot better than kill, but the fact he spoke with a Brooklyn accent and didn't once swear made him a terrifying figure.

No-one confessed to having thrown the beads at him. I mean, I was too scared to confess.

The management talked him down – explained who we were. Girls tied things to our bus all the time, and this love-gift had probably been there for a while and just worked loose. The biker was interested. 'A band?' We were charming. He was charming. We made friends with him. He was a lawyer. International copyright. We knew people in common. Lawyers, mostly. He liked some of our music. He thought our international legal set-up was *risible*. I never thought I'd hear a biker say *risible*. We invited him to our next show, and his girlfriend. Ah. That would be *boyfriend*. He went off almost happy, with a story. He left us the beads. 'As a souvenir.'

Which, of course, immediately turned them into the single most desirable thing on the bus – and that included eighteen-year-old Lula-Maybelline from Fort Worth and twenty-four-year-old Honey from All Over. When I said, 'But they're mine,' no-one believed me. Everyone now claimed them. I explained about the monk. No-one remembered him. Following the laws of physics of the *okay* tourbus, the most desirable thing always ends up with Syph – and Syph always ends up getting bored of it (them) and discarding it (them). But for some reason he took an unusual liking to the beads. He began to wear them on-stage. I was afraid they would become his lucky beads, replacing the lucky pick.

I needed them back, and there was only one way to get them: ante up and rejoin, after five years' sabbatical, the perpetual back-of-the-tourbus poker game, catch some strong cards, go heads up with Syph, put him all in, win, bankrupt the motherfucker.

This took ten afternoons and cost me approximately twenty thousand dollars, Canadian (we have some loyalty). I'm a better poker player than Syph, not than the roadies. And Syph had some astonishing luck. When it came to it, he was reluctant to put the beads into the pot, but with no more cash left, he had no choice. Full house beats three of a kind every time. As soon as they were in my hand, I cashed myself out and left the table.

'There *was* a monk,' said Syph, getting up to hound me. 'I remember now – there was a monk, in a robe. He gave you those beads.'

I got in my bunk, pulled shut the curtains.

Although he really wanted to harass me further, Syph could not break Bus Rule #2 *If a band member wishes to be alone he may signal this by drawing the curtains on his bed-area shut. It is absolutely forbidden to disturb a band member who wishes to be alone – unless the bus is on fire and the fire is getting close to them and you give a shit.*

I held the beads in my hand. They were a little scuffed from hitting the highway – Syph's stage antics with the mic-stand had probably done some damage to them, too. But the night in the cistern didn't seem to have adversely affected them. I stared at the beads. Why had I tried so hard to get rid of them and then so desperately to get them back? I put the beads on.

Nothing changed. I didn't become an insta-Bodhisattva. My behaviour, truth to tell, worsened – but only because the tour was continuing and, by then, all sensations were null.

Syph stole the beads a couple of times. With some help from my buddies the roadcrew, I got them back. They'd seen me win the beads – and although Syph was their blow-and-pussy God, they refused to let him resort to theft. They wanted a God they could respect. (Don't we all?) Eventually, Syph lost interest. Still nothing changed.

Nothing changed and the beads stayed the same. I wore them all the time, even in bed, even in the shower. They became a still-point in a tumble-dryer world. During radio interviews, I silently counted through them, just numbers, not prayers. There were twenty beads before the two separated by an elastic knot. I wondered, vaguely, if twenty *meant* anything.

I began to think about the monk – not about trying to track him down, ask him the meaning-of-life question. No, I began to think about him as a thing, a living thing, giving thing. He had come to see me and hadn't wanted anything from me – not a conversation, an autograph, a handshake, not even a thank-you. Which was lucky because I hadn't given him any of those. Not even a thank-you. And that was what made the gift so amazing.

They were cheap beads, I knew – I thought I knew. He probably gave them away by the dozen. He was probably famous for it, in San Francisco.

But when I asked around, no-one on the scene had heard of a monk who handed out beads.

I began to wonder if they really were worthless.

On the next free day, I took them into a pawnshop.

The guy (who looked like the kind of pawnshop guy you'd buy from a pawnshop) offered me ten dollars. I told them that wasn't enough, that I wanted a hundred. He offered me fifty. I knew then they weren't cheap giveaways. I said I'd give him fifty dollars if he told me what they were really worth. He looked at me strange, then told me they were antique ebony – black all the way through. Their monetary value was high. He'd have to check. That was enough for me. They were expensive. But maybe he'd been a rich monk.

The beads were working on me. Just by being a pure gift, they had made me realize quite how cynical I'd become – always looking for undeclared motives.

You could say, the monk *did* want something from me. He wanted to make me a Buddhist, convert me.

But that's not how Buddhists operate. They're not out on the street corners telling you their way is the only way, and any other is a sure-route excursion to hell. (Oh, Texas, I remember your million churches.)

The monk wanted only one thing from me, the acceptance of what he had to give.

It was a beautiful gesture – like writing a song you know people will really love, and not fucking it up in the recording studio.

By this time the American tour was coming to an end, glorious and debased.

A one-night stand at Madison Square Gardens...

I was in bits.

Nothing meant anything.

Rock'n'roll was dead.

Thank God.

etc.

I could count up to twenty.

People congratulated me. It took a second to figure they meant a sold-out night at Madison Square Gardens, not owning a set of elasticated ebony beads.

There were lots of fans in the audience. Full house. A saffron-wearing monk was not among them.

What I had around my wrist outweighed the adulation.

Retrospectively, I was grateful to the Frisco girl who'd picked the beads up from the dressing-room table. Or floor.

I was sorry I hadn't confessed to the biker.

Ebony is a very dense and dark wood.

Encore, encore, encore, curtain call, off.

I caught the red-eye to Vancouver, skipping the end-of-tour party.

It was necessary for me to be alone with the fact that I was alone with the beads.

Back in my apartment, I took all my clothes off and then, for the first time in weeks, took the beads off, too.

I put them in the very centre of the circular glass dining table, clearing away a bowl of fruit someone had left for me.

Then I went and had a short shower, unable to relax for the thought they might be gone when I got back.

The water could not wash away what I had done, but it could give the illusion of starting to do so.

When I emerged, I felt morally a little less repulsive –

– and the beads were still there.

I put them back on, starting from them, originating a new self – a self that had pursued and caught me, though I had tried to evade it – a self more like my old self than my current self – an attempting self.

In my bedroom, such a strange room in its familiarity, I carefully chose clothes – un-tour clothes: a good black suit, a pressed white shirt, a black silk tie, patent-leather shoes.

Dressed, overdressed, I went for a walk.

It was towards dawn.

Nothing happened during the walk.

Let me repeat that.

Nothing happened during the walk.

Let me repeat that.

HER

I met her, finally.

Her.

I met *her.*

My long-awaited.

She isn't a fan. It didn't happen because of who I am or what I do. It happened, you could say, in spite of those things.

This is how:

You join a band to meet girls. Then, after a while, you realize the girls you're meeting are the kind who want to meet men who are in bands.

For *meet* read *fuck.*

And usually not just one band but a series of bands. Which suggests, maybe-maybe, that what they're looking for ain't the Chapel of Love but the House of the Rising Sun.

In my experience, boys-in-bands react to this discovery in different ways: some punish the girls for being so screwed-up and needy, some try (and fail) to rescue them from themselves.

Myself, I've been through many phases, from mild abuse to all-out rescue missions. My ground rule with contempt-fucking was: Leave no permanent physical scars. But niceness, as I've learnt, can be the most murderously cruel thing.

What you come to realize is that, when you arrive in town, you probably look to them very like the solution to all their problems *but* that all their problems have been living with them in that town (which is probably the main problem) since whenever – and anyone who seeks a cure-all is probably on a deathtrip, anyway.

Now, there's a big difference between aspiring to be Casanova and joining the end of the gang-bang line.

And so musicians on tour are just as likely to hit on the

forty-year-old mother-of-five waitress refilling their coffee as the swimsuit calendar model in the booth beside them.

Because the waitress, unlike the model, hasn't advertised to them just by *being there* that seduction is unnecessary.

Syph had one girl who, at the moment of orgasm, cried out, 'Oh, Mr Liebowitz!' The fact she was underage only confirmed his suspicions. Liebowitz was her surname.

But he told this as *a funny story*.

If you can't see it as *a funny story* then it's whatever the opposite is. Beyond unfunny. Maybe not quite reaching tragic. An anti-funny story.

Anti-fun, I've had a lot of that. It becomes pornographic. A matter of stats, not flesh even. Sweaty accumulations.

I wanted this to end.

By myself I managed up to a month of self-imposed (and freakish, to Syph) road-celibacy – then I got bored, drunk, lonely, curious, all of the above.

You see, I couldn't make it alone. I needed a reason to believe –

I needed *her*.

Her, whose name turned out to be Esther Cloud.

There's that Liza Minnelli song where she goes on holiday, hoping to meet a man, heads for Dubrovnik, and *does* meet a man – who turns out to live in the very next-door apartment to her in New York. Norm Saperstein, his name is.

It wasn't exactly like that. For a start, my mother was intimately involved. But there was something of Liza's haplessness.

Since my dad died, Mom has become manically social. Not that he ever used to repress her or hold her back. His company most of the time was all she wanted. They call it *happy*. With that gone, there was a need for the making of new friends (widows, mainly) and for the collective avoidance of loneliness.

Hence, antiques.

She goes to these talks by visiting lecturers, sometimes

from as far away as England and Russia. A whole set of suave silver foxes, who tell the assembled ladies about ormolu, Louis XIV, bureau bookcases, pewter or Toby jugs. (She has books by said foxes on her shelves, from which I took these details.)

I even went to one of these hoedowns. Got stared at a lot, and learnt more than I'll ever need to know about commodes. Throughout three whole hours, no-one mentioned what they were *for*. I felt about twelve. 'Is that for taking a dump?' I wanted to ask. 'Do you ever find antique poop in them? What's a really high-quality, original-condition piece of eighteenth-century do-do worth?'

After the talk, coffee was served. Everyone tried to get talking to the commode-fox.

Everyone except my mother, whose sneaky reason for persuading me to come along was suddenly revealed.

'This is Joyce Cloud,' she said. 'She has a wonderful collection of antique lead-crystal glassware.'

'How fascinating,' I said, half twelve-years-old and half imitation silver fox. 'What attracted you to that in the first place?'

Mother gave me a mother look. You might be famous and all, but I can still . . .

'She also has a *beautiful* daughter.'

'Really?' I said. 'Are you collecting those, too?'

'Her name's Esther,' Mrs Cloud said, ignoring the rudeness. 'Your mother and I were talking last time, and we thought it would be a wonderful idea if we got you two together.'

Mrs Joyce Cloud looked like every other woman there. Grey-haired, well turned-out, cool and calm in the way of widows with enough in the bank to start antiques collections. Mrs Cloud looked like every other woman there, especially my mother.

Of course, I was trying to work out from Joyce what Esther The Beautiful might look like. All that kept coming into my mind was a picture in one of our family albums of me being breastfed. There was my mother, at twenty-two; there, as far as I was concerned, was Esther.

I turned to, or more accurately *turned on*, my mother: 'You're matchmaking me?'

'We think you and Esther would get on splendidly. She's thirty, single, likes music. You'd have a lot in common.'

Really, I thought, I should go to the bathroom, check I wasn't unexpectedly circumcised. Since when had my mother become so Jewish, already?

'You could come round for coffee,' Mrs Cloud said.

Was Cloud a Jewish name? Perhaps she was influencing my mother – who had never, through all my adolescence and later youth, *ever* tried to fix me up.

Just then the silver fox came over and asked for my autograph. He'd heard from one of the other ladies, who'd heard from my mother, who I was and what I did. In that room, we shared a vague celebrity – and it was enough for a few moments' conversation.

A second or two later, we were sharing something else, in that Mrs Cloud was trying to matchmake us both. The fox, it seemed, had met the new Mrs Fox – my mother.

Although he must get this all the time, he seemed more than a little fazed.

I realized why as the minutes passed. The Fox had come over not to talk to me but to get an introduction to Mrs Cloud. Sly is not the word.

My mother mentioned Joyce's glassware.

'How fascinating,' said Mr Fox. 'Do tell me more.'

Have mother will travel – out the door, into the parking lot and over quite a large emotional distance.

'I appreciate the thought but I don't need your help to meet women.'

'Yes, you do,' my mother said. 'You're back here, on your own, living in that messy apartment. You don't have many friends.'

'I do.'

'You say you don't like them. You complain.'

'Do I?'

'Let me be honest,' she said. We were talking across the roof of her SUV – I could see the top half of her head. I think we both felt that if we actually got *in* the car, this would become a real proper argument. 'I'm fed up waiting for grandchildren. There's only you, and it's possible you've become a father several times over –'

'Mom.'

'I know what goes on. But I'll never get to meet those kids.'

'There aren't any.'

'Right now, even if they turned up with a lawsuit, I'd welcome them. You don't realize the effects of your rock'n'roll lifestyle on those close to you.' This stunk of prepared speech. 'My friends all have the interest of another generation following on from their children. I like your music fine, for what it is, but it won't fill a photo album.' I waited for the phrase *those long winter evenings*. It didn't come. Matchmaking might have been a novelty but the central accusation of my relationship with my parents has been unchanging, probably as far back as breastfeeding: *You're so selfish. All you ever think about is you.*

'And you'd like me to meet this young woman, fall in love, get married and have babies by when? By Hanukkah?'

'Would it be so awful?'

We were doing okay for a real proper argument, even without getting in the car.

'What are the chances I'll like this girl?'

'Well, I like Joyce.' (Oh, the logic of mothers!)

'And what are the chances I'll fall in love with her?'

'Probably better than you think. I've seen her photograph, don't forget.'

I was rolling – I wasn't going to be halted by brute curiosity. Not just yet.

'And what are the chances, after I *do* fall in love with her, that she'll fall in love with me enough to want to marry me and have my children?'

'Perhaps you're right,' said my mother, wounded and intending to wound – a rarity with her. 'No-one else has.'

Antiques ladies walked past us to their SUVs. 'Bye-bye,' they said. And there went Joyce with Mr Fox following close behind.

The drive home was the most silent, ever. More silent even than the moment after Mom interrupted band practice by stepping up to the mic and singing along with a fifteen-year-old Syph.

Still, the next day, on reflection, I continued to refuse to meet Esther Cloud, the future love of all my incarnations (I hope). It was now a point of principle. What if I did like her? The lifelong humiliation of a relationship based on maternal interference. And then the farce began. Or maybe it was just a romantic comedy.

'If that's what you want,' said my mother. 'Loneliness.' And put the phone down on me.

There was just one thing: My mother had said she'd seen Esther. And I wanted to know exactly what she'd seen. But I knew, given the phone slamming, that I could never risk asking.

So – guiltily, after midnight – I went online. I googled 'Esther Cloud', checked her name in White Pages, scanned High School records. Cloud is an uncommon name.

And this is what I came up with:

No photos.

(I like to discuss with Esther what would have happened if, at this point, I'd got a look at her. She says I would probably have left the country rather than risk meeting such a monstrosity. Esther is photogenic but won't believe it. Personally, I think I'd have been visiting a very high-class 24-hour florist's on the way to my mother's – or romantically stealing flowers from someone's front garden. Peace offerings would have been required.)

Esther Cloud. 32. Originally from small-town Manitoba. Good qualifications. Currently working in the paediatrics department of Vancouver Hospital. Specialization: Autism, Asperger's Syndrome, Behavioural Disorders. Co-author of several papers with titles involving the words 'outcomes', 'therapeutic', 'recent' and 'positive'.

If my mother was looking to send me messages, they couldn't have been much clearer.

Esther did good. I was evil – and infantile.

I made up with my mother – did, in fact, visit a florist's, though not late-night.

But she's a stubborn woman. I arranged to go round for dinner that weekend, to demonstrate our reconciliation. (I didn't even pretend my many friends, who I liked, wanted me elsewhere that Saturday.) And, in the kitchen, when I arrived, helping with the vegetables, was Mrs Cloud. With her, offering his worthwhile opinion, was the Commode-Fox – these days my father-in-law, so I should be a bit careful.

Esther passed unmentioned until the end of the evening.

'She'd like to meet you,' Mrs Cloud said, on the porch, touching my arm. 'And, after getting to know you a bit, I'd be happy to introduce you to her. I was a little reluctant before, but you're nowhere near as wild as I'd expected.'

After they'd driven off, I turned to my mother and said, 'Could we just consider that argument as *had*?'

'What argument?'

'The one we could have now.'

'You apologized. I can invite who I like to my house. What have you got to lose?'

I didn't say, 'My dignity, in front of *you*.' And I didn't add, 'And any sense of running my own life.'

We kissed warmly because otherwise we'd have kissed coldly.

Back in my messy apartment, I remembered how corny the Fox's chivalry towards Mrs Cloud had been. Pushing her chair in behind her, helping her into her coat, flattering her intelligence and taste whenever the inevitable subject of antiques came up. But I also remembered the way he looked at her. Through his eyes, I distinguished her from the crowd of his audience. Mrs Cloud was whatever the female equivalent of a silver fox is. Although she still looked a bit like my mother – this sentence is going badly wrong. At eighteen-years-old, Mrs Cloud must have been . . .

At thirty . . .

During the following week, I found the car had started to want to drive me past the hospital. Somehow, the internet had decided to tell me where the Paediatrics Department was located.

I seriously considered heading for Dubrovnik.

My mother felt that Saturday's dinner had been such a success (she believed she was bringing Joyce and the Fox's romance on apace) that we should all meet again the following Sunday – and bring Esther into the party. Mom's deal – she offered one – was that the Fox would be inviting a blind-date for her, so the embarrassment would be shared 50/50 between us.

Sure, I wanted to meet someone. But I'd sat at that table with my father since my father had bought the table, thirty years ago.

Other false excuses occurred to me. I didn't bother making them. I thought about saying I'd be out of town for the weekend. I considered agreeing to turn up then not. Too childish. I don't like being estranged from my mother, even for short periods. What if she dies during one of them? You hear people talking about this, on TV.

I was watching a lot of TV.

'No,' I said. 'I'm not meeting her at our kitchen table.'

'We've thought about it.'

'We?'

'Joyce and I. You can take Esther out for a meal – on Sunday night. Then bring her round.'

'For what? The post-mortem?'

'So she can get a ride home.'

'No,' I repeated, until the message was through.

Then came the killer admission. Mom: 'I've already told them you're coming. And Esther's already accepted.'

'You will not win,' I said. 'You have made a big mistake.'

Sunday night, I watched TV. I couldn't work up the energy to go out of town.

And when the phone rang the first time, I didn't answer. (No message.) Nor, half an hour later, the second. (No message – maybe a sigh.) But on the third, I picked up – and found myself speaking to Esther. She said her name straight off, after the words *Listen, you, this is*.

Esther Cloud was angry.

'I'm insulted. Who do you think you are?'

'Where are you calling from?'

'What business is that of yours?'

'You're not at my mother's house, are you?'

'You must be very arrogant. My mother is quite upset. Your mother told her what you said.'

'I said nothing.'

'About me.'

'Believe me, *you* are not the issue. What did I say?'

'Even if she asked again, why would I want to meet an arrogant, selfish prick like you?'

'Don't worry. You don't have to. Why did you call?'

'I don't know. To see if you were as hopeless as they said.'

'You've talked to my mother about me?'

'A girl's got to do her homework. How do you think I got your number. She's very disappointed in you.'

'So you know who I am?'

'Yes.'

'Did you know before?' I asked. 'Before our mothers started –'

'I'd seen your face around. Don't flatter yourself, you're not that famous.'

This was a conversation. We could never meet, but we were talking. I wanted to ask what she thought of my face.

'Why are we still talking?' I asked.

'Because it's funny,' she said, and she sounded amused. 'You are now the person I must never meet. It would be too terrible if I liked you.'

'We have *that* in common,' I said. 'If I ever went on a date with you, my mother would have won. Total annihilation. I've been fighting her since –' I didn't want to say breastfeeding.

'Where do you live?' Esther asked.

'Why?'

'So I can avoid it.' She laughed. 'So I can never go down that street again – in case we *meet*.'

I told her the address. Then said, 'But you knew that already, didn't you?'

'How did you know I knew?'

'More homework.'

'So, where do I live?' she asked.

'How should I know?' I said, then felt the conversation begin to tumble. I didn't want it to hit the floor, smash. I made a grab for it. 'I'm not a stalker . . . But I did admire your paper on the proven links between artificial sweeteners and ADD.'

'Bitch!' she said. 'You total bitch!'

'I was curious,' I said. 'I know that I can never have children in this city – we cannot *meet*.'

'Never,' she said.

Something in her voice told me what to say, it was echoey with the boom of the future.

'Not next Friday,' I said.

'Definitely not.'

'Not at eight o'clock.'

'Never going to happen.'

'And not in complete secrecy, so no-one ever knows if we don't get on.'

'Uh-uh.'

I named a French restaurant I wasn't going to reserve us a table at.

'I would rather die than be there,' Esther gleefully said.

Later, a lot later, my mother told me she, Joyce and Esther had sat around on Saturday morning discussing the best way for her to trick me into asking her out. Scripted it. They *knew* I wouldn't make the dinner.

But on Friday, at eight, finally, innocent of my dupedness, I was there, in the restaurant, waiting. We'd talked on the phone every day in between. For hours. Laughing. Cackling. And, by the time she sat down opposite me, it didn't matter she was beautiful.

KID

I have more observations on the subject of heartbreakingly-heartbrokenly beautiful young women, but not here. (Enough has been said about that.)

Also, I have much I would say regarding – and *to* – their fathers, but not now. (Not enough has been said to them.)

Men is what I'm interested in: men – alone – together – travelling. Because that's what the whole *okay* experience has really been about.

For every hour we've spent in the company of women (and Mono's marriage to Major certainly boosts our average) we must've spent ten with each other.

Truly, we would have known more of female-kind had we become hair-stylists.

Casanova, Don Juan, Screamin' Jay Hawkins, Syph – they *leave*, that's the point of them.

Most women pretend to hate this. They fuck the going-men in a desperate attempt to make them stay – or so we're meant to think. Probably, they use faking an attempt to make them stay as a way of getting the really desperate sex they crave.

It's only recently, since the Buddhism, that I've realized how much what we do is about departure. We wanted to get out of Vancouver, sure. But to be always leaving is a weird state to achieve – to start seeing yourself as a going-man, and then to stop being able to see yourself as anything else.

That's why the practice of meditation has been so difficult and so rewarding for me. It means stopping.

And from the centre of that stopping, I can see the whole *okay* thing with much greater clarity.

We all – as kids – had problems, and those problems were

similar enough to bring us together. (Boredom, misery, hate and lust, if you really need to know.) We formed a band. We became successful. We still had the same problems.

Sometimes, in order to write the next album, we had to make those problems worse. Syph has trashed perfectly good relationships for the sake of a dozen song lyrics.

I suspect that if we had no problems, we would also have no fans. Us being emotionally adolescent keeps us emotionally relevant to adolescents. Who aren't, as you might have noticed, very together people, on the whole.

Of course, as you get older, you start lusting after the moms, not the daughters. Or as well as the daughters. But now it's the values of *our* moms I've started to yearn for. Not in a sexual way – in a way that yearns for a lack of sex.

Ultimately, I want an end of all yearning. That's a stage which resembles age not youth, wisdom not enthusiasm, grandmothers not groupies.

(Oh God, what's going to happen when people around the band read this? If the roadcrew got hold of it, they'll be bringing candyflossy ladies backstage to meet me and joking about how much I must be looking forward to Florida.)

But I'm still more on the subject of women than of me and the other guys in the band.

It's not that we love each other in a gay way, although living as we do there have been occasional kissings, gropings, suckings and more.

No, it's this: after so many years, we still find ourselves objects of mutual fascination.

Take Crab – an infinitely less charismatic creature than Syph. Yet it's him I look to for the truth of the matter in hand: I watch his face for grimaces of commentary. Even when soaked, he has a strong instinct for exactly what to reject. In this, Crab has remained the most Canadian of us – the quickest in quietly ditching the extraneous. He is mostly drunk, these days, and I think it's because that, too, fascinates him. Sober, he bores himself; sober, he knows the drunk in him would reject him; sober, he believes intellectually that he *should* be rejected.

And Mono. He's more of a fucking Buddhist than I'll ever be. He squats on lakesides, waiting to catch fish which he knows he'll put back – teasing them with the prospect of death and reincarnation. In Major, he has found someone truly stalwart. She won't allow him to ruin his life. Out of all this shit, they have a relationship that is as indestructible as a tank in cloudcuckooland.

We thought we formed *okay* for the music, but it was for the escape – the escape with one another. When we re-form, it's for the return to one another. Sadly, it has very little to do with the music any more. Even the money is irrelevant, except that it allows us to spend long periods of time in company.

There is an enjoyment, still, in thinking – from some hotel bar somewhere – how far we've travelled, how much we've accomplished.

This isn't *said.* I'm talking about the talk of men.

Our success materializes at the table, a fifth band-member. We all acknowledge he is there (our success is male, too) but without even a nod.

Perhaps it's in the carelessness with which we order drinks and food. No bill will ever touch us – the amounts are irrelevant.

Crab pays for his drinking, pays a stupidly high and every morning increasing price, but he'll be an elegant wino for the rest of his life, never a penniless street bum. If he gets into life-threatening situations, liver-wise, our fifth member will come to rescue him.

So what is it that *is* said, between us?

Not a great deal. Nothings that are sweet because uncruel. We have such vicious armouries of ammo, if we wanted to go to war. There is the mellow-illusion to be maintained: the illusion that things have always been this cool.

Untrue that.

Syph doesn't know but Crab once tried to arrange a hit on him.

That's not the story I'm interested in right now, though.

There had been a couple of quick cut'n'paste jobs, but never before the full vanity of a book.

What is it about pages of paragraphs without the relief of pictures that makes musicians go so pretentious?

Syph tried to seduce the writer, then to impress her, then to scare her – finally, he ignored her. This was where Crab and Mono had started, but only because they were desperate to maintain mystique. They knew that silence and distance were all they had going for them. A single face-to-face interview and they would have to confront, in print already, the terrible fact of being ordinary.

They weren't always ordinary.

We all started out as odd – marginally odd fish, within a small bowl (Vancouver, apart from Syph). But time passes, you leave behind your first, second and third set of contemporaries, you travel, maybe you become famous, someone invents the internet, you go online – and you find out that, all along, there were others just like you, that your odd wasn't.

Everyone is an average, if you have a wide enough range of standards by which to judge them. Average serial killer. Average conjoined twins.

The most terrible thing is finding out that The Parents were right in some of what they said. They understood, all along. Their questions weren't really questions; their questions were sewn seeds – were preaching-in-disguise.

'It's very loud, isn't it?'

'Yes.'

'Why does it have to be so loud?'

'It just does, okay? Look, could you step out of my room?'

'But do you enjoy it?'

'Yes. It's the best. Now –'

'Won't you get bored of it, eventually?'

'No. Never. Absolutely not.'

'Why don't you consider getting a proper job? Just in case –'

'Fuck you.'

But the you of *Fuck you* comes closer and closer to being the true you. And that you can't avoid post-adolescence for ever – and when you become unmistakably middle-aged, you realize you can't avoid saying the words *kids today* and that you're doing so as a non-kid.

I've watched many documentaries about the birth of rock'n'roll. Read quite a few books, too. And what I'm starting to realize is, those who opposed it weren't without their reasons.

Things were lost, because of it.

For us, it's easy to mock the Viennese-accented psychologists who were coaxed blinking into bright TV studios to expound on the *inzezzant chunkle ryzzms of zis rocking and rolling music*. But the Herr Professor *vasn't hrong*, the rhythm is the thing you can't get away from.

I know – I've lived a life almost exclusively in 4/4 time.

Faster, slower, a little breakbeat influence creeping in around 1996, incessant.

'Won't you get bored of it, eventually?'

In the end, yes, it gets a little dull.

I remember an interview with Yoko Ono, about when she first met John Lennon and heard his music. (I have been rude about Yoko in the past. I followed the party-line on her being the archetypal band-breaker. Yoko, I apologize.) What she said was that she found it difficult to listen to The Beatles because, unlike both the Japanese classical and New York avant-garde stuff she was used to, it neither slowed down nor sped up. *Thump*-and-*thump*-and.

And that's me. That's my home address.

Yoko and the Herr Professor knew something that, at twelve, when I made my pact with the Devil of Garage Rock,

I was ignorant of: life, unlike *okay*'s music, slows down and speeds up. Mostly, it slows down.

Rock music is a fight against that. An insistence on excitement and a battle against entropy.

But constant excitement is boring, entropy is inevitable.

The battle is worth it (The 1956-vintage Parents were wrong about that) – the battle *is* worth it, for a while.

Ten years.

Ten max.

The battle is not worth it for twenty – twenty years of road, of *thump*-and-*thump*-and – not on into your forties – not when you are about to become a parent – not when you are me.

I intend to surrender.

I want to enjoy slowing down.

McCartney was wrong: the Road (the Rock Road) may be Long but it is far from Winding.

Life slows down and speeds up, sweeps left, cuts right, has switchbacks, breakdowns, crashes.

The Road of 4/4 is a straight line from rainy windscreen to flat horizon. Cover of Springsteen's *Nebraska*.

For a drummer to leave a band and cite *musical differences* would be ridiculous, or so you'd think. The differences are in the melodies and harmonies and styles and influences, not in the positioning of the *thump* and the *and*.

When I announced I was leaving *okay*, I cited musical differences – I cited my deep desire for them.

I had been listening to classical music and feeling like a savage in the jungle, *shtuck wiz my inzezzant ryzzms*.

Percussionists are such untermensches within the orchestral Reich – except in something like *The Rite of Spring*. I wasn't quitting to join the Vancouver Phil. I was quitting because maybe I'd made a mistake, back at the beginning.

I had no talent for anything other than basic rock drumming. Maybe I didn't have enough talent to be a musician at all. I should have done what The Parents – in the person of my parents – wanted: become a professional. My mother wanted me to be a doctor, my father a lawyer. I tried to imagine myself as either. Couldn't.

Esther, the one, was seven months pregnant.

I told the band I was leaving.

We were at Band HQ. No longer an ironic reference to the small office from which our first managers operated. This was a company employing twenty, and looking to expand. Tinted glass, a woman on front desk who doesn't know whether to treat us as The Boss Times Four or as the Coolest Cats in Town, Man. Not a fan – a fan would make really bad front of house.

More specifically, we were in the unironic Boardroom – around the long black table that I couldn't help but see, the second before I opened my mouth, as a coffin-lid.

'No!' said Mono.

'You sure?' said Crab.

'See you,' said Syph.

They should have known it was in the post. At the previous couple of rehearsals, I'd tried to introduce some musical differences. Changes is what jazz musicians call them, though I didn't try anything of that complexity: I'd have been kicked out, not quit. What I attempted just confused them.

I think they thought I'd lost my ability to keep time – and maybe I had.

Or maybe it was that I'd lost my will to 4/4 discipline. I was outmoded. A drum machine did what I did, and so much better. There was a glory to Mo Tucker, my favourite skin-thumper – there was something transcendent about the strictness of her tempo. Half an hour of 'Sister Ray', undeviating. Each beat that didn't miss was a brick in a Great Wall of Rhythm. I loved Mo. She was motorik before krautrock. She danced to the machines. She found joy in repetition, like a true American. I would never be Mo. I didn't dare keep it simple, stupid. I had to have my fill of fills. Sorry, Mo.

I'd discussed it with Esther, before I quit.

In the kitchen.

She, give her credit, thought I was making a mistake. In all the years I'd been in the band, I'd initiated nothing, musically. (Had I initiated *anything*? In the mid-eighties, I got Syph to try sushi. The thought was terrifyingly sad.) She said it was time I brought something to the table – thought the others might be receptive to it. They knew we'd gone stale. How could they not? I tried to explain what stupid and stubborn bastards they were. I implied their contempt for me. She had more faith. It was justified.

'No!' Mono had said.

My lack of faith was also justified.

'See you,' Syph had said.

What to do next?

I didn't want to travel but I did feel a need to explore. I put on big fat headphones and set off into the deep north of the string quartet: Haydn, Mozart, Beethoven, Schubert, back to late Beethoven, Debussy, Bartók, back again to Mozart to hear what I'd missed, Janáček, all the way through all of all Shostakovich (to the death), Webern, Cage, Messiaen. The end of time. It sounds pretentious. It was wonderful. I was a postulant – a junior monk. I wanted to be allowed to kneel at the temple gates, in the snow and rain, in the mud, in the hammer sun, for a year, until they saw my faith, until they let me in, until they started to show me what enlightenment really was.

Mono came round and found me with the big fat head-phones on. He hadn't had to travel far – he and Major kept an apartment in Kitsilano, as well as the house in Northern Ontario. They stayed in each for six months of the year. Best of both.

Mono was as close as *okay* comes to a deputation.

'We want you back,' he said.

'I don't even understand it any more,' I said in honest reply. 'I don't understand how I ever did. I'm lost.'

'We can get you into a programme,' said Mono, kindly.

'Like the one Crab went on last year. It worked – for a while.'

For Beethoven's 'Grosse Fuge'? A programme?

'How's Major?' I asked. 'You should come round to dinner.'

'Are you on downers? What is it? We can help.'

'I'm trying to understand everything I haven't been doing.'

'And you're taking them, one by one. A drug encyclopaedia. I get it. Just tell us when you're finished. Where you up to?'

'It's *not* drugs.' The painkillers were beside the point – they were for rheumatism, in my kick-drum foot, in my snare hand. 'It's . . .'

I almost saw the continuation dots float out into the air, and I knew that, right then, I was unable to chase them down with any meaningful syllables.

'Tell the others – tell them what you like. That I've had a breakdown, got religion, Catholicism this time, not Buddhism. Tell them I've lost my nerve.'

Sad-faced, Mono picked up one of the records. The Alban Berg Quartet. I was listening to everything on vinyl – warm analog, through a valve amp.

'You really like this stuff?' he asked.

'I do,' I said.

That was my marriage vow, right then and there. Mono didn't even know he'd spliced me and Ludwig, until death do.

'They're really pissed, the others. We've got an album to record – that's fine. We can get session drummers in.' I wasn't even offended. 'But then there's a tour.'

The thought – the thought of the repetition.

'Never,' I said.

Mono stood up. 'You'll be back,' he said.

'Not as me,' I replied. 'Not as the me I now am. I will have to be different.'

'You're crazy, man.'

'Tell Major to bring you round to dinner.'

Amazingly, he did.

Esther cooked. Big rich beef stew. It was midwinter. Thick red wine. French cheese. I chose the background music. I was respectful – only music the composers would have expected not to be listened to: divertimenti, minor stuff. No-one noticed, just as I wanted. We talked about the old days. Esther was amused. Major asked for the stew recipe. I felt civilized. Mono looked awkward. I think he thought I was trying to be something I wasn't – domesticated or European. I felt such love for him, across our dining-room table. What I wanted least of all was for him to lose his musical faith like I had. Like I had when I had a breakdown, got Catholicism, lost my nerve and married Beethoven. It would be too cruel to wish these changes upon him – wish him away from what had brought him such a good life.

He told the story of the kid.

We were on tour in America. Some city. He said it was Pittsburgh. I thought it was Detroit. I'm sure Syph and Crab would have added two other cities. 'Heavily industrial,' we agreed upon.

'And we finish the show, get back into the dressing-room, and there's this child there.'

'A child?' asks Esther, interrupting but only to keep the story moving, not annoying.

'A boy,' Major adds.

'About seven or eight,' Mono says.

'Or six,' I joke.

'Maybe six,' Mono concedes. Six makes the story better. Six makes the story worse.

'Yes?' says Esther.

'You're awful. Tell the story *properly*,' says Major. 'Describe him.'

'He was small.' Major goes pah! 'Dark hair. Flat, not spiky. Pale skin. A little weak-looking, but intense. Bright. He seemed older than he was.'

'Five, maybe,' I say.

'Six.'

'Yes,' says Esther.

'He's there, eating peanuts from our rider. He has an *okay*

T-shirt on. Now, we didn't make them that small. But it looks perfect. A miniature version of the tour before that's T-shirt. And the kid looks at us when we come in, and he says –'

I join in on the chorus: '"Hi, guys."'

Mono continues, solo: '"Where's your mother?" asks Syph. I think maybe he sees the kid isn't too bad-looking, and wonders if she's worth checking out. Is she in the bathroom? No. "I don't have a mother," says the kid. "What about your father?" asks old Clap over there.' The women look at me, with approval. 'And the kid says –'

'"I don't have a father."'

'So I ask, "Then who brought you here?" And he says, "I came by myself. You guys are great. I'd like to hang out with you." "Are you a midget or something?" asks Syph. "Fuck you," answers the kid. We all ask his age, but he refuses to say. He just wants to talk about the set we've just played. He says he thinks we played too many obvious songs – should be more rarities in there, for the real fans. He names some old ones even *we've* forgotten. And however old he is, these were written and recorded before he was born. "How old are you?" we keep asking. The kid just won't say. We're amused by him, now. But we also want to move on, get something to eat, go to a club. The kid wants to come. We say no, he shouldn't even be here. "But I am here," he says. "And I was there in Minnesota, too."'

'"Detroit,"' I say.

'Whatever,' Mono says. 'Location isn't the point of this story.'

'And what is?' asks Major.

'Destination,' says Mono, quick as that. 'And I'm getting there as fast as I can. We're impressed by the kid. If nothing else, he's a great liar. People come to take us away. We wave goodbye to him at the stage door – and he's there to meet us outside the restaurant. Swear to God. The kid gets there *before* us. Our limo didn't drive slowly, either. And he's *in* the restaurant. "How did you get here?" we ask. "You tried to dump me," the kid says. "That wasn't fair." We figure he's earned a meal. The management at the restaurant don't seem to mind. Probably think he's a son or a cousin. We eat. The kid talks. He's very confident, and witty. He flatters us by being cleverly critical of our last couple of albums.'

'It's all true,' I say.

'I think you're right,' Mono says to me. 'I think he was probably six.'

'From the mouths of babes,' says Major.

'We give him autographs. We buy him food. He's offered burger and fries but has, get this, asparagus followed by veal. He is this evening's amusement. Again, outside the restaurant, we try to say goodbye. The kid gets upset. "I thought we were friends." "We are," Syph says. "But where we're going, you cannot go." Into the limo. Wave, wave. Halfway to the club, we decide to go somewhere else – just in case the kid has heard our plans and taxied there. We ask the driver, take us somewhere funky. He understands. Spins the wheel. Does a 180 there and then. It's a little hole in the wall place, when we get there, and –'

'The kid!' says Esther, wowed.

'– is in our booth. Behind the ropes. In VIP. We ask how he got there, he won't say. Crab is starting to believe the kid's a ghost, or a group hallucination. Syph has other ideas. Secretly, he's paranoid that he might be the kid's father, and this is some bitter mother's way of introducing them – before the lawyers get involved. We ask the doormen how he got in. They say they never saw him before. "Are you a millionaire?" I ask. "You've got a helicopter outside." "I just want to hang out with you guys," the kid says. "Quit trying to ditch me." "Can we be arrested for this?" Crab asks. "Only if we buy him drinks, I think," I say. "It's okay," the kid says, "I'll have Coke. I don't want to get you into trouble." So, we're amused. We let him stay. We have a great time, talking. It ends about three. He doesn't reappear back at the hotel. He's called it a night. But he's there after the next gig, backstage. He follows us from city to city.'

I am privately thinking of the beads around my wrist, but I say nothing.

Mono concludes: 'He follows us for the rest of the tour. We give up trying to escape him, after a few more switchbacks. He's too much. He's a phenomenon, even if he isn't supernatural. We joke about whose kid he is. On the last night, Hollywood Bowl, he says –'

'"Thanks, guys. It's been great."'

'And he hugs us around our middles and walks out of the dressing-room. And we've never seen him again.'

The women look at me. 'It's true,' I say. 'Every word.'

'And you have no explanation?' Esther asks.

'None,' I say.

'Zero,' says Mono. 'The kid is the strangest thing to happen to us, any of us, in almost twenty years.'

'How old would he be now?'

'Sixteen?' I say. 'Or a bit more.'

'Wow,' says Esther, my beautifully pregnant one.

'He's told me the story before,' Major says. 'And the details are remarkably consistent.'

'Why would we make that up?' Mono asks.

'What do you think?' I ask everyone. 'Ghost or millionaire or . . . ?'

'Ghost,' says Major.

'Millionaire,' says Mono.

'A friend,' says Esther. 'A true friend.'

I don't want to have to decide.

After this, the evening dies slowly. No story can compete. But it's been great. I kiss Major on both cheeks. She is Mary Magdalene and more. (Esther knows about my worship.)

When they've gone, I talk a while longer with Esther about the kid. Like I said, she is seven months pregnant, and we've done a lot of talking about kids, recently.

'What if he's this one?' she says, holding her big tummy. 'Come from the future to take a look at his daddy.'

'But he didn't single me out. He loved us all.'

'That should tell you something,' Esther says.

'This isn't a point of argument,' I say.

The next day, I put the big headphones back on – I listen to opus 133, to Deutsch No. 810, to Köchel 465. But I can't forget the kid. He is incessant. His image keeps repeating, thumping.

I made the right decision in leaving.

Two months later, I call Mono and tell him to tell the others I'll do the tour.

We meet. They say no. I explain. They say yes.

Not millionaire. The other.

Oh my little son, my lost son.

FUCK-UP

It wouldn't be me if I weren't alone, lonely, lovesick and forlorn – a long long way from home.

I fucked it up, bigtime.

Deliberately.

With Esther.

Well, kind of deliberately.

Esther has short, thick, very black-but-not-dyed hair with – when she doesn't pull them – one or two lightning-slashes of silver. She likes to paint her toenails a particular shade of damson which she can only achieve by mixing two cheapo brands of nailpolish. At a Chinese restaurant, she will order Peking duck; in Starbucks, decaf latte grande with nutmeg on. Born in the year of the Aardvark (private joke), Esther is Bette Davis the Second, Field Marshal Monty Python, the Queen of the Tambourine, Sexual History 101, a tigerskin mouse and a moon-harpoon (all private jokes).

As Elvis put it, I've forgotten more than you'll ever know about her.

She didn't ask for faithful, just truthful.

That was the motto in our imaginary sampler up on the real wall in our actual dream home.

NOT FAITHFUL,
JUST TRUTHFUL

But this nineteen-year-old girl had come all the way from Osaka Japan, just to see me. She'd spent her savings since she was twelve and first heard one of our records ('Sea-Song #3'). I felt some responsibility, you understand. I also felt horny. Esther was out of town, visiting her parents. I was drunk. She was cute enough. There is no excuse.

Esther minded that I lied about it, when she asked. I have no idea how she found out – perhaps it was in my face, the fact that I was trying to keep out of my face the fact I was trying to keep anything out.

I fucked it up. I tried testing it. I couldn't believe the sampler was telling the truth about not faithful. So I did half the opposite of what I should've.

Esther minded enough to push the big red button.

I thought I'd get more than one strike.

'When trust is gone,' she said, 'it very rarely comes back – ever.'

I was out.

She left the apartment, but I was the one in the cold.

And so I did bad things, to make it seem to myself like I wanted it to be over.

For example, I went to Osaka. And not for the seafood.

That lasted all of five days. Awe is not an appealing quality, not for more than three days. Awe so huge that the feeler can't make sentences. I'm very good at taking my feet of clay and moulding obscene objects out of them, firing them, presenting them as gifts – gifts which no woman could possibly ever want. Ceramic atrocities. Besides, none of our songs were there on the karaoke machines. (She hated karaoke, my visited visitor. I had to force her to go. She wanted romantic walks over meaningful bridges in small parks.) When I met her parents, I was older than her mother by exactly one week. There was steam on the windows of the kitchen as I ate a week's wages. I could touch the ceiling with my elbow, at a stretch. In her eyes, still awe. Even after a particularly fine clay figurine of a drunken drummer, vomiting down a demure Japanese girl's back. Her parents' acceptance of me was heart-breaking. They were far from Canadian.

Day five, I bought her a wedding ring, arranged to go out for dinner that night with her grandparents, and left for the airport. Only hate, I believed, could make her sell the diamonds and get back the money she'd spent on airfare.

How wrong I was.

Three days later, seen through the fisheye lens of my front door, her whole family, including grandparents. I never quite got the details straight, but someone had sold a fishing boat to book their tickets.

She looked at me with awe, because I played drums on some songs she loved.

The ring was on her ring-finger.

I could see only one solution: I introduced her to the rest of the band. Syph, at my request, stole her from me. (He'd probably have done it anyway – for free.) I took her to the rehearsal studios, without accompanying blood relations, and she cried for joy. Syph said he would write a song about her, because she was so beautiful.

The wedding ring was returned to me – such a beautiful red box, and tightly wrapped in black paper with delicately drawn marigolds.

When I asked at the hotel, the family had checked out.

But what if I'd made a mistake? Perhaps what my sordid soul needed above all things was innocence. That awe, it was almost as good as grown-up love, wasn't it? No-one else would ever want me. I was throwing away the only –

Another trip to Osaka.

I made it as far as the staircase of her apartment block before I realized that, so far, I'd messed up ten people's lives, but, right now, I was one cheery doorbell-chime away from destroying them altogether.

So there I was, again, alone, lonely, lovesick and forlorn – a long long way from home.

I turned around, and awe was standing in front of me, her mother to one side, her father to the other. Just as if my guilty conscience (I discovered, through her, that I still possessed one) had got action-figures of the three, and posed them.

'I came to apologize,' I said, to her father. 'I am very sorry,' I said, to her mother. 'Please translate,' I said, to her.

They invited me in for tea.

('Wouldn't the coolest thing now be to be Japanese?' as someone once said.)

I accepted.

We had what amounted to a business meeting. The daughter took no active part, merely translated the terms of my attempt to make up for lust, folly, vanity and cruelty.

'A bigger boat,' I said. 'With an icebox.'

We bowed for a very long time – my feet on the concrete of the stairway, theirs on the tatami of their hall.

The taxi took me to a nearby monastery, where I asked the Buddha, *Please, no suicides – no deaths of young girls who deserve better than me.*

Go home, the Buddha told me to tell myself. *Go home and try to do no more damage, to yourself or to others. Sit still.*

His voice was golden, like his face, like his toes.

I skipped the in-flight meals, fasting already.

There was a message from Syph on my answering machine, wondering if he could get that Japanese girl's number. 'She was cute,' he said.

There was no message from Esther.

I wanted to know how I could become good enough to deserve having her back. Until I was close, I daren't ask directly.

Sit still.

I couldn't.

I tried the Japanese way – went to visit her parents, mother and stepfather. They had moved back out to rural Manitoba. In penance, I set off to drive there. From Vancouver.

'I came to apologize,' I said, three days later. 'I'm very sorry.'

Perhaps something was lost in the lack of translation.

'Go away,' said her mother, Mrs Cloud. For a moment, when she opened the door, I'd thought it was Esther – aged by sadness.

'I've come from Vancouver to see you.'

'You've seen me. Now go away.'

'I brought you something.'

'How do you think she'd like it if I went accepting presents from you? I'm not going to say it again.'

'Please tell Esther I'm trying.'

'I will do you the favour of not mentioning this at all. Say hi to your mother. Poor woman.'

When she shut the door, the antique knocker on the outside rat-a-tatted about five times.

I got into my car, stared at the curtains for a while to see if any of them twitched in a way that I found totally loveable.

In the first motel I came to, I watched TV.

Actually, I watched a battle between TV and the Buddha. It was very like a Godzilla movie. TV hurled a series of beer adverts at the Golden One. He replied with universal love and compassion. TV countered with the bubble booty in a couple of rap videos. Buddha sidestepped this, offering a lotus flower in response. TV escalated to a full-on grunting treble porn-channel assault. Buddha said, 'Catch you later,' turned a sandalled heel and walked off into the haze of the empty minibar.

When the management refused to send any more drinks to my room, I tried to buy the motel.

The only thing that prevented me was, it being Sunday, there were no lawyers available. During negotiations, the keys to my car went missing (they were returned to me when I checked out, two weeks later, not having slept in my room again).

'I'll walk,' I said.

'Be my guest,' said the owner, a good man, with my car keys in his pocket.

'I *am* your guest,' I said. 'And there are rules of hospitality. If this was Japan —'

'This is Canada,' he said. 'And you are drunk.'

'Where's the nearest bar?'

This being Canada, he was polite enough to point me in the right direction.

'How far is it?'

'Don't worry,' he said. 'You'll still be drunk when you get there.'

He was right. When I got there, I was still drunk – but it was a day and a half later. In between the motel and the bar were two other motels, and I checked into, drank dry and got kicked out of both before I made it to what would become my regular barstool. It was summer, so I didn't even need a blanket to sleep in the alley alongside the bar. I slept on an old mattress I found. In the bar, there were beautiful neon signs in the dark between the mirrors. Four of our songs were on the jukebox. Maybe I could live there. The barman didn't believe I was who I said I was.

'Do you want to buy a car?' I asked. 'A good one.'

'No, thank you,' he said.

'Have you ever been to Japan?'

'No, but I've been to Thailand.'

'Japan is better,' I said. 'The people there are really decent.'

'I have no doubt about it,' said the barman. 'They have always seemed decent to me.'

Tuesday was a slow night. Wednesday, too. By Thursday, I was coming to suspect that it wasn't the nights that were slow but the town – more accurately, the outskirts of the town. But on Friday, people came and, if I hadn't been there already, I'd have had to fight for my barstool.

A drunk man coming through the door howled. 'Full moon out there,' he said, and perhaps saved my life.

I went to go look.

The sky was clear, horizon to horizon. Even at the edges, no decorative clouds.

Down the alley I walked. Up a dirt road. Through some trees to the top of the hill.

When I got there, I knew the Buddha had just left. I could smell the poems he'd been writing. Falling to my knees, I started to grub round in the grass. If I could just find a piece of gold leaf from one of his feet. I remembered Esther's toenails. I remembered the temple in Japan. I remembered the fog in Amsterdam or Rotterdam. I found something which shone, but the moonlight made it the purest, most beautiful silver. Next day, when I looked in my pocket, I found it was the wrapper from a stick of chewing gum. But up on that hill, I thought the Buddha was telling me to follow him. Leaving flakes. If I didn't follow him fast enough, all his gold leaf could come off bit by bit. Children visiting his temple would be disappointed by how dull he looked, though their parents would take it for wisdom. I would be responsible for the loss of glory. The way up and the way down are not the same. There is no bottom, and I was in danger of reaching it. If the flake wasn't Buddha-gold it was moon-silver. I sobbed then shouted to both of them: 'I came to apologize, I'm very sorry.' I was, very sorry. To show them how sorry I was, I pissed my pants. Or maybe I just didn't reach the zipper in time. 'I never wanted this,' I said, face down in the grass. After sleeping for a while, which I knew because the moon had moved further away from me, I tried rolling down the hill. This should be innocent. The grass was too long. I climbed back up, laughing. In the morning, there were deep cuts in my palms. At the very summit, I looked at the moon and howled. Waited. Howled. Someone howled back. It wasn't a wolf. How I would love to believe it could have been a wolf and not another drunk. They howled and I howled a reply and they did a very long howl and I tried to match them but my lungs gave out. 'Fuck,' I said, 'this is beautiful. This wouldn't happen in Japan.' The howling got louder, and turned into the man who'd come with a howl into the bar. He arrived friendly but when I staggered over to embrace him he thought I was attacking. I did have a rock in my hand, for some reason. He beat me but good. Saved my life a second time, I believe. I'd been doing too much relying on the kindness of strangers, this past week. How many people have heard the Buddha howl like a wolf? How many men have felt the moon's hard fists in their gut? He urinated, silver in the moonlight – not on my head but close enough so I could feel the warmth and taste the splash. 'Are you famous?' he asked, before he left. 'They told me in the bar you said you were famous. Well, I swam for the province – butterfly. Nearly got a trial for the Olympics. Next time, you be careful who you howl at.' I could see him thinking about kicking me. 'They know where you are,' he said, then walked down the hill. 'Thank you,' I said, pushing myself up into a sitting position. I wanted to howl but my wolf-spirit had left me. The moon was still there, lower in the sky, further away. Closing my eyes, I sat on a tatami mat of grasses. Sat still. Then I thought about the things I usually try not to think about. I was asleep within seconds.

When I woke up, the first thing I saw was the back of Esther's new stepfather's head – silver. It was the Commode-Fox.

He was driving me to hospital. I was in the back of his car, the car seat (a blanket under my sodden ass) holding me upright. The car's paintjob was gold.

'You awake, now?' he asked.

'Yes, sir,' I said.

'Don't give me that shit,' he said. 'How do you feel?'

'Like shit.'

'Good,' he said. 'I'm not doing this because anyone asked me to.'

I knew who *anyone* was.

'And I'm not doing it because I like you. I think you're disgusting.'

'You're right.'

'Agreeing with me doesn't make it any better. Do you want to die?'

I didn't answer.

'We were sorry about it. God knows,' he said. He didn't mean cheating on Esther. 'But you have to be stronger.'

'I can't,' I said.

'Then, please, if you're going to drink yourself to death, do it somewhere I won't hear about it. I don't want you on my conscience.'

'Thank you,' I said.

'For what?' he asked. 'I'm not doing you a favour.'

He left me without shaking my hand in the hospital lobby.

They took my credit-card details and gave me a room.

Just like with me, Esther was able to read what her step-father was trying to pretend he wasn't keeping out of his face.

She waited three days before she came to visit. I was shaky but part-way back.

Esther said, 'I didn't want to leave. I knew she was nothing. You gave me an excuse to punish myself. I hate what you've done to me. That was *our* baby. It was the most terrible thing. I blamed you even as I thought it was my fault. We did nothing wrong. We were unlucky. You didn't make it any better. How have you dealt with it? Like this? You stupid fucker. How annoying is that. Look at Crab – look at his life. I have something I need to say.' And then she said it: 'I *don't* trust you. I don't need you. But, unfortunately, I still love you.'

There were conditions.

I agreed to all of them.

In the black of Esther's hair, a real lightning-storm.

FAITHFUL AND TRUTHFUL
OR NOTHING, BUSTER

The way up.

GOLDEN

Twins.

Girls.

Non-identical.

Beautiful.

Which made a load of folks say *it must make up for losing one before* – which made us lose (fast) quite a few friends, or lose respect for them.

Sarah (11.33 p.m.) and Grace (12.12 a.m.).

Let me tell you *exactly* how wonderful they are.

Or, no.

You're pleased, but I can see you'll be even more delighted if I spare you the glorious details.

So I will.

Most of them.

On their birthdays, the world rebegan again – just as it's done on a trillion different days for a trillion different men. I was glad to join this great club of average transfiguration. I was glad to be so *normal*.

All through the pregnancy, all I'd asked for was *normally healthy*; I didn't mention *beauty, brains, athletic prowess* or even *being more like Esther than me* (which would be a cheating-way of asking for all the above).

What I cared about was that they emerge from the womb alive. After that, everything else was down to us, diapers to rehab.

Twin *daughters*.

Over the years, I've said and thought such terrible things about women. Let me take this opportunity to apologize.

Several revelations have come my way, since Sarah and Grace. First of these is –

Women are better than men.

And second, which I have to mention straight away, after that, is –

Women are nicer than men.

Men have meetings in restaurants and draw important arrows on important pieces of paper.

(Dear Esther, how can I ever . . . ?)

Men are overcome by a sense of their own importance, when examining the arrows they have drawn in important restaurants.

(Dear Esther, I am more sorry than I can . . .)

Women are different. They see things differently, and how they see things is a better, nicer, less arrow-dependent way of seeing them.

Women see differently.

(Dear Esther, I'll calm down soon.)

Jewellery taught me this, and the way Esther enters into it entirely. Women see it in greater detail than men, because they allow their eyes to change size. They look at a ring as if it were a building – as if the whole of the world might start again, from first principles, taking this small trinket as the beginning. Men stay as eye-giants, in comparison, lumbering, and are only impressed by cathedrals – which may be intricate but are never intimate. Except for God-the-visitor. (Cathedral-type buildings, I mean. Banks count, as do malls.)

A different hat; a different world.

This is the rule of clothes that women understand and men, most men, including me until recently – this is the rule men need to be told about and learn by heart.

If I wear this on my head, the atomic structure of Africa will alter. Not the butterfly effect, no. Avoiding chaos theory completely. Instead, there's a direct improvement caused by me (a woman) buying this hat and choosing the absolutely right occasion upon which to wear it.

Hence the horror, also never understood by giants, of turning up to a party and seeing another woman wearing the same dress, or hat; a parallel universe in which improvements overlap and so cancel one another out. Poor Africa.

To women, men are such a disappointment.

Why won't we rise? Women give us the utopian clues of their clothes. Silk as anti-war protest; pattern as plea for a more detailed and compassionate approach to human inter-relations. 'Don't rip the texture of the world – the textile of the world.' Jewellery to say to men: 'Stop and examine more closely *everything*. Me, especially. Beautiful me. Because if you find me attractive, you are less likely to do harm (to me but also, somehow, to others). And so, by my being beautiful, I save the world.' Distract the beast even in the moment it threatens to go berserk. As a justification for beauty, it is beautiful.

'No,' said Esther. 'You're being reckless again.'

She is so beautiful, as I've said before.

Women have always tried to save me, by being beautiful. One of them succeeded, temporarily. And now she's brought in two reinforcements. Sarah. Grace.

This was where I had reached, about a month ago. This was my new world-view. I was outlining it to Esther, and she was gently telling me how wrong I was, when the phone rang and Syph weighed in unwittingly on my side.

'Man, you gotta come over – you gotta come right over right now because I've got some weird shit I gotta tell you, I mean, this is some fucked-up shit, man, you're not gonna fuckin believe . . .'

Etc.

Come right over is easier said than done, as our house is almost an hour from downtown – where Syph bases his operations.

I knew better than to try and deal with him down the phone. When I've tried before, he's smashed the receiver at his end – resulting, once, in him being unable to call for an ambulance when his latest girlfriend OD'd. Which was what he'd been calling about.

She survived, luckily. Someone visiting the building (not a neighbour, they were used to weird noises) heard Syph's ranting and called the cops to report a domestic disturbance.

It was early evening by the time I made it to Syph's door. I hadn't been to his apartment in maybe half a year. He'd redecorated twice, or so I'd heard.

Around Christmas, Syph had a sudden revelation that anyone who didn't live in a cave or tent was pissing away their soul. So first the place was done out as a Neanderthal dwelling, with finger-paintings of buffalo on the walls; built-in cupboards for the entertainment media, however. And then, around Easter, this was re-done into the circular layout of a Mongolian yurt. Syph set up an ancestor-altar in the Northern corner – framed photograph of his dad at a Canucks game. Sitting on rugs, he sipped milk tea and told my informant (Crab) that he felt centred for the first time in his life. Reincarnation explained everything. Particularly the guilt. (A word I had never known him use before – not in reference to himself, at least.)

'Enter,' said Syph, who was wearing a kaftan of metallic pink. Above his forehead was a shiny disc, like a cartoon dentist might wear, only this disc was gold. Overall, he looked disturbingly like Sun Ra's honky flugelhorn player.

Behind him was something which, at first double-take, I took to be a high-end 1970s roller-disco. Then I realized that the flashing red and yellow lights were in fact control panels, and that the hallway closely approximated to the bridge of the *Starship Enterprise*. (*Star Trek: The Next Generation*.)

'Welcome to the *future*,' Syph said. His voice was very different to when he'd called me on the phone: calm, fruity, British-accented.

I was freaked. It was as if, when speaking to me before, he had done an impression of his usual untogether self in order to lure me to his space-lair.

Syph, who smelt strongly of rosewater, led me through into what he called 'the Receiving Area'. Here, the encircling walls of the yurt had been upgraded to include windows out into what, apparently, was deep space.

In the middle of the room was a circular rug populated by circular throw-cushions. Mono sat cross-legged on one, Crab lay with his head resting on another.

Approaching, I could see no sign of drugs, drink or even cigarettes – the usual accessories to Syph's chosen sitting-place. There was, however, a lime-green Ovation semi-acoustic guitar spangled all over with decal stars.

You bet I sensed danger.

'Thank you all for coming,' Syph said. 'I expect you're wondering why I asked you to join me here.' He sounded *just* like Lord Summerisle in *The Wicker Man*. 'I won't keep you in suspense any longer.' Obviously, the others had been hanging round till I got there. From the deep pockets of his kaftan, Syph drew out a TV-remote and pressed one of the buttons.

'Planet Earth,' he said, just as a beautiful image of said planet appeared on the twelve huge window-screens. 'Six billion people, and counting. I have received word from my Masters that this situation is what they call "unsustainable". An intervention must be made. And soon.'

Syph walked over to the lime-green guitar, picked it up and strapped it on. He then began to sing a song whose chorus ran:

Hail, the beloved starchild!
Hail, you harbinger of dawn!
Clear our polluted earth-senses!
Let us know we've truly been born!

We are born to a destiny
To un-iver-siality
We must leave our home planet
We can do it, if we but plan it.

'That's the opening track,' he said, almost as an aside. 'Me. Solo. Acoustic. Then there's an orchestral interlude, which I've got worked out already. And next comes . . .'

Next came:

> Message from the cosmos
> Knowledge from the gods
> Can we survive? Can we endure?
> Against such overwhelming odds?

And then:

> Confusion
> Illusion
> The Masterpiece of Doubt
> Come faster
> O Master
> And show us the Way Out

And so on, through all four sides of the album. Here is the planned track-listing:

SIDE A

Star-child (Brilliant Love)

Cosmic Wager/ 1000–1 at Least

Astral Travellers' Cheques

Madness! Sadness! (Possible duet with David Bowie)

The Wink of a God in Waltztime

Teeming Masses

SIDE B

December Morning (The Battle Begins)

Roundelay of Afternoon (The Battle Continues)

Yellow Interlude

Bad Metal Boogie (The Battle Reaches Its High Point)

Devastation Groove (The Battle is Tragically Lost)

SIDE C

But No, There is Hope!

Golden Music Teacher

Golden Section of Resurrection: Comeback Kings

Perfect People, Perfect Peace

Brilliant Love, Reprise

SIDE D

The Love Suite (parts I–VIII)

Rain of Hopeful Promise on Children of the Stars

'And I think *that* could make a good single,' Syph said, when the final chord (C major) had died away.

'What do you call it?' Crab asked.

'*The Masterpiece* colon *Message from the Golden Music Teacher* subtitle *Tales of Demographic Explosions*. I hear it as kind of "Ride of the Valkyries" meets "Ride a White Swan".'

'Hmm,' said Crab, and nodded. I have never witnessed a more sublime demonstration of deadpan. It was only awe which prevented me from pissing myself. 'What do *you* think?' Crab asked Mono.

'Yeah,' Mono said, playing along. 'I really like the riff for, what was it? Something Interlude.'

'But it's the whole thing,' said Syph. 'That's only a leitmotiv. The three-note structure is repeated emblematically throughout the piece, and it modulates from minor to major through contrasting keys.'

Personally, I thought it sounded like the 'Moonlight Sonata' as played by a doorbell.

'What about you?' asked Crab. He was focussing the full beam of his straight-man genius upon me.

'The Plan,' I said. 'The lyrics mention a Plan. Could you tell me, what *exactly* is the Plan?'

'I, as the Golden Music Teacher, must ask the world to change its ways. The perfect children *can* make perfect peace, but the imperfect children are the battle-bozos. We must gently rise, together, towards the light of intergalactic under-standing. We, by which I mean, "the Bright Ones", must prepare the planet for the journey to eternity. My Masters have told me this. Our feathers must be washed of the clay that holds us down. We are mired in conflict. This is because not enough of humankind is perfected.'

'Who isn't perfect?' I asked, dreading.

'The small yellow races,' replied the Golden Music Teacher. (I was trying very hard not to think of him as my old friend, Syph.) 'That is revealed in the lyrics to Yellow Interlude.'

'Aren't the, er, small yellow races more golden than us?' Crab asked.

'No. We are white gold,' said Syph. 'We are the pure.'

'Do you mean Chinese people?' Mono asked. 'I don't have any problem with Chinese people.'

'Chinese. Japanese. Korean . . .'

'Mongolian?' asked Crab, indicating the yurt.

'Yes,' said the Golden Music Teacher. 'Them, too.'

'And you want to kill them?' I asked.

'No. I want to allow them to die. Give them a generation or two. Make it humane, you know.'

'Why *allow* them?'

'They want to, really,' the Golden Music Teacher said. 'That is their purpose, galactically speaking. They make way so that the race of white gold may prove its worth to the Watching Ones. Then the Watching Ones will beat us into beautiful ornaments to adorn their breasts. The Watching Ones have large and shapely breasts.'

'What happened?' I said, looking at Crab and then Mono. 'What happened to him? Where did he go?' I didn't mean outer space.

'No idea,' said Mono.

'It's okay,' said Crab, oddly serene. He was still lying on the circular carpet. 'I can handle it.'

'The Golden Music Teacher will not be handled. I have called a press conference for tomorrow morning –'

'Fuck,' I said.

'I will announce *The Masterpiece* to the world.'

'Do they know about the' – I could hardly say it – 'small yellow part?'

'Of course not. For maximum impact, the Higher Knowledge must be injected directly into the media bloodstream.'

'Exactly,' said Crab. 'You *read* my mind.'

'They read *our* minds all the time,' said the Golden Music Teacher. 'Then they beam us back to us.'

'Like a superpowerful laser,' said Crab.

'I am like a lens,' said the Golden Music Teacher. 'Or a prism. Or a diamond. I can change shape at will.'

'Like a shaman,' said Crab. 'Like Jim Morrison.'

I couldn't believe what Crab was doing, encouraging the lunacy.

'You're going along with this?' I shouted.

Crab gave me a *shut up* look. 'Of course we must spread the great wisdom,' he said, rolling up onto his feet. 'Perhaps we should retire for a while, to let the Great One commune once more with the cosmos.'

'I do feel like I should check in,' said the Golden Music Teacher.

Crab grabbed my arm and pulled me towards the door. Mono followed. 'See you, man,' he said to the Golden Music Teacher.

'It's suicide,' I said, as soon as we were in the elevator. 'It's not even just career suicide. It's *actual* suicide.'

'Don't worry,' said Crab. 'It's never going to happen.' His amazing calm was, I figured, entirely due to not having taken in the absolute shitness of our situation.

'What if he mouths off to twenty music journalists about humanely exterminating China –'

'Relax. Just relax. I'm going out to pay a few visits –'

'To who? To the Masters of the Universe?'

'Yes,' Crab replied. 'You could say that.'

'We have to get him put away,' said Mono. 'He's not well. He can go to that place you went, Crab. Where was it?'

'Later,' said Crab.

'What's your plan?' asked Mono.

The elevator had reached ground-level.

'Trust me,' said Crab.

I drove home.

Maintaining trust in Crab took so much effort that twice I almost drove into oncoming traffic.

When the girls were safely asleep, I told Esther the whole thing, including track-listing – it was scorched into my brain. In reply, she told me to trust Crab.

'But . . .' I said.

'You are safe,' said Esther.

That night, I was never going to sleep. I walked around our house, looking at all the things that were soon to be taken away from me. Although I had spent a lot of time and money trying to overcome my materialism, the thought of losing *everything* still terrified me. When I stopped in on the girls, their sleeping bodies seemed so unprepared for the tsunami of hate they'd have to face, later in life.

I went outside and looked up at the stars – fuckers.

The press conference was set for 7 a.m. The Golden Music Teacher aimed to hit all the morning bulletins.

I got to our management's glassy offices early. Just as I arrived at the front door, a secretary I only vaguely knew was sticking a notice up:

> Today's press conference has unfortunately been
> cancelled due to ill health. The band wishes to
> extend its sincere apologies for any inconvenience
> this may cause.

'What's happened?' I asked.

'Crab just called,' the secretary said. 'From the hospital. He didn't sound all that ill.'

'How *did* he sound?'

She thought for a moment.

'Happy.'

I was there within half an hour.

In a very expensive private room, I found both Syph and Crab lying, side by side, on drips. Crab was awake, watching a breakfast show that – due to him – made no mention of a well-known rock band's cosmic concept album, or its ultra-racist message to the planet.

'And . . . ?' I asked.

'God bless cocaine,' said Crab. 'And God bless acid. And God bless heroin. The Masters of the Universe, who many mistake for humble drug dealers, came through. Cocaine. LSD. Heroin. In that order. Too much, but not *really* too much.'

'Is he still the Golden Music Teacher?' I asked, nodding towards Syph.

'We'll see when he wakes up. I kind of doubt it. We stayed up until four, listening to the Zep and Sabbath. I think by about three a.m. I'd brought him safely over to the dark side – temporarily, of course. Satanism's so much more respectable, in music circles, isn't it?'

Back at home, drained, I tried to apologize once again to Esther for the stupidity of men.

'But it was Crab who saved the world,' she said.

Three weeks later, sitting on a throne of plastic skulls, Syph claimed to have no memory whatsoever of the Golden Music Teacher. His apartment was black as hell. I thought it felt kind of homey.

Mono turned the 'Yellow Interlude' riff into a song called 'When I wasn't Me'.

I still think women rule.

I feel old.

My daughters are – of course of course – a different generation, and things young-me couldn't help but find new and exciting (the first Compact Disc in its display cabinet on the record-store counter – slice of silvery, rainbowy future) are relics that, to them, might as well be Victorian.

I will find it difficult not to try and impress upon them the importance, and even worse the superiority, of these bits of junk.

Not the CDs. The songs on them.

I love pop culture, still, but what if everything I've invested in it was a mistake?

Wouldn't it have been better for me to learn Latin and read the classics, or become an archaeologist and develop a relationship with the *really* old?

They will think me uncool, my daughters, probably using a less uncool word than uncool. Today, if they were tweens, I'd be *so over.* (Unless *so over* is *so over* and something new has popped up to take its place.) It's terrible to know that, because I have a bit of money, they'll end up speaking like spoilt Californians. Everyone speaks like that at the good Vancouver schools, that or like gangsta rappers.

Spoilt – not a concept the kids spend time worrying about.

One night four or five months ago, when they couldn't sleep, I was trying to come up with a new lullaby for them. There's only so many times you can sing Leonard Cohen's 'Suzanne' – and Esther had banned 'Chelsea Hotel No. 2' because of the oral-sex reference. I wanted something long-lasting, something folky – a tribal gift. Halfway through 'Rock-a-bye Baby' I realized how it ended, and stopped dead. I couldn't remember more than the first couple of lines of

'Lavender's Blue'. Is this my culture? What kind of heritage to pass on! Pop and fragments. I couldn't remember what my mother used to sing to me, so I called her up. It was only just gone ten. She told me she couldn't remember, either – then phoned back to say she'd remembered something. 'When you were about five, you used to love "I'd like to buy the world a *Coke*".'

Boy, that dates me. Man, that depresses me.

What do I have? What do I *own*?

Is Leonard Cohen it? The real thing?

Mom called back again, to say that when I was little I'd liked 'Nights in White Satin' and anything by the Mamas and Papas.

'Thank you,' I said, 'that's great. If you think of any more, please don't tell me.'

'I thought you wanted to know.'

'I did. I don't any longer.'

'You sound tired.'

She was right. Tired is how old people sound, because the young are exhausting them. They use us. We buy them stuff for them to lose interest in, quickly.

It's not that I don't want my daughters to make the mistakes I did. It's that I don't want them to make the mistake I *was* – to go with a guy who is the contemporary equivalent of the guy I used to be.

So, should I send them to violin lessons, ban rap music, have a *no tattoos no piercings until 18* rule? Should I install a smoke detector in their bedrooms?

(They are going to be two next week.)

I decided to reconsider Leonard Cohen. What was so bad about him? He wasn't shallow – an advance on buying the world a *Coke*.

When I was thirteen, Cohen was my God. His biography didn't mean much. Born Montreal, 21 September 1934 – that detail-crap. Author of esteemed books of poems with ornate titles, ahem, *Let Us Compare Mythologies*. Not important. All I cared about was the *Songs from a Room* long-player, and the clues it offered a lonely boy of a possible future. I know now that it's bad art whose greatest achievement is to make you envious of the life of its creator. Biggest clue was the back-cover photograph: a bare-bottomed blonde, dressed only in a white towel, seated at a typewriter, at a desk, in a white painted, shuttered, pale-floorboarded room. Also present were a table, some books, a chessboard, a burnt-down candle-stick, a sheep's skull and a white-sheeted bed. To pick out the important details was not difficult. Here was a woman and here was a bed. The two things could be linked. The woman might get into the bed. The woman might just have gotten out of the bed. And then, above the desk, typed out life-size, perhaps even by *that* typewriter, were the ten song titles. One of them, 'Seems So Long Ago, Nancy', contained a woman's name. Yet somehow the information had reached me that the blonde at the desk was Marianne, not Nancy. On another album, his first, Cohen had bade her farewell – so long, so long ago. This was Cohen's *ex*-girlfriend! Once upon a time, they'd had sex – probably in that bed. (And this did seem distant enough, from me, to be a once-upon-a-time fairy story.) I gazed at the back-cover and was all envy. If Marianne stood up and pulled at that towel, it would drop to the pale floorboards. (Women in Cohen's early songs are more likely than not to get naked, even nuns.) Perhaps, after the photograph was taken, that's exactly what she'd done. Cohen had then placed the camera down on the table, along-side the skull, and they'd had sex – or made love. At thirteen, I was still working on that fine distinction. Cohen, I knew, must have taken the photograph: there was a credit (John Berg) for the cover photo but none for this. To be in that room with that woman and that typewriter and that bed, holding a camera! I wanted it all. It was an injustice that I didn't live Cohen's life. His *ex*-girlfriend! There is no express-ing the glamour of such sadness, when it seems so unattain-able. So long. Past-tense Marianne wore a white towel she could drop, and I wanted that sexual availability for myself. To live in the scent of women no longer girls, women with children by other men. (I'd learnt this information, too: Marianne's son, not pictured, was called Axel.) Emotional complications far beyond those available in my suburb, to thirteen-year-old me – although my parents' generation was deep in the blue tangle of them. Being young is all about wanting to be older. I wasn't Leonard, eye watching shutter go click and Marianne reappear, still smiling, towelled. What more could life hold? What else could I aim for? One thing: to have had it and lost it. Typical for an envy-artist, Cohen's song of total ownership was one of renunciation. With great contempt, 'So Long, Marianne' wasn't even *on* this album. The photographer was already gone from what I might never have. At thirteen-years-old, not confident in my looks, it seemed entirely possible that no woman would ever tell me she could take no more betrayals. I was so far from female embrace (not my mother's), and I missed it so much – the fragrance and softness and cold burning of it. This was where Cohen's other renunciation song, 'Seems So Long Ago, Nancy', came in. That the young woman addressed had worn green stockings was neither here nor there. Bohemianism, in my future lover, would be desirable but I wasn't going to make it a without-which. No, what *really* got my attention was the line saying that Nancy had slept with *everyone*. And if she really *had* done that, then, if *I'd* been around, she would have slept with *me*. This seemed an epic promise. All I had to do was put myself in the vicinity of such women and it would happen. Listening to 'Nancy', I felt a new hope. Previously infinite distances became at least imaginable, astral. Sex, as far as I was concerned, was the moon. Men had been there, young men, some of them I even knew. Romance, however, was Alpha Centauri. And regret, erotic regret, was probably a parallel universe. Yet, learning from my envy of Leonard Cohen, I desired erotic regret far more than I did sex or even romance.

And I sing these songs as *lullabies*?

Not any longer.

Not after I'd thought it through, done a little research.

My daughters weren't called Marianne and Nancy, but imagine if I'd subconsciously insisted.

As a father, what I felt nostalgic for now was my ignorance and my idealism. I longed for my longing because all I had now was *having*. Unless I started having something else: affairs. Which would be having it all and more. I didn't want more. Esther and two daughters was more than enough. I idealized my earlier lacks – and that's what Cohen had done, too. He was such a fake, such a schlockster. It was all a line. He was saying *so long* to Marianne in the hope that, after writing such a sad and catchy song, he'd be attractive to a huge number of new women – all hoping he'd love them and leave them and immortalize them. Poet and novelist wasn't enough. He wanted the more I didn't. And I'm pretty certain he got it: singer-songwriter, modern-day troubadour, ladies' man.

The Cohen of the photograph was, I now knew, the Cohen of the Greek isle of Hydra, 1961–1965. That came before Cohen the Rake. But I wasn't interested in him: I'd been him, stroked the acres of smooth female flesh until my hands were calloused with it. Maybe his total *was* greater than mine; I knew the scented territory. No, it was a different, later Cohen that fascinated me – and almost as much as photographer-Cohen had: monk-Cohen.

In 1996, the cocksman retired up Mount Baldy in Southern California. He went Zen. Entered the monastery.

Now, his biography began to fascinate. Born Montreal. Father dies when he is nine. After a lifetime's sensual indulgence as a touring musician, gets Buddhism. What happened? Someone visit his dressing-room and slip him some beads? He renounces it all. Is ordained as a monk. Is known, get this, as Jikan, 'the Silent One'. And a couple of years later, he's back on the angelic streets of Sin City. And enlightenment? What of that? Carried in his suitcase or left behind?

I wanted to talk with him. People I knew knew people who knew people he knew – Canadians in exile, snow-nostalgists. Messages were sent. Was I sure it wasn't Joni Mitchell I wanted? Two weeks passed. Jikan stayed true to his name.

I wrote Mr Leonard Cohen a letter. One of my people had slipped me his email address, but what I had to say needed heavy laid paper and a smooth-flowing fountain pen. Courteously, I sent it via his management, marked personal. Then, a month later, I re-sent it direct to his home address, an address given me by one of the more sympathetic people my people knew. It was a letter about sensuality and Godhead. He had come down from the mountain. Was there any point me starting to climb it? Flesh of my flesh, daughters two. I live with three women, am outnumbered and loving every hysterical second. Had women, in the end, been a greater nirvana for monk-Cohen than the empty mind?

Jikan remained Jikan.

I took silence as my answer and was content.

Until I happened to find myself in LA with an afternoon free.

I went to his house, which was modest, and looked at the lawn out front. For the first time in years, I felt what fans must feel when approaching me: nerves like I was going to puke through my arse and shit out my nose.

Getting back in the rental car, I tried to calm myself down enough for a second try.

I could see the door, plain enough. There was the doorstep, where I would stand.

But I knew I wasn't capable.

I'd opened my door often enough on People Looking for Answers – opened it whilst thinking maybe this was the pizza delivery boy, or Fed-Ex with those new cymbals I ordered, or anything but fronting up as myself.

How could I expect Lenny shirt-sleeves to be Leonard 'Songs from a Room' Cohen, on demand?

I of all people should see the unreasonableness of this.

I started the car.

And then I saw him.

He came out the door, let it close and lock behind him, patted his jacket pocket (keys? cigarettes?) and didn't break stride until he'd reached his ride. Leonard fucking Cohen. His eyes were behind dark glasses. This was the ex-monk. Those eyes had looked upon Marianne, through the view-finder. He hadn't replied to my question, my letter. Sincerely, L. Cohen.

The car started up and he pulled past me down the street. Without thinking, I turned the ignition and began following him.

A left, a right, another right, onto the freeway.

Has he seen me?

LA is not a place you want to be tailed.

I'd been followed, too, plenty of times, by People Looking for Answers, and People Angry for No Clear Reason, and People Who Think It's Funny to Follow Minor Celebrities, and People with Cameras and Kids to Feed, and all sorts of other People.

Whatever he did, wherever he went, I'd be disappointed. Unless it was right back to Mount Baldy. Unless he'd just that afternoon thought, *I've made a terrible mistake.* Unless I'd caught the issue of the epiphany. He was probably gone for groceries.

I slowed down and took the next exit ramp.

What if I'd tailed him to Wal-Mart? Would that have been more crushing than if he'd wound up at a fantastic little kosher deli? Or a titty bar? Or his record label?

Soberly, I completed my business in LA.

When I got home, among my mail was a short handwritten note from Leonard. In it, he politely thanked me for my letter. These were deep questions. They took a lot of time, and he was a slow thinker – and an even slower writer, if that were possible. He was sure that when I needed to I'd make the right decisions. How wonderful to have twin daughters.

He liked my band. Good to see some fellow Canadians flying the Old Maple Leaf. If I was ever passing, please to drop by . . .

This was a good man, a man whose songs any father could sing to his daughters.

Again, I sang them.

(. . . drop by, but call first.)

I don't even know if I should record this next bit.

A few weeks earlier, my thoughts had become so Cohen-saturated that I even remembered him whilst changing my daughters' diapers.

Infant sexuality is what I was probably thinking about, really. Their little slits look like boxer's eyes, closed up so much the fight has to be stopped. But although they seem swollen they are not bruised. As I cleaned the mustard-poo off, wiping the cotton-wool in one direction, I thought of whether I would be happy for a young Leonard Cohen to witness the nakedness of a grown-up daughter of mine.

No, not whether I would be *happy*, whether I could *bear* it.

When they were just born, Syph came over and I gave him them to hold, took a few photos. 'So beautiful,' he said, like everyone else. Such an unholy terror, I felt. Those hands of his, and where they'd been, and what they'd done when they got there. Was this fatherhood? It was so violent.

My daughters' cunts. Here, in future, young men I distrust and older men I fear will trespass – or be invited. It's possible the older men may even be older than me. Imagine that.

We don't take bathtime photographs any more, even digital ones, for fear that if someone official gets to see them we'll be arrested as paedophiles. None of that smut on my hard drive. Looking at them, even as I wiped away their practical poo, my eyes felt guilty. I've thought such terrible things about women. The girls who slept with me, the underage-ish ones, wanted to – at least in the sense they were never drugged or physically compelled. But maybe larger forces were angry with them. Maybe it was a sky-high father with thoughts of previous wrongdoing.

Being Jewish, Cohen is big on atonement.

I try to be good, singing.

???

I saw it in a desk-calendar – one of those chunky ones with a quote for every date:

NOVEMBER 26th
Everything not given is lost.

And I was embarrassed to find it so true.

I've read some very respectable books, great works of world literature, which moved me far less.

Forget the fact that the 25th said *Smile and the world smiles with you* and the 27th *A journey of a thousand miles starts with a single step.* I know these both for clichés of corporate spirituality – just the right sort of uplifting sentiments for the hungover office worker, ripping away another yesterday and hoping for some hope. And November 26th – *Everything not given is lost* – is probably no less of a cliché. But, and here's the thing, it was one I'd never heard – that I came to fresh as a new-mown daisy on crisp white snow.

Felled me, that's what it did. Like the good old tree in the forest with no-one around to hear.

For what have I not given? What have I tried to keep on keeping? What have I sought to bury away, and ended up just burying? What have I still to lose?

The date this happened wasn't November 26th, it was some time in May. I had been left alone in one of the offices of our record company, and there was nothing else around to read – apart from other bands' gold and platinum discs, on all four walls.

What I wanted was a quick laugh at some sentimental trash, a little superiority-buzz.

I confess: I ripped November 26th right out of that calendar.

Only afterwards did I wonder what effect this would have on the record-company executive who'd been keeping me waiting. It wasn't that I *liked* him – quite the opposite. He was a knob. Plus, he wouldn't leave one of his real top-selling artistes alone for a second. If he couldn't be there personally, he'd send the most attractive girl in the department across to keep them amused. But maybe the very words he needed to begin the long task of extracting himself from the samsara of knobhood were the ones I'd stolen from him. Eventually, I got to feeling so guilty about the possibility that he would suffer the continued damnation of being a complete knob, however rich, successful and handsome, that I photocopied November 26th and sent it back to him – along with an apology for secretly removing that day from his desk-calendar. I did this, I should say, before the end of October.

Next I heard of it, our management were on at me, really pissed, for carelessly 'if amusingly' interfering with the delicate process of contract renegotiation. Mr Executive, you see, had taken the motto as a coded warning that we felt we weren't being paid (*given*) enough untaxable cash, and that if this situation didn't change then we'd soon be gone (*lost*).

Knob.

I kept November 26th in my wallet, behind the photographs of Esther, our daughters and Ringo Starr's 1964 Ludwig drumkit – all of which are there to keep me honest, keep me safe, and remind me of what I love the most. Faithful *and* truthful.

. . . not given . . .

What did that mean? If I didn't want to lose my family, I had somehow to give it away? To whom? Or didn't Esther and my daughters count, not being *things*? But 'everything', I knew, included things which weren't things. Everything, definitely, included me. And I'd given myself to them. Maybe not enough, though. Esther and I had talked about getting married, after the girls were born, but I never formally asked, and I think Esther was waiting for that. I'd tried to make it so she could be sure of having me, for ever. She and the girls were the only beneficiaries of my will. And, in a way, by giving me children, Esther had given herself to me. But I couldn't be sure I wouldn't lose all three of them.

Gifts are so terrifying.

There are shows I've played where not one single beat was for the audience, for the music itself or for my bandmates – money is what I wanted, and if the promoter had been fool enough to let me, I'd have taken it and left without even *seeing* the stage.

There are relationships I've entered with my exit strategy not only planned but already put into operation. Two-timing two perfectly nice women, as a way of being simultaneously discovered, dumping both and ensuring that neither would come back for more. (Okay, I did this once.)

There are prayers which I thought would make me look good, in front of Buddha. Like I really *did* feel that generous to the rest of the violent world, rather than pleading again and again for those I love to be spared the worst of it. *Oh-mani-padme-humbug.*

: . . . is lost . . .

As a young man, in fact as a handsome young prince, the Buddha did something usually done only by bastards: he walked out on his wife and kid.

What he said to them, in no words at all, was *I am more important than you.*

And he *was*, because he was the man who would become, after some while of wandering, the Buddha. But . . .

I never understood this, not properly. That each seeks

enlightenment entirely alone – fine. That the Buddha had to give up everything – okay. That that *everything* included his family – hold it right there.

This was an undeniably cruel act.

I've never read anything about how his abandoned wife got on, or what happened to his disowned baby. Did they gain from the harsh lesson of him leaving? *Unless you give me up, I will be even more lost to you than I am now.* Is he saying that? *If you love me, let me go.* Surely he should have given them his life, as he had pledged to do.

Whatever – it makes it pretty hard to forget that the Buddha, like all men, was from time to time a fucker.

Perhaps that's the point, exactly.

Of course, this took place when he was an unenlightened being – but after he sat under the Bodhi tree and became enlightened and saw whatever he saw, did he go back? Did he apologize?

No – because he must have realized there was no reason to. He had given them his absence; cosmically, seen from the point-and-no-point of view of an enlightened being, this was as good as his presence.

I guess.

But I'm still troubled. What sort of religion would his wife have started? Or his son? Or wouldn't they just have gone off and started a war?

Crab left his family, too, and this isn't the only thing he has in common with the Buddha.

He often sleeps in the open, under trees. But the Buddha's main hang was balmy India/Nepal. Crab is out there for Vancouver autumns. (He's not so dumb as to freeze to death November through February.)

Whenever Crab manages to gather together some material possessions, he ends up giving them all away. Sometimes I accept some of them, just so I can try to give them back when he realizes he's left himself with absolutely nothing.

And most importantly, Crab is a teacher. I don't just mean

guitar lessons, though he has always been humblingly generous with his time – never too busy to show some kid the
tuning for 'Honky Tonk Women' or 'Gimme Shelter'. In
comparison, I have been a miser and a recluse. Making that
Indie-Rock Drumming for Beginners video was no equivalent.

I try not to sentimentalize Crab, or sanctify him, but he
has given everything – not just to the band, to *everyone*, to the
world, to (more accurately) the universe.

He has been our teacher.

I am, in the language of that great neglected band, The
Minutemen, *boozh* (translation: bourgeois). I do not *jam econo*
(translation: travel light), as they would have put it. This
means that, at some point, I must have sold out and become
mersh (translation: commercial).

Every morning, without fail, the fact I own an extremely
good espresso-machine makes me feel suicidal. And it does
this by reminding me that Crab, because he doesn't own
anything, doesn't own an espresso-maker. If he requires coffee,
he steps into a diner – and *if* he requires coffee, it is usually
because he has a definite objective he wishes to achieve, for
which he needs to be sober.

Otherwise, beer. Otherwise, bars and parks.

One average everyday evening, not November 26th, after
the girls were in bed, I tried to explain to Esther about the
desk-calendar. I went the roundabout way, and began by
saying, 'Esther, would you marry me?'

'Of course,' she said, without missing a beat – conver-
sationally, she keeps better time than I do. 'Any time you
want to ask.'

'I thought I just did.'

'Try again.' She said this with a true smile. Her words look
harsh, written down, but didn't sound that way.

'I don't get it,' I said.

'Yes, I *would* marry you. Under certain circumstances.'

'What circumstances?'

'Well, first you've got to ask . . .'

'Would you be my wife?'

'I *would*.'

'Do you want to get married?'

'I do.'

'So, have I asked you yet?'

'No. But you're closer than you were. I'm sure you'll get there in the end.'

I understood.

'Esther, *will* you marry me?'

'That's right.'

'Will you?'

'In the right circumstances.'

'What circumstances?' I asked again.

Our main downstairs living room – the family room – is in a style Esther calls 'please God anything but minimal'. One wall is framed photographs of people we like, the opposite is pieces of fabric that Esther likes, which leaves the mantelpiece with the large painting above it and a wall of glass leading out, when slid back, into our garden. The large painting is by me, as Esther thought I should try it at least once. (Once is exactly how many times I'm going to leave it at.) We have a big squishy sofa which is guilt-makingly leather. And I am half-responsible for choosing it. On either side of this, to make things worse, are matching chairs. Mostly, I graduate towards the left-hand one. Esther, without wishing to pun, is usually seated in the right.

Esther asked, 'Do you want to marry me?'

'Of course, or else I wouldn't have asked.'

'But why are you asking me *now*? Have you been having an affair?'

I don't know why I hesitated before saying, 'No.' I hadn't even flirted with the idea of another woman since the girls were born.

'There's something . . .'

And finally, as I'd known all along it would, the conversation came round to the desk-calendar. (This is how compatible Esther and I are.) I pulled November 26th out of my wallet. It was the first time I'd shown it to anyone. 'Don't laugh,' I said.

Esther read the words carefully, then laughed. 'Sorry,' she said. 'I was really trying not to.'

'I am terrified by this, as a thought. I don't know how to work my way around it.'

'Through it, I think you mean.'

'Are we still getting married?'

'Because of this?'

'You could say that.'

'Terror is not a good basis for marriage.'

'Isn't it the only basis?'

Esther stood up and went into the kitchen. For one terrible moment, I thought she was heading towards the espresso-maker. I didn't want to complicate matters even further by mentioning my feelings about that. But, no, she was just running a glass of water. In this way, with great simplicity, and also giving me time to think my way a little further *through* my stupidity, Esther answered my question.

She waited until she had sat down before she provided a gloss. 'I'm not in the least bit scared.'

'You're not?'

She shook her head and took a sip. For some reason, it was the sip which made me believe her.

'The girls could die,' I said.

'Yes,' Esther said.

'They could die horribly.'

'Mmm.'

'And it could be my fault.'

'That is true.'

She was forcing it all out – every last bit.

'It could be *your* fault,' I said.

'I'm still not scared.'

'How can you not be?'

'Because you are.'

'What? So, you delegate the existential angst to me. I sub-contract –'

'No. Because if we both were, life would be unbearable. I made a practical decision. Your angst is more productive than mine. It makes you a better drummer. It makes you a drummer period.'

'You can't just *decide* not to wake up pissing yourself with fear. I think of horrible things . . .'

'So do I. But I don't let them horrify me. I go on.'

'Could I . . . ?' I asked, meaning take a sip of her water. My sip was more like a gulp. Afterwards, I said, 'You're protecting me.'

'More myself. And even more the girls. Enough horror in the house could probably kill them.'

'It's like we're already married, and you're doing what I should really be doing.'

'You do more than enough.'

'What do you think of that, then?' November 26th was still in her hands – she'd carried it into the kitchen and back.

'It's cheesy, a little simplistic.'

'How do I *not* lose you?' My tone was unashamedly pleading.

'You keep me.'

'But how do I do that?'

'You've done it so far.'

'If we get married, things won't have to change.'

'*If* . . . ?'

'*When*, then.'

'I still haven't said yes.'

'I thought you did.'

'We don't *need* to get married.'

'We just want to,' I said. 'I want to.'

'Yes,' said Esther. 'I think you probably do.'

She picked up the glass of water and put down November 26th.

'Does that mean the conversation is over?' I asked.

'No,' said Esther, and walked out into the garden.

There was moonlight. We have a very big lawn. Strangely, this doesn't make me feel as bad as the espresso-machine does. I went to join Esther. We strolled.

After a while, she said, 'If the girls die, I will mourn them.' And then, after a significant pause, she added, '*If*.'

I put my arm around her. It fit.

'You mean don't mourn things which aren't dead. Don't mourn your own life.'

'Now *that* would be a good thing to put in a calendar,' she said.

'Tell me how I should ask you to marry me.'

'Oh, I think you know well enough,' she said.

And it turned out that I did.

The next day I was checking, for the third time, that I'd strapped the girls safely in the back of our station wagon.

'Yes,' said Esther, coming up behind me. 'I will.'

It took me only a moment to realize where I was: engaged.

We found the nearest marriage commissioner, phoned them, asked for the next available date.

Crab was best man.

I gave him November 26th, framed, as a souvenir. He kept it, of course – by giving it away to the first person he could find.

There is still an espresso-maker in our kitchen, but I had one of our lawyers draw up an extensive document assigning the full moral responsibility for it to Esther.

She drinks water.

SCOTLAND

I went to Barcelona, Bucharest, Hong Kong, Melbourne, Perth, Buenos Aires, then returned home.

Esther believed I was the same; I knew I wasn't, but didn't know exactly how I'd changed.

Nothing had happened during the promotional tour – no significant encounters had taken place; no story-worthy incidents; no more girls or kids or monks.

But something changed in me.

What it was only became obvious when they asked me to go away again: I'd finally had enough.

Enough Club Class passenger-lounge complimentary aromatized wafer biscuits; enough last-bag-to-arrive-on-the-carousel; enough misspelt versions of my name awaiting me just beyond immigration; enough radio interviews where the hairy DJ has been deludedly expecting and heavily trailing Syph; enough tipsy PAs telling me how they envy creatives like myself – how that's what their boyfriend does, when he's not designing corporate websites; enough eyes of expectation in faces of delight wobbling on bodies with which I am familiar, typically if not specifically; enough phonecalls long-distance to tell Esther where I've been; enough of Sarah and Grace crying in the background, and not coming to the phone to talk to me; enough of how good I am at so many things my younger self would have hated my present self for being good at: meet'n'greeting, recording stacks of station idents for W-ANK and K-RUD, jamming with local percussionists (well, that's not so bad), accepting well-intentioned compliments which are actually vicious put-downs ('I really love the B-side to your second single – I think it's the best thing you'll ever do').

I'd had enough of that goo-goo stuff, enough already, enough *enough*.

Not enough for the moment, enough for good.

When I told Esther, beautiful known wrinkles at the corners of her eyes, my home in this world, she was delighted and terrified. (She was also standing at the breakfast bar with a mouth full of yogurt and granola – I picked my moment.) The cause of both emotions was the same: I'd be around the house a whole lot more.

I called a band meeting, usual place, usual booth, early enough in the day for Crab to be conscious if not sober – and they didn't take me seriously. (It wasn't like it hadn't happened before.)

'Anyway,' said Syph, across a double espresso, 'I want to go back to Japan next year. My rope-mistress is expecting me.'

'Don't believe me,' I said. 'Just watch. I'll be the empty seat on the plane, next time you fly out. This is it. I'm done. No longer participating. Over.'

'And the new album,' asked Crab. 'What about that?'

'As long as we record it at a studio within driving distance of my house – and I don't mean Seattle.'

'That's cool with me,' said Mono, who hated to leave Major in either Northern Ontario or Vancouver.

Syph gave me a look of dominance.

'Just watch me,' I said. 'I'm not there.'

And three months later, I wasn't. An air-ticket to Tokyo was in the trashbag at the bottom of the drive. The answering machine was flashing like a cherry-top cop-car in hot pursuit. I'd given my cellphone to the girls to play with. 'Hello, this is Barbie,' they said, to anyone who rang. 'What would you like to wear today?'

When the management arrived, I spoke to them through the front door.

'Well, get another drummer. Good-bye.'

Twenty-four hours later, they'd flown in Yoyo (hi Yoyo!) to plead from the fans' perspective: a sneaky trick.

I gave her coffee, bagels and a long explanation, which she posted on the website: 'He seems to be full of strong decision. Very proud, like a man. We must respect him even as we are sad too. See you soon, drummer boy.'

After a week, the management faxed me a grossly shitty legal document, fifty pages of it, which they'd had some mafia lawyer draw up. They claimed to own my Vancouver house – and have stakes in both my other properties (New York apartment, log cabin up North). My marriage, they stated, was in breach of contract – because I hadn't informed them of it in advance. If I didn't fulfil my obligations, see Coda A, paragraphs 1 to 33, they would be left with no option badda-badda-badda but recourse to the judicial system.

I called Syph and told him how disappointed I was, slowly and calmly.

'Come back. It solves everything,' he said. 'We miss you. This new guy, he's technically way better than you, but – just come back.'

'I haven't *gone* anywhere,' I said. 'You have.'

'That's a lie. Moving is our staying still.'

Wasn't that the truth?

'You saw the empty seat,' I said. 'Did you believe me then?'

'We believe you – we believe you. You are a strong, powerful, independent-minded motherfucker. Now fall in line.'

'I love you,' I said. 'Use a condom. Goodbye.'

Then I paid a visit to the most expensive lawyer I'd ever heard of and instructed her to terminate with extreme prejudice.

Her secretary had ordered me an infusion of mint leaves, whilst I waited. It tasted so delicious it was almost worth the fees for an hour of the woman's time.

'You have nothing to worry about,' she said as I sipped.

'I know that,' I said.

She smiled and offered me another drink.

When I got back home, after a long, happy trip to the

record store, there was a message from Syph on the answering machine. He was sobbing. Counter-suing, for some reason, had always upset him. 'You didn't have to start fucking World War Three,' he said.

A fax came through from the mafia lawyers. 'The band *okay* has dispensed with our company's services.'

If I wanted to, I could grant myself the illusion of being free at last, free at last.

For a couple of weeks, the girls climbed all over me on the couch and told me that everything I thought was wrong and everything I said was stupid, and I agreed.

'Let's go away,' Esther suggested, when she'd taken a good, assessing look at me and my TV-eyes.

'I can't fly,' I said. 'They'd crucify me.'

'Fine,' she said. 'We don't fly.'

Brochures arrived.

We took a Caribbean cruise, after a flight to Florida: I compromised.

On board ship, the girls invented their own new game, under-the-table-tennis – which kept them happy all day.

The map of headless-legless-chicken-shaped Barbados showed a place called Scotland. We drove up there in a rented Moke, drinking *Coke*. It was quiet – a shaggy craggy hillside. There was a shack available. If we stayed, the girls could consumer-detox (no more pink purchases), I could gibber in my own sweet way, and Esther could walk round in bare feet looking holy. So we ditched the cruise and bought more insect-repellent.

Sitting on a deckchair looking out over the rough Atlantic, where surfers were patient and sometimes rewarded, I tried to relax.

Couldn't.

Two days went by.

Still couldn't.

'Come and talk to me,' I shouted to Esther after she'd put the girls to bed.

But when she sat down, cross-legged in the doorway, we stalled after about five minutes.

'Does my life have too little resistance?' I asked.

'With those two?' she said.

'Shall we try for a boy?'

She hesitated but then said, 'No.'

'Why not?'

'I like the gender imbalance. I like seeing my feet – and eating anything.'

'You eat hardly anything.'

'But I can eat whatever of it I want.'

'You are beautiful.' And then, a little later. 'I feel wrong. My head feels wrong.'

'You need to do something – you can't do nothing.'

'I have no transferable skills. When the world ends, who's going to want a drummer?'

'The world has ended. Here we are.'

'Really?'

'Well, you seem to think so,' she said.

Grace started to cry in her sleep, and Esther went to comfort her. She always did this. I'd tried, failed. When the girls were learning to be comforted, I wasn't there to learn how to do it.

Twilight came and we resumed our conversation, drinking white rum – brewed less than nine miles away (that's how long the island is).

'You want a challenge?' said Esther. 'Be a good father.'

'Shalom,' I said, my usual greeting to her Jewish mother persona. 'Am I not trying – by quitting touring?'

'Don't congratulate yourself too much. That decision was mostly selfish.'

'If we had another baby, it might be a girl.'

'You'd probably leave us.'

'Always outnumbered, always outgunned.'

I got up from the deckchair and joined her in the doorway – it was just wide enough for our two sets of hips.

I asked: 'Is it inevitable that as we get older we get sadder?'
She didn't answer.

'I feel I did things better when I didn't know so much about them.'

The sky was the colour of amethyst. Around us, the shadows were making noises of insects as big as small animals. In one of the shacks a little nearer the water, music started up. It was not by *okay*. Neither was it surf music. And neither had it been made on the tropical island paradise of Barbados. It was American hip-hop. We sat and listened. After a while, they turned the volume up full.

'It'll wake the girls,' Esther said.

'Hold it,' I said. 'I recognize that.'

'Will you go and tell them to shut it off?'

'It's me,' I said. 'I've been sampled. They've sampled me – my beats.'

'Really?' Esther said.

'"Holding",' I said, naming the track off our second-last album. I'd been pleased with that break – it sounded like I was playing backwards, even though I wasn't.

'Oh yeah,' said Esther, and smiled. I love her – she's my happy. 'Go and introduce yourself, then ask them to turn it down.'

She went inside to check on the girls.

I picked up the bottle, still half full, and ambled down the hill. My limbs moved in a more Barbadian way. Hey, I wasn't some washed-up indie honky – I was down with tha mutha-fuckin' MC Whoever.

The surfer shack was smaller than ours, funkier. Up five crooked wooden steps, the door was open and a low light shone amber.

'Hey,' I said, and rapped my knuckles on the threshold. 'Hello?'

Through a beaded curtain I saw buttocks rising and falling, female hands cupping and pulling; I saw beaded dreadlocks swaying and bright blue fingernails digging; I saw very young firm smooth tanned Caucasian flesh, dark brown above and golden below.

'Oh, I'm sorry,' I said.

Their rhythm skipped.

I turned away, wanting to get into the dark before they made it to the door.

'Whu?' the young man shouted. But I didn't hear him coming after me.

I decided to take the long way back to our shack. The music went quiet whilst I walked along the beach, feet in the cold sea.

Esther was asleep when I got back.

Next morning, down on the beach, I saw Dreadlocks carrying his board out of the waves. Blue Fingernails, who looked about eighteen, was sitting in the shade of a tree, watching him and breastfeeding a tiny baby. There was a burnt-out campfire beside her, with crushed cans encircling it.

Esther and the girls came down to join me, and I knew I wouldn't have to make any introductions myself.

'How old is the baby?' asked Sarah, running straight over. 'Can we hold him?'

'Sure,' said Fingernails, 'when I'm finished.'

'How old is he?' Esther asked.

'Two months tomorrow.'

'Hi,' I said, and shook Dreadlocks' hand. 'Congratulations. These are ours. Sarah. Grace.'

His hand was still salty-wet. He undid the elasticated band linking his leg to the board. Then he said: 'Craigie, Jenny and Boo.'

'He doesn't have a proper name yet,' said Jenny.

'Your accent,' said Esther.

'Scottish,' Jenny said. 'That's one of the reasons we're here. Who wants to hold him first?'

They both did, but we made them take turns. The baby's chin was still milky and Jenny took her time about putting her nipple away.

'Look at him stretch,' said Grace.

'Was I like that?' asked Sarah.

We became holiday-friends.

I could tell that Esther thought Jenny was wonderful; I envied Craigie – envied him his body, the surfing and Jenny.

They came round for dinner that night, bringing warm rum (no fridge) and baby Boo.

After we'd finished eating, I put the girls to bed. They resisted, wanting Mummy tuck-in, but this was the new fifty-fifty regime. In the end, after a yowling half-hour, sleep took them.

'We heard your music last night,' said Esther, doing my detective work for me.

'Was it too loud?' asked Jenny. 'I said it was too loud.' The baby was asleep in her arms.

Neither of us wanted to say anything.

'Sorry,' said Craigie, 'we'll keep it down.' He was very young to be a father – a good father, better than me. But they lived in a shack without a fridge, and he surfed all day long. How good a father was that?

There's always an atmosphere of sweet panic around very young parents, even if they themselves don't feel it. *Keep life away from them*, everyone thinks, *keep them safe from realizing what they've lost.* For the first time ever, I felt grandparental emotions.

'What album was it?' Esther asked. 'Only . . .' And then she explained who I was and what I did. Tssk-Boom-Tssk-Tssk.

Jenny looked doubtful, but a moment later said: 'I recognize you.'

'It's not an album,' said Craigie. 'It's a mix-CD someone gave us in New York. Doesn't even have a track listing.'

'Can I borrow it?' I asked.

'I can burn you a copy,' said Craigie.

I must have looked surprised.

'I have my laptop,' he said.

'No fridge,' said Jenny, 'but email.'

'Satellite phone,' Craigie explained. 'If you want to call anyone . . .'

'Definitely not,' said Esther. 'But thank you.'

Boo started to wake with animal stretches. Jenny fed him. I saw Esther's look. I was not mistaken.

'I've been thinking about that baby,' she said, when we were in bed later on.

'The boy?' I asked.

'The girl,' she said.

'As long as it's not twins,' I said.

We tried to keep it quiet.

The CD was slipped under our door the following morning.

I borrowed the girls' CD-player and listened to myself coming out of the pink speakers, via who knows where.

'Don't sue them,' said Esther, meaning the rappers.

'What makes you think I'm going to sue them?'

'Mint tea?' she said — I'd told her all about it.

'Not even for that,' I said.

I listened to the track again. It was good enough to be a hit. Perhaps it already was, underground.

'I'm the new funky drummer,' I said, buzzed.

'It's good,' said Esther. 'We're going to the beach.'

I listened a couple more times then went to join them.

When Craigie came out of the waves, after catching a couple of monster rides, he sat down beside me and accepted a beer. I could feel his coldness and salt-wetness.

'I saw you,' he said quietly. 'The first night when you knocked. Don't think I didn't see you. There's a little mirror at the top of the bed.'

'I didn't watch for long.'

He looked at me sideways. 'But you watched,' he said.

'I watched,' I said.

He went back to looking at the sea.

We stayed another two weeks. Craigie and family moved

on before that – the surf, they'd heard, was up off Hawaii.

As soon as I got home, I had someone start tracking down whoever had used the 'Holding' sample.

In a week, they came back to me with a name and a cellphone number. I made my plan, checked with Esther, dialled.

'Yo-wassup?'

I explained who I was, why I was calling – that I was flattered he'd liked my beats enough to sample them. I stressed that I wanted nothing from him.

'How much you don't want?' he asked.

'No, truly,' I said. 'I'm just pleased I'm still relevant in some way – however tangential.'

'Yeah,' he said.

I'd lost him already.

'Can we meet up?'

'Sure, man.'

He lived in Manhattan.

I suggested a place I thought we'd both be comfortable, Starbucks near Times Square.

'Four o'clock, Thursday.'

'Yeah, sure.'

I knew he wouldn't show, but I flew down, stayed Wednesday night in a hotel that made me feel incredibly white and unstreet.

At four o'clock precisely, a man walked up to my half-hour-occupied sofa in Starbucks. He wasn't the man I'd spoken to on the phone. I knew because that sweet, light voice would never come from this body – from his *amount* of body, vertically and horizontally. They call them body-guards but his was a body-weapon, tactical, nuclear. Big Boy.

'You him?' he asked. 'You him the drummer?'

He was carrying a new briefcase.

'Yes,' I said.

'He ain't coming. This here's for you.'

The suitcase was placed in front of me.

'Don't be calling him again, or we come and take it back. You got yours, now.'

'I just want to say thank you,' I said. I knew what was in the briefcase – pretty sure. To within the nearest ten thousand. 'That's all I want. I don't want this.'

Big Boy kept going, and when he went out the door it was as if the room had lost a wall.

I cracked the briefcase.

I'd been right, to within the nearest ten thousand. It was a very generous settlement, though infinitely less generous than the handshake and smile and musicianly conversation I'd been hoping for. I'd needed that so much more than I needed this.

In sadness, I walked out of Starbucks, taking the briefcase. I could have left it behind, to change a barista's life, but I didn't. I could have given it to the next needy person I came across, but I didn't. I took it to a large bank where I have an account.

It was only when I was standing in line that I looked down at the carpet and realized what I should do. This was the same pattern carpet as in our record company's corporate headquarters.

Outside the bank, I gave half the dollars to the first needy person I saw and the other, with the briefcase, to the guy working the till at Starbucks.

Two months later, the song made it to Number One on the Billboard Hot 100.

okay's highest position was seven, and that had been six years previous.

Big Boy was there in the video, sipping Cristal, enjoying a slo-mo lapdance, nodding sagely to the beat.

My beat.

Maybe I'd made a mistake by quitting.

LA

There's this moment – and if you're lucky enough to be in a half-decent band, you'll know it.

It comes when you're playing a gig, can be near the start but never right at the start, can be during an encore, but usually it comes halfway through the second verse of one of your best songs, for some reason not your *very* best.

You stand there, playing whatever instrument you play, and at the same time you're able to sit way way the fuck out towards the very back of your mind – and you're able to watch everything around you.

The music isn't exactly playing itself, but during that moment it feels as if it could, possibly, with one more push.

And sometimes, just then, when this is upon me, someone else in the band will feel the exact same thing at the exact same moment, and they'll turn their back on the audience, and we'll exchange a glance that says it all.

And after this moment, whether there's been a glance or not, what I always feel is best is to look out into the audience – if the lighting allows – and find someone there who saw the glance and understood just what it meant: that this, for us, isn't just another gig, this is the very reason we go through all the other shit.

There is a moment – I know there is a moment; I remember it pretty well, it's just, it's been so long since I've experienced it, since I've made any kind of eye-contact with another member of *okay*. (Our image doesn't exactly require us to be chummy-chummy. I know that certain fansites have compiled lists of the gigs we broke off halfway through, after throwing our instruments at one another's feet or heads.)

This, the above, is why I thought it was time to tour again – not, I repeat, not for the money; there is enough of that, given our back catalogue and the eventual decision to let them use 'Sea-Song $^{\#}3$' to advertise that cranberry juice.

No, I wanted to feel the moment, be in it, and then do a little dance around its precinct.

I'm thirty-nine now, and I've only got a limited number of little dances left – or a limited time in which to dance them, without loss of dignity. (Dignity, surprisingly, is important to me – even the controlled loss of it: children bring this upon one.)

When I dance these days bits of me move that never used to, because they were never there, or because they were more securely attached.

I don't want to be an embarrassment to anyone, least of all my daughters, who will see the footage when they grow up, and already like some of our records (the early ones, the little bastards) – but I do need, for what feels like the last time, in California-speak, to reconnect.

And so I called Syph, and I called him, and I called again, and after a week, when he probably thought I was his dealer, he picked up.

'Hey,' he said, a *Hey* which seemed to go on for at least ten seconds.

Although we are famous together, and I am one quarter of the reason he is ten times more famous than I am, it took me a minute to get him to show any comprehension of who I was.

'Oh,' he said. 'Hi.' He wasn't unfriendly, he was just speaking long-distance, and not to me, to his own mouth: I could tell; I knew him and his drugmoods well enough. It was antidepressants with God knows what layered on top: drugs of focus, drugs of obliteration – a careful balance that no longer worked, certainly not for me, probably not for him.

I explained what I was thinking – a tour of smaller venues – and Syph didn't say no: whether he'd still remember this conversation the time after the next time he lost consciousness ... I decided to fax him a reminder, then called the others.

Mono was out of the house, probably fishing with Major. Since she quit the cosmetics counter and moved into his lakeside shack, that's mostly what they've done. I left a message on his machine, faxed, emailed and wrote him a letter on fluorescent paper, just so I could be sure.

Crab wasn't easy to get, either. I tried calling but his phone just rang and rang. Eventually, I went down to his neighbourhood bar – and there he was. Getting his agreement wasn't hard. He lives for the road and dies without it. 'I'll be there,' he said, before I'd even said where.

LA – two weeks later. Crab having taken the red-eye, gone to hang out with Syph and try to get him both straight and in the mood. Mono having had the letter, and the fact that he owned an answering machine, a fax and a computer, drawn to his attention by the delightful Major. Perhaps she wanted him out of the house. Now I see what made Syph fall for her – she's a solid woman. She'd put any man right, even Syph.

Not like the matchstick I found him with when I arrived at his off-Mulholland (please, don't do it, Syph – but I just love the view) mansion. I can never remember who it used to belong to, but they were very famous and waited till they'd moved out before drinking themselves to death. Syph wasn't intending to make the same mistake. The windows were painted black, I saw from the outside, and also covered with tinfoil, I saw when I cleared a space on the couch and sat down – very grateful not to have spiked myself on a needle, of which there were many. I hadn't known it was this bad. Crackhouse chic – burns up some of the walls, Jackson Pollocks of dried blood, a sea of takeout containers, mice. It can be a terrible thing, when the cheques keep coming in without you having to leave the house. Syph was wearing the darkest pair of glasses I've ever seen.

I remembered wanting the moment back, but I also wanted to save my friend from himself, from the matchstick girl, the Mexican with the Virgin of Guadeloupe white-sparkling on his chest.

Crab had got Syph onto the JD, so he was at least not raging. Whilst I talked, he did what passes with a lead-singer for listening: wait for the sentences that include his name and then follow the content from then until the next period is reached. I had long known how to deal with this, and so began every other sentence with, 'If Syph agrees . . .' or 'Syph, of course, is important here for . . .' This pisses both the others off, but they know it has to be done – otherwise decisions are reached that Syph later claims never to have been consulted about. Legally, this causes problems; worst of all was the cranberry juice ad.

I told Syph that Syph had been really fired up by the idea of a small-scale tour, first time I called Syph, and Syph seemed to believe me. The other two knew I was lying but didn't mind; checking with them later, I confirmed that, seeing the state our old friend was in, they'd decided to join me on my mercy mission: get him road-ready, get him away from all the jewel-encrusted amigos and matchgirls.

'We'll just turn up in a van,' I said. 'Let the college radio station hear about it, accidentally, a few hours before. Appear under a different name, play covers, or hardcore versions of our songs, or whatever the fuck we want.'

'Whatever the fuck we want,' said Syph, with a smile, then nodded off. I'd forgotten to include his name in those last few sentences.

We had made a start. The following afternoon, the band reconvened. Syph was very different – completely lucid, focused, aggressive and wanting to be in charge. From what he said, it appeared he now believed that he'd called us together, that the small-scale tour was his idea and that, out of the other three, I was the one being obstructive.

'Er, Syph . . .' said Mono, but I shook my head at him. Although he was delusional, this was fine – I didn't mind Syph beating up on me; better that than dying before our eyes.

Syph had been up all night. Our management, who I was interested to find were still interested in us, had taken an early morning flight over from New York – were due to arrive within an hour. Good old Tony and Jordan were long gone. This latest pair were far worse – straight out of *The Matrix*.

'They'll deal with all the shit,' said Syph, who hadn't sat down once since we arrived. 'The bookings, the fees, the equipment.'

'Of course they will,' Mono said. 'That's their job.'

'And we can just . . .' said Crab. He closed his eyes, nodded and mimed a descending bass part that I think I recognized.

'Fucking *exactly*,' screeched Syph. 'They can talk, we can rock!'

I remembered a time, long ago, when we only used the work *rock* ironically – verb or noun, it didn't matter; the word referred to something bands did to please fans who made evil fingers back at them. When I looked at Syph, now on the point of raging, I realized what a Monster of Rock really was. I also realized exactly what kind of price, in terms of personal humiliation, I was going to have to pay to save Syph's life – or temporarily delay his death, long enough to give him a choice to choose it, again. The management should be doing all this.

The management arrived. They talked almost exclusively to Syph, and once they were over the disappointment of not making the maximum amount of money possible, they began to agree with everything he said. Weirdly, Syph gave them my speech of the day before, about why we should do this tour – word for fucking word. I didn't think he had that kind of memory left. Mono looked at me and shook his head, Crab didn't. They nodded and smiled and said *absolutely* and sipped drinks that contained no caffeine.

'We need somewhere to rehearse,' said Syph, and one of them made a note in his palm.

*

Five days later, we were in some purpose-built rehearsal facility with everything we might want – especially everything Syph might want. Heavy men with devotional jewellery came and went throughout the afternoon, and Syph spoke to them in a unisex toilet with more horizontal than vertical mirrors.

'It's comfortable,' said Mono, lying on a long leather couch. I didn't know whether he meant the couch, the studios or our life in general.

'How's Major?' I asked.

'Pissed,' he said. 'But I had to come. It's what I do, isn't it?'

'I thought you caught fish,' said Crab.

'Or not,' I said.

'Or not,' said Mono. 'How are the girls?'

'They rock,' I said, ironically, and was glad to see the other two smile. It was bizarre we hadn't had this conversation the moment we saw one another. Since the last meeting, we hadn't hung out much; we knew that, if we were going to be touring soon, time alone would be a rarity.

'How's Ginger?' I asked. Ginger was Crab's on-off girlfriend. On when she was out of rehab.

'In a wheelchair,' he replied.

Just then, Syph banged out of the bathroom. 'Okay,' he shrieked, 'let's rock'n'roll!'

We picked ourselves up and moved slowly across to our instruments. I have to say, it was good to be reunited with our old equipment. It had been a year and a half. My kit had been lovingly treated by some hi-grade drum-tech – the last I'd seen of it, it was scattered across the stage of some arena. I've never trashed my instrument before, but it was the end of the tour and God did I need the release.

From the moment the bass intro to the first song started up, we were *okay* again. No matter how many sessions I do with other musicians (it pays well), there is something fated about how we work together – as a rhythm section, as a band, as a sound. I looked around for someone to make eye-contact with, but Mono and Crab were entirely heads-down no-

nonsense boogie – and Syph was working an imaginary audience.

We played through our setlist, with smiles, jokes and sips from *Cokes* in between. Syph only went to the bathroom twice, and we accommodated this by jamming whilst he was away and kicking into fast numbers the moment he came back through the door, raging. That's us: part-band, part-nurse.

I tried to ignore the management, who stood somewhere off to our left – nodding, as if they liked music. We sacked our first manager because he wasn't getting us bookings on television, and never since had we dealt with anyone in possession of an undamned soul, not even Tony and Jordan. Oh, we made so many mistakes – and this, I was beginning to feel, was another of them.

'Come round to my room,' I whispered to Mono and Crab at the end of the rehearsal, 'about one o'clock.' We were all staying in the same hotel, so they didn't have to cross town or anything.

'What is it?' said Crab, who joined me and Mono around quarter after two. Mono, thank God, hadn't asked me anything – I think he knew already. We had just sat and watched a movie, buddies.

'I don't think we should tour,' I said.

'The fuck, man,' Crab said.

'It won't help,' I said.

'I agree,' said Mono.

'The tour was your idea,' said Crab.

'It was,' I said. 'But this' – I gestured around the tasteful beige interior and out over the grid of LA lights – 'this wasn't.'

Crab said, 'Yes, but –'

And Mono said, 'Clap is right. We're not helping Syph. This isn't what he needs. It's turning into a monster already.'

'*He's* turning into a monster.'

*

After the rehearsal, we had gone back to Syph's house to celebrate. Without him making a single call, people began to arrive for the party, none of them had to ask where the bathroom was, and by the time I left, about a hundred were there. I was surprised Crab had remembered our meeting, or thought it urgent enough to attend. Perhaps there was something still in there.

'I don't care,' said Crab. 'I just want to play.'

'So do I,' I said. 'That's why I started this – if you remember. But we've lost that before we've even started. We can't just do anything any more.'

'We're not real,' said Mono. 'We've stopped being real. This isn't real.'

'It's true,' I said. He had put it too well – it was the sort of comment that changes your life. These days, I tried to avoid hearing those. It's been changed enough already, thank you very much.

'Well, fuck, yeah, hey, man, we're keeping it real for our brothers on the street.' Crab was more drunk or something than I'd noticed. 'We were never *real.*'

'We tried to be,' said Mono. 'At least, I thought we tried. What have we got left to be true to?'

Crab said: 'The music. The fans.' Because it was something he would say in an interview, we knew it was a lie.

'Each other,' I said. Mono had been saying everything I'd meant to say, and better than I could have said it, right now. Major had trained him well. I needed to put in at least one comment that went in advance of him.

'We are,' said Crab.

'Syph needs help,' said Mono. 'He doesn't need more drugs and fun. He needs to lead a very boring life, supervised by people who are paid lots of money to make him forget he's bored.'

'We can talk to him,' said Crab.

'God can talk to him, perhaps,' said Mono. 'He won't listen to anyone else.'

'So it's all over. We just pack up and go home and wait for this to happen again in a year's time.'

'No,' Mono said. 'We stay here – at least, one of us stays here to be around Syph. We try to get him through.'

'Yes,' I said. 'That's what we should do.'

After a long while, Crab said: 'I disagree.' Then he walked out.

Mono and I stayed in my room and decided to do what needed to be done.

The management had been partying with Syph, or pretending to party, but they were up and bright at ten o'clock when Mono and I made a surprise visit to their LA office. We explained our position to them, and watched them cope first of all with the idea that we might be important enough to interfere with their plans (a three-month itinerary already roughed out on the wall), then with the fact we were asking them to behave like responsible adults and finally that there were very good reasons, even of profit, why they had to admit we were right. They agreed to nothing, formally – but they said they'd see what they could do. We left, aware we'd have to fire them pretty soon, and that it would take money and lawyers and more money.

We went for lunch, then drove to the rehearsal rooms together. Mono had rented a Mustang of some sort, I don't know cars. It was red and made a boom of blissful bass. The sun was shining in a blue sky on grey roads and off-white buildings. I wasn't tempted for a moment.

In the parking lot was an ambulance. We ran towards it, expecting to find Syph in a coma.

We'd only got about halfway there when two men got out of the cab, walked round and opened the back doors of the ambulance.

It was Syph, on a gurney but fully conscious – raving. Beside him, crying, was the matchgirl.

'No,' she said.

'What's this?' asked Mono.

'Hi,' said Syph, pushed up onto an elbow.

'He refused to go to hospital,' Matchgirl said. 'He made them bring us here.'

'Rock'n'roll,' Syph said, and grinned – his eyelids were twitching, there was no flesh on his face.

'Is this true?' Mono asked one of the ambulance guys.

'He said to bring him here. He said he felt fine.'

'Half an hour ago, he stopped breathing,' the girl said.

'I think I'm going to write a song about it,' Syph said. 'I've got the chorus.'

The management came out through reception, followed by Crab. 'What's going on here?' the management asked.

'And you brought him here?' said Mono, very angry.

'He insisted,' said the same ambulance guy. 'And he promised us tickets.'

'What if he died?' I asked. 'Your tickets wouldn't be much good then.'

The ambulance guy smiled as if he knew better, which he probably did.

'I'm not going to die,' said Syph. 'I just want to go and play some music.'

'Hey, man,' said Crab, 'are you okay?'

'Never better,' said Syph. 'Breezy.' He sniggered. 'Can I have some more of that oxygen?'

The matchgirl put her huge face in her huge hands and her tiny body bounced with sobs.

I turned to the management. 'He needs to go to the hospital, immediately.'

'We need to think about this,' said one of the management.

'No, you don't,' said Mono. 'You need to make sure your number-one client doesn't die.'

'What do you want?' the other half of the management asked Syph.

'Like I said, man . . .'

The management took a step or two away, to consult in private.

It was then that the girl shrieked, 'He went blue! He

stopped breathing and I didn't know how to make him start again. I didn't know. He was blue all over.'

'I'm okay,' said Syph.

'I just hit him on the chest, like they do on the TV.'

'Thank you,' said Mono. 'We're very grateful. You did exactly what you should.'

'You'll definitely get tickets,' said one of the management. 'Backstage pass, too.'

The girl held Syph's hand. 'I love your music.'

'He goes to hospital,' said half the management while the other half made a call.

'Thanks, babe,' said Syph, to the girl. He lay back and closed his eyes.

'Do your job,' said Mono to the ambulance guys. 'We'll follow you.'

'What do you want?' the ambulance guy asked Syph.

'He's doing it again,' sobbed the girl.

'No, I'm not,' Syph said.

'Give him some oxygen, for Christ's sake,' I said.

'Are you taking him here?' asked the management making the call and pointing to the address on the side of the ambulance.

'Who are you phoning?' asked Mono, in the management's face. 'The *LA Times* or *Variety*?'

'The publicity department,' the other management said. 'They always handle this kind of thing.'

Mono turned to Crab. 'How fired are these fuckers?'

'Very fucking fired,' said Crab.

Management looked at me, their last chance.

'Third vote,' I said. 'You're out. I never want to see you or hear from you again.'

'You'll hear from our lawyers,' the management said, both together.

Crab got in the back of the ambulance and one of the guys closed the door on him and the matchgirl, whose name it later turned out was Celia.

Management walked away. The siren started up – and I wondered how much extra that would cost us. Didn't matter. It was worth it.

I looked at Mono and he looked at me, and that look said it all.

We walked together towards the big red car, although part of me felt like doing a shameful little dance.

ORANGE

When I arrived in Mexico City, the day before our seven-date arena tour, there was a vast bowl in my hotel room, containing apples, oranges, a bunch of bananas, some seedless green grapes, a single kiwi. A bowl of plastic wood – wood-effect plastic.

It was still there when I came back, two weeks later, although those specific complimentary fruit items had – I'm assuming – been replaced, once if not several times.

(I think about those lost, uneaten fruits, and where they might have ended up. On the spotless gingham tablecloth of some maid's grandmother's *apartamento* deep in the *barrio*? Pigfeed? Anywhere but the trash, I hope.)

The night before we flew home, I sat cross-legged on the bed in my hotel room and ate one of the oranges.

Here is the truth:

I remember that orange better than I remember any of those gigs – the whole of that tour, in fact. At some of the arenas, there was an attendance of forty thousand people. (*okay* is big in Mexico. We have just the right amount of melancholy for them, is my theory.) They came, applauded, screamed, screamed louder (when Syph told them to), waved banners that had taken them hours to paint, held lit lighters aloft, jumped up and down, hugged each other, wept, experienced the most profound emotions – and I forgot them.

Worse, I didn't bother acknowledging them even when they were right in front of me. My contact lenses out, I failed to focus on a single adoring face.

Let me describe the orange. Curving around and around so fully in the low lamplight, its delicately dimpled skin was shiny with wax and God knows what other crap. It was quite a bit larger than I'm used to at home. (Esther buys organic, when she can.) It was a display-case orange. Where the stalk had been removed, a perfect star-shape of green remained behind.

I don't know why I plunged my thumb in and began the laborious process of peeling. If I'd wanted a quick vitamin C fix, I would have gone for the grapes.

If you eat an orange with your hands, you know you'll have to wash them afterwards. That may have been part of it. I might have wanted to do something sensuous, sensual, one or the other, or both together, I always get them confused. I think I might have felt it a good thing to be forced to wash my hands. They weren't dirty, even symbolically. I hadn't slept with anyone I shouldn't have. Faithful and truthful, I'd called Esther and the girls several times a day. I was alone in the hotel room.

Since the twins came along, I have been much more enthusiastic about getting dirty. The visual isn't enough, and my ears are fucked. I want experiences which involve intense smell, touch, taste. As Richard Manuel of The Band put it, 'Can't we have something to feel?'

During concerts, I don't even *hear* the applause any more. It's like, I know it's there, but really it doesn't exist outside me any more than my tinnitus does. Intellectually, I know that the person in the back row – Juan, Juanita – clapping so hard, hands above their head, is thanking the four of us for choosing the life we did. But it gets to a point where that gratitude seems contemptible. And then it gets to another point, where it seems contemptuous.

People *envy* me.

I know this from the way they behave towards me (by paying me much too much attention, or ignoring me completely) and from the things they write about me, but most of all I know it from the questions they ask me.

They are what I call the Bob Dylan Questions – the ones he asks in his songs about where you are tonight and what you know and don't know and, mostly, how it feels?

And to them I give the Bob Dylan answer, which is to ask them once again what it was they wanted?

'You're the drummer,' that's what my questioners imply, and sometimes even say. 'You don't even write the fucking songs. How come you get to go along for the ride? You're not that good-looking. You're not such a great drummer.'

To be famous is to be put in a position where failure is your only option. And when you've failed, and fallen completely out of view, it's not too bad – you achieve total has-been status, and are ignored. But the way down is the roughest ride, not the same as the way up in reverse, not at all. Up is booster rockets and G-forces. Down is spine-jangling bumps and bouncing reality checks. They hurt, and you develop a soul-wince – a wince back in the direction of fame and its safety harnesses.

When I got home from Mexico, I walked through the front door and said to Esther, 'It's happened. We've turned into The Eagles. We are Corporate Rock Cocksuckers.'

'Say hello to the girls, why don't you?'

'Hello, girls.'

That night, I couldn't sleep. I could imagine them, out there – wherever *out there* is, these days; younger bands, all of them saying, 'We're never going to end up like *okay*, just touring fucking stadiums for cash. We're never gonna sell out.'

And some of them won't, the failures, and some of them will, also the failures. You cannot but fail if your true premise is this: *We're never going to grow old.*

I remembered a journalist – not from Mexico. From years ago. Finland, I think. 'You must feel very lucky,' he said. And I didn't want to tell him the truth, because that would have made us seem either a. grasping (no, we fought damn hard to get here) or b. ungrateful (yes, it's been a breeze). I referred instead to the loyalty of the fans – it was they who made the choice in favour of longevity. We exist by their good graces. Blah blah blah.

At least I wasn't talking to a fan. Try telling a group of

them that what you have isn't what they *think* you have – see how they react. Demented are go. They will destroy i-and-m. We exist as a projection of their desires, from the most mundane (*I hate my job and want to quit and tell the boss to go fuck himself*) to the most extreme (*I want to two-time Miss August with Miss World*). The trick is knowing which is which; navigating between.

I know. I started as a fan; if I betray anyone along the way, it's myself-as-a-fan.

How early did I realize it wasn't going to be what I dreamt it would be?

Dreamt here, isn't a figure of speech. I remember whole night-visions of me, blinded by the lights, counting the band in, 1–2–3–4, and then hearing an awesome crowd lift in recognition of our latest hit.

My dreams came true, they were very accurate predictions. And *so* many fans out there must be experiencing the same, night after night. But would you think I was lying if I told you the dreams were better than the reality? In the dreams you always think, 'Wow, this is really happening!' whereas in reality you think, 'This is just a dream – it can't be happening like this.'

In dreams you take all the credit and are fully present in the moment; in reality, the mind doesn't react well to dreamlike situations – mine doesn't, anyway.

Fans, though, aren't half as bitter as contemporaries. Early on, you learn the road has a wayside, and you see nine-tenths of your generation heading for that fall, and leaning frantic-ally away from it, towards the other side of the road – and you learn that there's a wayside that side, too.

How do we know what we're doing while we do it? We don't. How do we know the effects it will have on other people – not just immediately but in a future so distant that we too have become other people? We don't.

In late September of last year, three months after the orange, a fourteen-and-a-half-year-old American boy called

Otis Wallace-Benjamin committed suicide whilst listening to our first record. His big sister Caroline found him – he was hanging from one of the ceiling struts in his basement den. There was a note. In it, he said that he knew *exactly* how his future life would be, and didn't want any of it.

'Read my diary,' he said. 'Then you'll understand. I hate being me. It's a really shitty option.'

Option, followed by three kisses, was the last word Otis Wallace-Benjamin wrote.

The next day, sedated, his parents, Aaron and Jean, sat down together with the diary. What they found was nothing terrible; it didn't seem as if Otis had been abused or bullied at school. Instead, there were repeated mentions of *okay*, and how much our songs meant to him – how the songs kept him alive.

When Caroline looked at the Recently Played list on his iTunes, she saw that – for as far back as it went – Otis had listened exclusively to us. She told her parents and, taking an earphone each, they tried listening to a few songs. They thought it might help them to understand.

The following day, they called our record company, who passed them on to our management.

'We don't want to sue,' Aaron said. 'Don't worry about that. We just want to talk to someone.'

Syph was in rehab; Crab was on a bender; Mono couldn't be contacted; it fell to me.

Along with the telephone number, I was given what amounted to a briefing: 'Our lawyers have stressed that you should not admit to any kind of culpability or offer any form of compensation.'

Oh, take *off*.

Caroline answered the phone.

I told her who I was.

'Really?'

'Yes,' I said.

She called out, 'Mom, Dad! It's him!'

The next voice was an older version of Caroline's. 'Thank you so much for contacting us. We're so grateful you could take the time from your busy schedule.'

'We're both listening,' said Aaron. 'I'm in my office. It's on speakerphone. Jean is in the hall.'

I imagined my voice in their echoey house.

'I'm so sorry to hear,' I said. 'You have my, and our, deepest sympathies.'

I'd discussed with Esther what to say. All I could think of were clichés. 'If you make it too ornate,' she said, 'it'll come across as phoney. It's not what you say, it's just the fact that you're saying it – and meaning it.'

'But I feel phoney. I've never met them. I never met him.'

As it turned out, I started thinking about the girls as soon as I heard their parental voices. This is what I'd sound like, if Sarah or Grace died: disturbingly normal, but not – like a ghost pretending to be an accountant.

'Thank you,' said Aaron. 'We appreciate your kind words.'

I heard noises, clatterings.

'My brother thought you were way cool,' said Caroline, shouting into the speakerphone.

'Yes, I was told that. I'm glad.'

'The funeral is in two days' time,' said Jean. 'We thought we would invite you.'

'We're inviting you now,' said Aaron. 'That's what we mean. Could you come? We want to honour him . . .'

The father was crying.

'Of course,' I said. 'Tell me how to get to you.'

Chicago, then a two-hour drive. Iowa.

'We have a bright-blue front door,' said Jean. 'You can't miss us.'

I took Esther and left the girls in the care of Esther's parents.

I had tried again to contact the other band-members, but they were all hiding, in their various ways. Not hiding from this, just hiding.

'You don't think they want me to speak, do you?' I said, as we waited in the departure lounge. 'At the funeral.'

Esther said she was sure they didn't.

'I can't just arrive and take over. I'll distort everything.'

'I think that's probably what they want you to do.'

'I'm not being immodest.'

'I know you're not. This is one of the consequences of what you do, of what you are.'

'Of who I am.'

'No, of *what*.'

On the flight, I had time to listen back to our first album. Somehow the detail had got through to me that this was Otis's favourite, and the one he chose to kill himself to. And perhaps that was why, for the first time ever, I was able to hear the songs as if I'd had nothing to do with creating them. A couple, 'Click' and 'Sea-Song #1', I've played live at every concert since they were written. But still, I *heard* them.

They were satisfying, that's the best word. The melancholy in them was true. I couldn't really tell if they were good or not. That didn't seem relevant. They communicated. I recognized them.

'How was that?' Esther asked, when I took the earphones out. She knew what I'd been doing.

'Strange,' I said. 'Very strange. Maybe I see why he liked us.'

At Chicago, we hired a decent-sized car. I said that I would drive. I wanted something to do.

We got to their town mid-afternoon, and checked into a bed & breakfast they had recommended. There were images of lilacs on almost every surface, and it smelt of lilacs, too.

A man in a grey suit approached me when I went outside to get our bags. He had followed me from the B&B.

'I'm an uncle,' he said. 'Thank you for coming. It really means the world to Jean and Aaron.'

I shook his hand. He was undecided about whether to hug

me – I could feel that. I came from a world of common hugs, but held off.

'When you're ready, I'll show you over to the house, if you'd like that.'

'That would be good.'

'Let me help,' he said, taking Esther's case.

'You're Jean's brother,' I said.

'I am.'

'How is she?'

'You got kids?'

'Two.'

He gave a grunt meaning, *So . . .* Then, because that wasn't clear enough, he said, 'She's a strong woman, Jean, but you can't expect too much. These are the first days.'

The uncle carried the bag upstairs in front of me.

Esther was in our room.

'Chester,' said the uncle. 'I'll be at the funeral.'

'Esther,' she replied, and they both laughed sadly.

'I'll leave you to get ready,' said Chester.

We met him outside fifteen minutes later – and followed his car in ours. I felt self-conscious about my very expensive black suit.

The B&B was only five minutes from the house with the blue door. It was a small town. We drove past a church with a graveyard.

Aaron and Caroline were waiting at the bottom of the drive. I guess Chester must have called to warn them. Jean came out just as we stopped, a cloth in her hands.

There was a basketball hoop above the white garage door.

We got out.

Chester reversed until he was close to us.

'I'll leave you,' he said, and drove off.

We all shook hands.

'Well, come on in,' said Jean.

The house was as I'd imagined, perhaps a little smaller. A well-adapted American home, not built to last for ever. It smelt very clean. In the kitchen there were unopened bags of potato chips in bowls all along the counter.

'This is Marjorie,' said Jean. 'She'll be doing snacks.'

'Would you like to see the basement?' Aaron asked, from behind me.

'Yes,' I said.

I realized, as he led me through to the back of the house, that the basement was one of the main reasons I had come.

The next room was a utility room, with large white goods. A door to the left was painted red and covered in radioactive waste decals. Aaron opened it, flicked a light-switch, and I saw wooden stairs with a strip of shaggy orange carpet running down them.

'Would you like to go alone?' Aaron asked.

I looked round for Esther, but she had stayed in the kitchen.

I grunted a yes.

'Take your time,' Aaron said. 'We don't have to leave for an hour or so.'

He went straight back into the main part of the house.

I wanted a cigarette or something.

There was a bike on its side in the mud of the backyard.

I went down into the basement.

Part of me suspected this might all be a trick to get me here – and Otis, alive, would be waiting downstairs with a group of his friends.

The large room was unoccupied.

Around me, the walls were hidden by shelves, and the shelves were full of tools and toys.

I sat down on a couch covered in a tartan blanket.

When I looked up at the beams, there was no way to tell which Otis had used. One towards the middle, I guessed.

There was a low table in front of me. All of our CDs were laid out across it in a line.

There was an acoustic guitar on a stand.

At first I didn't play it, and then I did.

The guitar was still in tune.

When I finished, it was as if the room were suddenly filled with applause.

But for Otis.

C$_2$H$_2$OH

The first time Crab pissed his pants on-stage, I thought our career was over, right then and there.

Denver Colorado.

Second time, two gigs later, Sioux City Iowa, and I was able to take in the fans' reaction: abandoned screaming of wild delight.

Third was the same.

Fourth, he was showboating, and fifth it was an established part of our act – missed if not performed.

And get this: some of the audience, women and men, had already started to copy him.

(Word spread via *okay* noticeboards and chatrooms.)

The man has problems, but no-one seems to have a problem with that. His problems make him more, more something. Edgy, perhaps – a quality yearned for by sixteen-year-olds.

Edges cut.

I've known for quite some time that Crab was in serious trouble. But it never really hit me until he started up with the piss-routine. And then, about halfway through this tour, I overheard him, drunk on the plane, being interviewed by a journalist from Melbourne Australia. The words Crab said were these:

'Whenever I get out of rehab, I like to . . .'

Didn't matter what he liked to.

Whenever.

If I could have gone home right then, I would have done – I would have strapped on a parachute and bailed; I would have quit the band again, crawled back to Esther, howled in her arms, and then tried to figure out the right thing to do. The right thing for Crab.

Probably I shouldn't be saying this. I should be saying I would have intervened straight away. But what could I do? What could I do? Cancel the tour? Get him checked into rehab? Come on. Rehab, clearly, was now part of the problem – part of the rhythm and routine of his addiction. Another clean-up, another relapse. Tssk-BOOM.

Whenever.

On the afternoon of his tenth birthday, the boy who would later become Crab rode over to show me his new bike – golden leaves stuck between the spokes, because he had cycled straight through several piles of them.

His face gets brighter, the further away it is. His ten-year-old's face.

That bike made him happier than any other material object.

When it goes, Hope leaves a very clear outline, like a cartoon character running through a puff of smoke, like a God-shaped hole in the universe.

Two weeks later, his father took that bike and threw it off a river-bridge. He did this coldly, and without anger. It was a lesson.

Being an alcoholic, you could say that Crab was dying from the day he first took a drink.

Over the last couple of years, it has gotten much worse.

People say, after he leaves a room, *My God – he looks like Death.* But he's looked that way for so long I've started to think, *No, actually, Death looks like him.*

We all *drink*, the band, but for some people it's just a different substance – more necessary, more beautiful. It is *Good Morning, Vietnam* and *Goodnight Vienna.* It is *Happy House* and *Sad Café.*

Guitar is Crab's day job, a way of financing his vocation: C_2H_2OH.

So, I waited until the end of the tour, and then the end-of-tour party – and then I went back to Vancouver with Crab, and I stayed with him.

The first night, in a bar, he thought I just didn't want to go home.

'See your kids, come on. You haven't seen them in weeks. Go be Daddy.'

But I had already okayed it with Esther. She knew why I wasn't where I wanted to be.

'No,' I said. 'I thought I'd have a few more.'

I had a few more. Then we were invited to a party. Crab tried to lose me there, but I kept him in sight. We took a taxi to a casino. He tried to appal me by losing a vast amount of money – most of his takings from the tour – on the roulette table. I said nothing. Next came dawn, and coffee in a diner.

'Are you ready to go home yet?' he asked.

'No.'

So he led me off on further adventures. Around noon, we stopped at a fleapit motel for some sleep.

'I like this place,' he said. 'I may stay here for a while.'

The whole Bukowski thing.

He snuck out some time that afternoon.

I caught up with him back at the bar.

'Oh, hi,' he said. And the chase began again.

That night was little different to the night before, only a woman was involved. Around 4 a.m., she became maudlin and tearful. We ended up back at yesterday's motel, friends once more.

I turned in, slept and woke.

From the room, I called Esther.

'How's it going?'

'I can't keep up.'

'Talk to him.'

He had checked out, and disappeared for the rest of the day. I thought I'd lost him but he turned up back at his regular bar that evening. The woman wasn't with him. He was drunk. Yet, when he spoke, it was with absolute clarity.

'Look, I know what you're trying to do. I appreciate it. I love you for it. You will fail.'

I have never been that good at lying. Never have I wished more for the skill.

'I don't know what you mean.'

It wasn't the words themselves; it was the rhythm with which I said them. And a good drummer always knows when he's out of time.

Crab smiled, falling back into the woozy. But he knew exactly what he wanted to say: 'Give up. Go home.'

'No,' I said. 'I'm with you.'

There was a football game up on a screen at the end of the bar. One of the teams scored. Crab did not allow himself to be distracted.

'It's not a place to be,' he said. 'You're a good man.'

'I'm not.'

'Compared to other men, you are.'

'This isn't about me.'

He looked at me, focussed again.

'Of course it's about you. Come on.'

The barman brought us another couple of beers. I believe Crab ordered them telepathically.

'Come on!' he said, getting loud for the first time.

I'd misunderstood.

He led me across to an empty booth.

When we sat down, I found we were out of sight of televisions.

'What's this about?' he said.

I hesitated.

'No, tell me, what's this about?'

It all came out. My worries. The interview on the plane. The *whenever*.

'It's quite understandable,' said Crab. 'I make you feel bad. You want to be able to help, but there's nothing you can do.'

Lit from below, from a small lamp on our table, I couldn't help but see that Crab had started to look quite like a pig. His face was pink, bloated. The nose was bigger than it had been. I could kind of see up his nostrils.

He continued to talk. 'But you also feel other things. One of them is guilt. It's not guilt about me. It's guilt about yourself. Because I'm doing what you feel, in your heart, you should be doing. Not for you. You're not a person like me. You don't have my reasons. You don't have those reasons at all.'

I knew what he meant.

'We made a contract with the fans. They expect us to be like me. And Syph. No-one's interested in a Buddhist. Everyone thinks a Buddhist's a waste of time and everything. No offence. I respect you. I think you have it just about right. It's a better life. But you're too fucking clean, man. And nothing's going to come of that, is it? You've always been kind of clean-cut. It's a good look, when there are other people around you to rough it up. Make it attractive. But you've removed yourself from the fray.'

At *fray*, a bubble of spittle landed on the lamp's lightbulb and went fz.

'It's not what's wanted. The fans are important. I understand that in a way you don't. They have requirements. I'm not making up for you – those aren't my reasons. But . . .'

He needed a run-up to what he was about to say.

'There's Syph and there's me, and then there's you and there's Mono. And he has Major and fishing, and you have Esther and Sarah and Grace and the lord Buddha.'

Imaginary figurines were arranged in front of me on the tabletop. Mine, though it didn't exist, was the most grotesque.

I said, 'And you, you have drinking.'

'And I have drinking,' he said. 'I quite agree. Absolutely, old chap. That's what I have.' (Comedy Englishman was beside me.) 'Corking, what? And Syph has whatever the current drug *du jour* is. But we also have something else. Call it freedom. It's a shorthand but we're living the dream, baby. And if we don't, you can't. We're the guarantee of quality. One hundred per cent the real deal.'

This time I caught the finger-lift that brought us another

round of beers. What I couldn't figure was how that gesture had also added whiskeys to our order. Trebles.

'The people want to see you're living the life. If that's not happening, then they think you're living the lie. I know you look down on what I do. But I am devoted. We need to survive, as an entity. The band is my life. I love it.'

'I do, too.'

It sounded feeble.

'Look at me,' Crab said.

I did my best.

'Say it again,' he said.

'I love the band.'

It sounded more feeble.

'Is it *everything*?'

'No, of course —'

'You don't *love* the band. You *have* the band. You take it or you leave it. You love your family. I have no family. I love the band. Let's not try to compete because I'm going to win.'

To prove this, he drank off his whiskey.

To at least stay in the conversation, I drank mine off, too.

There was no coughing. My eyes hardly watered. But I felt my soul sag like the back of an old mule. I was carrying unaccustomed burdens.

'I'm not trying to compete. I'm trying to —'

'Rescue me.'

'I didn't say that.'

'No. You didn't *say* that. But that's what I *heard*. You're not comfortable here. This is a public place. I like to live where I can be seen. There's always someone can pick you up, if you need it. They'll rob you, as well. But people are astonishingly kind, when you're needful. I don't want to be on any other level. I'm not after enlightenment. You understand?'

I had got so used to him monologuing that, for a moment, I had no answer. I kicked the soul-mule. It moved, slowly.

'There's a difference between that and killing yourself.'

'Most people are killing themselves, or hadn't you noticed?

If you haven't got that far, I can't help you. I'm sure the Buddha –'

'Yes, he knew,' I said. 'That's what he's all about.'

'And you love me. And you don't want to see me die. Well, thank you. I'm flattered. And I am more moved than I can possibly allow myself to show you.'

For the first time, he wobbled along the winding wall-top of a sentence. To recover, he went simple:

'I like my life. I don't want your life, or any other man's life.'

'You're in denial,' I said, and immediately regretted it. He was making me feel priggish.

'I'll let that pass,' he said. 'I'm in denial of nothing. What am I in denial of? I'm in a bar and I'm drinking. I know what it's doing to me. Shall I describe it? I've had it talked at me enough times. My liver. I'm not Superman. There is damage. There is pain. I am being true to my freedom.'

This last statement seemed conclusive.

I began to speak, but Crab spoke for me, and against me.

'It is not enslavement. Please don't say it's that. I am gliding. I am gliding slowly down. This is not a crash. If it was a crash, I wouldn't be here.'

More drinks arrived.

'Will you listen to me?' I said.

'Of course,' said Crab. 'But there is nothing you can say that will change a damn thing. I am the person you see before you.'

He waved across the bar to someone he knew.

It was this gesture which defeated me. He was right. This wasn't my place. I was disgustingly superior, in attitude. I couldn't ditch that.

The Buddha took clothes from a dead man, when he gave up being a prince. But he washed them before he wore them. He washed them until they were clean.

I stood up.

'Well, at least you tried,' said Crab.

I sat down again.

'You are breaking my heart,' I said.

Crab let that hang, until it answered itself.

I stood up again.

'You will have nothing to blame yourself for,' said Crab. 'You did everything you could. Tell Esther hi.'

I came out from behind the table and took his right hand. It was covered in small cuts and gouges from hitting the strings so hard.

'That was a good tour,' I said. 'You were excellent.'

'Thank you,' said Crab. 'You weren't bad yourself.'

With that, I left.

A taxi took me home.

The driver recognized me, and told me about his son's band. They were good, he said. I should check them out. I asked what they were called. Then asked again, because I'd already forgotten. After that, I let him talk.

At home, Esther took me upstairs. The girls had been asleep for several hours. Esther chaperoned me into their room. Crab had been right. This here was my band, now.

'Tell me,' said Esther, when we relocated to bed.

'He's wise,' I said. 'He's beyond me.'

'How come?'

I went back over our conversation. How everything I wanted to say to him, he said first.

'He made me feel uncool,' I said.

'That was his tactic.'

'It worked.'

'But that doesn't change anything. He's still what he is. You tried to give him an opportunity.'

'No, I just slotted in line, along with all the other people who try to tell him what to do. I repeated the pattern. I made it worse. I wanted his bike. Oh God, I feel –'

I made it to the bathroom.

I mostly missed the toilet.

'I'll get a bucket,' shouted Esther.

Together, we cleaned it up.

Then Esther made me drink as much water as I could. Then we went to bed.

I woke up in a clean house.

I did not hate it.

MYSELF

I don't believe in myself any more.

Not in a gung-ho, dream-the-impossible-dream-and-fight-the-unwinnable-fight kind of way.

Not even in an I-will-survive way.

I don't believe in myself in the same way I don't believe in fairies at the bottom of the garden.

The difference is, I *never* used to believe in the fairies, but I seem to remember thinking that I had a worthwhile self and that that self, if it so chose, could do things to things that would affect things and perhaps even improve things.

Right now I don't even make it to ghost.

I wish I did – then I could haunt someone worth haunting: Esther.

I could buy odour of lavender from the ghost-stores, and drop it for her to smell in the passageways of our house.

She would know it was me, because I've told her that's how I'll communicate with her from beyond the grave.

I think, today, I am beyond the grave; beyond in the sense of the grave no longer being really relevant to me – if I tried to get into my own long home, I would just fall through: through the dirt, through the rock, the mantle and core, right through to the other side of the world and off into space.

This isn't what I should be feeling, husband of one, father of two: I remember the opposite – when every sensation, even the teensiest, was so intense it was like getting tattooed.

Look, needles on a tall tree, glittering in the frost: the greatest fucking most amazing thing I've ever seen!

Drugs did this, sometimes – for other people, never for me. Never truly.

Good cocaine, I admit, was Snow White, and on it I occasionally felt like a Handsome Prince, but all the other

drugs turned me into one of the Seven Dwarfs: dope, predictably, made me Dopey, ecstasy made me Happy (but in a
really depressing way), heroin made me Sleepy, alcohol made
me Doc (diagnosing everyone else's problems, governing the
world), caffeine made me Grumpy, crystal meth made me
Bashful (because I was so hyper-aware it should be having
the opposite effect, hubba-hubba) and bad cocaine made me
Sneezy.

I won't say *and then I discovered meditation* and I won't add
and it did everything for me that I'd ever wanted drugs to do. I won't
patronize you with a recommendation to try it or disgust you
with a hippie testimonial.

You're on your own path, as they say. You can walk on
gilded splinters all you like. You can choose to spend your
alive-time doing what you wanna do. For example, you could
go up to Lexington 125 and wait for your man. Or you could
taste the whip. Or you could get on a clipper ship and sail.
Your desires are your desires, whatever they may be. You can
sometimes get what you want if not exactly what you need.

I don't have a story about drugs. Leastways, not one I want
to tell.

Looking back, I can see that I was gradually on the way to
where I am now. But I've been cuntishly slow in getting here.

The years have helped. Thank you, 2003.

Becoming middle-aged is like waking up, I mean regaining
consciousness, halfway through writing a rock opera – forget
dignity, forget cool. Instead, there's the distant prospect of
much money and the comfort that's meant to bring. There's
some laughs to be had, mostly at your own expense. There's
a whole lot more drama backstage than ever crosses the
footlights. And there's the inescapable awareness that you've
become a person you would never ever have wanted to be.

I should know.

This I'm going to tell you about took place after six days
of a two-week-long retreat – one of the ones where no-one
speaks to anyone.

I won't even tell you where on earth it was because *it doesn't matter*. The time of day I'll give for free, early evening.

At the moment we join me, I am kneeling on the floor of my deliciously bare cell (one bed, one chair, walls bare apart from a photograph of the face of a statue of the Buddha) – I've been trying and failing to meditate, thinking too much of my distant family, when in walks someone I really don't want to see: me, aged twenty.

'Hey, maaaan,' baby-Clap says, 'reached enlightenment yet?'

Was this really me?

I am surprised at how good-looking I once was (shiny hair, clear-ish skin, good teeth); less surprised to meet myself this way – it is a showdown that's been in the offing for several years.

Still and all, I am not ready for it.

'Take a seat,' I say. 'Take *the* seat.'

Clap Jr chooses not to. He goes and inspects the Buddha-photograph with his head aggressively tipped to the left and then to the right. I have a body memory of doing this, the cocky confidence it was meant to express; the awkwardness it was meant to cover over.

The Buddha is Buddha Maitreya, the Buddha of the future.

I give up on the meditation but stay where I am, close to the floor.

When he doesn't speak, I know Clap wants me to be the one to start it. 'Are you here for any particular reason?'

'What?' he says. 'Ghost of Christmas Past? Kind of.'

'You have life-lessons to teach me?'

'Not exactly. It's about the music, the band.'

This last sentence makes my stomach and guts feel like leaving my body and going for a walk in the monastery grounds – maybe take in the Zen garden.

'What exactly about the band?'

'Stop it – just stop it. *Now*. Find lock and clawl under, Glasshopper.'

'What do you think I've been trying to do for most of the past decade? They won't let me.'

'Who's *they*? Because you're always blaming them −'

'The band,' I say. 'The management, the employees.'

'Boo-fucking-hoo. I haven't even put a record out and you're letting them release this musical turd with your name on the cover.'

He means the last album, of which I am truly ashamed. We should never have tried to update to a contemporary sound, involving hip-hop − not even after my number-one sample.

'I said no to that at the time.'

'But you didn't nix it.'

'I couldn't,' I say.

'Why not?'

'Tax. The girls needed new things.'

'Then sell a house.'

'I like my houses. Each one has a different function.'

'You used to exist in one room.'

'*Exist*, not live. You should know that.'

'True. But my dreams of life are a lot more noble than your nightmare of a reality.'

His lines sound more rehearsed than mine. Perhaps he's had more time to prepare.

'I'm not aware I ever thought much about *nobility* when I was your age −'

'Of course, because you've forgotten everything you ever knew that was worth knowing. It's all about nobility − it's about nothing else. We wanted to say something worth saying, not just fill the space. Make way for youth.'

'I do. Every day. My daughters.'

'Quit the band. And don't go back. Not like last time. Let them make fools of themselves by themselves.'

'How would you handle it different, if you were me now and not you then?'

The sun is going down outside, splashing a stretched circle of gold up the wall.

'I'd be a private citizen. I would go to Savile Row, London, and get them to make me some bespoke suits – not wear that semi-rock star crap you do. Ditch the bracelet –'

'They're beads. They're important to me.'

'They make you look old.'

'They're not about looks.'

'Bull*shit*. Learn to do something else, and do it well.'

I feel calmer than I should do – six days of solid meditation and garden-inspecting have achieved something.

'Why are you so eager to silence me? Isn't what I have to say as valid as –'

'No, it's not. It's not as valid as anyone. I want to silence you because you're embarrassing yourself – fucking up your own reputation. At one point, you were pretty good. And now people are just laughing at you. You're no longer valid. Fetch the mop-pushing porter from your local high school – *he's* got a story. You just have more anecdotes of weaknesses indulged and privilege taken for granted.'

'I don't disguise them as anything else.'

'Get real. Meet some *real* people – people who aren't successful – people who are going down, rapidly.'

'Believe me, I've met enough of those.'

I tried very hard not to think of Crab.

'You have *no idea*, man. You're so up yourself.'

'I know that.'

'What are you doing about it?'

'Well, for a start, I'm talking to you – correction, I'm listening to you and taking you seriously.'

'And?'

'I'm considering quitting, as you suggest. I don't think I'll be ordering the suits, though.'

'Just a suggestion, man. Have some dignity.'

Clap Jr has now moved across to the chair and sat down. From the side pocket of his jacket, he produces a packet of tobacco – and begins to roll himself a joint. I don't try to stop him.

'How did I lose my dignity?'

'The first time you did something without putting your whole soul into it, that's when.'

'Not when? How?'

'By deciding to rip off the fans – short-changing them.'

'Did I?'

'As good as. You've admitted as much yourself.'

'And how are you going to avoid this?'

Long pause. 'I'm not. I'm you. That's why I'm so fucking pissed at you.'

'I'm sorry.'

'You should be.'

'And you will be.'

'I am already.'

He lights up. The smell brings back further memories. I feel a powerful anti-nostalgia.

'So everything you do right now contains your whole soul? You must be exhausted.'

'And exhaustion leads to weakness – which is how it happens, the sell-out.'

'Can I tell you a story?'

'No. I've had enough of your excuses.'

'I am less angry than you. Stories may be one of the reasons why.'

'Very clever. No.'

'But I'm also less bitter. Even though I have a lot more to be bitter about – twenty years more. You're bitter in anticipation of things that won't even happen.'

'They might have done. I didn't avoid them out of virtue.'

'Listen – I made a decision – or perhaps it was all just an accident. Around your age, I invested my entire life in pop culture –'

'– in the music. No-one talks about "pop culture".'

'– in a sound that attracted me as much as anything ever had or would, apart from –'

'– pale and interesting young women.'

'Correct. But that investment, while paying dividends, also was subject to taxation.'

'You're talking like an accountant.'

'I've spent a lot of time in their company.'

'You shouldn't have.'

'Some of them are decent people –'

'And the majority deserve –'

'No worse than I do. Anyway, I am paying that tax now. It is larger and larger in proportion to my income, which itself is shrinking fast. Those first older generations that reacted to rock'n'roll, the spectacled back-from-the-war bunch, the Herr Musik Professors and the Church of the Holy Gook Ministers they got some things right when they condemned this primitive and lustful new artform. They didn't *understand* it, because they never fell in love with the sound like we did, but they knew that it was part of a general decline in Western culture –'

'Oh –'

'You see, I call myself a musician, but I'm not. I'm not anything like as good as I should be – as I could have been, if I'd practised, if I'd had a discipline to practise. And I might still be improving, rather than getting worse and worse, as I am.'

'Now you're just making me sad.' He says it sarcastically, but I can tell that he means it.

'Fathers and mothers have reasons for saying the things they do – about settling down and getting a proper job, marrying and putting a little away for your retirement. They've counted a few more costs than you have.'

He begins to sing: 'Sometimes you cannot count the miles till you can count the cost.' Our lyrics.

'You're not wrong.'

'But you are.'

'And I'm you.'

'I know. I know you're me. That's what's so hard.'

We sit for a long while without talking. The light has gone

from the wall and from the window, too. 'We find ourselves and lose ourselves in the dark, in the dark.' More of our lyrics.

'I will quit,' I say. 'Maybe it will take a little time, but not longer than a year.'

He starts on another rollie.

'Maybe you shouldn't. Maybe I'm being too hard on myself. I'm not perfectly noble. Like you said, why am I so keen to shut you up? What am I afraid of?'

'You're just trying to protect me. And I thank you for it.'

I feel him considering his memory of what this room looks like, although I can't see him moving his eyes or head.

'Do you really like it here?'

'I love it.'

'That's good. It's good to find a place like that.'

'You will.'

'I'm sorry I got angry at you. I just feel frustrated. I want to get into what you're already beyond. I hate it that you're beyond it.'

'It's been a long time since one song took over my life – told me how to dress and live and how to *be* inside. But it still happens, sometimes, if only for the length of the song. I can be driving along a road, and, until it finishes playing, I'll be a completely different person. I'll drive in a different way. Often, it's a worse person I've become – more aggressive, more angry. Songs make me younger. Some of them make me you again.'

I become aware that he has gone without leaving, but I continue talking, to myself.

'When people write to us, as fans, I know that's what they're saying, or trying to say – that we change them in a way they want to be changed. They want to say thank you. But we didn't get anyone saying thank you about the last album. So, that's why I'll quit. Not because of you.'

I raise my voice.

'So you needn't feel guilty, maaan!'

I lower my voice.

'Not any more than you usually do.'

I don't speak again for the next eight days.

Q&A

A Swedish music magazine sent us a questionnaire. Our tour publicist, Karla, waited until we were stranded in the departure lounge of Reykjavík airport before presenting it to us.

With nothing else to do, the band sat down at four tables in the bar and applied itself to answering.

I don't know exactly how many of these things I've tried to be cool, clever, amusing or profound in, since we began. Let's say, one every three days, on average – which totals around twenty-five hundred.

The fog that was keeping us on the ground thickened, and, after another hour, we were told a decision had been made: we were returning to the hotel.

On an impulse, I asked to look at the answers the other guys had given. This was a mistake. I started to cry, although I made sure no-one noticed – I put my head in my hands.

'Can you photocopy these?' I asked, handing them back to the publicist as I got off the minibus. I had on my dark glasses.

'Sure,' she said, puzzled.

They were delivered to my room later that night. I sat up with them, a *Coke*, a vegetarian burger and fries, and Elvis Presley's Sun Sessions on my iPod.

I noticed that Karla had censored some of our answers, and filled in spaces we'd left blank.

Name?	**Syph**
Born?	**Yes! I was! Isn't it great?**
Star sign?	**Leo. What else? Roar!**
Place of birth?	**Saturn.**
First crush?	**My mom, of course!** **Then the midwife.**
First record bought?	~~**Hey, I always stole them!**~~ *Sex Pistols, Pretty Vacant*
First job?	**Explosives expert.**
Favourite colour?	**Paint it black!**
Favourite animal?	**Any party animal. Yow!**
Favourite book?	~~**Hitler. A study in Tyranny**~~ *Hammer of the Gods* *by Stephen Davis*
What do you usually do when you are bored?	~~**Heroin**~~ *Go to a club*
If you could go anywhere in the world, where would you go?	**The Playboy Mansion** **Hi, Hef!**
Would you rather have the ability to fly or be invisible?	**To fly. It would be so cool for concerts. Whoosh!**
Do you collect anything?	**Digits, baby! What are yours?**
Most frightening experience?	**Nearly dying in LA.**
Funniest experience?	**Nearly dying in LA.**
Desert island single and album?	**AC/DC, For those about to Rock!** **Led Zeppelin IV**
Hero/heroine?	~~**Myself**~~ *Jim Morrison*
Have you ever seen a ghost?	**No.** ~~**But I have made one**~~
Do you have final words of wisdom?	**Stay cool, children!**

Name?	**Crab**
Born?	**[Blank]** *1965*
Star sign?	**Scorpio**
Place of birth?	**Don't remember**
First crush?	**My English teacher, Miss Ullshawn**
First record bought?	**The Ramones, Rockaway Beach**
First job?	**Always proudly unemployable**
Favourite colour?	**Don't remember. What's that yellowish one?**
Favourite animal?	**Skunk**
Favourite book?	~~**The wine list**~~ *The Catcher in the Rye.*
What do you usually do when you are bored?	~~**Start a fight**~~ *Call up a friend.*
If you could go anywhere in the world, where would you go?	~~**Cognac**~~, **France**
Would you rather have the ability to fly or be invisible?	**Fly, fly, fly away**
Do you collect anything?	**Parking tickets**
Most frightening experience?	**[Blank]** *Losing my voice*
Funniest experience?	**Waking up this morning**
Desert island single and album?	**The Ramones, Rockaway Beach/Rocket to Russia**
Hero/heroine?	**Jesus Christ**
Have you ever seen a ghost?	**Yes. Seriously. I don't want to talk about it.**
Do you have final words of wisdom?	**Study hard**

Name?	**Mono**
Born?	**1965**
Star sign?	**Pisces**
Place of birth?	**Vancouver**
First crush?	**Paul McCartney**
First record bought?	**Pink Floyd, Wish You Were Here**
First Job?	**Assistant drum majorette**
Favourite colour?	**Blue**
Favourite animal?	**Rainbow trout**
Favourite book?	**Izaak Walton, The Compleat Angler**
What do you usually do when you are bored?	**Talk to my wife**
If you could go anywhere in the world, where would you go?	**The Great Barrier Reef**
Would you rather have the ability to fly or be invisible?	**Be invisible**
Do you collect anything?	**Nature books. Matchboxes**
Most frightening experience?	**Never been scared**
Funniest experience?	**My future wife not being interested in Syph**
Desert island single and album?	**Paul McCartney, Maybe I'm Amazed I don't like albums any more**
Hero/heroine?	~~**My wife**~~ *Jaco Pastorius*
Have you ever seen a ghost?	**No. I don't believe in ghosts**
Do you have final words of wisdom?	**Keep calm**

Name?	**Clap**
Born?	**June 29th 1966**
Star sign?	**Cancer**
Place of birth?	**Vancouver Canada**
First crush?	**Mrs Sylvie Ullshawn, English teacher.**
First record bought?	**Snow White and the Seven Dwarfs soundtrack**
First job?	**Paper route. Lasted two weeks.**
Favourite colour?	**Tortoiseshell.**
Favourite animal?	**Cicada.**
Favourite book?	**e.e.cummings, Selected Poems**
What do you usually do when you are bored?	**Drum.**
If you could go anywhere in the world, where would you go?	**Home. Bed.**
Would you rather have the ability to fly or be invisible?	**But I can fly, and I've always been invisible. You'll have to try harder than that.**
Do you collect anything?	**Sad stories.**
Most frightening experience?	**Syph's overdose.**
Funniest experience?	**That's private.**
Desert island single and album?	**Fleetwood Mac, 'Tusk' Joni Mitchell, 'Blue'**
Hero/heroine?	**The Buddha, obviously**
Have you ever seen a ghost?	**Yes. Recently.**
Do you have final words of wisdom?	**Yes. See over.**

Okay, here goes – my good advices, my road apples:

Always shave in the direction the hair is growing.

Look before you leap, but look *over your shoulder* – because that place you're leaping from, you'll never see it again.

Instinct will serve you better than any committee, even a committee of your best friends convened to decide what is in your best interests.

Be careful what you ask for, it'll get you. In fact, if you want it badly enough, it'll track your weary footsteps through the snow and ravage you until you're nothing but a pile of red mush.

Heartfelt experience concentrated to a diamond-like essence cannot be expressed as anything other than cliché. Sorry. This is a fact.

As Bob Dylan once said, 'Keep a clean head and always carry a lightbulb.' I don't know what it means, either.

Most people, as you'll learn, are essentially good; most people, you'll discover, are innately evil; most people, you'll find, are morally ambiguous. Kids, too.

I don't know what the sound of one hand clapping is, but I know it makes a lousy rhythm track.

If a tree falls in the forest, and no-one hears, no lawyers need be involved; with the creation of any other recordable sound, that is not the case.

Life is very short; life is very long; life is as long as a piece of string.

Beware those who moralize their incapacity.

Don't – whatever you were thinking just then: *don't*.

Be true to *who you really are*, unless *who you really are* turns out to be Adolf Hitler or Ted Bundy, in which case repress yourself as much as you possibly can.

Find your inner beauty and offer it the once-in-a-lifetime opportunity of plastic surgery.

If you're scared of clowns, don't run away to join the circus.

All will be revealed, but only if you tuck $20 in her garter.

It happens fast or it doesn't happen at all.

Don't mourn your own life.

There are no short cuts. Let me repeat that: There are no short cuts.

As soon as I was finished, almost as if it had been preordained, I coughed up a small black spot of blood.

There had been a few flecks before, but nothing to worry about. This was more like a haemorrhage.

It was midnight. Still evening for Esther, however. So I called her. She told me to see a doctor, immediately.

After I'd put the phone down (the girls are *fine*, I am *fine*, see a doctor *now*), I spoke to reception.

By quarter past, the doctor had arrived.

By ten the next morning, I had a diagnosis of lung cancer.

By three o'clock, I was on a flight home.

It happens fast or it doesn't happen at all.

*

On the airplane, I thought about death. I often think about death when I'm on airplanes – in fact, I rarely think about anything else. But this was different. This time it was as if Death were in the passenger seat beside me. It was as if Death were flying the plane – quietly steering us towards a mountainside in Greenland. It was as if the plane itself were Death.

I tried to calm down, be casual.

So, I might be leaving the party early. Well, that's always been my way, hasn't it? Because of which, I've missed out on some pretty wild stuff (after hours), because of which I've ended up with fewer regrets (Sunday morning coming down).

I didn't even regret having been the kind of guy to leave parties early.

I got out my notebook and wrote down my wishes for my funeral:

No music. No eulogies. No sadness. In fact, no funeral.
Cremate me somewhere crappy – where they ask cash or cheque *when you walk in and then give you fifteen minutes for the service.*

My will was in good shape: Esther got the lot, including my ashes –

– these she could dispose of as she wished, which would probably be somewhere shady in our garden. I knew the spot she'd choose, and wouldn't have been able to dissuade her even if I'd wanted.

It meant she'd never be able to sell the house but, my money being what it was, she shouldn't ever have to.

Over the next week, I found myself interviewing myself. Questions. Always more questions.

Are you angry?
Yes, I am angry.
Do I feel it's unfair?
My whole life has been unfair – entirely in my favour.

This counts as a minor belated adjustment. What I had, all of it, I did not deserve.

Am I going to fight this thing?

Yes.

Do I have a message for the fans?

No.

Haven't you learnt anything you wish to pass on?

Yes. And I wrote it all down. Looking back, I think that was a foolish thing to do. If I'd kept all my wisdom secret, I might have been granted a little longer.

Has your faith given you strength?

It's shown me how pointless is the quest for strength.

God, that came out pompous.

How did the band take it?

Those guys – they never believe anything I say, thought it was a put-on, that I was shitting them.

I don't feel all that great. Can we end here?

One final question: How would you like to be remembered?

On my bedside table is a bowl of flowers – their roots are in earth, not water. I've asked, and they're called marguerites. They have a dial of propeller-shaped petals, twelve or thirteen, arranged around a disc of egg-yolk yellow. They are a very simple flower, like one of my girls would draw and be dissatisfied with. Their leaves have a difficult-to-describe shape: dragon's feet. Coloured a very delicate silvery green, they are far more complicated and morally ambiguous (if you want to have it like that, and right now I do) than the flower-parts. Lure those bees in with a happy face but then what those buzzers are keeping alive is actually a bit monstrous. I haven't seen a bee in a while. I haven't been in a summer meadow. I didn't last summer (on tour). I would like to and it's likely I won't unless I insist – unless I make it through to next spring, or fly to somewhere where it's a different season. But then it wouldn't be a real meadow, just a rich man's fake.

I am forty-two years old.

BENEFIT

Genital warts.

The joke between me and Esther is that this was the first gift I ever gave her.

Since then, I have been desperately trying to make up for it – really *desperately*.

I have given her three houses, a half-dozen cars, a piece of silver jewellery from every city I've been, a forest of flowers.

The first thing I remember Esther giving me was an old fob-watch her great-grandfather had kept thirty years in his waistcoat pocket. It didn't work, hadn't since the 1940s, but I found someone to fix it.

I don't know why she entrusted me, wart-bringer, with something so important to her and her family; this was only a month after we'd met – perhaps because she saw that responsibility was what I needed. (In that, she wasn't wrong.) And I have managed, so far, not to lose or destroy the watch. Mainly by having it screwed to the music-room wall, framed behind tungsten and bulletproof glass.

I have given Esther every getable object mentioned in her favourite-ever song, Dylan's 'Sad-Eyed Lady of the Lowlands': one copy of the *Missionary Times*, a silver cross, some silk, some glass, some Arabian drums, some metallic sheets, a deck of cards (I removed the Jack of Hearts and the Ace of Spades), some clothes bought from a basement store, a specially commissioned Victorian-style silhouette of Esther in profile, a matchbook that plays a tune when you open it, a recording of gypsy religious music, a list of Australian convicts (not easy to source), a rug made only between the hours of midnight and 6 a.m., her mother's drugs (antihistamines, I should point out – that took some explaining), a signed first edition of Steinbeck's *Cannery Row*, a picture of someone's husband cut out of a magazine *belonging* to one of her friend's husbands, a medallion bought from the Vatican and personally blessed by the Pope – is that holy enough for you? etc.

She, of course, topped all this by giving me the girls – although she hates it when I speak of their birth as a gift.

'We made them together. You gave them to me, just as much as I gave them to you.'

Didn't look that way in the delivery suite, I'll say.

And now, to put an end to all gift-competition, she – along with about eighty thousand other people – has given me a second death; the first one, so it seems, has been dodged.

Yippee! Whoopee! Whoop-de-doo!

Let's be silly.

I feel that now, let's be really silly, having faced down **THE FEAR** – as Stephen King would no doubt put it.

𝕿𝖍𝖊 𝕱𝖊𝖆𝖗!

Tinkle-tinkle goes the music box.
I am going to die.
La-la-la go the spooky children.
Black fear.

I am as good as dead.
Slam goes the metal door. Clank-clank go the chains.
Solid fear.
There is no hope.
Not fear like mist or water – fear like a slab of marble that you have to try and walk through. And you know it's impossible but suddenly you find yourself inside it – black marble – and you're obliged to keep moving, and you don't know how: if you think about it, you're paralysed; if you don't think about it, you can't move. You begin to be afraid of thought itself, so you try to stop thinking – which takes a lot of thought.

𝕿𝖍𝖊 𝕱𝖊𝖆𝖗!

After my prognosis came in, Esther hit the internet so hard it flinched. She spent all night in medical chatrooms, three at a time. She gathered enough information to write several PhDs. She emailed clinics across the world – and, when they didn't email back, she called them.

Eventually, she found the hint of a possibility of a treatment.

It was experimental. It involved lasers. It was expensive, even for us.

To make the treatment worthwhile, at least nine other people had to undergo it as well. And we would have to pay for them. A new hospital didn't have to be built from scratch, but the cost wasn't far off.

And then, even though only band-members can call a band meeting, Esther called a band meeting.

The other guys showed. Usual booth.

'No shit,' said Syph.

'At least there's hope,' said Crab.

'Of course we will,' said Mono.

And, with that, the benefit concert was put into play.

All bands re-form eventually: The Velvet Underground, The Sex Pistols, The Who, The Beatles (sort of).

Their reasons are, usually, not complicated. Usually, they are the reverse of complicated.

Dylan's '78 tour was known as the Alimony Tour; our second-last jaunt was privately known as the Paternity.

I am not the only member of *okay* to have become a father. But I am the only one to be personally raising his children.

Crab went out to get the I-divorce-you-I-divorce-you-I-divorce-you pack of cigarettes. He sees his son, maybe once a year. Not Christmas.

At the last count, Syph had nine legally certified offspring, sprinkled far and wide across the world – five girls and four boys. Most were conceived before DNA-profiling became widely known and used. Not all – Syph, as you know by now, takes a long time to learn his lessons. There are three more suits pending.

Mono won't and, fittingly, Major can't.

The Paternity Tour had been a cynical, and remunerative, exercise.

This re-formation was different: my life depended on it.

True friends, I've realized, are the people who will come and visit you in hospital *more than once.*

If I'd known this a while ago, I'd have included it among my good advices.

Yoyo (hi Yoyo!) came more than once – as did ex-roadies Monkey Boy and Shed, Clarissa Publicist and Maggie Marketeer.

Mono and Major were at my bedside around the clock. I know that, because we often spent the wee small hours playing backgammon. (For some reason, I became obsessed with the game – as if it, too, could help save me.) The two of them moved in with Esther and the girls. They were a great help at home, cooking and babysitting.

'But we're not *babies,*' I can hear Sarah and Grace say, together.

Ever since the Golden Music Teacher incident, Crab has had a phobia of hospitals. We spoke every day on the phone, however. Behind him, I could hear the sounds of bars – they made me feel bad, but he made me feel good. He told me I was tough, and, coming from him, I took that as one of the highest compliments I've ever received.

The real surprise was Syph. He used to hang out all the time, partly because he was going through a medical fetish phase, and wanted to meet nurses.

He met nurses.

But he also sat and talked to me in a way that was so intimate and compassionate that – well, I won't say it made being ill worthwhile, just to see; that would be untrue: I wouldn't for a moment wish myself back in that white condition. It was one of the unexpected gains, let me leave it at that. Syph is a true friend. He even wrote me a song. ('Isn'tism'.)

Being ill, like becoming a parent, makes you realize just how normal you are. To the outside world, you can be Mr Big Stuff, but your lungs could care less – and, neither, for the most part, could the medical professionals.

I had one guy, a consultant, who, after telling me that my prognosis was much worse than it had been two weeks previous, wanted to discuss the wrist technique of flams, drags and paradiddles. (Technical drummer stuff, don't worry.) Apart from him, though, everyone treated me like a totally run-of-the-mill rich-and-dying person.

I'm under no illusions that a poor version of me, given the same cancer, would have faced a completely different world of shit and pain.

As a famous person, I'd been called upon, in my pre-illness life, to visit the sick'n'dying – also the perfectly healthy but vastly disabled.

Confession: I never felt comfortable.

There's excruciating footage of John Lennon, on-stage during The Beatles 1964 American tour, doing what these days would be called 'spazzing out'. He sticks his tongue down behind his bottom lip, smiles with his cheeks, crosses his eyes and puts his head at an angle. Then he contorts his arms and legs until they look sufficiently palsied. And then, to make it even funnier, he does a little sideways spazz-dance towards Paul and George.

This happens so frequently that, even on *The Beatles Anthology*, it can't pass unmentioned. (It looks, at points, like Lennon couldn't face a camera without first making a spazz-face.) One of John's talking-head chums helpfully explains that, although the popular image of Beatlemania is of four moptops singing *oooh!* to stadiums crammed full of screaming teenage girls, in actual fact, the first three or four rows at each concert were usually taken up by the severely mentally and physically handicapped. When they played, this was what The Beatles saw – a glistening sea of wheelchairs. Lennon, the head-friend says, was just trying to cope.

I, too, finding myself confronted by ill people all day every day, spazzed out. Not physically, mentally.

THE FEAR!

'I can't cope,' I said.

Actually, I screamed it.

Esther was called.

'You can cope. You have to cope.'

For a week, I stayed in my private room.

Sedated is the word.

Then I went out again into the communal spaces.

Here, I met Mike.

He was fifteen-years-old, wheelchair-bound and thought my band sucked. Mike liked only the heaviest grindcore. (Cannibal Corpse was, he said, 'shitty pop'. His favourite group was Anal Cunt.) Apart from that, we had a lot in common. For instance, we both played backgammon, and we both had only six months to live.

'Your band are pussies. You don't rock. You're easy listening, man. Hey, six and six. I'm doubling up.'

On top of serious-as-fuck cancer, Mike also had really bad acne and braces. I couldn't see the point of inflicting braces on him, seeing how his teeth would never be sorted. His parents, although divorced, were united in wishing to see him die with an orthodontically satisfactory smile.

You might be expecting me to say that Mike made me realize how lucky I'd been, in my life. Even if I were to die, I would at least know that I had achieved something.

And he did make me feel that. But not in an obvious way.

'You suck. And you're playing too slow.'

We talked about him and what he wanted to do – what he would have done, if he hadn't been in hospital, in a wheelchair.

Mike was without ambition.

He didn't make me feel as if I'd lived his dream. He made

me feel as if I'd lived way beyond anything he was capable of dreaming. In a way, his modesty was Zen.

Yes, he loved grindcore, but he was happy to leave the playing of it to other, more disqualified souls.

In 1996, Anal Cunt released an album called *40 More Reasons to Hate Us*.

'What about travel?'

'I can see pictures. Why would I want to be there? I don't like it to be too hot or cold.'

Checking first to see there were no nurses around to overhear, and report me: 'What about losing your virginity?'

'Oh, come on. I did that years ago.'

'Years?'

'When I was twelve. She was fourteen. She was so ugly no-one else would do it to her.'

'What was her name?'

'Jane McManus. It was in the basement of our building. There's an old couch there that everyone uses. It's gross.'

'That's a very romantic story, Mike.'

'She sucked my cock, too. So I've done that, as well.'

'I'm glad.'

'Were you going to offer to get me laid? You can still do that, if it makes you happy.'

'No,' I said, though I had considered the possibility.

We resumed our conversation a few days later.

'What about growing up? You want to grow up, don't you?'

Mike didn't answer. At first, I thought I'd really upset him.

'I'm sorry,' I said.

'I do want to live longer,' said Mike. 'But I don't want to become, like, old. I don't want to be like you.'

'What am I like?'

'You're kind of finished.'

'Is it that obvious?'

'There's stuff for you to do, but you're not as into it as you were into stuff before.'

'They call that middle age.'

'I don't want that.'

Again and again, he beat me at backgammon. He wasn't just lucky, he was way better than I was. But, when he lost, he didn't even seem to notice.

A third time, I tried finding out his ambition.

'Food?'

'My parents bring me McDonald's when they come.'

'Drugs?'

'I've had enough of those.'

'Money?'

'What for?'

Mike's six months, so it turned out, had been more optimistic than mine. After two of them, he went into renal failure and caught pneumonia.

Towards the end, I contacted Seth Putnam from Anal Cunt through a friend of a friend of Syph's. He flew in with the band and played a short set for Mike. At his request, they finished with a cover of Motörhead's 'Killed by Death'.

'Thank you,' said Mike, the next day. 'They were quite good.'

He died the following week.

Soon afterwards, the benefit concert went ahead.

Eighty thousand people in GM stadium.

I joined the band on tambourine for a gentle acoustic version of 'Sea-Song #2'. It was all I could manage.

I've never heard an audience like it.

FUCK THE FEAR!

All I had to do was stand there.

Hanks.

The money came in.

Yippee!

I got treated and went into remission.

Whoopee!

Five out of the other nine people are still alive.

I invited all of them, and all their families and true friends, to a costume party at our house. It was clear we had very little in common, except gratitude. But we had the greatest time. Esther came as the Virgin Mary. I went as a skeleton.

Whoop-de-doo!

ROADKILL

Roadkill.

For Canadians, it's a fact of life.

And, of course, death.

Pet Heaven only knows how many bugs, birds and beasts I've massacred in my twenty-two years of qualified driving.

Since becoming a Buddhist, however, I mind about it more.

My Religious Studies teacher, a committed Christian, once told an anti-Buddhist story in class – in a blatant attempt to try and put us off this rival religion. He said that a friend of his knew a Buddhist monk, and this monk had just bought a car. The friend asked the monk how he was going to square his belief in reincarnation with, essentially, roadkill. Wasn't it terrible karma even to hit all those bugs? The monk had a simple solution: get someone else to drive. Then it would be *their* karma that was impacted.

Even aged twelve, I didn't believe the teacher. For a start, I didn't believe he had any friends at all – let alone one who knew someone as cool as a Buddhist monk. Misguidedly, I imagined the monk-friend as a cross between Obi-Wan Kenobi and David Carradine in *Kung Fu*.

To be perfectly honest, I still haven't worked out what I think about this. It's not orthodox, whatever that may mean. I can't really believe that some guy who leads a really shitty life, and comes back in the form of a slug or a rat, isn't going to want to get out of that body as soon as possible.

I would.

Some reincarnations are better than others. But then, I suppose, some – like my current one – give you a bigger chance of majorly fucking up.

Pretty often, I look back over what I've done, over the totality of what I'm guilty of, and I can almost feel myself metamorphosing into a cockroach. On bad days, an amoeba.

It's not for me to judge, luckily.

And I know what I should believe – that every existence is of infinite individual value, that the smallest single cell creature is beyond glorious.

So, therefore, avoid doing harm to others, including life-forms you would hate to be.

Like, I'm sure there's a lot of warmth and camaraderie among rats. You get to spend time hanging out with your extended family. But I have enough trouble remembering birthdays as it is. And if I had any residual consciousness of how much Esther hated me and my kind . . .

And what about viruses? If Sarah or Grace go down with throat infections, I'm not going to worry that I'm prolonging the samsara of strep. They get dosed.

There is a hierarchy.

Yes, Buddha-nature is in everything.

Yes, I can just about imagine sparing a mosquito that I catch chowing down on my forearm.

But should I give up my car completely and walk every-where just because a couple of dozen bug-reincarnations are going to move on up to a higher level for each mile I travel?

To the voices who say, *Yes, if that's what you believe*, I say, *Gimme a break, I'm still working all this shit out.*

To the voice inside which says, *You don't know exactly what's wrong with your spiritual life, but you know it's pretty much in the vicinity of everything*, I say, *Shut up for one fucking second, won't you?*

So, I am driving down an empty moonlit road, between trees, returning home from a friend's – call him Fred. He lives in Southern Alberta. I have a ritual of flying there and driving back. I like the empty time.

There's music in the hire car: Nick Drake's *Pink Moon*, appropriate to the night and the way I am feeling.

Fred is almost divorced. He has reached that stage where he looks back and thinks of all the good times.

The rear-view mirror is an empty black. I always feel this

is wrong, and there should be at least a smear of the car headlights in it.

I am driving and not thinking.

It has been a sunny summer's day, and for much of it I have worn a hat – a grey fedora to go with the suit I've recently returned to wearing, along with a white collarless shirt. I did, after all, go up to Savile Row to buy it.

Dignity uniform.

As I drive, the hat sits in the passenger seat. But I can feel the ghost of it all around the circumference of my head. I have to keep checking that it's there and not there.

From my left, two suddenly incandescent rabbits rush the road, diagonally. They are moving too fast for me to avoid them. The lead rabbit, smaller of the two, makes it to the opposite verge. But rabbit the second doesn't freeze, as cliché would demand. Rabbit two goes between my front wheels and keeps on running, until it meets my rear right wheel.

I can't say I really feel a bump. There is a sound, more of a thud than a crunch. I become aware of a death, behind me.

Roadkill.

Like I said, a fact of life.

But because I'm increasingly bothered, I pull over, stop the car and walk the twenty yards back.

I am carrying my glove-compartment flashlight, but the rabbit is clear in the moonlight.

I feel as if I can see every detail of it more perfectly than by daylight. Each hair on its still body seems to be illuminated from within.

The rabbit is dead – I don't need to touch it to know that. However, there is no blood. The wheel didn't squash it in any way.

Sad to say, it's a beautiful sight, the paleness and stillness of it. If it were alive, I'd never get this close.

I kneel down, aware that I have to listen out for other cars – even though (despite the tinnitus) I'd hear them a mile off, at least.

I don't touch the rabbit. I don't want the guilt of its warmth. And pretty soon, I've gone from *I don't touch the rabbit* to *I can't touch the rabbit.*

It isn't disgust that stops me. The emotion is something much more like terror. This, here, is the fact of death. However many times we encounter it, it's always the first time, because we are only born into the present moment an instant or two before.

But I know I should at least carry the rabbit over to the ditch. Some critter or other will probably have it before the night's out. If I leave it where it is, a truck will flatten and splatter it – destroying its perfect intactness.

I leave it.

I walk away, following the flower-shape my flashlight makes on the ground: chrysanthemum.

There is no good explanation. Maybe I just want to do a worse thing than kill it, out of self-disgust.

Esther is asleep when I get home, and the next morning I tell her about the divorce, not the rabbit.

I certainly haven't forgotten.

When I don't tell her, I'm deliberately *not* telling her, just as I'd keep an affair secret, although I've never cheated on her, not since the Japanese girl.

A day passes, then another, and the rabbit becomes the affair I've never had but was secretly having.

It would be humiliating to tell Esther now. She thinks vegetarians are essentially rampant egoists who hate society and use food as a means of revenge. I'm not sentimental.

Two weeks later, Major calls me and tells me straight out, Crab is dead.

I ask how:

'You won't believe it,' she says. 'A lightning strike got him. He was asleep in Stanley Park under a tree, and it just got him.'

'How did you hear?'

I am jealous – I want to know why I haven't been called first.

'Someone from the Vancouver police department called an officer here. It hasn't been announced anywhere. He drove right over to tell us. He's still here. Can you contact Syph?'

How much don't I want to?

'Okay,' I say. 'Thanks for calling.'

Then I ask, 'How's Mono taking it?' but Major has already hung up.

I don't know how *I* am taking it. For so long, I have expected to hear that Crab was dead. He has been hospitalized increasingly frequently, during the last couple of years. (Not as much as me, though.)

'Esther,' I shout, and she knows from my voice that death is involved.

She has been having lunch in the kitchen with the girls.

One of them starts whining; Grace, left with macaroni cheese and no access to ketchup.

Esther hugs me hard, then has to go back to them.

I think about calling Syph, then decide I need to see at least one member of the band face-to-face that day.

All through the drive, I think of how long I'd known Crab and how long it had been since I'd really known him.

Traffic is backed up, after a truck rollover, and the journey takes an extra hour.

'I know,' says Syph, opening the door. 'I heard.'

We talk as we enter the circular room. He has redecorated, again. It is 1930s modernist, very restrained.

'Did someone call?'

'I was online. Yoyo messaged me. Condolences.'

'How do you feel?' I ask. The question is again for myself.

'I feel, *the bastard, how could he do this to us?* I feel, *here is an excuse for drugs.* I feel, *I will never have a better friend.* I feel, *shouldn't I be feeling more?*'

It is a long time since I've heard Syph this eloquent. His words are almost like his song lyrics.

We sit in leather and metal chairs.

'What about you?' he asks.

'The same,' I say. 'It's quite a cool way to die.'

This is what I would have said, aged seventeen or twenty-five. I should have something different to say, now.

'He always thought he was going to be electrocuted on stage, like Keith Richards in 1965.'

'Remember that rainstorm over Glastonbury?'

'I heard him chanting the Lord's Prayer all through that gig,' says Syph.

'Really? I never knew.'

Syph makes some coffee and the calls start to come in. We let the management write a response for us. There is a brief conference call with Mono.

'We have to talk about the band,' says Syph.

'What band?' asks Mono.

Syph doesn't press him.

I can remember the thunderstorm the night before. Half-woken by it, I had worried that the girls would start freaking out. The next time I had any kind of conscious thought, the skies were silent. How could I have known anything significant had happened?

We buried him.

His father, tough old fucker, was still alive to see the day. I had never known him sober before. His mother I won't describe, out of respect.

There was resignation and pointless anger and black humour and something missing. The service was very traditional. It surprised me to learn that Crab had often gone to this big old Catholic church. When the priest spoke, briefly, it was clear he'd known the man.

Crab had made a new will only two weeks before. Half of everything went to his mother, the other half went to establish a music school. Classical music, not our stuff. Acoustic instruments only – that was what the will stipulated. This fact moved me.

Little else did.

Mono stayed a week after the funeral but refused to talk about the future.

The management suggested a memorial concert.

Syph liked the idea.

Secretly, I did, too.

Over the next month, Crab's death became like the ghost-hat. I wore it all the time, consciously.

I tried crying and it just didn't work. Tears came, but they felt forced.

I made further efforts at grief.

I went to the charred tree in the park and stood there for an hour.

I played all our old albums. I watched the tour video. I read the distraught emails and letters from fans.

And then the hat was gone.

One night, about three months later, I am driving back from Fred's, from my now-divorced friend's house. There is no moon. The night is different than before. That was summer. Now it is December and snow everywhere. It is a little stupid to be driving back in a blizzard. But I have chains on the wheels, and the 4×4 I've hired is a mean old bastard.

When I reach the point in the road where I hit the rabbit, my foot comes off the gas.

I cruise to a halt, unable to see for strong crying.

The front right wheel hits the soft shoulder.

I get out and stumble back up the road.

I am a wailing thing, not myself at all.

The words coming out are a song more than a sentence.

'I should have moved you. I should have moved you even if I didn't bury you. I'm sorry. I'm sorry, rabbit. I shouldn't just have left you there, all dead. I didn't mean to kill you.

I hate those fucking trucks. Did they mess you up? I hope you're okay. Why didn't I bury you? I wasn't being disrespectful. And you were such a beautiful rabbit.'

DOG #2

'Rpt ad lib to fade'
(No specific song. Most of our songs end this way.)

'A three-legged dog is still a dog' – that's what Syph said, with sorrow, in one of his post-Crab interviews, quoting Michael Stipe, without acknowledgement, ha ha.

And so, when we went back on the road, earlier this year, we called it 'The Three-Legged-Dog Tour'.

But the sound was too empty, too exposing. No middle. We found that we needed another leg, and we ended up with another couple: ex-roadies Monkey Boy and Shed were recalled to active service.

It was a much better solution than employing some session musician.

okay went slightly folky, which chimed with the times.

Still, we missed Crab like hell. All of us.

Syph had stood to his right for over twenty years, was regularly jabbed by his elbow, cut across the face by his swinging-round headstock; when he looks to his left these days, Crab is missing – even off-stage, he's not where he should be.

His life, the end of it, was more complicated than we initially thought.

In what turned out to be the final year, Crab met a woman – the one he introduced me to, that night I tried to keep up. Things must have moved fast, afterwards. Perhaps he was in control of them, and himself. I like to think so. It went something like this: Courvoisier courtship, Moët et Chandon marriage, Jack D divorce.

But he hadn't signed the papers, because he'd lost the papers, because he was drunk, because he was an alcoholic, because he hated everything so much, because nothing would make it go away, so she is claiming all the money.

Until we use our mint-tea lawyer.

Then the money will go to his mother and the music school.

This may take time.

As for my own children, I'm sometimes asked whether becoming a parent wasn't a huge shock, after the cosseted life that people assume I'd led.

In fact, being the drummer in a mid-level indie rock band was the best preparation for parenthood: the general sense of bewilderment and disorientation, the hours of boredom, the moments of all-redeeming joy, the ubiquity of bodily fluids, the subservience to endearingly unreasonable ego-monsters, the love of exhaustion and the exhaustion of love.

I like touring, but I prefer being at home.

I've never really enjoyed pleasure.

I realized this recently. It's too re-re-re-repetitive. The moral of debauchery is always the same: *It's not worth it, in the end.* And I think I'm intelligent enough to have picked that up from other people, ones around me.

Restraint (mine) leads to curlicues of moral ambiguity. I think that's why I've spent my life – ignoring certain well-documented periods – just saying no. There were binges, like after Esther left me, but they were anomalous: I was being weak, and to do so took a certain strength of character.

Where does Syph get the energy?

I still love the music.

I love the music so much I've made myself deaf.

When I go in to check on the girls, I can't hear their breathing from the door – I can't hear it bending over them – I probably couldn't even hear it with my head an inch above their chests.

No, to tell they're still alive, I have to touch them (sometimes because of this they wake up) – in the quiet of their room, I can hear a piledriver being used by a banshee while an air-raid siren warns of a whistling bomb which never lands: tinnitus.

In this, among drummers, I am far from alone.

But the convention is, we don't talk about it. It's un-rock'n'roll and ungrateful.

When you're fifteen, the stage is the only place you want to be. At forty-four, consider it as a working environment. Some nights, you might as well be shovelling iron ore into a blast furnace.

Drumming is manual labour.

Boo-fucking-hoo.

In *The Last Waltz*, Robbie Robertson – bullshitter *extraordinaire* – called The Road 'a goddamn impossible way of life'.

That may well be. But you certainly meet some interesting people out there.

I don't have a story from the Three-Legged-Dog Tour. We now have enough money to protect us, by and large, from amusing events.

And so, I thought I might bring you up-to-date on a few of the interesting people we've met along the way, interesting and otherwise.

Because of publishing these ramblings as a book, I had to check out with most of them (those who could be traced) that they didn't mind me including them. Names have been changed to protect the innocent, and the guilty, and the morally indeterminate but shy.

Of course, this is going to be sad, in parts. But, here goes.

Cast in order of appearance.

WHERE ARE THEY NOW?

MINOR CHARACTERS

I've never managed to track down *Inge the Beautiful Dog-Rescuer of Rotterdam/Amsterdam*. (Probably for the best.) And I might as well dispose, here, of all but one of the other untraceables:

Ginger who was Crab's On-Off Girlfriend, Celia the Matchgirl who was around for Syph's Overdose, Lydia Who Fell in Love with Me and Whom I Cruelly/Kindly Left, The Girl in Room 333, Shirley from Lubbock Who Introduced Mono to Jesus, The Buddhist Monk Who Gave Me the Beads, Lula-Maybelline from the Tourbus, Honey Ditto, and *The Butterfly Swimmer Who Kicked My Ass and Saved My Life.* It's just, you meet so many and remember so few. I remember you all. Be in touch, if only to let me know you're still around.

Lindsay the Librarian sent me an invitation to her wedding, c/o the record company. I got it two days late. It turns out she moved to Nottingham, England, and met a Recruitment Consultant called Colin. They now have a daughter, Bryony. Lindsay published her first book of poetry, with a small Scottish press. It's called *Our Hosts.*

Miss Watts the Head Librarian is still working. At eighty-five.

For *Yoyo from the Fanclub,* see the entry on Syph, below.

Syph's Mom has remarried, twice. There's no-one out there good enough for her.

After school, *Katie Proudhon (aka Catty Proudhorn)* had a brief modelling career. Then she took an MBA, and is currently very dull.

It's impossible to separate *Shed* and *Monkey Boy,* so I'll do them together. After the Three-Legged-Dog Tour, they went and recorded their ninth album. Thanks to you, the buying public, it was a hit, like always.

Kerrie Who was Crab's Ex is doing a fine job bringing up Crab's son. We have seats near them at Canucks games.

Our Management from the Time of Syph's Overdose are still in LA, and welcome to it.

The Divine Miss Sylvie Ullshawn Who was Crab's and My English Teacher, and Our First Crush took early retirement, and moved to New Zealand, where she gardens and paints. She has never married.

Scary Asian PA from Our First Big European Tour Who Mono Fell in Love With has become one of the world's leading designers of S/M figurines. It is a growing market. She specializes in latex-clad nurses.

My Mother's Friend Betty, Who was Around When My Father Died, herself died of breast cancer a couple of years ago. I will always be grateful to her memory. She made a bad time slightly more bearable.

My Mother is fine, thank you for asking.

Skullfukk, the Deathmetal Band in Whom I Took Solace split, sadly. But their monster of a drummer went on to become a mainstay of Maggotdikk.

Dorothy in South Africa Who Introduced Me to Her Aunt, and Set Up a Drumming Party for Me is HIV-positive but getting antiretrovirals. She was raped, which is how she became infected. She stopped to give the guy a ride. He pulled a knife. I warned you this was going to be sad.

Barbra, the Model Trying to Figure It All Out made lots of money and retired aged twenty-five. She does take photographs, but not professionally. From what I hear, she will soon be coming out of retirement.

Friend One, Friend Two and Friend Three from the Black Forest email me occasionally. They've all completed their educations. Two of them have children. Slowly, they are becoming less Goth.

Crab Senior outlived his son, but only by two weeks.

Tony and Jordan, Our Ex-Management are once again our management. More, I cannot say. And *Cindy, Their Former Assistant* is now managing other bands, and doing very well thank you.

Clarissa the Publicist remains a stalwart friend and supporter of the band. She has a good man – Jeremy-of-the-firm-handshake – who is big in sports equipment, and two lovely daughters, who are small in flowery dungarees.

Maggie the Marketeer wants to know what's so horribly wrong with her. (That's what she asked me to put.)

Irina the Russian Superfan turns out to have been working for the Russian secret service all along. After bringing off a major-league mafia bust, she had to go into hiding. I do not know her whereabouts. She is not in Canada.

Joyce Cloud, Esther's Mother cannot be praised highly enough. I think I have been forgiven.

The Commode-Fox, Esther's Stepfather has taught me a thing or two. And not just about antiques.

The Kid Who Followed is the one I left out of the list of people we couldn't track down. Of course we couldn't track him down.

The Japanese Girl I Almost Married, and Her Fishing Village Family are doing fine. The financial settlement helped them no end.

They now have three boats. And she married the boy she should have married all along. They have a button-cute son.

Leonard Cohen aka Jikan, the Silent One is back up Mount Baldy. In fact, I think he never fully left – I was misinformed about that.

The Record Company Executive with the Inspirational Desk-Calendar is still, I am sorry to have to report, a knob.

Mint-Tea Lawyer is still TCB.

Craigie the Surfer and *Jenny* and *Boo* came to stay last Easter. Boo got on very well with Sarah and Grace, despite the age gap. After we met in Barbados, Craigie managed to become an exhibition surfer, but hated the commercialization of his art. However, he'd earned enough to set himself up as a board designer and manufacturer. After building the business up to the third biggest in Hawaii, he sold it off. Currently, he is fronting a surf-forecasting website and learning high-end yoga.

Jenny has written two very successful novels, *The Wide Wide Blue* and *Spillikins*.

Boo likes horses better than waves.

As for *the Rapper Who Sampled 'Holding'*, I can't tell you how rich and successful he is.

Big Boy, Sent to Meet Me by the Rapper Who Sampled 'Holding' was still there in the videos, last time I checked. Still nodding in slo-mo, looking both venal and smug.

Jean Wallace and Aaron Benjamin, Parents of Otis are fine – though fine, I have to say, on a fairly modest scale. These things never go away. I mostly hear about them through their daughter, *Caroline Wallace-Benjamin*, who came to work for *okay* as a sound-technician. She will go far, if she turns the kick-drum up just a little more.

We exchange Christmas cards with *Chester, Otis's uncle*. He runs a successful business servicing golf-carts.

Karla, Our Tour Publicist in Iceland drowned whilst swimming off the coast of Croatia. She was only twenty-six.

Fred, Call Him Fred, My Friend in Alberta is just about over his divorce. I have never told him about the rabbit, so he's going to learn something about me if he reads this book. (So is everyone.)

MAJOR CHARACTERS

Major. Rocks. Majorly.

Mono (along with Major) has become a committed environmental campaigner. It happened like this: during the winter months, when he couldn't do much fishing, he started to become obsessed with levels of chemical emission from nearby factories. He is now campaigning for tighter restrictions on industry, not just in Canada but right across the world. He has Bono on speed-dial.

Get this: *Syph* hasn't taken a drink since the day after Crab's funeral. And I'm pretty sure he's kicked his other addictions, too. For a few months, after coming out of rehab, he went to live with Mono and Major. They tell me he did a lot of fishing, and crying. Then he turned up on our doorstep, in tears. He told me – he told my right shoulder – that he'd always loved and admired me. And this was before I'd even invited him in. Once over the threshold, he became even more distraught – telling me that, really, he'd always wanted to *be* me. 'You're so solid – and I'm hardly there at all. I feel like I've been absent for the past fifteen, twenty years. Right from our first success. Look at what you have. Your beautiful wife and your family. You have a support network.' After he'd calmed down, I gave him a couple of these anecdotes to read – just to show him how solid I really wasn't. (If you're interested, they were 14, 22 and 25.) 'These are great,' he said, when he returned them, late that evening. 'You should publish them.' I told him they were entirely private. He dropped the subject immediately, then brought it up again a few days later. Meantime, he had been quizzing me about Buddhism. He'd seen me go off to meditate, and had asked if, next time, I could teach him. We did some basic mindful breathing together. After that, he went completely wild with it, sitting for hours on my *zafu*. He wanted me to become his guru. I told him to stop shitting around. 'Please,' he said. 'I need your wisdom.' I gave him a couple of books to read – other people's wisdom. He'd finished them by the following morning. 'More,' he said. When he'd exhausted my small library, he started ordering all the other books by the same writers. It only took him a fortnight to manage the full lotus; those slinky hips of his. Also, he'd asked to read the rest of my stories. 'They're all great,' he said, when he was done. 'You really should think about putting them out there. I think they'd help a lot of people understand what it's like.' He could only mean *What it's like to be a drummer.* Before this, though, he acknowledged my justifiable resentments against him. 'I'm so sorry,' he said. 'I can't tell you how sorry I am. I was in a lot of pain. I had a lot of anger.' In number 16, he came across the mention of Mount Baldy. He left us for California a few days later, having cajoled his way in there. 'Please,' I said, 'whatever you do, don't mention my name to Leonard.' 'I promise,' he said. The next we heard, a month later, he had been joined there by Yoyo (hi Yoyo!). And then they got married. And then, two months later, they got divorced. But they're still together. And Syph still meditates, sometimes. He's back in Vancouver, though. I see him around. He keeps dropping by. He wants to do a new album. 'Mono's in,' he says. 'All we need is you.'

Sarah and *Grace* have made me promise not to say anything embarrassing about them. But what else are dads for? They are the most oodlesome girls in the world.

Esther is love. Esther is pregnant.

And *Me?* I play the drums in a band called *okay*. And that's cool.

OKAY DISCOGRAPHY, INCOMPLETE

OKAY

Sea-Song $#_1$

Work

Gustav Klimt

Withdraw

Walls

Sea-Song $#_2$

Sea-Song $#_3$

Into Space

Click

With Strings

Queen Victoria

Sea-Song $#_4$

ARRIVE

Anæmic

Blissfully

Call

Thousand

Jane-Jane

Beachcombed

O

Arrive

Moon

Waltz

August

Haven't

Motherhood

Zero

THE SOCIETY FOR MUTUAL AUTOPSY

Different Types of Sugar

Isn't, Wasn't, Won't

Prohibition

Nikki's Gone to America

The Unhip

Vancouver Drug-Hoover

SS

Cutey π

Gnostic Jewellery

Easel-Weasel

Art-junk-shop

Groteskimo & His Penguin

   Gimp

Nature vs Nurture

Rat Mansion

4ᵀᴴ

Cleaning up	Giggling
Spangle-jangle	Save it
I love love love you	Wolves (The Most Honest Words)

LIVE ALBUM (DOUBLE)

Isn't, Wasn't, Won't	Sea-Song $^{\#}1$
Idiot Boy	Sea-Song $^{\#}2$
Giggling	Sea-Song $^{\#}3$
Anæmic	Sea-Song $^{\#}4$
Jane-Jane	

The Unhip	Waltz
Haven't	Beachcombed
Queen Victoria	Wolves (The Most Honest Words)
Click	Rocks Off

SONGS AND SNOGS

Retro-futurism	Gunk
Jealous	Unnamed
My Dead Shoes	Bitterness
She Spat Me	Exit Strategies
Bitte Schön	
With You (Out of Doors)	

UNDERLINGS:
B-SIDES & EARLY RARITIES

Celibacy

You are the girl

Cicada

Underlings

Saw you last

Castor & Pollux

Chicken Rhythm #2

August Strindberg

Vancouver Drug-Hoover

2 a.m. song

Hippie Summer

Bookends

Helicopters

Take me away (from you)

Hush-hate-hum

Wipeout

TREE

So holy

Woods

Green again

Rust

Cassette

Tree

Back to where

Holding

Battery

Envelopes

Long-shot

Mist

9ᵀᴴ/DARK DARK DARK

6-6-Sixties
Lord and Master
Heaviosity
Spunk-burger
Hello, Hell
The Subterraneans
Hole of Nobody Knows
When I wasn't me
Shadow-walker
Incandescent Twilight
Blinder than Thou

Masterpiece of Pain
Agony Threnody
The Scream (We all scream)
Killingly
Luciferous
Ride the Metal Steed
Zero Sum Game
Decimate
Planet-killer
Total Blackout
SS Nature

SONGS OF DEFEAT A.K.A. COUNTRY ALBUM

Sleeping on the sofa
The Drinker's Song
Long Cold Lines
The Heels of Her Shoes
Where I'm Calling From

The Song
Thanks a Million
What Daisy Knew
6
Saved by the Bell

ISN'TISM

O Love

Lindsay

(I used to be your) Poster Boy

Caravaggio

The Left-behind

LA (OD)

Unsaid

Confessional

Better than Not

Isn'tism

OKAY: MTV UNPLUGGED

Sea-Song $\#_1$

Waltz

The Left-behind

Long Cold Lines

She's Lost Control

Kooks

Click

When I wasn't me

Woods

Holocaust

So Long Ago, Nancy

Wolves (The Most Honest Words)

Sea-Song $\#_2$

SOLO ALBUMS / SIDE PROJECTS

MOUNTAIN MEN
BY MONKEY BOY AND SHED

Basement Testament

Hung Up on Glory

Grunky Girls

So English It Hurts

Spare

Back of my Truck

The Cold Fire

Moshpit Romance

In Sunderland

Wilfulness

Mountain Men

Honcy Child

The Revolution

Hymnal

HOOK, LINE & SINKER
BY SYPH

Coup de Fou

I can't even talk to you

Perfume

Drum Majorette

Beatbox Romeo

Croix de Guerre

My friend, the winner

No hard feelings

Bastard

What I Wanted & What I Got

Pull Out the Roots

The Yearning

Nothing, No-one, None

Spendthrift/Spindrift

TOBY LITT

GHOST STORY

Agatha and Paddy were to have a baby. They bought a new house on the south coast. But then something happened and they found they couldn't fill their new home – no matter how they tried. That emptiness threatened their relationship, and they began to ask: how was it they could be haunted by something that had never existed?

'Unsettling, extraordinarily vivid . . . makes you remember what reading's all about' *Daily Telegraph*

'One of the most compelling books of the year. Litt's finest novel so far' Ali Smith, *The Times Literary Supplement*

'Beautifully written, moves and intrigues and cracks along at a galloping pace. A striking portrayal of how bereavement can overshadow life' *Guardian*

TOBY LITT

HOSPITAL

The end of the world doesn't come with a bang or a whimper, but with the chukka-chukka of a helicopter coming into land . . .

Hospital is about blue murder and saving lives, having sex and surgery, falling in love and falling from a great height, crazy voodoo and hypnotic surveillance – it's about the last days and the first days. And the Rubber Nurse knows you've been very naughty and is going to teach you a well-deserved lesson.

It's the story of a lost boy wandering the corridors of a strange, antiseptic building, looking and hoping for a chance to get home. And also of a man who won't wake up despite the best efforts of the hospital staff – and while he sleeps, a threatening darkness settles over everything . . .

'Litt has created an extraordinarily vivid comic nightmare, an apocalyptic vision for our own weird times' *Guardian*

'A mind-bending trip – like a shot of morphine . . . a dark, absurd fairytale . . . an epic nightmare' *London Lite*

'Vivid, hallucinatory, startling and humane. Defibrillating fiction' China Mieville

He just wanted a decent book to read ...

Not too much to ask, is it? It was in 1935 when Allen Lane, Managing Director of Bodley Head Publishers, stood on a platform at Exeter railway station looking for something good to read on his journey back to London. His choice was limited to popular magazines and poor-quality paperbacks – the same choice faced every day by the vast majority of readers, few of whom could afford hardbacks. Lane's disappointment and subsequent anger at the range of books generally available led him to found a company – and change the world.

'We believed in the existence in this country of a vast reading public for intelligent books at a low price, and staked everything on it'
Sir Allen Lane, 1902–1970, founder of Penguin Books

The quality paperback had arrived – and not just in bookshops. Lane was adamant that his Penguins should appear in chain stores and tobacconists, and should cost no more than a packet of cigarettes.

Reading habits (and cigarette prices) have changed since 1935, but Penguin still believes in publishing the best books for everybody to enjoy. We still believe that good design costs no more than bad design, and we still believe that quality books published passionately and responsibly make the world a better place.

So wherever you see the little bird – whether it's on a piece of prize-winning literary fiction or a celebrity autobiography, political tour de force or historical masterpiece, a serial-killer thriller, reference book, world classic or a piece of pure escapism – you can bet that it represents the very best that the genre has to offer.

Whatever you like to read – trust Penguin.

Clear
Skin

Clear Skin

A Step - by - Step Program to Stop Pimples, Blackheads, Acne

Kenneth L. Flandermeyer, M.D.
Illustrated by Monique M. Davis

Little, Brown and Company   Boston—Toronto

First Edition

Library of Congress Cataloging in Publication Data

Flandermeyer, Kenneth L
  Clear skin.

  Includes index.
  1. Skin — Care and hygiene.   2. Dermatologic agents.
I. Title.
RL87.F55   616.5′3   79-486
ISBN 0-316-28545-5
ISBN 0-316-28546-3 pbk.

BP

Designed by Janis Capone

Published simultaneously in Canada by Little, Brown & Company (Canada) Limited

Printed in the United States of America

For Clara, Norbert, Sandy
and my acne patients

Acknowledgments

Many people were involved in the writing of this book and I sincerely thank all of them. Unfortunately, space does not allow me to recognize each of them by name. Scores of my acne patients and other friends not listed here were directly involved in the preparation of the manuscript. I am also aware that my acne patients were my real teachers in the development of the treatment program.

The largest credit, though, goes to Caroline Davis, who treats acne in my office and whose continued support, advice, research and editing were invaluable as the work on the manuscript progressed.

I am grateful to Bobbie Diebold, who originally suggested I put my ideas about acne treatment into a book, and to Grey Darden, Cheryon Inglehart, Juelie Loftin and Gerard J. Hassenfratz, M.D., for encouragement and help at the beginning of the project.

During the evolution of the manuscript, the faith, confidence and patience of my parents, Clara and Norbert, and of my wife, Sandy, were indispensable to my efforts. They — as much as anyone — are responsible for the completion of this book. Lorane Lee deserves special thanks for her support. Marion Wolff's enthusiasm and writing experience were important in the organization and development of portions of the manuscript. Marjorie Jannotta, Joyce Graf, Nancy Clingan, Mary Barnes, Eva Rollins, Judy Brauner and Henry G. Coors IV contributed with suggestions and criticisms. I wish to thank Rhoda Weyr, of the William Morris Agency, for all her assistance.

I am indebted to the following dermatologists who gave freely and generously of their time to read the manuscript and offer suggestions: Philip C. Anderson, M.D.; Larry E. Becker, M.D.; Cary M. Barnes, M.D.; Alan C. Blaugrund, M.D.; Gary J. Brauner, M.D.; Robert C. Clingan, M.D.; Samuel L. Fort, M.D.; Lawrence J. Gaughan, M.D.; Jack Graham, M.D.; Charles F. Merwin, M.D.; Joel D. Nash, M.D.; Ralph F. Powell, M.D.; Edgar B. Smith, M.D.; James J. Stagnone, M.D.; and Darl E. Vander Ploeg, M.D.

Pediatrician Richard Green, M.D., critiqued the manuscript and educator Ronald Fuchs circulated it among young teenage students.

Kenneth R. Pelletier, Ph.D., with his excellent book, *Mind as Healer, Mind as Slayer*, inspired the section on stress. David E. Bresler, Ph.D., and Barbara B. Brown, Ph.D., gave of their time and expertise to further advise me about that section.

Monique Davis deserves special thanks for the excellent illustrations. Brenda Castello and Isabel Reno spent long hours patiently deciphering my scribbling and expertly typing and retyping the manuscript through the many revisions.

Genevieve Young, Senior Editor at Little, Brown, was most helpful and a pleasure to work with. She is responsible for significantly improving the content and readability of this book. Betsy Pitha's copyediting was thorough and expert.

I cannot forget Don and Pat Hatfield, who helped at critical times.

K.L.F.

Contents

1

To the Reader

No matter how old you are, this book will help you if:

- you suffer from *any* skin blemishes — whether severe acne, or just a few blackheads;
- you have treated your acne before, but your skin is still breaking out;
- you want a safe, simple, inexpensive treatment you can do at home with preparations you can buy without a prescription;
- you want a treatment that is virtually 100 percent effective.

The treatment program explained in this book is based on scientific facts; by following the directions you can virtually guarantee yourself success in treating your acne.

Your goal in following the program should be complete clearing.

You must take two steps to achieve this goal:

First, you should read the whole book so that you can understand the causes of acne. Successful treatment is based on a thorough understanding of how blemishes form so preventive measures can be applied intelligently.

Second, you must carry out the treatment program consistently. This program can completely clear your skin, but it is not magic. If you fail to continue treatment faithfully for the period of time required, the program will not work. On the other hand, if the treatment is followed diligently you can expect to clear all your skin blemishes: blackheads, whiteheads, pimples and even the large red bumps that look like boils.

There is simply no reason to accept pimples as a fact of life — something you have to live with and can't do anything about. All it takes is the desire to be free of the disease and a determination to learn the treatment and carry it through.

If you really want to, you can fight acne and win!

2

Answers to Some Questions You Might Have

Q: I have just a few pimples and blackheads. Do I have acne?

A: Yes, you do. Acne varies in severity, ranging from just a few blemishes or an occasional "breakout" to the severe cases with large red bumps and cysts covering large areas of the face, chest and back. Blackheads, whiteheads, pimples, red bumps and cysts are all part of the disease process called acne, and, as you will learn, all these different types of blemishes begin in the same way. All types of blemishes are also stopped in the same way.

Q: Will I outgrow acne?

A: Acne is a disease, not just a normal stage of growth. It is a disease that affects the majority of adolescents — 86 percent of all adolescents have some degree of acne by the age of seventeen — and it *is* true that the disease tends to die out in the early twenties. But there are millions of exceptions to this general rule, and acne cannot be simply classified as a teenage disease that is outgrown; 43 percent of those who consult a doctor are over twenty and a third of American females between twenty and fifty have acne. Sometimes acne does not even begin until age thirty or forty, and I have had acne patients in their seventies.

Q: Will this treatment really clear my skin as completely as the girl's on the cover?

A: The girl on the cover has severe acne and, as you can see, even severe acne will clear with this treatment. Whether you have severe or mild acne, if you follow the directions in this book and treat your acne aggressively, you too should achieve *complete* clearing.

Q: I don't really have pimples — but I do get large blackheads — will this treatment help me?

A: Yes. This treatment prevents conditions that cause blackheads and whiteheads to form.

Q: I am thirty-two years old and I have had pimples since I was twelve. Is it ever going to stop? Will this book help me?

A: As already stated, your case is not unusual. This disease can last a long time. No one can tell you when the process will stop, but this book can and does tell you how to control acne — how to interrupt and block the process so that pimples no longer form.

Q: You talk only about the "control" of acne. What is the difference between "control" and "cure"?

A: When a disease is cured, you don't have it anymore. When a disease is controlled, you still have it but the signs and symptoms of the disease go away. While acne cannot be cured, controlling it is just as good as a cure for all practical purposes. When you control your acne, you have no pimples and no one will ever suspect you have acne.

Q: My son is twelve years old and just beginning to get a few pimples. Should he begin treatment?

A: Absolutely! The sooner the better! The treatment is much easier when started early. Severe acne begins as mild acne; the severity increases gradually and tends to peak three to five years after onset. Treatment should begin at the earliest signs of the disease.

Q: Can I really treat myself successfully with nonprescription acne preparations? I have tried some and they have never worked before.

A: Certain over-the-counter, nonprescription acne products are excellent and very effective. Others are nearly worthless. Even the effective ones have to be used correctly. This book will show you exactly how to do that.

Q: Is this treatment going to be a lot of work?

A: No, it is simple and easy. If you start early, it is *very* easy. And, no matter when you start, once you are clear, you may drastically reduce treatment to a maintenance level which is, again, very easy. If you are not starting early or if you already have severe acne, the initial treatment may require that you wash your face as frequently as four times a day and apply an acne medicine after each washing. Even this doesn't require much time and I encourage aggressive treatment at first because you achieve clearing faster.

Q: What about after I am clear? If I stop treatment, do the pimples come back?

A: They may, because, as already stated, this treatment is not a cure. But in my experience, no matter how severe the acne was before treatment, once cleared it is very easy to keep it cleared. Maintenance therapy is extremely easy, usually involving just one or two washings per day followed by application of some acne medicine. I will encourage you to do no more than you absolutely have to in order to stay clear.

Q: Until I am clear, what is the best makeup to use for covering up my acne?

A: It is best to use no makeup at all while you are fighting an active case of acne. Cover-up makeups usually contain oily and greasy substances that can actually *cause* acne. The acne you have today could, in fact, be due to the makeup you used to hide your acne three to six months ago. Don't camouflage your acne, clear it! However, see "Grease Is Out" in Chapter 6, if you feel you must wear some makeup.

Q: How long will it take for my face to clear?

A: With aggressive treatment, you should achieve control in three to eight weeks. Your control/ clearing time will be determined by: (1) how aggressively you treat and (2) the type of acne you have. After you have read Chapter 3, you will understand what I mean by "type of acne," and you will be able to understand the more detailed answer to this question given on page 108.

Q: My case is too severe. I have already been to four doctors and I still have acne. What can this book do for me?

A: You will probably find the reasons for past failures in these pages. Go back to one of the doctors and apply these principles to the medicines he or she prescribes. This time it will work!

Q: Is this book only for home treatment or can it be used along with my doctor's treatment?

A: It can be used either way. A recent study shows that 89 percent of people with acne never go to a doctor. Most of those people, however, are treating their acne at home, by themselves, with over-the-counter products. If you are one of those people, you will learn which products to buy and, more importantly, how to use them.

Q: Should I see a doctor about my acne?

A: The emphasis of this book is on home treatment, but there are many ways a doctor can help you. He or she can speed up clearing, especially if you have a severe case. A doctor can provide medicines and treatments too strong to be used without medical supervision. If you are an adult female who has suddenly developed acne, you should definitely consult a doctor (see page 56).

Q: Can I be sure I have acne?

A: There are other diseases that mimic acne in appearance but are not acne and must be treated differently. These other diseases are not nearly as common as acne, but they do occur. One clue is that if you have no blackheads and no closed comedones (the next chapter will show you how to identify closed comedones), you may not have acne. Some diseases that resemble acne :

Perioral dermatitis, a disease characterized by small red bumps around the mouth, but sometimes involving other parts of the face, looks a lot like acne. This disease occurs almost exclusively in females, has no comedones (defined in the next chapter), and frequently, unlike acne, itches.

Rosacea, a disease with redness *around* and *between* the pimples or on the nose, is frequently confused with acne. In acne, the redness is limited to the pimples themselves. Rosacea usually occurs in middle-aged or older individuals and affects only the face, and there are no or few comedones.

Ingrown hairs in the beard area of males with curly hair cause little bumps that are sometimes confused with acne.

There are additional diseases that may look like acne but they are even more uncommon. It is also possible to have two diseases: acne plus another disease. The treatment in this book works for common acne; it may not work for other diseases. If you are in doubt about the diagnosis, you should see a doctor.

Q: Will my doctor approve of the methods explained in this book?

A: Your doctor may be delighted that you have read this book — it makes the doctor's job easier. The methods in this book are based on scientifically sound, medically approved procedures and many doctors use these methods. There is nothing wild, untried or dangerous about this approach. Remember, though, that doctors are protective of their patients and are trained to be skeptical. Any doctor not familiar with this book will be skeptical. Appendix A is written specifically for doctors and summarizes the book in medical terminology.

Q: How do I know this treatment will work?

A: You won't until you try it. If you have been repeatedly disappointed, it is only natural to be skeptical. I can only tell you that I have been treating acne as a dermatologist for over eleven years and that I have used this approach for the last eight years on thousands of acne patients. I have also tried every other medically approved approach to treatment. I am now thoroughly convinced that the best treatment for acne is the one explained in this book.

3

What You Need to Know about Your Acne

Why This Chapter Is Important

Acne frequently lasts six years; ten years is not uncommon; and some people have it for as long as thirty or forty years. Almost no one can afford constant professional guidance for that length of time. Therefore, your best bet is to understand the disease so you can control it yourself.

This book explains the fastest, safest, most effective and least expensive way to treat acne. The treatment program is based on understanding. The purpose of this chapter is to give you the facts that you need in order to understand your disease.

If you are the impatient type and anxious to get on with the treatment, you may skip to Chapter 5 and start on the program. But be sure to come back to this chapter and the one that follows. There are no complicated concepts to learn and nothing to memorize. A comprehensive explanation of the physiology of the skin is not necessary. Only necessary facts are included here.

Even if you go to a doctor and even if you go as often as once a week, the process that causes acne occurs on a daily basis. Almost everything you do in your daily activities can affect your acne. Without knowing it, you may be doing things that make the doctor's treatment less effective and more difficult than need be. You are a partner with your doctor in attacking this disease and you want to be a good teammate.

By understanding the disease you will understand the treatment and you won't waste time and money on ineffective remedies.

There is much misinformation circulating about acne. The disease and its treatment often seem very mysterious. To eliminate myths, misinformation and mystery, you need know only a few facts.

By learning a few basic facts about this disease, you can become an expert at treatment. Remember that the goal is *complete clearing*, not mere improvement. To accomplish that goal, you can't make a lot of mistakes. You have to know what you are doing.

Normal Skin

Your skin is composed of basically two layers, as shown in Figure 1. The bottom layer is called the *dermis* and the top or surface layer is called the *epidermis* (the prefix *epi* means "over").

The epidermis provides us with a tough outer covering and protects us from the outside world. The dermis contains blood vessels, nerves, sweat glands, oil glands and follicles. The supporting structure of the dermis, the stuff that holds it together known as

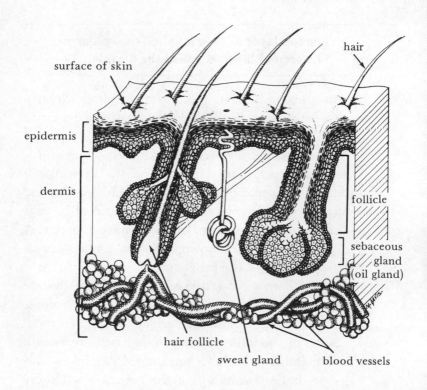

Figure 1
Normal Skin

connective tissue, is not shown in the illustration. All the blank white spaces are not really empty but are filled with connective tissue.

> **The top layer of skin is called the epidermis. The second layer is called the dermis.**

Sweat glands have their own openings directly onto the surface. These holes at the surface are too tiny to see.

The oil glands, however, deliver their oil into follicles (commonly called pores) and the openings of follicles are sometimes large enough to see. For the purpose of understanding your acne, realize that follicles go deeper than you may have thought. A follicle is hollow, as shown in Figure 2, and goes all the way down to the oil gland.

The oil comes out of the oil gland into the follicle and flows outward through the follicle until it comes out the other end onto the surface.

Some of the follicles contain hair and are known as hair follicles. Follicles are shaped like tubes, and in one that contains a hair the tube wraps closely around the hair. That gives you some idea of how small follicles are.

In medical terminology, oil glands are called sebaceous glands. They produce an oily or greasy substance known as sebum. The oil may act to lubricate the surface of the skin and the hair, if the follicle contains a hair. Oil glands are shown in the illustration in cross-section — as they would appear when

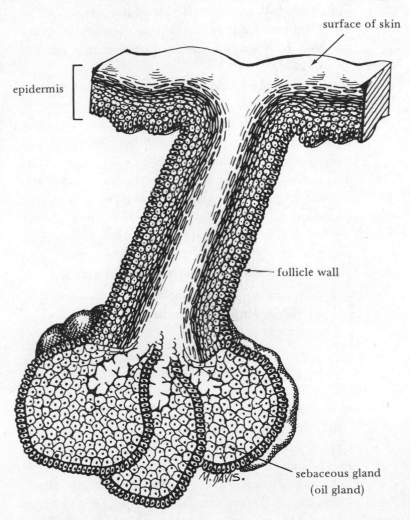

Figure 2
Normal Follicle and Sebaceous Gland

cut through the middle. If you could dissect out an oil gland and see it in three dimensions, you would see that it is shaped like an upside-down head of cauliflower.

Oil glands are found in the skin over most areas of the body. They are tremendously concentrated in areas where acne commonly occurs: the face, back and chest. There can be as many as 2,000 oil glands per square inch in some areas of skin on the face! They are also very numerous on the back and chest, but not as plentiful as on the face. The sebum (oil) excretion rate on the forehead is five times that of the back. There are oil glands on the arms and legs but not nearly as many as on the face, back and chest. The palms and soles have no oil glands.

> **Oil glands empty into follicles. Follicles are commonly called pores.**

Now, let's take a closer look at the epidermis and the walls of the follicles. As Figure 2 shows, the walls of the follicles are extensions of the epidermis. The epidermis simply turns in to line the follicles. The circled area in Figure 3 shows an even greater magnification of a small section of epidermis or follicle wall. The cells at the surface are flat and dead. These dead cells are constantly falling off and being replaced by new ones moving up from below. These new cells are born in the very bottom or deepest part of the epidermis, the basal layer. As new cells are thus formed, they push their neighbors upward and

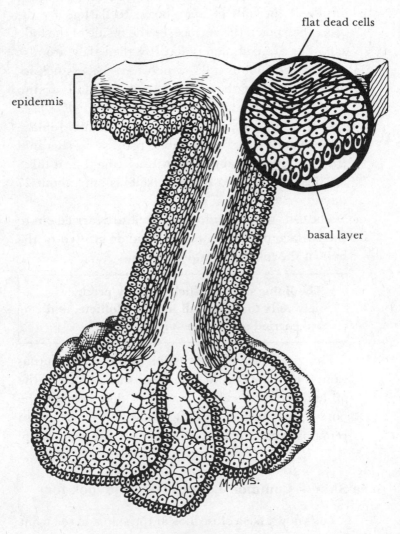

Figure 3
Enlargement of Epidermis

outward. As they approach the top of the skin, or the inside of the follicle, they begin to flatten. By the time they reach the surface, or the inside of the follicle, they are completely flat. By then they are also dead. These lining cells, which have been stuck together, now lose their attachments and fall off into space or into the follicle.

In this manner, the lining cells constantly replace themselves. This replacement process is so rapid that the "epidermal turnover time" (the time it takes for the epidermis to replace itself) is only about 27 days.

The cells that fall into the follicle are carried out to the surface by the flow of oil and/or growth of the hair, if the follicle contains a hair.

> **The lining of the follicle rapidly produces new cells that die, fall into the follicle, and are carried out to the surface.**

This concludes the discussion of the normal situation. It is important to remember that as long as the oil and the dead cells continue to flow through the pore to the surface, nothing bad happens. The skin remains completely normal and pimples do not form.

Acne Skin — Common Lesions (What to look for)

Let's now take a close look at the skin and see what happens to cause acne. Acne occurs when a follicle becomes plugged.

Every type of acne blemish, no matter how severe or how large, begins in a follicle. That is, all pimples, all blackheads, all whiteheads, all large red bumps and all cysts start in follicles. All these types of lesions, everything that happens in acne, begins with the plugging or clogging of a follicle. The word *lesion*, as used in this book, means any type of acne blemish.

Acne is a disease of plugged follicles.

It is known that within a follicle affected by acne, the sebaceous or oil glands are large and overactive. This results in the production of more sebum or oil. The excess oil can frequently be seen or felt on the surface of the skin. Therefore, people associate acne with oiliness of the surface. As a general rule, this is a valid association, but there are exceptions. An acne condition is usually, but not always, accompanied by oiliness of the surface.

Some people whose skin is very oily on the surface do not get acne; conversely, some people who feel dry on the surface get a lot of pimples.

How can this make any sense?

Acne occurs only when the oil doesn't get out!

Microcomedo (comedo, pronounced kom-ee-doe)

In acne, the dead cells and oil do not flow smoothly out of the follicle to the surface. Instead of

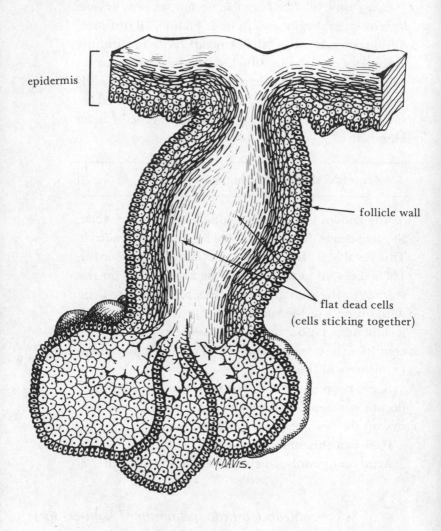

epidermis

follicle wall

flat dead cells
(cells sticking together)

M. DAVIS.

Figure 4
Microcomedo

falling apart, the cells stay stuck together and begin to build up along the wall of the follicle. The follicle wall thickens. When this happens it spells trouble. *This is how all acne starts.* This process will eventually completely plug the follicle with dead cells and oil. Figure 4 shows how the plug looks when it first starts forming. While the follicle is not yet completely plugged at this stage, pressure from the oil and dead cells has already caused the follicle walls to bulge.

All acne starts when the cells that line the follicle remain stuck together. This is the beginning of a process that will plug the follicle.

These beginning plugs are tiny. You can't even see them with the naked eye. They are microscopic in size and are not red; that is, they are not inflamed. These are baby pimples, the earliest zits.

Dermatologists call acne plugs *comedones* (singular, *comedo*). Since an early plug is so tiny that it requires a *micro*scope to see it, it is called a *micro*comedo.

These developing plugs are extremely important in terms of understanding the treatment program. Microcomedo formation is the single most important concept to remember about acne. The primary reason the treatment program outlined in this book is so successful is that it stops these plugs from developing. Stop microcomedones and you have whipped acne!

Acne begins with the buildup of dead cells along the inner wall of the follicle. If the acne process were to stop after the development of microcomedones, there would never be any ugly pimples since microcomedones are not visible.

Unfortunately, the process does not stop. New cells are constantly being made in the basal layer and, therefore, the buildup of dead cells continues.

It is interesting that pimples do not form in follicles that contain large hair (such as beard or mustache hair). Pimples form only in follicles that contain no hair or only tiny "peach-fuzz" hair. Apparently, if the follicle is filled with a large hair, the outward growth of the hair drags the oil and dead cells with it.

Closed Comedo

As dead cells and oil continue to build up along the wall of the follicle, they cause the walls to bulge more; what was originally a tube-shaped follicle balloons into a tiny round ball, as shown in Figure 5. Eventually the ball becomes large enough so that evidence of it may be seen on the surface even without a microscope. It appears as a very small skin-colored or slightly white bump. It is still not red (not inflamed) and, therefore, not very noticeable. Sometimes these are more easily felt than seen and

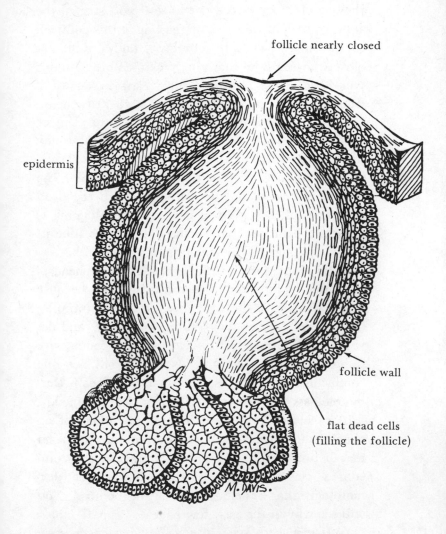

follicle nearly closed

epidermis

follicle wall

flat dead cells
(filling the follicle)

M. DAVIS.

Figure 5
Closed Comedo

they are frequently easier to see if you stretch the skin. You might wish to stop reading at this point, go to the mirror, stretch your skin, and examine it closely to see how many tiny skin-colored bumps you have. They are very important in terms of treatment and you need to be able to identify them.

These little bumps usually do not get any bigger than 2 mm (about the size of a pinhead), and it may take them months to get that big. Thousands of cells have to build up before they become visible. The follicle is now completely plugged with the dead cells and oil. But, as you can see, the plugging is *beneath* the surface, *within* the follicle. The tube itself gets plugged — not the opening of the tube.

Some people call these little bumps "whiteheads." I feel that "whitehead" is a confusing term because it is also used to describe other forms of pimples. (Red pimples, after they "come to a head" and develop a yellow or white cap in the center, are sometimes called whiteheads.) To avoid possible confusion, I will not use the term whitehead. Dermatologists call this type of plug a closed comedo.

It is "closed" because there is not much of an opening at the surface. In fact, even in the big ones it may be impossible to see the opening. Closed comedones cause lots of trouble. One clever dermatologist has labeled them "time bombs." You will see why in the next few pages.

You can already see why *you should never squeeze a closed comedo*. The opening at the top is essentially closed and you will not be able to force it open by squeezing. Instead, you may force the comedo to burst beneath the surface. You may force the contents so deep into the skin that when it finally heals, you will be left with a scar.

> **As the plug grows, it may become big enough to be visible on the surface.**

Open Comedo (Blackhead)

With continual accumulation of oil and dead cells within the follicle, sometimes the hole at the top is slowly stretched open (Figure 6). As the opening thus enlarges, one can easily see the opening and the follicle appears filled with a dark cheesy substance. The common name for this is blackhead; doctors call it an open comedo. The cheesy stuff inside is primarily dead cells and sebum. There are bacteria there also, but these will be discussed later (page 157).

The dark color at the top of a blackhead is not dirt. *Blackheads are not due to being unclean.* The dark color is simply due to the normal pigment (melanin) that is present in the skin. Active melanin-producing cells are present only in the upper part of the follicle so only the top is black. The color of open comedones tends to parallel skin color: it is white in albinos and darkest in dark-skinned people. Part of the color may be due to oxidation of sebum, but it is not dirt! Also, washing alone is not the answer to treating black-

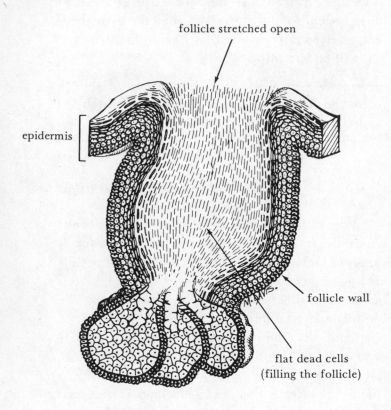

follicle stretched open

epidermis

follicle wall

flat dead cells
(filling the follicle)

Figure 6
Open Comedo (Blackhead)

heads. They extend 2 to 3 mm (⅛ inch) below the surface, and, therefore, washing alone will not get rid of them.

Because the hole at the top of a blackhead is open, one can usually successfully squeeze out the contents. But this is painful and it does not eliminate the blackhead. Since the wall of the follicle remains and continues to produce new cells (which again stick together in a diseased follicle), the blackhead re-forms — it fills up again in a month or so. If you feel you must attack it, the safest way to empty a blackhead is with the use of a "comedo extractor," which is available at your local pharmacy. Be careful, and, if the contents do not come out easily, don't force it. If you are going to do this, I urge you to wait until you have been treating your skin a few weeks. The contents will then come out a lot more easily.

Blackheads form as a result of continual growth of the plug.

By the time a blackhead can be seen it may already be several months old. The appearance of a blackhead tells us that a tiny invisible plug was there perhaps as long ago as six months. Knowing this, we are then concerned about how many other plugs have already started. How many micro-comedones and closed comedones are present? Since it is much easier to prevent these plugs from forming than it is to unplug them once they are formed, it is time to start treatment. You can now see why an eight-year-old who has only a few blackheads should nevertheless start treatment immediately.

Now you are an expert on comedones (plugs). You know exactly how they form, and you know that there are three types:

1. Microcomedo (invisible)
2. Closed comedo (sometimes visible)
3. Open comedo = blackhead (visible)

Inflamed Papule (Small Red Bump)

We dermatologists do not like comedones — especially closed comedones — because we know what's coming next. However, most of my patients, before they become experts, become concerned only about lesions that are more noticeable: the red inflamed bumps.

What makes a hateful, conspicuous, bright red pimple?

Inflammation!

What causes inflammation?

The follicle explodes! It pops like a balloon. With a continual buildup of oil and dead cells inside the follicle, something eventually has to give. So the follicle wall sometimes ruptures and the dead cells, bacteria, sebum and tiny hair get out of the follicle and into the dermis, as shown in Figure 7. This is the first time the acne process gets *inside* the body. Before this, everything has been occurring outside the

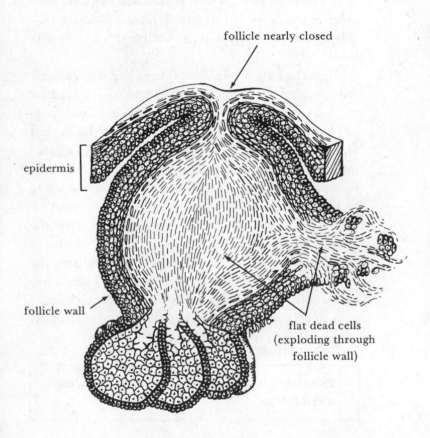

Figure 7
Inflamed Papule (small red bump)

body since the follicle wall is nothing more than an indentation of the epidermis. Acne starts on the outside and inflammation does not occur until it gets inside.

When the follicle explodes things begin to get serious, and the dermis gets redhot and angry because the bacteria, dead cells, sebum and hair simply do not belong there. They are "foreign" to the dermis and the dermis becomes inflamed. As part of this inflammatory process, microscopic blood vessels in the area get bigger, or dilate, so that more white blood cells can be brought to the scene to clean up the mess. White blood cells engulf and destroy the cells, sebum and bacteria. The increase in the size of the blood vessels, bringing more blood cells to the area, is what makes it red. These red bumps are called inflamed papules. A papule is a "small bump" to a dermatologist; but to some of my patients it seems more like a mountain.

> **Eventually a follicle may explode, producing a red bump.**

These red bumps should never ever be squeezed. They *do not* heal faster if you squeeze them; in fact, they heal more slowly. You never get out pus, you only force the bump to bleed. And, most importantly, you force the bacteria, dead cells and oil deeper into the skin, which tremendously increases the chance of scarring. Leave them alone!

Inflamed papules frequently develop out of closed comedones. In spite of the fact that the follicle is already filled with dead cells and oil and the walls are bulging, the walls just keep making new cells. But there is no room for these cells so one of two things happens: the opening at the top may be forced open, creating a blackhead, or the wall simply breaks down. Closed comedones frequently "explode" in this way, and that is why they have been called time bombs. They may sit there for months not doing anything and then suddenly the clock runs out and they blow up into full-fledged, bright red pimples. When multiple closed comedones choose to do this at the same time, the results can be quite shocking.

Inflamed papules sometimes develop from blackheads, but not as commonly as from closed comedones. It is not all bad news if you have a lot of blackheads. Sometimes blackheads just stay blackheads and never become inflamed. In blackheads, there is an escape route open and the contents can get out through the hole at the top. If you have a lot of blackheads, it means that your follicle walls are tough; they don't rupture easily. If they ruptured easily, they would never have become blackheads. So there is at least some good news for you if you have lots of blackheads, in that you have a certain resistance to the development of red pimples, which are more noticeable.

On the other hand, people whose acne consists mostly of inflamed papules usually don't have many blackheads. Such individuals have follicle walls that break down easily and, therefore, blackheads rarely form. In other words, there is an inverse relationship between the number of blackheads and the number of pimples.

It is also possible for inflamed papules to develop directly from microcomedones. From observing thousands of acne patients, I have the impression that sometimes microcomedones can convert to inflamed papules rapidly. Exactly what causes the wall to rupture in such cases remains undiscovered. Further research may give us the answer soon. Obviously, the plug does not need to become so large as to be visible before it ruptures.

Pustule (Small Red Bump with Yellow Cap)

When a comedo ruptures, white blood cells move into the area and begin ingesting the dead cells, oil and bacteria. Pus then forms (pus is merely white blood cells plus the products formed as a result of the interaction of the white blood cells with the bacteria, sebum, cells, and so on). With the formation of pus, the pimple sometimes comes to a head. It gets "ripe." The pus rises to the top and you then have a red bump with a yellow cap. This is called a pustule and is illustrated in Figure 8. When this happens, it is usually the end stage; the last thing to happen before healing occurs. This is a mature pimple.

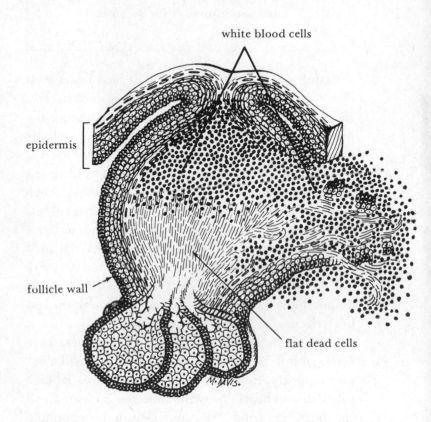

white blood cells

epidermis

follicle wall

flat dead cells

M·DAVIS.

Figure 8
Pustule (small red bump with yellow cap)

> **Red bumps sometimes come to a head, forming a pustule.**

Pustules can be drained and will heal faster as a result, but you must be careful if you do this. You should first sterilize a needle and then puncture the pustule in the center. (You can sterilize a needle by holding the tip over a flame, but don't forget to let it cool.) Make the hole exactly in the center of the yellow cap, where the epidermis is quite thin. Then squeeze *very gently*. You will get out a little bit of pus and you must be satisfied with what comes out easily. Don't force it. Keep the fingers at least ¾ inch apart from each other, so that any exerted pressure will be in an outward direction. You don't want to do anything that might force the dead cells, oil and bacteria deeper! Don't use your fingernails.

By removing some of the pus in this manner, there is less of it to be absorbed and the pustule will clear more quickly. But even without doing this the pustule will still heal. The white blood cells clean up all the bacteria, dead cells and sebum by engulfing them, destroying them and carrying them away. This may sometimes take weeks or months, during which time there may still be a bump there and it still may be red. Once all the foreign material has been removed, healing occurs when new connective tissue forms to fill the space. It may heal quite well and end up looking completely normal again, or it may heal to form a scar (see page 45).

As you have probably observed, some papules heal without ever becoming pustules. In these cases, the break in the wall was probably only a small one, with so little material leaking into the dermis that the white blood cells quickly cleaned it up and there was no noticeable formation of pus.

Acne Skin — More Serious Lesions

You now know everything you need to know to become truly expert at acne treatment. You have seen how all pimples originate as tiny invisible plugs within the follicles. Since the treatment is primarily aimed at preventing those early plugs, you will never have to deal with any of the things that follow; so if you are impatient, you may skip the rest of this chapter.

However, we have not yet discussed *all* the things that can happen in acne. Some acne may develop into more serious problems — for example, large red bumps that may look like boils and stay around for months. Once these have formed it is difficult to treat them at home. You would be better off going to a doctor. Dermatologists, as a general rule, are more knowledgeable and up-to-date on acne treatment than are other doctors. However, certain other doctors, particularly some family practitioners and pediatricians, are true experts at the treatment of acne. Even if you have very large red bumps and even if they have already been there a long time, doctors have special procedures to make them go away.

But if professional help is unavailable to you, don't despair! You can still manage your disease. Even the very largest acne lesions, with very rare exceptions, disappear eventually. *And you can stop the development of new ones!* As the old ones gradually shrink and go away, your skin will become completely clear.

Even the more serious lesions that occur in acne start out as microcomedones.

Nodule (Large Red Bump)

Where do these larger, more chronic lesions come from? They begin in exactly the same way as all the other lesions I have already explained. A nodule is simply a giant papule; the only difference is size. When there is a large break in the follicle wall and a lot of the foreign material gets into the dermis, you get a large red bump instead of a small red bump. A nodule feels firm when you touch it. *You should never ever squeeze a nodule.* A nodule will probably heal by scarring anyway, and if you squeeze it, you practically guarantee the scar will be deeper and larger.

Cyst

As the inflammatory process proceeds within a nodule it becomes soft. Pus has formed, making the contents somewhat liquid, and at this point it is no longer called a nodule. It looks and feels like a boil. Doctors call this type of lesion a cyst. It is true that a cyst will heal faster if the pus is drained, but this is best left to a doctor or nurse. In order to get all the pus out one must make quite a large incision into the cyst, and by doing so, you risk scarring (from the incision) and it may bleed profusely. *Leave cysts alone.* Go to a doctor if you have acne with cysts.

Secondary Comedo

Another thing can happen after a comedo ruptures. The ends of the follicle wall may grow out and join again, thus enclosing the material that has leaked into the dermis (Figure 9). The same process occurs with the surface epidermis when it grows back together after being cut. You have seen this happen as cuts heal. If the ends of the follicle wall meet, the lesion is once more entirely encapsulated and is called a secondary comedo. This type of comedo has an eccentric shape that reveals where the blowout occurred. If you have a red bump (inflamed papule) and you think it is healing because the redness goes away, but you then discover that a bump

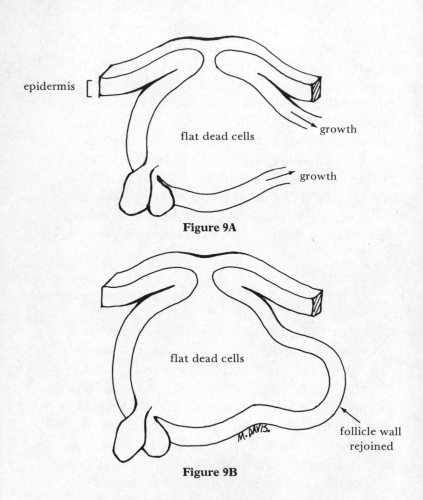

epidermis

flat dead cells

growth

growth

Figure 9A

flat dead cells

follicle wall
rejoined

Figure 9B

Secondary Comedo

remains, a secondary comedo has formed. This is a type of closed comedo and should not be squeezed.

Polyporous Comedo

A polyporous comedo is a type of secondary comedo with more than one opening to the surface. These form when adjacent comedones blow out and the blowouts face each other. As the follicle walls grow out, they may meet and join as shown in Figure 10. This is a permanent lesion and can only be treated surgically. More than two comedones may be involved in this process and the entire lesion may be quite large.

Sinus Tract

If a polyporous comedo ruptures and becomes inflamed, it may drain pus for a long time. It heals very, very slowly. It is then called a sinus tract or draining sinus.

Pitted Scar

If the break in the wall of the follicle is very close to the surface of the skin and is not large, it will probably heal without a scar. However, if the break in the wall is large and deep, scarring is likely.

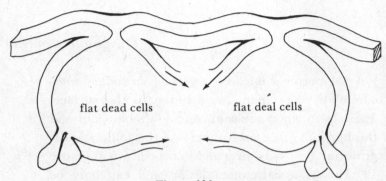

flat dead cells   flat deal cells

Figure 10A

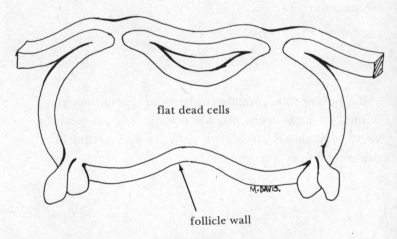

flat dead cells

follicle wall

Figure 10B

Polyporous Comedo

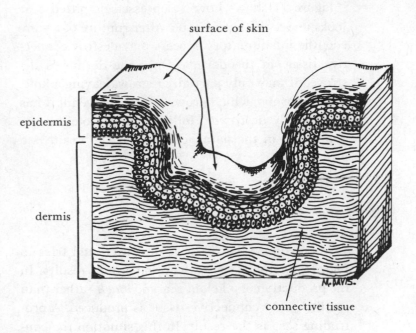

Figure 11
Pitted Scar

Whether or not a scar forms is partially determined by luck since some people simply heal better than others.

Figure 11 shows how a depressed or pitted scar looks under the microscope. After rupture of a comedo, the inflammatory process may destroy connective tissue in the dermis. Once the dermis is destroyed it may only partially regrow, leaving a hole. The epidermis, which grows out again even if it has been totally destroyed, follows the contours of the depression in the damaged dermis. The result is a pitted scar.

Keloid Scar

When connective tissue is destroyed and tries to regrow, another type of scar sometimes results. In the production of a keloid scar *too much* rather than too little new connective tissue is produced. A protruding scar is the result. In this situation the connective tissue overdoes the healing process and doesn't know when to stop. The tendency for this type of scarring is greater in people with dark skin.

Buried Scar

Sometimes when a comedo ruptures, the white blood cells do not engulf and destroy all the foreign material that has leaked into the dermis. Instead, scar tissue or remnants of the follicle wall may encircle and wall off the foreign material. A bump then forms beneath the surface of the skin and, unfortunately, it is permanent. The only treatment is surgical removal.

4

What Causes Acne: Fact versus Fiction

Now you know exactly how pimples form. You have followed their development from birth to maturity. All the necessary background information needed to understand the treatment is now yours. But you may be asking:

- What *starts* the process leading to pimple formation?
- Is there something I am doing to cause my acne?
- Why do I have acne at age thirty-five?
- Does my acne mean I have a hormone imbalance?
- If I eat chocolate or french fries, will I get acne?
- Does masturbation cause acne?
- What effect do birth control pills have on acne?
- Is acne due to "nerves" — is it an emotional problem?

This chapter will answer all those questions, and others, by explaining how certain factors may or may not play a role in acne.

Heredity

Is acne a hereditary disease? Did you get it from Mom or Dad? Or Grandpa? Very likely. As a general rule, your chances of developing *severe* acne are increased if one or both parents had (or have) *severe* acne, but many exceptions occur. Severe acne can be found as well among offspring of parents who never had a noticeable acne problem.

The hereditary factors involved in acne are so widespread throughout the population that almost everyone gets at least a few pimples. Hereditary factors can more easily be studied in diseases such as diabetes or asthma because only a small percentage of people get those diseases. Since almost *everyone* gets pimples at some time in their lives, what can be said about heredity? Don't waste time feeling guilty about giving your kids acne, and don't waste time blaming Mom and Dad for your acne problem. Spend your time treating it and clearing it instead.

It is difficult to evaluate the hereditary aspects of such a prevalent disease.

Sex Hormones

Myths regarding acne have been common for a long time. For hundreds of years people thought that marriage and sexual intercourse cured acne. Millions of married men and women with acne would like that myth to be true, but of course it isn't. It is interesting that this notion was not *scientifically* disproved until 1949 (!), when it was conclusively shown that acne does not get better following sexual intercourse. This disease is not caused by a lack of sexual activity!

> **Acne is not caused by unfulfilled sexual desires.**

The truth of the matter is that a sex hormone called *androgen* does indeed play a leading role in the development of acne, but that role has not been found to be related to sexual activity.

Androgen is the hormone primarily responsible for normal male sexual development, but all normal females also have androgen. This hormone is absolutely necessary for acne to develop (eunuchs do not get acne), and only a very small amount of androgen is needed. Androgen's role in acne is to stimulate the sebaceous (oil) glands, causing them to produce more oil. It does this in all people, male and female. Before puberty, sex hormone production increases dramatically and, therefore, the oil glands are stimulated. They grow larger and begin producing increased amounts of oil. Increased oil sets the stage for the development of acne.

Now you can understand what causes the relationship between puberty and acne — the great increase in sex hormones. But this increase is not abnormal. This happens to everyone! Since girls tend to reach puberty earlier than boys, they also tend to develop acne sooner. All you need for acne to develop is the normal amount of androgen. And, for females, having acne almost never means that a hormone imbalance exists.

One exception must be noted. Androgen-producing tumors in mature women can cause an acute onset of acne and the acne may be quite severe. Therefore, an adult female who suddenly develops a significant acne problem should consult a physician, especially if other signs of excess androgen appear, such as menstrual irregularities, appearance of facial or chest hair, loss of scalp hair or enlargement of the clitoris. The acne may precede these other abnormalities and could be the first sign of an androgen-producing tumor in the adrenal glands or ovaries. Such tumors are quite rare, but when they occur, it is helpful to make the diagnosis early. Again, for emphasis, if you are an adult female who develops acne, the safe thing to do is consult a physician.

Birth control pills contain sex hormones and can, therefore, play various roles in acne. Since so many women take birth control pills and because some birth control pills are used to treat acne, I have devoted more attention to them later in the book (see page 169).

Masturbation

Absolutely no connection exists between masturbation and acne. Masturbation does not make acne better and masturbation does not make acne worse.

> **Masturbation does not cause or aggravate acne.**

Chocolate, Greasy Foods, Colas, and Such

Diet is a controversial subject in the treatment of acne. Doctors and parents have preached for years that chocolate, greasy foods, colas, dairy products, peanuts, and almost everything that tastes good cause acne. They apparently feel that if you put more fat and grease in the mouth, it will eventually find its way to the oil glands in the skin.

For years diet has been rated as one of the "stars" in the acne drama; a famous actor with a leading role as the villain. However, this role has not been convincingly portrayed in recent years, and many critics consider this actor a has-been. He should be allowed to retire quietly. Dietary restrictions are *not* necessary when treating acne. Chocolate, colas, french fries, and so on do not cause acne.

Doctors Gerd Plewig and Albert Kligman, who have researched this disease extensively and have published a book for doctors on acne, state that fats which enter the body through the mouth do not exit through the skin, and that the fats in the sebaceous glands do not resemble the fats in the blood. Even complete starvation will not shut off the sebaceous glands. These oil factories continue to produce despite almost any attempt to close them down.

I suspect that even those acne patients who are truly convinced that chocolate or french fries makes them break out frequently eat those things and nothing happens. But when there is no breakout, they forget that they ate a forbidden food a day or two earlier. The fact that they got away with eating chocolate may go unnoticed. However, if their acne should suddenly get worse, they might then think *back* to a day or two earlier and will frequently be able to remember doing something wrong . . . ah ha, there it is, those french fries from Mary's plate two days ago.

Doubt was first cast on the diet theory of acne at the University of Missouri in 1965. Doctors J. D. Grant and P. C. Anderson chose volunteers who agreed to eat a very large amount of chocolate. All of the volunteers were highly confident that chocolate made their acne worse. Before eating the chocolate, the subjects' faces were carefully charted to indicate the location and type of each acne lesion. Then on two successive days each of the individuals ate a 9¾-ounce chocolate bar (these were the very large bars, equivalent to about six of the regular-sized chocolate bars). In a 48-hour period they ate almost twenty ounces of chocolate. What do you think happened? To the surprise of the patients involved in the study, nothing! The expected flare did not occur.

Following that study, I did essentially the same experiment with peanuts. Again, nothing happened. Milk was also studied at the University of Missouri with the same result.

Some years later another experiment was performed at the University of Pennsylvania. Doctors Albert Kligman, James Fulton and Gerd Plewig fed chocolate bars containing ten times the amount of chocolate in a typical bar to both acne and nonacne subjects. Nothing happened to either group.

> **Chocolate, greasy foods, colas, etc., do not cause acne.**

Perhaps you have been fortunate and have never had an opportunity to see a list of foods acne patients have been forbidden. All of the following have been, at some time, blamed for acne:

Chocolate	Carrots
Fatty foods or fried foods	Egg yolk
Milk and dairy products — cheese, butter, ice cream, etc.	Alcoholic beverages, including beer
	"Sweets"
Cola drinks	Popcorn

Coffee	Shellfish
Nuts	Saltwater fish
Citrus fruits —	Spinach
Oranges	Cabbage
Lemons	Lettuce
Grapefruits	Artichokes
Limes	White bread
Tomatoes	Fats
Tomato catsup	Carbohydrates
Yellow vegetables	

It would be practically impossible and even dangerous to your health to avoid all the items on the above list. It is not necessary to avoid any of them. I never restrict a patient's diet, and the treatment still works.

If you don't have a weight problem or a medical problem that restricts food intake, don't punish yourself by unnecessary dietary restrictions because of your acne. But don't get all of your calories from chocolate bars and colas. That is unhealthful for other reasons. You have to pay attention to the nutritional value of the food you eat.

Oil and Grease

The following comments do not apply to dietary oil or greasy foods as discussed in the preceding section. What is meant here is the oil and grease that come in contact with the skin, oil and grease purposely or accidentally applied to the surface of the skin. It doesn't seem to matter how they get there; not only can they aggravate an already existing acne condition, they can actually *create* one. The evidence is overwhelming:

In the old days, parents rubbed camphorated oil on their young children because they thought it was healthful. Result: acne.

In India, mothers put certain vegetable oils on their children's bodies. Result: acne.

The scalps of certain Israeli immigrant children were repeatedly treated with a paraffin oil. Result: acne.

John had no pimples until he landed a part in a local theater production and began daily applications of greasy stage makeup. Result: explosive acne. Some stage makeups can be dynamite!

Certain jobs that involve oil coming into contact with the skin place the person at risk. For example, mechanics, machinists, refinery workers, and those who work with tar as in tarring road surfaces may get acne. So may short-order cooks, and it may be limited to the neck and jawline, where grease is more likely to splatter.

Oil and grease on the skin may cause or aggravate acne.

But, you may ask, how does this apply to me? I am

not a machinist, nor a short-order cook, nor a child in India or Israel.

Are you black? Are you male? Do you use greasy pomades on your hair? Do you have an acne problem on your forehead and temples?

Are you white? Do you sunburn? Do you use suntan *oil* to protect yourself from burning?

Do you use makeup to cover your blemishes? Is it a "water-base" makeup? Is it "greaseless" or "oil-free"? Do you use a moisturizer? Do you cleanse your face with "medicated cream" at night?

Many of us put oily and greasy substances on our skin without even thinking about it. Some of those things definitely plug pores and lead to acne. Since oily substances can sometimes be the cause of acne, as well as a reason for treatment failure, they will receive further attention in Chapter 6.

> **Ordinary moisturizers and makeups may cause or aggravate acne.**

Pressure

"Doctor, I have followed my treatment program and now my cheeks and forehead are clear, but I still get new ones on my chin." Why? "Doc, my shoulders started breaking out about the time school started." Why? There is a common denominator for these two patients that could also be a factor in your acne: *pressure* on the skin.

Your acne may have an unusual distribution or may persist in one particular area because it is being aggravated by external pressure. If you have a problem with "chin acne," you may find that you have a habit of resting your chin on your hand while studying or watching TV. A recurrence of acne on your shoulders or chin may coincide with the start of football season and the wearing of shoulder pads and helmet straps.

The exact mechanism whereby pressure causes acne is not known. Some doctors feel that friction rather than pressure is the important factor. I can understand how friction might cause existing comedones to rupture, but I doubt that friction would create new comedones. Pressure might. Pressure on the skin causes moisture to be retained in the surface skin cells. If the cells on the surface swell with the additional moisture, the size of the follicle opening would be reduced. The smaller the opening, the more difficult it is for the dead cells and oil to get out.

No matter what the mechanism, pressure *can* increase the number of pimples you may have in a particular area and slow down the rate of clearing, causing you more aggravation and frustration.

Do yourself a favor: tune into your habits to see if there isn't some pressure factor that you could eliminate. If you can't do that, perhaps you could at least minimize it.

You do not need to give up football, stop playing the violin, throw away your baseball cap, or quit using your backpack because of acne. Nor is it necessary for you to change a vocation that contributes to your acne.

You may find it necessary, however, to counter the damaging effect of the pressure factor in some way. This counterattack may include using stronger acne medicine, or applying the medicine more frequently to the affected area. This type of adjustment will be covered more completely later.

Pressure on the skin may cause or aggravate acne.

Drugs

Drugs are not a familiar or frequent actor in the acne drama, but they do sometimes play an important role in this disease. By "drugs," I mean medication being taken internally or applied topically (to the surface of the skin). Certain drugs can cause acne or can make an already existing acne condition worse. It is not within the scope of this book to discuss at length all the drugs that have been implicated in this disease, but I will discuss briefly those that have received the most publicity. The important thing to remember is that all acne, whatever its original cause, will respond to the treatment described in this book.

Cortisone and Its Derivatives

Cortisone is kind of a magic medicine. By acting as an anti-inflammatory agent, cortisone produces dramatic improvement in a wide variety of diseases. Therefore, this medicine is used frequently by almost all doctors. Cortisone is administered orally, intramuscularly (by injection) and topically (on top of the skin). It is injected directly into inflamed joints, or into diseased tissue as in bursitis.

One of the unwanted side effects of cortisone is acne, and it can occur fairly rapidly. I have administered a cortisone shot to an individual and seen that patient's existing acne condition flare within one week. Others have stated that it usually takes at least two weeks, more frequently a month. However long it takes, there is no question that cortisone can cause acne. This drug is sometimes the reason behind a sudden appearance of multiple pimples.

Even cortisone applied to the surface of the skin will cause acne, and the more potent the cortisone, the quicker the acne appears.

If a doctor has prescribed cortisone for you, and you observed a flare of acne, do not discontinue using the medication on your own. Consult your physician. In the meantime, start the treatment described in this book.

Iodides and Bromides

The role of iodides and bromides as causes of acne has become somewhat controversial. In the past it was thought that even small amounts of those substances could cause trouble. Some doctors even restricted the use of iodized table salt for their acne patients. However, all humans need a certain amount of iodine and it is comforting that most of the more recent evidence suggests that it requires very large amounts of iodide or bromide to cause acne. The amount that we routinely encounter in our food and water or in iodized salt is almost certainly not enough to induce acne.

However, some doctors still feel that any medication that contains iodides or bromides is a potential source of trouble. Nonprescription drugs that contain iodides or bromides are common and include certain cough medicines, sedatives, preparations for the common cold and pain relievers. Some doctors are concerned that kelp tablets, which contain iodine, can cause acne. If you are concerned about something you are taking, you can check the list of ingredients on the package. Just look for the words "iodide" or "bromide."

In my experience the role of iodides and bromides has been overplayed and I feel they are rarely a problem. I always ask my acne patients about what medications (prescription or nonprescription) they are taking, and in the thousands of acne patients I have treated I can recall only a handful in whom I thought iodides or bromides *might* be playing a role.

Birth Control Pills

Certain birth control pills cause or aggravate acne. These are discussed more fully in the special section on birth control pills on page 169.

Others

Other drugs have been implicated as a cause of acne, but in most of these cases it is more important to control the disease being treated than it is to have a clear complexion. For example, Dilantin, a drug used to control seizures, can cause acne. So can isoniazid (INH), a drug used to treat tuberculosis.

Even if some drug truly is causing your acne, don't despair. You can still treat it successfully.

Certain drugs such as cortisone may cause or aggravate acne.

Stress

Nancy, a very attractive thirty-year-old, came into my office one day because of a severe flare of her acne condition. She had been a patient previously, but had not been in for several months because she hadn't needed help. Initially, I could not explain Nancy's sudden flare. She had continued her maintenance-level treatment; no medicines had been changed and she had not skipped any treatments. She had not been exposed to anything such as theatrical makeup or acne-causing drugs. Only later, on a subsequent visit, did I learn that another kind of change had occurred in Nancy's life, a change that could have influenced the severity of her acne. Nancy had been dating David for several years and they had been engaged to be married. Just before her acne flared the two of them had encountered difficulties in their relationship, quarreled, and split up permanently.

Scott, a twenty-one-year-old university student, whose disease had been completely controlled for some time (he had not had any new acne lesions for four months), came in one day with about fifteen rather large red pimples on his face. Why? What had happened? Scott convinced me that he had not in any way decreased or slacked off his treatment. But he also told me that he had just finished a week of final examinations.

Lisa's acne had been difficult to treat but was eventually completely controlled and remained so for three months. Then she got a new job. The job required that she handle complaints from dissatisfied, sometimes irate, clients. At the same time, her acne flared and was again difficult to control until she acquired more confidence in her new position, and thus experienced less stress.

Examples such as these have convinced me that emotional stress (anxiety, worry, tension, psychological trauma, being "uptight") can sometimes play a very important role in the disease of acne. Additionally, my beliefs have been reinforced by patients who voluntarily tell me that they think stress is partially responsible for their disease. Some time ago I made an effort to document exactly what percentage of new acne patients felt stress to be a factor in their disease. When asked about it, 72 percent stated they had observed that at stressful times their disease seemed to get worse.

Stress may cause or aggravate acne.

To show you in terms of anatomy and physiology how the mind may play a role in this disease, I refer you to Figure 12.

At the lower portion of the brain is a small structure called the hypothalamus. This structure is influenced by other parts of the brain and in turn regulates the pituitary gland, which is the master gland of the body. The pituitary, through chemical messengers called hormones that travel through the bloodstream, controls other glands in the body, including the adrenal glands located just above the kidneys. When stress occurs, the hypothalamus stimulates the pituitary to produce more hormones. One of these hormones stimulates the adrenals to manufacture and release certain other hormones,

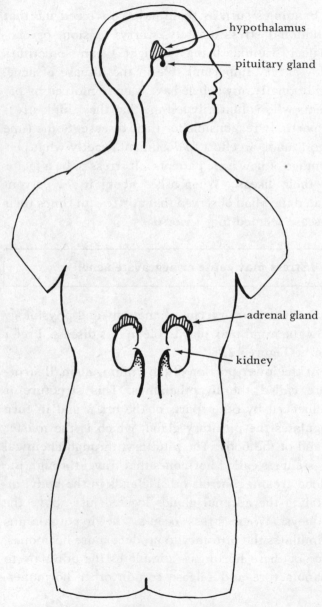

Figure 12

including the sex hormone androgen.

As we know (see page 55), androgen stimulates the sebaceous glands of the skin, causing them to grow and produce more oil, and thus add fuel to the acne process. It can be summarized diagrammatically:

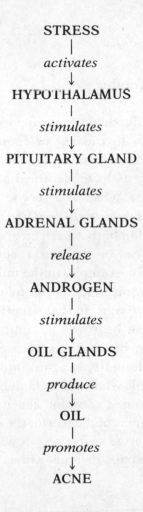

STRESS

|

activates

↓

HYPOTHALAMUS

|

stimulates

↓

PITUITARY GLAND

|

stimulates

↓

ADRENAL GLANDS

|

release

↓

ANDROGEN

|

stimulates

↓

OIL GLANDS

|

produce

↓

OIL

|

promotes

↓

ACNE

If you feel that stress is a big factor in your acne, you should attempt to reduce the stress, but otherwise the best treatment for your acne remains exactly as detailed in this book. The treatment works no matter what the cause of the acne.

Climate and Geography

No one really knows how important climate and geography are in causing or improving acne, because the evidence is mixed and conflicting.

Dermatologists have identified a condition called "tropical acne," which is a very severe form seen in areas of great *heat* and *humidity*. A lot of tropical acne occurred in both American and British soldiers in certain areas of the world during the Second World War. For example, in the military hospital in Guam, 20 percent of the dermatology patients were there *because of acne*. In that situation, however, factors other than heat and humidity — for example, pressure from backpacks and stress — have to be considered. Humidity is again implicated when we note that people who work in laundries, for example, seem more prone to develop acne.

In certain areas of the world, the incidence of acne has been reported to be very low, almost nonexistent. These areas include Korea, Peru, Ecuador,

Spain, Turkey, Eskimo villages and Okinawa. Is the reason climate? Heredity? Diet?

Most people with acne get better during the summer. Is the reason sunlight? Heat? Relaxation? Yet 20 percent of acne patients get *worse* during the summer. Why? We can speculate, but no one has the answer to these conflicting findings. We know that acne can frequently be treated successfully with ultraviolet light (or sunlight), so it is confusing when some acne sufferers get worse after a week at the beach. Suntan oil?

We have had a number of patients in the arid Southwest whose acne flared when they visited a place like Houston, which is much more humid. But the reverse has also occurred: people moving to Albuquerque from a much more humid environment may experience a flare of acne. Is this the psychological stress of the move? When the prevalence of acne in different areas of the United States was studied, it was found to be nearly the same all over the country.

As you can see, there are many unanswered questions and conflicting reports regarding the role of environment, climate and geography. Further research in this area is obviously needed.

Climate and geography may be important in acne, but evidence conflicts.

Dirt

If you have acne, you have probably been told a thousand times not to put your hands near your face, not to let your hair fall over your face, not to do anything that might bring dirt to your face. The notion that dirt causes acne is firmly ingrained in our society and leads to the mistaken belief that if you would merely wash your face often enough, you would not get pimples.

Washing affects only the surface and the disease is *beneath* the surface. Acne cannot be washed away.

> **Dirt does not cause acne.**

5

Your Own Home Treatment Program

Now Comes the Payoff

Now that you know exactly how pimples form, you are ready to start treatment. You know what's going on within your skin to cause pimples so it will be easy for you to understand how to interrupt and block the process. Now comes the payoff for the time you've taken to read this far.

So many people who are trying to treat their acne really have no clear-cut idea of what they're trying to accomplish. Their efforts are wasted because the steps to reaching their goal are ill-defined. When people do not understand the disease, they do not understand the treatment and consequently they fail. However, you are now in possession of all the pertinent facts about acne. As you treat yourself to complete clearing, you will know exactly what's going on every step of the way.

Remember, *you* must become the expert on *your* treatment. Take the time to read Chapters 5 through 8 carefully. They contain everything you need to know to rid yourself of pimples. You should be able to control your acne and keep your skin clear for the rest of your life.

Your Treatment in a Nutshell

The details of the treatment come next, but the basic principle involved can be explained here briefly.

You remember that acne is essentially a plugging disease, that the plugs all occur *within* follicles, and that the plugs are composed of mostly dead cells and oil. It is the sticking together of those dead cells that starts the process of plug formation. You have also learned that when the plug first begins forming, it is invisible (microscopic in size) and that it is called a microcomedo.

Suppose you could stop the formation of microcomedones? What would happen? Your acne would clear!

If you can keep the oil and dead cells moving out of the follicle and to the surface, then you reestablish the normal situation and *no pimples can form!* Remember, as long as the oil and dead cells get out, there's no problem.

How do you accomplish this?

It is actually very easy and requires very little time. You already wash your face. The only added thing you must do is apply an acne medicine after you wash. That requires only a few additional seconds of your time.

Sounds easy? It is! But you must use the proper medicine, the one just right for you, and you must use it correctly.

The effective acne medicines work because they contain chemicals that, when applied to the surface of the skin and rubbed in, get down *into* the follicle and break apart or peel apart those dead cells that are trying to stick together. The oil and dead cells can then flow out to the surface. Although you won't be able to see the peeling that is occurring deep within the follicles, you *will* be able to see the effects on the surface because the cells there will also be peeled apart. You will know the medicine is working as you observe the surface peeling.

These medicines prevent the formation of plugs and can even break up plugs that have already formed.

As you use your medicine, you will notice a "drying" of your skin. Since the effective medicines *dry* and *peel*, they are called Drying-Peeling (DP) agents. Doctors call these desquamating or exfoliating agents.

To fight acne and win, you must peel apart those dead cells that are sticking together within the pores.

Drying and peeling will not harm your skin in any way. It will not cause the skin to age faster, and it will *not* cause wrinkles. A full discussion of this matter will be found on page 126, "Peel Is In"; the important thing for you to understand here is that *dry-ness is the key to clearing your skin.*

Now let's go through your treatment program step by step.

Step One: Determine Your Skin Type

There are three factors you use to determine your skin type: oiliness, skin color, and severity of acne.

In estimating where you fall into each of these categories, don't worry about making a mistake. You only determine your skin type so you can advance to Step Two and intelligently select the strength of DP agent you will use to start your treatment. After you start, you can easily make adjustments. Even if you make a mistake, your selection will still be better than if you had blindly chosen an acne medicine from the drugstore shelves.

The following directions apply only to your face. Certain special considerations apply to the back and chest and will be discussed later.

Oiliness

Decide whether you have dry skin, oily skin or average skin. If your skin is very sensitive, easily irritated, dries out with ordinary soap and water, or if you have truly needed to use moisturizers to keep your skin from flaking, you have "dry" skin. If you have dry skin, circle number 1 below. On the other hand, if your skin feels slick as you rub your finger across your face, you have "oily" skin and you should circle number 3. Be sure you are not sweating when you do this as that will also make your skin feel slick. If you think you fall somewhere in between dry skin and oily skin, or if you are not sure, or if certain areas seem dry and other areas oily, call it "average." If you have average skin, circle number 2.

If your skin feels oily constantly, or if it feels oily again less than one hour after washing, or if it is so oily it actually looks shiny, call it "very oily" and circle number 4.

Dry 1
Average 2
Oily 3
Very oily 4

Skin Color

Now judge your skin color. For example, if your skin is very pale and sunburns easily rather than tans, if you have blond or red hair, if you have freckles, you have "light" skin. Circle the appropriate number on the next page. If you can't decide whether to call it "medium" or "dark," call it "medium."

```
Light ............... 1
Medium .......... ②
Dark  ............... 3
```

Severity of Acne

If you are just beginning to develop a few pimples, blackheads or closed comedones, call your acne "mild." If you have more than a few, you can, if you wish, actually count the number of lesions.

Counting can also be used as a log by which to measure your progress. But it has its limitations in that you cannot count existing microcomedones because they are invisible. Some of the microcomedones you have now will develop into papules and pustules.

Estimate the severity of your acne or count the lesions thus:

Date of Count_____

Number of closed comedones_____

Number of blackheads_____

Number of papules_____

Number of pustules_____

Number of nodules_____

Number of cysts_____

TOTAL LESIONS_____

If you have fewer than 10 total lesions on your face, your acne is "mild." If you have 10 to 30, call it "moderate." If you have more than 30, call it "severe." If you have even one large nodule or cyst, call it "severe." Circle the appropriate number below.

> Mild .... (1)
> Moderate 2
> Severe 3

You should have numbers circled under the three headings: *OILINESS*, *SKIN COLOR* and *SEVERITY*. Now total these numbers to determine your skin type.

For example, say your skin is easily irritated. You decided it was "dry," identified your skin color as "medium," and counted only six closed comedones, plus two pustules, on your face. Your skin-type determination would look like this:

OILINESS

> Dry ....(1)
> Average 2
> Very oily ... 4

SKIN COLOR

> Light 1
> Medium ...(2)
> Dark 3

SEVERITY

> Mild ....(1)
> Moderate 2
> Severe .. 3

OILINESS 1 + *COLOR* 2 + *SEVERITY* 1
= *SKIN TYPE* 4

Remember the number that represents *your* skin

type. You will use it to determine the strength of the DP agent you are going to start with.

Step Two: Select the Strength of Your DP Agent

One factor that will govern the strength of the DP agent you choose will be your skin type, which you have just determined. The other factor will be how often you are accustomed to washing your face each day.

Look at Chart 1. Read across it until you come to the number of times you are washing your face, then read directly down that column until you are across from the number that represents your skin type. The box you land on will tell you the strength of the DP agent suited to your particular needs. For example, if you are presently washing your face twice a day and you have skin type number 6, you will select a *moderate* DP agent.

Step Three: Purchase Your DP Agent

Now you know the *strength* of the DP agent you will start with. Individual products are ranked by groups according to strength in Chart 2 on page 88.

In order to help you find the product best suited to you out of the confusing welter of acne products of-

CHART 1

SELECTING THE STRENGTH OF YOUR DRYING-PEELING AGENT

Washings per Day

		1	2	3	4
	3	weak	*	*	*
	4	weak	weak	*	*
S **k** **i** **n**	5	moderate	weak	weak	*
	6	moderate	moderate	weak	weak
T **y** **p** **e**	7	strong	moderate	moderate	weak
	8	strong	strong	moderate	moderate
	9	strongest	strong	strong	moderate
	10	strongest	strongest	strong	strong

*This is too many washings per day for your skin type. To start with, you should decrease the number of times each day that you wash.

fered for sale, I mention specific products by brand name. Chart 2 is by no means inclusive; those listed are simply the products I have used in my practice and have had a chance to evaluate carefully — something I could not do for every acne product on the market. Other products, not listed, will be found to be equally effective. A method by which you can select a product not on my list, if you wish, is explained on page 94. Either purchase one of the products listed on page 88 or purchase an alternate product of equal strength.

The credit for ranking the products in order of strength goes to Caroline Davis, who has worked closely with me for the last three years and has treated over a thousand acne patients in my office. We are aware that, while the ranking may not be completely scientifically accurate, it should be helpful. Caroline arrived at this ranking by doing hundreds of "half-face" studies. That is, volunteers were asked to apply one product to the left side of their face and another product to the right side. We observed for surface peeling and the products were used until there was a clear-cut difference between the two sides. In this way each product was ranked according to strength.

We cannot guarantee absolute accuracy of this ranking in terms of relative strength of these products in any one given individual since there was some individual variation. We are also not implying that any of these products is either better or worse than another — it was merely more or less drying when Caroline tested it. Remember, those in the top category are not necessarily the best, just the strongest.

The acne medicines listed in Chart 2 are in the form of a lotion, gel or cream and, after application, dry clear — they leave no trace on the skin. You won't have to go around looking as if you're wearing pancake makeup or calamine lotion.

Some drugstores do not stock all the products mentioned in this book, but most will stock at least one product listed in each of the four groups in Chart 2. Before you go to the drugstore, copy the names of all products listed in your group, or take this book with you. For example, if you need a *moderate* DP agent, you should buy either Klaron, Komed, Microsyn or Xerac. You may find only one of these on the shelves but it does not matter which one you use. They are approximately equal in strength.

If you do not find a product listed in Chart 2 (or other products I mention later), ask the pharmacist if he has it. It may be that the pharmacist has the product but just hasn't displayed it on the shelves. If he does not have the product you want, he will gladly order it for you. Ordinarily he can obtain whatever you want from his supplier within 24 hours. Ask the pharmacist if you have any problems whatsoever. Before you buy a product not listed on Chart 2, consult your pharmacist and ask him to read "What Makes Your DP Agent Work" (page 92).

CHART 2

RANKING OF DP AGENTS BY STRENGTH
(Canadian readers see Appendix B, page 195)

STRONGEST
†Benoxyl 10
†Epi*Clear Antiseptic Lotion 10%
†Persadox HP Lotion
†Persadox HP Cream
 PiSec
 Saligel
 Transact

STRONG
 Acne Aid Lotion
†Benoxyl 5
 Epi*Clear Acne Lotion
†Epi*Clear Antiseptic Lotion 5%
†Fostex BPO
†Persadox Lotion
†Persadox Cream
†Vanoxide

MODERATE
 Klaron
 Komed
 Microsyn
 Xerac

†Contains benzoyl peroxide. See page 95.

WEAK
    Acno Lotion
    Komed Mild

The products within each of the four categories are approximately equal in strength. Within each group the products are listed alphabetically.

Step Four: Get Started

Now, begin your treatment. Just wash your face at the time you are accustomed to washing it and pat it dry. Then apply the DP agent with your fingers. That is all there is to it: apply your DP agent after each washing, and do it every single day.

A Word about Washing

You may use your hands to wash or you may use a washcloth. It is not necessary to scrub hard; gentle washing is sufficient. You may use a complexion brush or BUF-PUF if you like, but it is not essential. Steaming, facial saunas and the like have never been proved to have any value.

The soap or cleanser you select is not critical except that you should not use cleansing creams because they contain oil. Don't use any cleanser that is advertised as good for "dry" or "sensitive" skin because these also frequently contain oil.

Special acne cleansers are available and are listed on the next page. Those listed frequently contain chemicals that have peeling powers, but rinsing largely dilutes and washes off the chemicals. The DP agent that *stays on* does most of the work.

I usually have my patients use a special acne cleanser, but if your acne is mild, if your skin dries easily or is easily irritated, or if you are looking for ways to save money, start out with ordinary hand soap. You probably won't need any special acne cleanser.

Some of the special acne cleansers are abrasive. They contain particles or granules that make them feel gritty or sandy. Some patients with severe acne or a lot of comedones or severely oily skin prefer these. They feel the abrasive cleansers do a better job of cleaning. Other patients object to the roughness of the abrasives and feel they are too harsh and too irritating to the skin.

The decision about which cleanser to use is yours. I feel that if the principles in Chapter 6, How You Make It Work, are followed, it doesn't matter which cleanser you use as long as it contains no oil.

The DP agent, not washing, does most of the work.

CHART 3

SPECIAL ACNE CLEANSERS
(Canadian readers see Appendix B, page 195)

ABRASIVE
†Brasivol
Epi*Clear Scrub Cleanser
Ionax Scrub
Komex
Pernox
Polybrade Scrub
SAStid [AL] Scrub

NONABRASIVE
Acne Aid Soap (bar)
Brasivol Base
Fostex cream or bar (cream is twice as drying as bar)
Fostex liquid
Ionax Foam
Neutrogena Acne Cleansing Soap
SAStid Plain
SAStid Soap (bar)
Sulfur Soap (bar)

†Available as "rough," "medium" or "fine," depending on the number of particles per unit volume.

How to Apply Your DP Agent

Washing removes surface oil and dead cells and facilitates the action of the DP agent. It does this by hydrating (adding water to) the dead cell layer, which allows the DP agent to penetrate better. Washing is an important part of the treatment, but not nearly as important as the DP agent. The disease is deeper than the surface so surface cleansing alone will not stop the disease.

Apply the DP agent to the entire area where you get acne, not just on existing pimples. Rub the DP agent in until it disappears. If you have applied too much, you may not be able to rub it all in and you will need to wipe off the excess with a tissue.

Avoid the sensitive areas around the eyes, the corners of the mouth, and the folds that run at an angle from the nose to the corners of the mouth (Figure 13). Try not to get any DP agent on those areas. Also, try to avoid letting the DP agent run down onto the neck unless you have acne on the neck.

Certain areas of skin are quite sensitive and should be avoided when applying DP agent.

What Makes Your DP Agent Work?

A tremendous number of over-the-counter acne products are available. Between the pharmaceutical

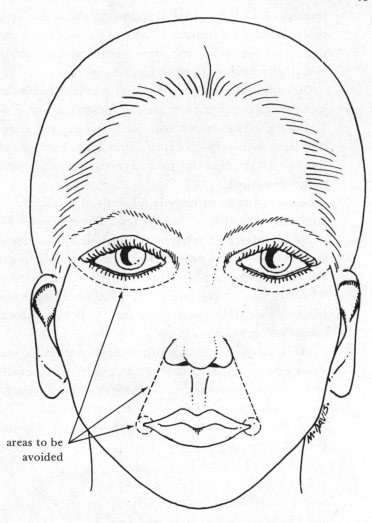

areas to be
avoided

Figure 13
Areas To Avoid

industry and the cosmetic industry, there are over three hundred products that are supposed to be beneficial for acne and new ones are constantly being launched on the market.

One might expect that the products which sell the most do so because they are the most effective. Unfortunately, this is not true. Advertising, not effectiveness, is the key to capturing a large part of the market. The companies that advertise the most tend to sell the most.

Some of the most heavily advertised products are worthless or, at best, worth less. For example, alcohol is not a bad astringent and will help remove surface oil, but it's not been shown to be able to get down into the follicle and stop the acne process. Nevertheless, products that are really nothing more than alcohol have been advertised as being "strong medicine" for acne.

There are five chemicals that make your DP agent work effectively, and four out of the five are available without a prescription. The fifth, vitamin A acid or tretinoin, is available only by prescription. The four that are available over-the-counter in the United States are:

1. Benzoyl peroxide
2. Sulfur
3. Resorcinol
4. Salicylic acid

These are the drying and peeling chemicals that will stop acne when used correctly. If you wish to select a DP agent on your own, one that is not included in Chart 2, make sure the product contains at least one of these chemicals.

A Word about Benzoyl Peroxide

Benzoyl peroxide is truly one of the most effective medicines available for treating acne. Because benzoyl peroxide is found in so many acne medicines and since there are special problems unique to it, I will discuss it separately. Unfortunately, one person out of a hundred becomes allergic to benzoyl peroxide. I have never seen an allergic reaction to sulfur, resorcinol or salicylic acid. If you are allergic to benzoyl peroxide, you have to use a DP agent that does not contain it. The ingredients are listed on the package and I have also indicated on Chart 2 which products contain benzoyl peroxide.

Many of the effective DP agents will burn or sting a little as you apply them and there may be a slight reddening of the skin. These things are normal, but if you experience severe burning or stinging or if excessive redness occurs, you may be allergic to the medication. If this happens, discontinue use until the reaction subsides. Then reapply a little of the medication to a small area about the size of a quarter. Do this for several days and watch for any reaction before you reapply it to a large area. If you have a severe reaction or the skin around the eyes becomes swollen, stop using the medication and see a doctor.

Benzoyl peroxide is a bleaching agent. Sulfur, resorcinol and salicylic acid are not. Benzoyl peroxide may bleach clothes, pillowcases, hair, and so on. Bleaching of fabrics is usually avoided simply by allowing the medicine to dry before it comes into contact with a colored fabric.

All benzoyl peroxide products lose strength when exposed to heat and, therefore, they should not be stored in a warm place. If you have more than one tube or bottle on hand, you should refrigerate the one you are not using. The one you are using can be kept at room temperature for several weeks, but don't place it on top of a radiator or a windowsill where it is exposed to the sun.

Do not let the above comments discourage you from using benzoyl peroxide. The one real problem — allergy — affects only one out of a hundred people.

Step Five: Establish a Baseline Record

The main object of this treatment program is to prevent the formation of new pimples. But even as you do this, you still have to look at those pimples that already exist. Some cases of acne clear in a week with good treatment. But unless you are one of those lucky people, the first few weeks of treatment can be discouraging because the changes may be so gradual that you don't believe you are making any progress at all. When patients don't believe the treatment is working, they lose their enthusiasm and get sloppy and irregular with the treatment, and the whole program falls apart.

In weight-reduction programs you always know exactly how well you are progressing. You merely step on a scale and read the numbers. In an acne-reduction program it is different. It is sometimes very difficult to determine how well you are doing. The reason is that you see your own face too often. We all look in a mirror several times a day — sometimes only a few hours apart — and we cannot detect the changes that have occurred since the last time we looked. No one can do this! From one glance in a mirror to the next you look exactly the same. This can easily fool you into thinking the treatment isn't working. Other people who see you frequently are also no help. They also cannot judge how well you are doing.

In order to measure your progress — and you *will* be making progress — you need to establish a baseline record, to make a record of what you looked like when you began the program. If you have mostly inflammatory lesions (red ones like papules and pustules), I recommend that you have photographs taken before you start — close-up photographs that show every blemish. In my practice we commonly take photographs on the first visit, and we find them extremely useful later in boosting the morale of our patients. Who can argue with a photograph?

Photographs are not particularly helpful if you

have mostly comedones; in fact, they can be misleading. Comedones don't show up well on photographs and may turn into papules and pustules, in which case you *appear* to get worse after starting treatment (see "Time Bombs," page 136). In my practice this happens to about 20 percent of my patients. If you are in this minority, you should have the photographs taken *after* the comedones have converted to red lesions.

If you have mostly red lesions, photographs can be very helpful in judging your progress.

Step Six: Adjust Your Treatment

Adjusting Treatment Upward

Your goal is clearly defined: peeling within the follicles. Since you cannot see into the follicles, you can only judge follicle peeling by the amount of surface peeling you see. You want to achieve a visible flaking of the skin surface. *If your skin does not begin to peel after about five days with the treatment program you started on, you will need to make an upward adjustment.*

To do so you may either increase the frequency of treatments (for example, treat three times a day instead of two), or you can buy a stronger DP agent (for example, move up to a *strong* DP agent if you have been using a *moderate* DP agent).

After getting started, most readers will have to adjust their treatment upward.

You may need to adjust your treatment more than once to get it just right for you. In making any adjustments, just remember there are two factors that determine the "dosage" of your treatment:

1. *Frequency* of treatments — how often each day you wash and apply a DP agent.

2. *Strength* of the DP agent.

Change *one* factor *one* step at a time. Increase the number of times you wash your face by one. Or increase the strength of your DP agent by one category. Do not do both, and don't jump more than one step at a time. The point of this step-by-step procedure is to discover exactly how much treatment you need.

Maintain treatment at the new level for five days. Continue at this level if peeling results. If it does not, increase the frequency or the strength by one more step.

Adjusting your treatment upward will also be necessary when "toughening" occurs. After you begin treatment and establish peeling, you will reach a point when the peeling stops even though you have maintained the same level of treatment. When this happens it means your skin has developed a tolerance to, or has toughened somewhat with, the use of the DP agent. At this point, increase your treatment one step.

Increased treatment is also required in young teen- agers as they grow older and their acne gets worse. What works at age twelve may not be strong enough at age thirteen. If you notice increased oiliness of the surface or decreased peeling, you need to increase the treatment.

When you are launching a counterattack against some factor like pressı (see page 62), which causes you to break out more ın one particular area, in- crease your treatment in just that area. For example, if your chin starts breaking out from your football helmet strap, treat the chin an additional time (or two) each day. Or use a stronger DP agent on the chin.

If emotional stress causes your acne to get worse, you should likewise increase your treatment.

The idea is to stay one step ahead of the disease and you must judge how well you are doing by the peeling you see on the surface.

You will need to increase your treatment if:
1. **You do not peel**
2. **Your skin "toughens"**
3. **Your acne gets worse**
4. **Your acne is stubborn**

When you begin treatment, you must continue peeling as long as new lesions appear. If you are already clear — using only maintenance treatment (page 141) — and new lesions appear, you should increase your treatment and peel again.

Various degrees of peeling occur. With minimal peeling you cannot see that you are peeling, but the skin will feel somewhat drawn. You will notice this more as you smile or otherwise wrinkle your face. With more aggressive peeling a superficial flaking is obvious — you are able to *see* the skin peeling and it will feel tight. With the most aggressive peeling the skin comes off in large flakes, somewhat as it does following a sunburn.

Any discomfort is generally limited to the first two weeks of treatment and the vast majority of my patients have not complained. If peeling bothers you at first, realize that your skin gets used to peeling and any discomfort should subside.

You alone will determine how aggressively you treat your disease; it is your decision. Remember that the more aggressively you treat, the sooner you will clear, and remember that peeling does not harm the skin in any way (see "Peel Is In," page 126). Certain cases respond quickly and easily — visible peeling may not even be required. But if you have a lot of blackheads or closed comedones, or if your disease is stubborn, I urge you to be aggressive. Surely a few weeks of peeling is a small price to pay for clearing and controlling a disease that otherwise you may have to chase for *ten years*. Jump ahead of it and attack the disease head-on. Once you have conquered your acne you no longer need to peel.

If you are adjusting upward but are reluctant to buy a new DP agent and find it hard to treat more frequently during the day, you can try merely putting on more DP agent and/or rubbing it in better.

When you increase the frequency of application of your DP agent, don't worry about the fact that you may be applying it more frequently than directed on the package. The directions on the packages of DP agents usually say something like: "apply once or twice a day or as directed by your physician."

Be aware that the directions supplied with DP agents are written for anyone who may purchase that product, including people of all skin types. The manufacturer must caution against overuse to protect those users who have sensitive skin and peel easily. People who have more trouble peeling and who are using one of the weaker DP agents *must* apply it more frequently or change to a stronger product.

If you do buy a new DP agent, don't throw the old one away. Save it. You can use it again later when you are clear and you decrease your treatment to a maintenance level.

Adjusting Treatment Downward

Several situations may require that you adjust your treatment downward:

1. If you are peeling so much that it becomes

painful or you develop intolerable itching, you should decrease the dosage.

2. If you are going skiing and are already peeling, you should adjust treatment downward to avoid a bad sunburn. You are more likely to sunburn when peeling because your skin is thinner.

3. If summer arrives and you are going to be out in the sun a lot, you should decrease your treatment for the same reason. When you are exposed to the sun, it is like putting on more DP agent since sunlight also causes peeling of the skin.

4. After you stop forming new acne lesions you may begin decreasing treatment, although I recommend, as you will see in Chapter 7, that you do not until your skin is completely clear (all flat red spots have disappeared).

The majority of readers will have to treat only once or twice a day, but some will need to treat three or four times a day — at least during the early part of the treatment. If you need four treatments a day, you should try to space them evenly. To keep the spacing approximately equal, you should treat: (1) when you get up in the morning, (2) around noon, (3) sometime after work or after school, and (4) before going to bed.

Don't be discouraged if it takes you a little time to arrive at your exact treatment schedule. You *will* eventually, and in the meantime you are not wasting your time. Even though it may not yet be obvious, you have already helped your acne and you may already have completely stopped the development of new microcomedones. Although you do not *see* peeling, you are probably peeling on a microscopic level, which is frequently enough to stop the formation of microcomedones.

Adjusting treatment is an essential part of the program.

Area Acne

For reasons that are sometimes not entirely understood, your acne may be more severe in some places than others. The cheeks, forehead and chin are not always equally affected by the acne process. In such situations the treatment must be adjusted to accommodate the special needs of each area.

Begin treatment by following Steps One through Five in this chapter, washing and applying DP agent to the entire face.

When peeling starts, examine your face carefully. Make sure that all areas are peeling. You may notice that the relatively clear areas are dry *and peeling*, but that the area with the most pimples is not even *dry* from treatment. Obviously adjustments are in order.

Any areas affected by acne must be made to peel. You can do this by applying more DP agent to such areas, or by rubbing it in better. If this doesn't work, wash and apply DP agent to those areas more frequently, or use a stronger DP agent. For example, if your chin has many lesions but isn't peeling like the rest of your face, you may need to wash and apply DP agent to the chin two (or even three) times each day, while applying it only once to the cheeks. Or you may want to apply a *strong* DP agent to your chin while using a *moderate* agent on your cheeks.

The acne process sometimes zeroes in on certain areas while sparing others. If an area is not involved with acne, don't treat it.

In adult women it is quite common for the acne to be localized on the chin: the chin may be breaking out with pimples while the cheeks are completely clear. When the acne is localized, only that particular area needs to be treated. It may even be permissible to use moisturizers on certain dry areas while using DP agents on the acne area. Just don't use an oily or greasy moisturizer on the acne area.

Different areas of your skin may require different dosages of treatment.

If You Have Trouble Achieving Peeling

I have advised you to build your treatment program around the number of times you have been accustomed to washing your face each day. This works for everyone except those who have trouble achieving peeling. If you are already using one of the strongest DP agents and you are not peeling, you can:

1. Increase the number of times each day that you wash and apply DP agent;

2. Rub the DP agent in better;

3. Go to a doctor for a prescription for an even stronger DP agent.

Some people can't find time to wash more frequently than twice a day. This I can understand. But some of my patients don't want to wash any more frequently than once a day. Treating the skin only once a day may work for very mild acne, but unless you fall into that category, you should count on at least two treatments per day.

If you can't find time to wash more frequently, you should apply a DP agent without first washing. But remember that washing facilitates the action of the DP agent. Therefore, when you wash before every application, you are in effect increasing the strength of the DP agent. Consequently, if you can't or don't wash before each application, you may need to use a stronger DP agent.

As long as you achieve peeling it doesn't matter how you do it. Be sure, however, that you are not trying to do it with washing alone. Washing can make the surface peel, but it does not cause peeling within the follicles. A DP agent is absolutely essential and must always be applied at least once a day.

The important thing is to be consistent and *do the same thing every day*. The only time you should ever change what you are doing from day to day is when you are making a purposeful adjustment in your treatment program. After adjusting, you again do the same thing every day.

Back and Chest

If you have acne on your back and/or chest, special considerations apply to treating those areas.

To wash your back and chest two, three or four times a day is difficult or, at least, inconvenient. Additionally, the back is hard to reach and impossible to see without the aid of a mirror. When you take your daily shower or bath, I recommend that you use a back brush so that you can easily reach all areas.

Since you are limited by how frequently you can treat those areas, you will almost surely have to use one of the stronger DP agents. You may have to use a different DP agent from the one you use on your face.

Remember that DP agents *can* be applied without first washing. In this way you can apply the DP agent to the back and chest twice a day with almost no inconvenience, and three times a day with very little inconvenience. I am not discouraging washing those areas more than once a day, and for some who have very severe acne in those locations, it will be *necessary* to shower or bathe twice a day.

A thorough covering of the back with a DP agent often requires the assistance of another person.

The chest, especially in females, is frequently more sensitive to DP agents than the back. It often peels more easily. You can still use the same DP agent in both locations; merely decrease the frequency of application to the chest.

> **The back and chest are harder to treat than the face.**

How Long Does It Take to Achieve Control?

It varies tremendously from person to person. In my practice, some lucky patients stop getting new lesions after only one week of treatment. At the other extreme are a few who have to treat for longer than four months to achieve the same result. These are the extremes, but most patients are controlled in a month and the vast majority are controlled by two months.

Two factors determine how long control will take. One of those factors you can influence, the other is governed purely by chance. You alone regulate how aggressively, enthusiastically and regularly your acne is treated by following the points repeatedly emphasized in this book. What you cannot regulate is the type of acne you have. Some types are easier to control than others, and how severe the acne *looks* may be misleading in terms of how quickly it responds to treatment. That is, cases that *look* the most serious are frequently very easy to control and clear while, in contrast, some mild-looking cases are occasionally very difficult to control and clear. Acne that is all papules and pustules, with few or no comedones, may look terribly severe, when in terms of clearing and control it is not. In fact, control in such cases can be expected in only two or three weeks! Papules and pustules are easy.

Comedones of all types are more difficult to clear. Open comedones (blackheads) can sometimes be extremely resistant to treatment. Closed comedones are unpredictable. I have seen them disappear in a week; I've seen them sit there for months doing nothing; and I've seen them all turn into papules and pustules after treatment is started. In most people this treatment eliminates closed comedones, but sometimes it causes them first to explode, thereby "maturing" into papules and pustules. When this happens, it is somewhat alarming but, fortunately, the papules and pustules then clear quickly (see "Time Bombs," page 136).

Inflammatory red lesions usually clear more quickly than comedones.

The number of microcomedones you have at the time you start treatment is also very important. Because they are invisible, you have no way to determine how many you have to start with. If you are lucky, you don't have many or they will unplug easily with treatment. However, if they are firmly seated, and especially if you do not treat aggressively, they will continue their growth and eventually develop into more mature lesions (closed and open comedones, papules and pustules). Hopefully, you have only a few presently existing microcomedones; most importantly, you can expect that with good treatment, you won't be making any new ones.

Because of flat red spots (see page 134) or lingering comedones, you may achieve *control* before your skin is completely *clear*. *Control* is achieved when you stop getting new lesions. To be *clear* means not only that you are controlled, but also that all evidence of previous lesions has disappeared.

You should achieve control in three to eight weeks.

How You Make It Work: The Secrets to Complete Clearing

Now come the essential principles of treatment — the "secrets" that make the difference between 50 percent clearing and 100 percent.

You will have to follow most or all of these principles if you want to stop your acne totally. If you have had problems with past treatment, the reasons should become obvious as you read these pages. These principles apply no matter whether you're treating your own acne or a doctor is directing your treatment.

I have talked with many patients who have spent an unbelievable amount of time and money treating their acne, yet the treatment always failed and the reason was that knowledge of these principles was lacking.

The treatment of acne involves slightly more than taking a magic pill that will make it go away in a few days and never come back. We keep looking for that pill, but we don't have it yet. Until we get it, the method in this book is the best we have. It works! But it *does* require some effort on your part.

If you don't mind washing your face, it will be very easy for you because the only other thing you need do is apply a DP agent after washing. That requires only a few added seconds of time. The most that is ever required of you with this treatment is that you may have to increase the number of times you wash your face each day. And this applies only to those individuals who cannot achieve dryness and peeling in any other way. Surely an additional washing or two per day is a small price to pay for a clear complexion.

When we have the magic pill that will make acne go away and never come back we will have a *cure* for acne. This treatment is not a cure. It is as good as a cure because you will not look as if you have acne. You should have no pimples and your skin should be clear. No one will ever know you have acne. But your acne cannot be called *cured*.

We cure appendicitis when we cut out the appendix. That takes care of it forever, and the patient can never get appendicitis again. We do not cure diabetes when we give insulin. The patient still has diabetes and will need more insulin the next day. The diabetes is controlled, not cured. In the same way, this treatment successfully *controls,* but does not *cure*, acne. Even after your skin is clear and you are not getting any new pimples, the underlying condition that causes pimples will remain.

If you quit treating or treat too little, the evidence of the disease — pimples — will come roaring back. Therefore, you have to continue treatment as long as the disease lasts!

In Chapter 7, Staying Clear, I encourage you to decrease your treatment after your skin is clear.

There's no reason to treat any more aggressively than is absolutely necessary.

There are seven "secrets" of treatment. These are:

1. 24 and 7
2. Preventive Medicine
3. Grease Is Out
4. Peel Is In
5. Flat Red Spots
6. Time Bombs
7. Pick, Squeeze and Scratch

Now, let's have a closer look at each one.

24 and 7

The first secret is 24 and 7. To treat acne and win, it is important to realize that the process causing new pimples goes on 24 hours a day, 7 days a week, and there are no holidays!

In order to avoid a lot of frustration and a prolonged period of continuous breaking out, you must remember 24 and 7. You are involved in a battle with a disease process. One of the two of you will win. The disease does not rest. You cannot rest either. You have to keep after it all the time. If you treat it sporadically, if you skip days of treatment or applications of DP agents, you are inviting the formation of new microcomedones and thus new pimples.

When I see patients who have had treatment

problems, the cause is often that the principle of 24 and 7 was not followed.

Many acne sufferers spend a lot of hours working very hard to treat their acne, but then they go off for the weekend, or they go to a slumber party, or hiking, or camping, or whatever, and forget to take the medication with them. There is thus a period of no treatment. They resume treatment when they're home again and may work at it very diligently. However, they get new pimples! Those new pimples formed during that no-treatment period! The pimples may not show up right away but they began forming while there was no treatment to stop them.

Acne simply cannot be treated six days a week because new microcomedones may form on the untreated seventh day. Six-days-a-week treatment may result in only 50 to 70 percent improvement. Yet that extra little effort, that seventh day, can close the gap and totally arrest the disease.

So, remember, *almost* perfect treatment may result in only 50 percent clearing, whereas a perfect treatment program results in 100 percent clearing. It's so easy to make that extra little bit of effort.

You should not be satisfied with anything less than 100 percent clearing and that means you have to be diligent and consistent about your treatment. It has to become a part of your daily routine, just like brushing your teeth.

It is also important to remember that the disease is going on at night as well as during the day. It's risky business to be without treatment for the six or eight or ten hours that you sleep. There should be something on your skin to keep new plugs from forming. The products I have recommended have enough lasting power to protect you during the night. All you need do is apply the DP agent and leave it on to work for you while you sleep.

I know that some readers will persist in thinking, "Oh, surely it doesn't matter if I skip just a day or two of treatment." Believe me, that can be a very costly mistake, especially early in the program. Remember this: if you do skip a day of treatment and don't immediately see new pimples, don't think you have gotten away with something! A new microcomedo can form during the period of no treatment and not become visible for weeks or months. If you could watch your skin through a microscope, you could see that the new plugs were forming during the time that you slacked off.

Anyone who has a significant acne problem and wants to be completely clear will take the acne medications wherever he or she goes. If you don't like to carry around a large bottle or jar of medication, find a small bottle that will fit into your pocket or purse. Put a little of the medicine in the small bottle so you can have it with you while you're away from home.

New microcomedones can form any time you are not treating. This disease does not take holidays.

If you are on three or four treatments a day and something happens so that it is absolutely impossible to wash, there are other things you can do. For example, instead of washing, you could merely wipe your face with alcohol. Conveniently packaged alcohol wipes are available at your drugstore and they are effective in removing surface oil. You can then apply the DP agent.

If it's impossible to clean the surface first, apply the DP agent anyway. That requires almost no time. DP agents don't work as well without cleaning the surface first, but doing it this way is far better than doing nothing.

Just remember that microcomedones are always trying to form. You can stop them when you are treating, but if you stop treating for even a short time, a few will develop. Once these early plugs develop, they may go on to make full-fledged pimples.

Preventive Medicine

The ideal way to treat any disease is by preventing its occurrence. This approach is called "preventive medicine" and is initiated *before*, rather than *after*, the development of disease. It works by identifying situations that might induce or aggravate a disease and then alters that situation to prevent the occurrence. Preventive medicine is not only more effective, it is also easier. It is obviously simpler to prevent a disease than to try to cure it once it has developed.

The treatment described in this book is based on the principle of preventive medicine. It is less concerned with the pimples you now have on your face than it is with the new pimples that will continue to appear unless the process that causes them is altered. Patients with severe acne manufacture thousands of pimples during the course of the disease. These new pimples are the ones that must concern you and that you will prevent with this treatment.

This may require a drastic change in your point of view. You must shift your attention away from all the *old* pimples and concentrate only on *new* ones. Don't allow yourself to get trapped at the mirror, worrying about existing red bumps. Write them off in your mind. Consider them has-beens. They have already done their thing. They have made their play and they are on the way out. Don't fret about them! Worry instead about the adjacent skin (where there are no pimples now) and prevent pimples from forming there.

I want to emphasize that to be effective acne medicines must be applied to the *entire area* in which acne forms, and not applied just to the existing lesions. While applying DP agents directly to existing lesions will certainly cause them to heal faster, it does nothing to prevent the formation of new pimples and ignores the principle of preventive medicine.

Don't focus your attention on existing pimples. Stop new ones from forming.

What about those old ones? All the old pimples will go away. While it is true that existing acne lesions sometimes die a slow death, they *all* eventually disappear. Some will disappear in just a few days' time, but the more serious or deeper lesions can stay around for weeks or even months. All the more reason to prevent them from forming in the first place.

Do not allow yourself to get discouraged if you have certain lesions that seem to be hanging on forever. You cannot blame your treatment and you must not get discouraged about those lesions that existed before you started treatment.

Do not go looking for reasons to get discouraged. Maintain a positive attitude. You will win!

Can anything be done to clear old ones faster? Absolutely! As I have stated, you will be applying acne medicine to the entire area where acne is occurring. But you can dab *more* on existing lesions. You can put a small amount of the DP agent directly onto red bumps and thereby speed their resolution. You can do this as often as your schedule allows; there's no danger. You may also wish to buy one of the very strongest DP agents to use for this purpose. A doctor can inject or freeze existing lesions to make them clear faster.

In certain situations you may also wish to hide or cover existing acne lesions so that they are not so obvious. The safest thing to use for this is one of the products listed on page 124.

Be careful about makeup and if you use it at all, be sure it contains no oil (see "Grease Is Out"). And never allow covering or hiding to become the main object of your treatment. Remember the secret of preventive medicine.

Grease Is Out

Earlier it was pointed out that oil and grease are frequently important actors in the acne drama. When oily and greasy substances come into contact with the surface of the skin, they may cause acne.

The entire treatment program is aimed at keeping the pores from plugging, keeping the pores cleaned out. You want the follicles to stay open! It is against all reason to apply something to the skin that actually plugs pores. Oily and greasy substances do this! You must try to avoid getting oil and grease onto skin areas where acne occurs.

Products often applied to the skin that contain oil or grease include almost all moisturizers, most makeups, suntan oil and some hair preparations. When I see patients who have been "treatment failures" and I evaluate their past treatment, it is not uncommon to find that the only reason for failure was that they continued to apply some greasy substance to the skin. When I persuade them to stop the use of all greasy substances, the acne clears.

Greasy materials not only complicate treatment of an existing acne condition, they can actually create acne in someone whose skin was previously completely clear. Doctors use the term *acne cosmetica* to describe this situation. Cosmetics are frequently the reason why a thirty- to forty-year-old woman still has (or develops) acne. It is not surprising that adult acne is far more common among females.

What Kind of Makeup Is Safe to Use?

I believe it is no great sacrifice to go totally without makeup, but some of my patients wholeheartedly disagree with me. To me skin is more natural-looking without greasy makeup, even cleaner-looking. But the main reason for my belief is that because of our lack of knowledge and because certain products originally thought to be safe were later found to be harmful, I have an underlying uneasy feeling about almost all makeups.

It would be most helpful for all female acne sufferers if there were some easy and reliable way to test makeups and moisturizers to determine their safety. Unfortunately, there is no such test. The only sure test would be to repeatedly apply the makeup or moisturizer to human skin and see if it causes acne. People don't like being guinea pigs so this is not often done. Since laboratory animals do not get acne, we have no readily available test animal to use. The closest model doctors have found is the inside of rabbits' ears, which can be induced to develop blackheads. But we don't really know if information derived from experiments on a rabbit's ear can be directly applied to the human situation. For example, rabbits' ears do not develop inflammatory lesions, so obviously the "acne" we see in rabbits' ears is not the same as acne in humans.

Eye makeup can safely be used and I also allow my patients to use regular greasy moisturizers around the eyes, since acne almost never occurs close to the eyes. Powder makeups brushed lightly on the surface are safe and, of course, lipstick causes no problem. With those exceptions, I try to persuade my acne patients to discontinue using all makeup. If I am unsuccessful, I try to persuade them to use a tinted acne medicine, such as those listed under "Makeup Substitutes," page 124. If I am again unsuccessful, I insist that they use a "water-base," "greaseless," or "oil-free" product. Such products frequently do not spread as evenly or smoothly and do not cover as well as regular greasy or oily makeup; therefore, patients often do not like them as well as the oil-containing makeups. But some of the same ingredients responsible for easy spreadability and good coverage also plug pores and cause acne.

Do not use the cost of a makeup as a guideline

because some of the most expensive are very dangerous for people suffering from acne to use. Also, acne is not an allergic disease and it's of no consequence that a makeup is advertised as "hypoallergenic." When a makeup claims to be "medicated," it frequently is *not* safe to use. The term "medicated" is used very loosely. Don't expect such a makeup to be helpful in treating acne. It may actually be harmful.

If you use theatrical or stage makeup, be especially on guard. Some stage makeups are absolute dynamite and can cause or flare acne in just a few days' time. One of my acne patients, who had been controlled for a long time, flared within 24 hours after *one* application of stage makeup. If you must wear stage makeup, apply a strong DP agent under it and remove the makeup as soon as possible.

Makeup Substitutes

  Acne Aid Lotion (tinted)
  Fostril
  †Loroxide
  †Postacne
  †Rezamid
  Sulforcin Base 4%
  (Canadian readers should see Appendix B, page 195.)

---

†Comes with a special color blender that you add to the lotion so that it will match your skin color.

The above products contain drying-peeling chemicals. If you use one of these regularly, you are actually increasing your treatment.

The objection to using any of them is usually that they do not spread easily or cover well enough. However, some people are quite satisfied using one of the above. In my experience, the two most popular are Rezamid and Sulforcin Base 4%. If you are trying to hide an existing acne condition and want to be *sure* that you don't create more acne in the process, I urge you to try one of these products.

> **Do not cover your acne under heavy, greasy makeup. You may cause more acne.**

What Is the Best Way to Remove Makeup?

Cold creams and cleansing creams contain oil! They have no place in the management of acne and you should avoid them. Soap and water do a better job of cleaning. The only time you should ever use one of those creams is if you're trying to remove very heavy, greasy, waterproof makeup such as the theatrical type. Then you may find a cream useful. The oil-containing makeup will dissolve more easily in an oil-containing cleansing cream and will therefore come off more easily than with water. But you should follow the cream with a good scrubbing using soap and water.

I can summarize my feelings about makeup by

asking, "Isn't it much better to clear the acne than to camouflage or cover it? Especially since covering it can actually cause it?" The acne you're looking at today may actually have been caused by the covering you did a month ago.

Other Sources of Oil

There is an endless list of preparations containing oil or grease that might be applied to the skin. When oily or greasy hair preparations are used, some gets onto the forehead and temples. A few people with acne get worse during the summer and one of the reasons is suntan oil. Men with acne should be careful of the shaving preparations they choose. Brushless shaving creams contain oil. The *AMA Book of Skin and Hair Care* recommends either a lather-type shaving cream used with a brush or an aerosol foam.

Peel Is In

You may have been shocked as you read Chapter 5 to learn that you are being encouraged to dry your skin until it actually peels. I am aware that all sorts of horrible consequences are supposed to occur if you do anything that dries your skin. But this is *exactly* what you must do because this is what clears acne! You should speed up the treatment by using a DP agent strong enough and/or by applying it frequently enough to cause a noticeable surface flaking or peeling. It will not harm the skin in any way and it is only temporary. It does not age the skin faster or cause wrinkles!

Any concern you may have is probably the direct result of advertising by the companies that sell moisturizers. Cosmetic companies sell 500 million dollars' worth of moisturizers each year! That fact alone should give you pause.

I have nothing against moisturizers except that they should not be used on acne skin. Moisturizers will usually make your acne worse. It is a safe bet that anything that promises to be "moisturizing" contains oil or grease and, therefore, can cause acne. More arguments follow to convince you that peeling does no harm, but first let's consider why peeling is even recommended.

Why Is Surface Peeling So Important?

Because all acne lesions originate within follicles and since the basic abnormality is that cells stick together instead of flowing out of the follicles, it follows that if you stop those cells from sticking together, you prevent the development of acne lesions! You must *peel* those cells apart to control this disease.

Two thousand follicles per square inch are found on some areas of the face. The follicles not only are very numerous, but also are very small. It is into these thousands and thousands of tiny follicles that you must deliver the DP agent to control the disease. It is obvious that there is no way to get the DP agent into the follicles without rubbing it onto the surface of the skin. So you will be "treating" the surface as well as the follicles. Although you might prefer not to do so, you really have no choice. You will get dryness and peeling on the surface as well as within the follicles, and if you experience no dryness or peeling on the surface, it is a cinch there will also be no peeling within the follicles.

Because this whole issue is so closely tied to the use of moisturizers and the prevention of wrinkles, let's examine wrinkles closely.

Wrinkles: Their Cause and Prevention

Dermatologists have understood the causes of wrinkles for a long time. Three main factors determine how much wrinkling occurs in any individual's skin. Other factors are, by comparison, of almost no significance.

The first factor is genetics. Some of us are destined to wrinkle more than others solely because of the genes we inherited. Obviously, we have no control over this factor.

The second factor is age. The older we get the more wrinkles we have; it's inevitable and again we have no control over this natural, normal phenomenon.

The third factor is sun damage and, in terms of preventing wrinkles, this is by far the most important factor because we can and should try to control it. Sun always damages the skin, the more exposure the more damage, and the effects are cumulative. When you are forty years old, your skin reflects the damage done to it over the entire preceding forty years. That is, you have to pay the price at age forty for damage done to your skin, for example, at age nineteen (or ten or four). If you were a lifeguard during your teens you will have more wrinkles be cause of it and you will, incidentally, also have a greater chance of developing skin cancer. Your chances of developing skin cancer are directly related to the total amount of sun exposure you have received.

Returning to wrinkles: realize that sun damages the elastic tissue fibers in the dermis, which is the second layer of skin (see page 18). The ultraviolet rays of the sun pass right through the epidermis into the dermis. It is the dermis with its connective tissue fibers, including elastic fibers, that serves as the foundation or supporting structure of the skin, and damage at this level is what causes wrinkles.

Proof that sunlight damages skin and produces wrinkles is readily available to you. Notice the skin of people who work outside all the time and you have your proof. Observe the face or neck of a farmer, for example. Moreover, doctors have noted that in such individuals the part of their skin that is usually covered, the skin on the buttocks, for example, looks much younger and doesn't wrinkle nearly as fast.

Notice also the skin of black people. They get wrinkles much more slowly than white people. The reason is that black epidermis (outer layer of skin) is loaded with pigment (melanin), and this pigment stops the ultraviolet rays from reaching the dermis. The epidermis, in other words, protects the dermis. I have seen fifty-year-old blacks who didn't look a day past thirty.

The single most important thing you can do to retard wrinkles is to avoid the sun or protect yourself against it by using a sunscreen. Some of the most effective sunscreens contain PABA (para-aminobenzoic acid), and your physician or pharmacist can recommend names of those brands that do not aggravate or cause acne.

The above discussion concerns true wrinkles, permanent ones. Another type of "wrinkling" sometimes occurs with dry skin and may occur with acne treatment. It is not true wrinkling because it is not permanent and is easily reversible. Yet this pseudo-wrinkling sells millions of dollars' worth of moisturizers per year!

A superficial flaking or peeling occurs when you speed up the treatment as I've encouraged you to do. Along with the peeling and flaking you may notice very fine, "cigarette-paper" or "crepe-paper-like" wrinkles. Those are of no consequence and are nothing to worry about. They do not represent damage to the dermis. This "wrinkling" involves only the very outermost part of the epidermis: the dead cell layer. You don't need to be concerned about what happens to this layer since it is constantly being replaced. Also, you can reverse these changes in a few minutes anytime you choose, as you will see.

If you look closely at those "wrinkles," you can see that they don't even look like real wrinkles. They look more like roughness, crinkling, rippling or cracking.

What Moisturizers Do

Moisturizers work by eliminating the superficial pseudo-wrinkles and *temporarily* making the skin look smoother. When the flat dead cells come into contact with water they absorb some of the water and swell. They puff up and make the surface look smoother. The oily or greasy film that moisturizers provide holds in this water and preserves the smooth look.

There is an easy test you can do to demonstrate this. First, take a close look at your hands. Notice any roughness or wrinkling. Look at the backs of your hands as well as the palms, and notice the fingers also. Now moisturize the skin on one hand by placing the hand in water for five minutes. Then dry it off, without getting the other hand wet, and look again at both hands. Notice how much smoother the skin is on the hand that you moisturized. It looks better and will continue to look better for up to an hour and a half, but eventually all the absorbed water will evaporate and your hands will look exactly the same again.

You were able to produce a truly noticeable change by adding moisture, but not a permanent change. You probably also noticed that not all of the wrinkles went away on the soaked hand. All the changes you produced were superficial, involving only the dead cell layer. The deep wrinkles involving the dermis were not affected.

If, after adding moisture to your skin, you had applied an oily or greasy film, it would have helped to seal in the water and the skin would have stayed smooth-looking for a longer period of time. This is what moisturizers do. They really work and, even if no water is added first, they still help to hold in the water from sweat, which would otherwise evaporate. (Your sweat glands are always at work even if you're not noticeably sweating.) So, moisturizers hold water in the skin, but that is all they do, nothing more, despite any advertising claims. They work, but the results are only temporary and superficial. These is no evidence to show that they retard permanent wrinkles.

Another kind of "wrinkling" occurs if you leave your hands in water longer than a few minutes. As the dead cell layer absorbs more and more moisture, it continues to swell and it eventually buckles. These are the changes you have noticed on the skin of your hands, especially on the fingertips, after washing dishes.

Be assured that the "wrinkling" of the dead cell layer that occurs when you are treating acne affects *only* the dead cell layer. Remember that the dermis or underlying layer is what is important in true wrinkling.

> **Peeling does not cause wrinkles.**

You do not need to worry if you decide to follow this treatment plan and do it right and avoid moisturizers. Nothing terrible or irreversible will happen.

If you don't like the way you look when you are peeling, take a dry, rough washcloth or BUF-PUF and brush off the scales. *But don't ever let anyone tell you that peeling looks worse than having a face full of pimples.* Furthermore, you need to peel only for a limited period of time, just until your acne is controlled. Finally, peeling will get rid of the acne.

Caution!

When you are washing or applying the DP agent, remember to avoid the corners of the mouth, the folds that run from the nose to the corners of the mouth, the area surrounding the eyes and the neck, if possible (see Figure 13, page 93). Those areas are more sensitive and more easily irritated. If you have acne on the neck, of course you have to treat it, but otherwise try to avoid letting the medicine run down onto the neck.

Remember, too, that wind, cold, dry weather and sun exposure will increase the dryness and peeling. If you are going skiing, for example, you will want to temporarily decrease your treatment. *You are more susceptible to sunburn while peeling.* Remember this if you go to the beach. But don't use any oily suntan lotion on acne areas.

Blacks and others with dark skin must take extra caution and may have to treat less aggressively when using DP agents. The reason is that such individuals run the risk of hyperpigmentation (increased pigment in or darkening of the skin), and the chances of this occurring are even greater if there are already leftover dark marks from previous pimples. If you can see that you have already hyperpigmented, be careful! You should proceed cautiously or consult a dermatologist before embarking on a very aggressive peeling approach. The darkening, if it occurs, may take months or more than a year to clear. Doctors have bleaching agents that will sometimes speed up the clearing of those dark marks and they can also give you other methods of treatment.

Flat Red Spots (Macules)

As acne lesions disappear they may do so in two stages: first they may flatten and then they lose their red color. The second stage sometimes lasts a long time. Certain lesions linger as red or purple flat spots for months.

In dermatologic terminology those red spots are called macules. A macule is a lesion that is completely flat — not elevated. To the untrained eye those flat red spots look just as bad as the red bumps that were there earlier. But you cannot let the spots fool or discourage you. You must recognize them for what they are: burned-out acne. In terms of the end result, they are of no consequence! They *will* clear eventually! If you have ever sustained a cut or any kind of wound, you know that even after it has healed, the area remains red for a while. This redness is caused by residual inflammation and the same thing happens in acne.

Flat red spots are burned-out acne. Try not to let them discourage you.

Fortunately, these red macules are not a serious problem for most individuals with acne. Unfortunately, they tend to occur in those individuals who have already suffered the most with their disease, since persistent red macules are more common following the larger and deeper types of acne lesions.

I have had patients who were completely controlled (no *new* lesions) for months but who still had those very obvious red marks. Should this happen to you, don't despair. Always remember that when a lesion becomes flat, it is clearing — disappearing!

If you are not getting any new lesions but you still have flat red spots, that is, if you are *controlled* but not *clear*, I encourage you to continue peeling. It's acceptable to decrease treatment as soon as you achieve *control*, but from my patients I have the impression that those flat red spots clear faster if you keep peeling. If you are frustrated or bothered by the red spots, you may wish to hide them with one of the products on page 124.

Time Bombs

During the first few weeks of treatment, a small percentage of patients seem to get worse before getting better. If this happens to you, the exact percentage is of no consolation because the worsening affects *you* 100 percent.

Should you fall into this category, you will be glad to learn that there is an encouraging explanation. When you get "worse" after starting treatment, your acne is on the way to complete clearing.

From what you know about how pimples form you understand that before a lesion becomes inflamed (red), it is in a noninflamed state and not as noticeable. As microcomedones and closed comedones mature or "come out," they turn red.

The process that produced the red pimple was

going on for some time already, maybe months. A red pimple, even though it may pop up out of completely normal-looking skin, is never truly "new." To become a red pimple it had to go through the non-red plugging stage. Inflammatory lesions that appear after starting treatment come from comedones present before you started treatment, so do not lose heart.

Treatment can make early plugs mature faster. As the irritating DP agents get down into the plugged follicles, they may cause the follicles to rupture. Treatment does not create new lesions, but can "bring out" plugs that have already formed.

People already having multiple closed comedones who begin treatment are the most susceptible to this phenomenon. When it occurs, it usually does so in the first few weeks of treatment.

Already existing comedones may turn into red lesions after you start treatment.

If this happens to you, you will, of course, be disturbed, but now that you understand what's happening it should not be discouraging. Should this occur, you *know* the treatment is working! You know the DP agents are getting down into the follicles. Also, once all the comedones have "come out," they clear quickly and you will notice a dramatic improvement immediately following the apparent worsening. Remember also that those comedones would have ruptured anyway and all you've done is speed up the process.

Pick, Squeeze and Scratch

Some individuals find it nearly impossible to keep their hands off their acne lesions. It becomes a nervous habit for some and they are often not even aware that they are doing it. Others purposely and with the help of a mirror and various instruments boldly attack acne lesions, believing that the lesions will clear faster or not look so bad if squeezed.

There's nothing wrong with squeezing certain acne lesions, as we've already pointed out, but you have to know what you're doing. Certain acne lesions will resolve faster if they are opened and drained. However, other acne lesions will heal more slowly if irritated and it can be downright dangerous to pick, scratch or squeeze other lesions. You can cause permanent scarring, for example.

To learn which lesions must be left alone, read the section Acne Skin in Chapter 3.

Picking and squeezing acne lesions can be a dangerous practice.

7

Staying
Clear:
Your
Maintenance
Program

Definition

Maintenance treatment is treatment at a reduced level, using a weaker DP agent or fewer applications of the one you have been using. Maintenance treatment is usually very easy. No matter how severe the acne was to start with, almost all patients, once controlled, can remain so with only one application of DP agent per day (either at bedtime or in the morning). A few patients will require two applications per day to remain controlled.

With maintenance treatment you do not need to see any peeling. Your skin will look and feel completely normal! You *will* actually still be peeling but you won't know it because the peeling will be occurring on a microscopic level. Remember, it is *normal* for the skin to peel. Acne forms when the skin doesn't peel. People with beautifully smooth skin and no blemishes are constantly peeling; the dead cell layer is continously shedding. Your goal with maintenance treatment is normal peeling with beautifully smooth skin and no blemishes.

The difference between you and the person who has no acne is that you must continue to use DP agents to make your skin peel *normally*. When your acne goes away, you can completely stop all treatment, but until that time you must continue treatment. If you do not, new blemishes will form. Keep in mind that you still have the disease and it is controlled, not cured.

> **Maintenance treatment is easy but is absolutely essential.**

When

When should you decrease your treatment to a maintenance level? You could do this as soon as you achieve control (no new lesions), but if you have flat red spots, I encourage you to wait until you are completely clear. Flat red spots (see page 134), in my experience, disappear more quickly if you continue peeling.

How long should you go with no new lesions before considering yourself controlled? Caution dictates that you wait at least two weeks. After two weeks with no new lesions (and assuming you have no flat red spots), you are ready to start decreasing treatment. However, any female prone to premenstrual flaring should delay decreasing treatment until after her period starts.

Another consideration that applies to a few individuals is that some blackheads and closed comedones are occasionally quite stubborn. If you have been controlled for weeks but retain a few stubborn comedones that just sit there and do nothing, there are four things you can do:

1. Increase the treatment to cause even more peeling. If the stubborn lesions are limited to only one area of the face, as is frequently true, you need only to cause greater peeling of that area.

2. You may buy a comedo extractor and squeeze out the blackheads, but be careful to leave all closed comedones alone (see page 30).

3. Go to a doctor for acne "surgery" (see page 162).

4. Ignore a few stubborn closed comedones. If you have only four or five closed comedones remaining and you have had no new lesions for weeks, you may choose simply to ignore those few old comedones. They will eventually go away or mature into papules or pustules.

How

How do you decrease treatment? Slowly, cautiously, and step by step. Remember the dosage of your treatment is determined by two factors: the *strength* of the DP agent and the *frequency* of application. Either or both of these may be changed as you decrease treatment to a maintenance level.

Change *one* factor, *one* step at a time. Decrease the number of times each day you wash your face by one. Or decrease the strength of the DP agent by one rank. Do not do both, and don't jump more than one step at a time. Remain at each lower level of treatment at least two weeks before decreasing another step. Continue this stepwise decrease until you are no longer peeling.

Caution

As you decrease your treatment, if you get new inflammatory (red) lesions, you will of course notice them. But you should also be on the lookout for new closed comedones, which are not so obvious since they are not red. Occasionally you should take a very close look at your skin — stretch it and examine for closed comedones. If any kind of new lesions appear, you must increase your treatment.

These comments are especially applicable to the midteen years, when acne usually gets worse. A sixteen-year-old may achieve peeling and control with, for example, a moderate DP agent applied twice a day. But the acne may not have yet reached its peak of activity and decreased treatment may result in a new breakout. It is perfectly acceptable for teenagers to decrease their treatment when their acne is controlled, but they should be aware that they may have to increase the treatment again if the acne takes a turn for the worse.

Adults may also experience increased activity of their disease and, in such case, should increase their treatment. This is not as common as in teenagers, but increased emotional stress, for example, may trigger a flare of an acne condition that had been completely controlled. Regardless of your age, if you flare after decreasing your treatment, your immediate adjustment will be to return to the previous level of treatment at which you remained free of new lesions.

Premenstrual Flares

Without treatment about half of all female acne patients report a flare of their acne just before the menstrual period.

Usually these premenstrual flares are controlled with the peeling treatment. Occasionally, however, some women continue to develop new lesions premenstrually, even though their acne remains completely controlled during the rest of the month. The flaring in such cases is usually minor and the lesions tend to clear quickly. Nevertheless, premenstrual flaring can be very annoying. How do you deal with this?

You can probably stop this flaring by increasing

your level of treatment *five* days before your expected breakout. Increase the treatment by one step. If you tend to flare three days before your period, for example, increase your treatment to include another application of DP agent eight days before your period (five days before the expected flare).

You may have to use a calendar and keep track of your menstrual cycle and premenstrual flare time for a few months in order to do this properly.

Premenstrual flaring may require special treatment.

Don't be discouraged if you don't control the monthly flares the first time you try. It may take you a few months to figure out exactly what to do. Just realize that you have to increase the treatment *before* the expected flare.

If your periods are irregular, the above solution could be difficult. Should the flaring be severe enough to warrant further measures, go to a doctor.

Home Treatment Summarized

Acne starts when the cells that line the follicle stick together instead of sloughing off as they do normally.

You treat the disease by peeling apart those cells that are trying to stick together. You do this by rubbing peeling agents into the skin.

You cannot avoid peeling apart the cells on the surface as well as those within the follicle, but this does not damage the skin in any way and seeing surface peeling proves to you the medicine is working.

Expect to continue breaking out after you start treatment. Even after you have been peeling for a few weeks you may still get "new" pimples — inflammatory (red) lesions such as papules and pustules. These come from preexisting comedones and are not truly new.

Aggressive treatment in the initial phase will help to unplug existing comedones so that they won't rupture and turn red. However, if they are time bombs just ready to explode, the added irritation from the DP agent may actually cause them to rupture. Don't panic if this happens. They would have ruptured anyway — only at a later time.

The real goal of treatment is to prevent the formation of the earliest lesions, the microcomedones, and this is much easier than unplugging those that have already formed. Maintenance treatment is easy.

Since new microcomedones are constantly trying to form, you must keep after the disease on a daily basis. If you do not, new microcomedones will form and hence more papules and pustules will appear later.

Don't handicap your treatment by using oily or greasy makeups or moisturizers. Moisturizers should be used only around the eyes. When applying DP agents, avoid the areas around your eyes, as well as the corners of your mouth.

Remember that your first goal is to achieve *control*. Your acne is controlled when new lesions no longer appear. Even after *control* is achieved some flat red spots may remain. You must recognize those for what they are: burned-out acne.

As the residual inflammation dies out in these flat red spots, you achieve complete *clearing*. To stay that way you must continue to treat, but you can do so on a much reduced dosage. You must still treat daily or new microcomedones will form but you no longer need to be visibly peeling. You go on peeling with maintenance treatment, but on a microscopic level. Your skin will look and feel completely normal.

You may have to treat different areas of your skin differently. If you have acne only on the chin, treat only the chin. Be aware that picking, scratching and squeezing can be downright dangerous.

Do not overwash. Washing dries only the surface. It can actually cause *peeling* of the surface and can thereby mislead you into thinking you are treating adequately when, in fact, you are not. The disease is in the follicles *beneath* the surface, and you must use DP agents to cause peeling in the follicles.

The time it takes to gain control over the disease varies from person to person, but the vast majority of readers can expect control in three to eight weeks.

Doctor-Assisted
Acne
Treatment

If you are thinking about seeing a doctor to get help in treating your acne, or if you are already doing so, you may find the following pages helpful, with answers to questions you may have. The use of prescription drugs is discussed as well as special techniques and procedures employed by doctors in treating acne.

Whether you consult a doctor is, of course, your decision. As already discussed in the introductory remarks, if you have severe acne, if there is any doubt in your mind about the diagnosis, if you are an adult female who has suddenly developed acne (see page 56), or if you are having trouble treating it yourself, I recommend that you see a doctor.

But if you do not fit into any of the above categories, there is no reason you should not treat your acne yourself and, of course, home treatment and how to do it are the main points made in this book.

Prescription DP Agents

The doctor's prescription pad is a powerful tool

with which he/she can give you access to certain drying-peeling agents available only by prescription. If you have difficulty making your skin peel with over-the-counter DP agents, you may want to use one of the prescription agents.

Some readers will not peel with even as many as four daily applications of the strongest over-the-counter DP agents. If you are in this group, don't worry about it; you can clear your acne and there are several ways to do it. You can apply your over-the-counter product even more frequently, you can put on more when you apply it, rub it in longer or better, or you can go to a doctor and get a prescription for a stronger DP agent.

The most widely used prescription DP agents contain benzoyl peroxide. As you know, excellent benzoyl peroxide products are available over-the-counter, but certain of the stronger ones require a prescription. Another very popular prescription DP agent is vitamin A acid (tretinoin or retinoic acid).

Tetracycline and Other Antibiotics

If you have consulted a doctor about your acne condition, you were probably given a prescription for an antibiotic to take orally, since oral antibiotics have been the backbone of professional acne treatment for over twenty years. The best-known antibiotic is still penicillin, but penicillin is not effective in acne. The antibiotic most commonly employed in treating acne is tetracycline. More tetracycline is used than all the other antibiotics combined, and it has been in use since the early 1950s.

How Do Tetracycline and Other Antibiotics Work?

Tetracycline is the standard, prototype antibiotic, but the following comments apply to all those used in acne. Antibiotics, in general, work by fighting bacteria. Bacteria are organisms so small we cannot see them without a microscope. They are found in many areas of our bodies, including the follicles of the skin. Antibiotics kill bacteria, or stop them from reproducing, or inhibit them in a number of other ways.

As with so many other medicines, tetracycline was known to be effective in acne before there were any well-accepted theories about *how* it works. We still argue about the precise way in which tetracycline and the other antibiotics alter the acne process, but the most widely accepted theory has to do with their effect on the creation of *fatty acids* within the follicles. The role of fatty acids has recently become controversial, but most doctors still believe they cause problems. First, they are irritating and may help to cause the inflammation associated with acne. Part of the evidence for this is that if fatty acids are injected into normal skin, a red pimple forms at the site of the injection. Secondly, fatty acids may somehow play a role in the beginning of plug formation, when the cells of the follicle wall start sticking together.

Bacteria within the follicle break down the oil (sebum) into fatty acids. The theory about how antibiotics work is that they interfere with those bacteria that are helping to manufacture fatty acids. Treatment with antibiotics means fewer fatty acids and, therefore, less fuel for the acne process.

What Are the Side Effects of Taking Tetracycline?

Millions have taken this antibiotic and have done so for years without any side effects. Tetracycline is truly one of the safest drugs available today.

The only side effect that occurs with any degree of frequency is vaginitis in females. Vaginitis is a vaginal infection with an accompanying vaginal discharge that is troublesome and inconvenient; it frequently itches. But it is easily treated and does not necessarily mean that the individual cannot be treated with tetracycline. A reduced dosage, for example, may be just as effective in treating the acne without causing the vaginitis.

Other side effects are rare and include stomach and intestinal problems such as diarrhea, skin rashes, fingernail problems and blood changes.

Pregnant females should not take tetracycline because of possible damage to the developing baby. For example, if pregnant females take tetracycline past the fourth month of pregnancy, the baby's teeth will almost certainly be discolored. A yellow, gray or brown stain is the usual result. The same applies to mothers who breastfeed their infants. They must avoid tetracycline. Children up to the age of twelve should not take tetracycline because of the same risk of staining the teeth. Some doctors feel tetracycline is safe after age eight.

People with certain kidney diseases cannot take tetracycline because it may further damage their kidneys. Also, old tetracycline should be discarded since it can cause kidney disease. Taking someone else's medicine, or taking medicine that has been lying around for a long time, is never a good idea, and this general rule also applies specifically to tetracycline.

When Tetracycline Doesn't Work

Sometimes when tetracycline doesn't seem to be working, it is because of problems that can be corrected. Tetracycline must be taken properly if it is to be effective. Obviously, the medication has to be absorbed. It has to get into the blood before it can be circulated through the body and arrive at the follicles of the skin where it's needed. There can be significant problems with absorption of this drug. If tetracycline is taken at the same time that food or milk is ingested, it becomes bound to certain substances like calcium in the food or milk and passes through the intestines unabsorbed and wasted. If tetracycline is taken an hour before meals, it is completely absorbed before the food gets to the stomach. But if you've already eaten, you should wait two hours before taking the tetracycline if you want to ensure maximum absorption. Similarly, tetracycline may not be absorbed if it is taken with vitamin and mineral tablets. Antacids will also interfere with absorption. People who take such things as Gelusil, Maalox, Mylanta, Rolaids, Tums and others must take them at a different time from that when they take their tetracycline.

If more attention were paid to this important detail, perhaps many of the tetracycline failures would not be failures at all. Scientific studies have shown that in many acne patients who fail to respond to tetracycline, the concentration of tetracycline found in their blood was very low, indicating poor absorption.

Erythromycin

Almost all antibiotics have been tried in the treatment of acne. The second most important and most widely used one is erythromycin. Many doctors use this as the backup drug for tetracycline. If tetracycline isn't controlling the acne, they may switch to erythromycin. Erythromycin is probably as effective as tetracycline, but it's more expensive and not used as frequently.

Erythromycin is just as safe if not safer than tetracycline. Erythromycin is probably as safe to use as any drug on the market, but there is one form, erythromycin *estolate*, that can damage the liver.

The other forms of erythromycin are all free of this risk.

Minocycline

Minocycline is a chemical derivative of tetracycline. It has been shown to work many times in acne when plain tetracycline has failed. Food and dairy products do not interfere with absorption of minocycline, but antacids do. Since it is a derivative of tetracycline, the comments on page 158 about the side effects of tetracycline apply here also. A side effect much more common with minocycline than with plain tetracycline is dizziness. The dizziness may be eliminated by lowering the dose or taking the minocycline with food. If your doctor wants to change you from tetracycline to minocycline, the main difference you will immediately notice is the cost. Minocycline is much more expensive, but that may not concern you if it clears your skin.

Clindamycin and Lincomycin

Clindamycin and lincomycin are related antibiotics and will be discussed together. These drugs are very effective in the treatment of acne and enjoyed a period of popularity. However, it has been found that they may cause diarrhea and a few of the cases of diarrhea were associated with severe colitis (inflammation of the colon).

Topical Antibiotics

Topical means applied to the *top* or surface of the skin. Within the last few years a lot of research has been done using tetracycline, erythromycin, clindamycin and lincomycin on the surface of the skin. Research in this area continues, but some of the early reports are very encouraging.

Any topical medicine is, as a rule, much safer than a systemic medicine (medicine taken orally or given by injection so that it gets into your entire system). There is much less concern about side effects when these antibiotics are used on the surface.

Special Techniques and Office Procedures

Acne "Surgery"

So-called acne surgery applies to the opening or expressing of certain existing acne lesions, using such instruments as a scalpel (small surgical knife), a needle, or a comedo extractor.

As stated previously (page 40), existing pustules will heal faster if the tip is punctured and the contents carefully expressed. Doctors and their assistants are expert at this, and it can definitely effect a rather dramatic improvement. Sometimes larger lesions, if they are soft and fluid-filled, can also be drained in this manner.

Some doctors also like to express comedones and they feel it is quite helpful in the treatment. However, the effects may be only temporary. You probably have already noticed that when you squeeze a blackhead, it reappears later. Expressed blackheads are not gone, they are just temporarily emptied. But this procedure can provide a head start for the DP agents and your skin looks better instantly.

Intralesional Steroids

This procedure involves putting medicine directly into (*intra*) certain lesions by injecting them with a needle. It causes very little pain and is a good and useful procedure. The medicines used are corticosteroids: usually triamcinolone. Triamcinolone, because of its anti-inflammatory action, causes injected lesions to resolve more quickly. The results are sometimes quite dramatic and evident in only a few days' time.

Cryotherapy

Cryo means cold and the term cryotherapy usually refers to the freezing of certain inflammatory lesions with liquid nitrogen, liquid oxygen, or dry ice. Cryotherapy is another method of causing large inflammatory lesions (nodules and cysts) to heal more quickly. Without treatment, they may last five months or longer. Freezing them or injecting them frequently causes them to heal within a few days to two weeks.

Another form of cryotherapy involves freezing an entire acne area, such as the cheeks, forehead and chin; in other words, a broad superficial freeze that promotes peeling. Liquid nitrogen is used as a spray, or can be rolled on with an applicator. A form of this therapy that has been popular for many years is the use of dry ice. Dry ice is solid carbon dioxide (CO_2) and it can be used as is, or can be ground into a powder and mixed with such things as acetone and sulfur to form a slush that is then applied to the skin. Some readers may know this as the "doorknob" treatment.

Superficial freezing of the skin in this manner can be very effective and can be used for a short burst of intensified peeling or as an integral part of the current treatment program. However, the effects of this superficial freezing last only three to four days, and therefore if one relies on it to sustain peeling, it must be repeated at least twice a week.

X Ray

X ray damages the sebaceous glands, causing a dramatic decrease in oil production. The only other way we presently have of slowing down the prodution of oil is by using estrogen, which will be discussed later.

Prior to 1945, about 70 percent of acne patients who went to a doctor received X-ray therapy. X-ray therapy is very effective and the fact that it works so well supports the argument that oil production is very important in this disease. Later, X ray was replaced by tetracycline as the most popular acne treatment.

There are several reasons for the replacement. Unfortunately, the oil glands recuperate after being damaged by a course of X-ray therapy. So the effects do not last; they are only temporary. Furthermore, one cannot repeatedly receive X ray. Eventually it damages the skin and increases the chances of skin cancer later in life. X ray can damage other tissues as well, and therefore the eyes, eyebrows, scalp hair, thyroid gland and the sex organs must be carefully shielded.

Ultraviolet Light (UVL)

Most people with acne get better during the summer months and one of the reasons is the increased exposure to the sun's ultraviolet rays. Ultraviolet rays are known to be able to kill bacteria, and they also cause peeling of the skin.

Artificial sunlight in the form of sunlamps or ultraviolet lamps has been used for years by doctors in the treatment of acne and this method remains popular. Administered in the right dosage and frequency, UVL alone can frequently clear an acne condition. A side effect that patients like is tanning of the skin, which also helps camouflage the acne. The only problem is that ultraviolet rays, like real sunlight, speed up aging of the skin, cause wrinkles, and increase the chances of skin cancer later in life.

Ultraviolet light, like certain forms of cryotherapy, can be used for a short burst of intensified peeling or as an integral part of the current treatment program. But, again, if you are going to sustain peeling this way, you have to repeat it two to three times a week. It works best if pushed to the point of causing visible peeling of the skin. In essence, one must cause a mild burn of the skin, which, of course, once more raises the issue of damage to the skin. The same peeling can be accomplished with DP agents that do not damage the skin and do not cause wrinkles.

Other Medications

Diuretics

Diuretics (water pills) pull water out of body tissues and expel it in the urine. Theoretically, at least, diuretics might be beneficial in a female whose acne tends to flare before her menstrual periods. Many women tend to retain fluid premenstrually in certain body tissues. This leads to swelling in certain areas and it's common to notice a slight gain in weight. If there is swelling of the cells of the epidermis that surround the follicle opening, it will be smaller. Consequently, it will be harder for the dead cells and oil to get out, and thus comedo formation is increased.

So, theoretically, diuretics taken at the right time could alleviate the swelling and open the follicles again. If your acne gets much worse before your periods, or if it is completely controlled except for premenstrual flares, your doctor may suggest trying diuretics.

Diuretics should be taken only with a doctor's supervision because, in addition to pulling water out of the body, they also pull out potassium and sodium. If too much potassium or sodium is removed, the individual can become seriously ill.

Vitamin A

Vitamin A taken orally is to be distinguished from vitamin A *acid*, which is applied topically. As recently as the mid-1960s, this vitamin was widely used in the treatment of acne. Dosages usually employed ranged from 50,000 to 150,000 international units (IU) per day.

Controlled studies, however, have shown that usual doses of vitamin A are no more beneficial than sugar pills. Therefore, this form of therapy has lost most of its support. Some doctors still feel that vitamin A can be helpful in acne. However, they admit that it requires a dosage on the order of

400,000 IU per day. At that level there may be side effects, including headaches, nausea, fatigue, insomnia, dry skin, itching and redness of the skin.

Some people think that all vitamins are harmless and they are not aware that it is possible to be injured by an overdose of vitamin A. I caution you here because vitamin A is available without a prescription and occasionally an acne sufferer has overdosed himself because he read somewhere that vitamin A was beneficial for acne.

Tranquilizers

Mild tranquilizers taken for a short period of time are sometimes beneficial in acne. If you feel emotional stress is playing an important role in your acne (see page 67), discuss this with your doctor. The danger with tranquilizers is that one may become psychologically dependent upon them. Tranquilizers are not actually physically addictive, but if you take them too long, it becomes very difficult to stop taking them. Try to learn to relax without the aid of medication.

Zinc

We do not yet know how effective zinc is in the treatment of acne. Results are conflicting and this form of therapy must, as yet, be considered experimental. The original publicity was probably far too optimistic.

This medication is available over-the-counter, and I caution you not to overdose yourself with zinc. Zinc can be dangerous — it irritates the lining of the intestines and can cause intestinal bleeding. Be careful about treating yourself with internal medication! Learn the side effects and risks. Read the directions carefully and do not exceed the recommended dosage.

Estrogen and "The Pill"

Oral contraceptives (birth control pills) are extremely popular and have been used by millions of women all over the world. In recent years, there has been increasing concern over the safety of "the pill." Side effects and complications can be serious. Estrogen, the female sex hormone found in birth control pills, is the main component responsible for producing these complications.

Most of the side effects are not really serious, just troublesome and frustrating. One possible side effect of the pill is its influence on acne. That influence can produce opposite results. That is, when you are taking the pill, acne sometimes gets better, but sometimes it gets worse. Taking the pill causes hormonal changes similar to those of pregnancy and the same confusing response has also been observed in pregnancy: acne sometimes clears completely, yet in other cases, it breaks out.

No one can yet explain these paradoxical responses to pregnancy, but researchers have partially solved the mystery of the pill and its opposite effects on acne. Birth control pills can be divided into two types: one type tends to make acne worse, and the other type tends to make it better. This latter type is "estrogen-dominant." Estrogen is known to decrease the output of the oil glands.

However, even the most estrogen-dominant pills are not always helpful. They just are not always effective; even if they do work, it can take as long as five months to get a good effect. Further frustration is encountered in that they may actually make the acne worse the first month or two. Also, sometimes the acne "breaks through" after being suppressed by these pills for a prolonged time.

Estrogen (in any form) cannot be used by males, since it may cause enlargement of the breasts, loss of sexual appetite, softening of the testes and other feminizing changes.

Treatment of Scarring

The objective of this entire book is to show you how to treat acne effectively so that scarring does not occur. But what can you do if you are already scarred?

If your disease is still active, your primary concern is to stop the disease so that further scarring does not occur. You should institute a very aggressive topical treatment program and follow it diligently. Attempt to achieve control quickly and, if you have any degree of difficulty, consult a doctor. Scarring acne must be stopped since it is considerably easier and much less expensive to prevent scars than it is to treat them once formed. By treating aggressively you benefit further because, while bringing your disease under control with peeling, you will at the same time be treating your scars. Surface peeling, no matter how it is accomplished, noticeably decreases scarring.

Be aware that time alone is a "treatment" for scarring. Scars become less obvious just with the passage of time. When you are using DP agents and peeling, these changes occur more quickly.

Even so, the improvement that occurs with time or superficial peeling (with DP agents) is not very dramatic or fast; you may wish to do more. Many forms of professional treatment for scarring are available. The only limitations are availability of professional services and your financial resources. Doctors are getting better all the time at the treatment of scarring. Ask your doctor to discuss the various methods that could be used to treat *your* scarring, since such treatment needs to be tailored to fit each individual's need, depending on the *type* of scarring. Ask your doctor to estimate how much improvement you can expect, what the potential risks are, and how much it will cost.

Dermabrasion

The classic method for treating acne scars is dermabrasion. In this method, the skin is frozen (usually with a refrigerant spray) and then sanded with a wire brush or diamond fraise, which is mounted on an instrument much like a dentist's drill. Follow-up care varies, but the abraded area oozes and bleeds and quite a lot of swelling can occur. A crust or scab may form and when the crust comes off, the skin is rather raw and tender until completely healed about three weeks later. While healing, and even for some weeks after healing, the skin is much more sensitive to anything applied topically as well as to sunlight.

Theoretically, perfectly smooth skin should be the result after healing, but this frequently is not the case. Some scars are too deep and will not be eliminated with this procedure. People who have a lot of "ice-pick" scars, for example, should not expect such scars to disappear.

On the other hand, if all the scars are quite superficial, they may be completely eliminated. When there is only partial improvement this procedure can be repeated, producing further improvement. Adequate time for total healing must pass before a repeat dermabrasion.

The risks include infection, hyperpigmentation and hypopigmentation (an increase or decrease in the amount of color in the skin) and the production of tiny cysts called milia.

The main drawback, in my opinion, is that the results are disappointing in those who need improvement the most: those who have deep scarring. Appearance is misleading immediately after healing from dermabrasion, because of swelling within the skin. This swelling persists for weeks to months and makes the skin look smoother than it actually is. The immediate appearance is better than the true end result.

To summarize: for some people this procedure is great, but for others the results are disappointing. Your doctor can tell you how much improvement you can expect with your particular type of scarring.

Chemical Peeling

Chemical peeling is quite similar to dermabrasion, except that a caustic chemical, such as trichloracetic acid, is used instead of mechanical sanding. The chemical is applied and causes a severe peeling very similar to dermabrasion. The results and risks are also very similar to those of dermabrasion.

Chemical Exfoliation

When the term chemical peel is used, it usually

refers to a one-time application of a caustic chemical in strong concentration, such as 50 percent trichloracetic acid. Another form of chemical peeling that is less drastic involves applying a lesser concentration of the chemical, but applying it repeatedly. An example would be the application of 20 to 30 percent trichloracetic acid twice a week.

This produces a less severe peel, but the results can be gratifying if applications are continued for several weeks. There are fewer complications in removing scars this way. Furthermore, this form of chemical peeling, frequently referred to as chemical exfoliation or chemo-exfoliation, has the added advantage of being capable of treating active acne as well as scarring.

Chemabrasion

Chemabrasion is a combination of chemical peeling and dermabrasion. Combining the two methods may lead to better results.

Cryotherapy

Superficial freezing of the skin with liquid nitrogen, either rolled or sprayed on, causes peeling similar to chemical exfoliation. Sometimes it is done with dry ice instead of liquid nitrogen. This method is used to treat active acne as well as scarring.

Ringing

Some scars are more obvious simply because they have sharp-sided walls. If the walls of a scar are almost perpendicular to the surface, they cast a shadow in the depth of the scar, making it more noticeable. Very strong solutions, such as 100 percent trichloracetic acid, can be carefully applied to the edge of such scars. This causes a beveling of the wall of the scar. With the incline more gradual the shadow is decreased and this makes the scar less noticeable.

Surgical Excision

Certain scars are so deep or so large that they are best treated by cutting them out surgically and stitching the skin back together.

Excision and Elevation

Depressed scars can be incised (cut) with a scalpel or biopsy punch (a small cylindrical knife that works like a cookie cutter) and brought to the surface. A filler material is sometimes placed beneath the scar to help elevate it.

Financial Considerations

As stated, a limiting factor in the treatment of scarring is the patient's financial situation. Some of these procedures are quite time-consuming and expensive. Advances are constantly being made and much can be done for scarring, but it will remain far better and far less expensive to prevent scars rather than to try to eliminate them once formed.

Questions and Answers about Your Treatment

Maybe someday we will have an injectable medication, or a pill or some other treatment that can be administered just once and that permanently cures acne. If such treatment is discovered, and is also found to be free of dangerous side effects, it will be a tremendous advance in medical knowledge. But we have to live in the present and, at present, there is no such treatment. If you have acne *now*, you must treat it with the presently available knowledge, techniques and medication.

There is no magical treatment. What is available, if you want to control the disease completely, is a treatment *program*. Such a program is detailed in this book.

The treatment described in this book is the most effective, fastest, safest, simplest and least expensive program available today to rid yourself of acne. You have every right to expect complete clearing if you follow the directions given. If you have problems, do not achieve the results you want, or if you have questions other than those answered here, you should go back through the book again. Instructions are given *throughout* the book; all possible problems and questions are not answered in this chapter. The discussion here is limited to emphasizing certain points most commonly asked about by my patients.

Q: My husband objects to the odor of my DP agent. What can I do?

A: This has been a problem for a few of my patients. Both sulfur and benzoyl peroxide products may produce an odor. You should switch DP agents or apply it after he is already asleep. If you are already controlled and need to apply the DP agent only once a day to stay controlled, you could use the DP agent during the time when your husband is not home.

Q: My DP agent leaves a whitish film on my face. Isn't it supposed to dry clear?

A: Yes, it is, unless you are using a tinted DP agent. You may be applying it a little too heavily or not rubbing it in completely. Or it's just a problem of individual "skin chemistry" and all you need do is switch to another product.

Q: My DP agent burns and stings when I first put it on. Is this normal?

A: Slight burning or stinging is normal. It should last only a short time. If it is severe or persists, you may be allergic to that product, in which case a switch to an alternate DP agent is indicated.

Q: I have very large pores on my nose that look almost like blackheads. What can I do?

A: They are probably not truly blackheads because the pores on the nose are commonly quite large.

Many people have these but you haven't noticed, just as other people do not notice them on you. Remember, you look much more closely at your own skin and you are probably far more critical than anyone else would be. It is difficult to alter permanently the size of pores (follicles) and I challenge any claim you have heard to the contrary. This shouldn't be too surprising now that you know the microscopic anatomy of follicles. I *do* think that DP agents can be of some help because with the oil and dead cells flowing out, there is nothing to stretch the pore open.

Q: I started using a DP agent and achieved peeling, but the scaling skin is brown in color.

A: This happens sometimes on dark-skinned people and is almost never anything to worry about, although perhaps you should see a doctor since you may be causing hyperpigmentation (darkening of the skin color) and you want to avoid that (see page 134).

Q: I am peeling and the itching is driving me crazy. What can I do?

A: A small percentage of my patients complain about this. The itching is related to the degree of dryness and peeling. If the itching is so bad you can't tolerate it, you should adjust your treatment downward one step. See "Step Six: Adjust Your Treatment," page 98.

Q: Are you sure this peeling won't wrinkle my skin?

A: I am sure. This question is answered in great detail in "Peel Is In" (page 126).

Q: I don't mind the peeling except that it looks so awful. What can I do?

A: Does it look worse than the acne you had when you started? If you think it does, you should decrease treatment or go to a doctor. Remember, peeling is a means to an end — controlled acne and clear skin. Once you are controlled, peeling is reduced during maintenance treatment to an invisible level.

Q: What makeup can I use?

A: It is best not to wear any makeup when you're treating an active case of acne but if you feel you must, insist that the label on the makeup states "water-base," "greaseless" or "oil-free." Again, I encourage you to try one of the products listed on page 124.

Q: After starting treatment I got oilier. How can this be?

A: By unplugging pores more oil may now be getting to the surface. Remember, as long as it gets *out* there is no problem. I recommend, though, that you increase your treatment by applying a stronger DP agent or using your present DP agent more frequently.

Q: I haven't had a new pimple for a month but I still look terrible. When will I clear?

A: This is the problem of flat red spots (see page

134), which are merely residual inflammations. They will fade with time.

Q: I started treating and now it is three weeks later and I have more pimples than I had before. What's going on?

A: Your preexisting comedones are coming out. They would have done this anyway sooner or later. See "Time Bombs," page 136.

Q: The corners of my mouth are so dry and cracked that they hurt. What am I doing wrong?

A: The DP agent is being applied too close to the corners of your mouth. Put a colorless lipstick or ChapStick on them and from now on be careful to apply the DP agent so as to avoid those areas.

Q: You said this treatment would not cause wrinkles, but I can *see* the skin wrinkling around my eyes.

A: You haven't caused real wrinkles; don't worry! See "Peel Is In," page 126. Don't apply the DP agent close to the eyes and it is permissible to use your regular moisturizer there.

Q: How long will I have to peel?

A: It depends on how aggressively you treat and what type of acne you have (see page 108).

Q: My cheeks are dry and peeling but my forehead is still oily.

A: Put more DP agent on the forehead, put it on more frequently or rub it in better. You could also buy a stronger DP agent for your forehead.

Q: I should be treating three times a day but sometimes I simply cannot wash during the day. What can I do so I won't upset the treatment?

A: Apply the DP agent anyway, without first washing, or wipe your face first with a presaturated towelette such as Therapads. These can be carried conveniently in your pocket or purse.

Q: I started with a face full of closed comedones. Now about 80 percent of them are gone. The dryness and peeling are getting to me. Do I need to stay this dry to get rid of the remaining comedones?

A: Yes, if you want to get rid of that remaining 20 percent as fast as possible. No, if you are willing to have them around a little longer. The important factor is that you are controlling the formation of new comedones.

Q: I am completely controlled except just before my period. What can I do?

A: Treat more aggressively before your periods or go to a doctor (see page 145).

Q: I am convinced I am doing everything right but I am not getting any better. What should I do?

A: Go to a doctor. You may not have true acne or your acne may be superimposed on another disease.

Q: I have heard so much about vitamin E, but you never mention it in the book. Is vitamin E good for acne?

A: Vitamin E has never been shown to benefit

acne. This applies to vitamin E taken orally as well as applied topically to the surface of the skin. If you use vitamin E topically that is prepared in an oil base, it may make your acne worse.

Q: Not only is my face oily, I also have very oily hair and dandruff. What can I do about this?

A: Try shampooing more frequently and scrub the scalp — don't just wash the hair — as you shampoo. Scalp brushes are helpful in doing this. Additionally, you could ask your pharmacist to recommend a stronger shampoo — one that is recommended for oily hair and dandruff. If you have severely oily hair or dandruff, not controlled by what I have just suggested, go to a doctor.

There is nothing more I need to tell you. The next chapter is written for doctors and summarizes what I have said in medical terminology. With an understanding of your disease and a method to treat it, you are now fully equipped to fight acne — and win!

My sincerest best wishes,

Appendix  To the
Physician

The basic principle *which is the* foundation of topical
acne medication *is the achievement of a* continuous mild
nondisfiguring drying and peeling *of the skin to remove
and prevent follicular obstruction.*
— *Marion Sulzberger and Victor Witten,*
    Medical Clinics of North America, *43:895 (1959)*

Dear Colleague:

As you know, acne is a disease evolving from retention
hyperkeratosis of the follicular epithelium. The hyperkeratosis is due not only to retention, but also to increased
production, of squamous cells. Impactions form intrafol-
licularly and may eventually rupture into the dermis, producing inflammatory lesions. Not all follicles are susceptible. For example, the presence and outward growth of a
terminal hair are sufficient to prevent an impaction. While
these morphogenetic events are widely accepted, the precise and primary pathogenetic event(s) eludes us. The
exact roles of heredity, androgen, 5-alpha reductase,
sebum, free fatty acids, microorganisms and their en-
zymes, intercellular cement, keratinosomes, and Knut-
son's lipid inclusions remain ill-defined and controversial.
While questions remain and research continues, we already have extremely effective therapy for this disease and
that is the message of this book.

Hyperkeratosis can be successfully combated with desquamating or exfoliating agents. Older literature refers to
such things as sulfur, salicylic acid and resorcinol as being
keratolytic, but they do not actually lyse keratin and are
therefore not keratolytic. However, what *is* important is

that the agents we use be *comedo*lytic; that they break up the follicular impactions and/or prevent their formation. They may do this by altering intercellular cement, affecting desmosomal attachments, or inhibiting the synthesis of tonofilaments. The literature is sparse on the exact mechanisms of desquamation; nevertheless, anyone can readily observe its occurrence. Certainly we've all seen epidermal desquamation with the above agents as well as with the newer benzoyl peroxide and retinoic acid. Additionally, free fatty-acid measurements, radioisotope studies and observations of clinical efficacy convincingly demonstrate that follicular "penetration" and follicular desquamation occur.

Since the follicular epithelium is merely an invagination of the epidermis, this disease begins outside the body and consequently invites topical therapy. Systemic agents, if they are to combat retention hyperkeratosis, may need to be capable of penetrating the follicular epithelium.

This book espouses the peeling — desquamating — method of treating acne. Some have been reluctant to employ this approach because of the difficulty in achieving patient compliance. In my experience this is easily overcome in the vast majority of cases by patient education on the initial visit. Time thus invested is returned with interest on subsequent visits, not to mention the tremendous satisfaction that comes from helping someone to completely clear an acne condition — a task I find difficult without the patient's understanding and cooperation. As a further time-saving measure, one can train assistants to spend the necessary educational time with each new acne patient. Perhaps some of you will find this book helpful in training assistants as well as in educating and motivating patients.

I am fully aware of the doubts, confusion, questions, unrest and fears created in patients' minds by certain lay medical publications. Many of us are weary of interrogations regarding the latest cure for a disease as outlined in the daily newspaper, magazine or book such as this. We object to being forced to read what is likely to be speculative or premature. Since you may feel obligated to read part of this, I present my position here as succinctly as possible with candid attention to those items most likely to stir controversy.

In the text I do caution against certain treatment modalities. Thus: I point out that clindamycin and lincomycin have caused severe colitis. Oral contraceptives and X ray are both associated with significant risks. Ultraviolet light accelerates cutaneous aging processes. Dapsone and prednisone are not mentioned as treatment modalities.

One does what one feels necessary, but I am personally convinced that a lot of "necessities" would vanish if the peeling approach were first employed. I have nothing against the use of tetracycline or erythromycin but, as you know, antibiotics are not a panacea and do nothing for existing comedones. Tetracycline cannot be used in pregnant females, nursing mothers or children. James Leyden reports a 4 percent incidence of Gram-negative folliculitis with long-term administration of antibiotics and states they have never been able to cure that condition. This is not discussed in the text because these statistics are inconsistent with my observations, but if Gram-negative folliculitis is that likely, it is a potent reason to limit the use of antibiotics. Free fatty acids are probably not as important as was believed. Even so, benzoyl peroxide is more effective and sulfur as effective as tetracycline in reducing free fatty-acid concentration.

The reports on topical antibiotics are encouraging. One hopes Gram-negative folliculitis and sensitization will not become problems.

The book is consumer-oriented, since DHEW Publication No. (HRA) 76–1639, based on an examination of 6,768 youths age twelve to seventeen, reports only 11 percent of those with acne seek professional help. The text details the fine points important to a successful peeling approach whether accomplished with prescription or OTC medication. By increasing public awareness of the facts that acne is *not* normal but a true disease and that effective treatment *is* available, the book is certain to result in increased seeking of professional help. On the other hand, the book emphasizes what can be done at home without consulting a doctor.

You are encouraged to read the entire book, if you are so inclined, but I'm cognizant of your reading requirements. Therefore, I've attempted above to give you an overview of the goal and the philosophy behind it, along with my position on points most likely to interest you.

What follows is a short synopsis of the treatment program as detailed in the text:

The overriding principle of topical therapy is dosage. The goal is peeling, controlled exfoliation, on a 24-hours-a-day, 7-days-a-week basis. The superiority of any particular exfoliant has not been established. Some are stronger but that does not make them better. They must be matched to the individual. Incidentally, vast clinical experience obviates any concern regarding sulfur's comedogenicity.

Unwarranted concern about the additive effects of exfoliative modalities is avoided by remembering the principle of dosage. While it is true that a patient using retinoic acid will exfoliate more if the medication is applied to a hydrated stratum corneum, some cases require increased exfoliative action. Again, the end point of this approach is visible surface peeling. If there is no epidermal desquamation, it seems unlikely that intrafollicular desquamation is occurring.

There are three stages of treatment. During the *initial* stage, preexisting microcomedones, closed comedones and occasional open comedones will sometimes rupture, producing "new" inflammatory lesions in spite of (or even because of) aggressive topical therapy. The second stage is *control*, when "new" inflammatory lesions no longer appear. Frustrations are encountered because erythematous macules can remain during this stage and must be recognized for what they are: burned-out acne. With eventual resolution of all residual inflammation *complete clearing* is achieved.

Intensified bursts of therapy with CO_2 slush, Vleminckx's solution, liquid nitrogen spray or UVL are useful, but since new microcomedones are an ever-present threat, these modalities must be repeated at least twice weekly if they are to be the foundation of therapy. Sporadic desquamation fails.

After clearing, maintenance therapy is essential but is easy and is performed at a considerably reduced dosage. Clinically obvious peeling is no longer necessary at this point. The vast majority remain clear with BID (or merely QD) applications of the proper desquamating agent. Clinically, it is much easier to prevent microcomedones than it is to unseat those already established.

Stress is a factor in acne and must be dealt with appropriately. Instead of being embarrassed by the placebo effect, we should make every attempt to maximize it. Pressure, from football chin straps, for example, can trigger acne. Comedogenic substances including makeup and moisturizers must be eliminated. Dietary restrictions are not necessary although certain drugs can interfere. For example, steroids, topically as well as systemically, can induce an acneform eruption.

Acne does not affect all areas of the face equally; the distribution is patchy and changes. The forehead, for example, may require a different dosage from that for the cheeks or chin. The corners of the mouth, the periorbital areas and the neck (unless involved) should be avoided when applying desquamating agents.

For premenstrual flaring increased desquamation and/or diuretics can be tried, but should be started on about day 15 of the cycle.

This book was written to be helpful. I hope I have achieved some measure of success in that direction. I welcome your comments.

Sincerely,

Ken Flandermeyer, M.D.

Appendix For Canadian Readers

At the time of this writing, not all the products listed in this book are available in Canada. According to my sources:

Regarding Chart 2, page 88

A. All benzoyl peroxide products require a prescription in Canada.

B. Unfortunately, none of the *Strong* products listed are available in Canada. If you have determined that you need a *Strong* product, there are three things you can do:

1. Talk to your pharmacist about a Canadian equivalent of the products listed;
2. Decide to be slightly more aggressive as you start your treatment and use PiSec or Saligel. PiSec and Saligel are from the *Strongest* group and *are* available in Canada;
3. Decide to be slightly less aggressive as you start your treatment and chose a *Moderate* product, all of which are available in Canada.

C. In the *Weak* category, Komed Mild is available in Canada.

Regarding Chart 3, page 91

Almost all of those listed are available in Canada.

You will not find Epi*Clear or Polybrade. The others are available to you.

Regarding Makeup Substitutes, page 124

All except Loroxide and Sulforcin Base 4% can be obtained without a prescription. Loroxide is available but requires a prescription.

Glossary

Acneform — In the form of acne; acnelike

Acnegenic — Causing or generating acne

Adrenal gland — A small gland located just above the kidneys that manufactures several types of hormones

Androgen — One of the normal sex hormones responsible for male sexual development, but also found normally in females

Antacid — Something like Maalox or Gelusil that neutralizes or counteracts acids

Antibiotic — Medicine used to fight bacteria

Bacteria — Germs

Basal layer — The bottom layer of the epidermis or follicle wall where new cells are born

Benzoyl peroxide — A very effective drying-peeling agent

Chemabrasion — Combined chemical peeling and dermabrasion. A method of treating acne scars

Clear — To cause all evidence of acne to disappear; or, the condition that exists when you have blemish-free skin with no evidence of acne

Clearing — No new blemishes are forming and all old ones are disappearing

Clindamycin — An antibiotic helpful in acne but that may be dangerous when taken internally

Colitis — Inflammation of the colon

Comedo, closed — An advanced microcomedo with the follicle opening almost closed

Comedo, open — Blackhead

Comedogenic — Causing or generating comedones

Connective tissue — The foundation or supporting structure of the skin; found in the dermis; damaged when wrinkles form

Control — To stop the formation of new blemishes; or, the condition that exists when you have stopped the formation of new blemishes

Corticosteroid — A hormone like cortisone produced by the cortex (outer layer) of the adrenal gland, also produced synthetically and used as a medicine

Cortisone — A hormone with anti-inflammatory powers, found naturally in the body and also used as medicine

Cryotherapy — Cryo means cold; this refers to superficial freezing of the skin

Cyst — A large acne lesion with liquefied contents

Dermabrasion — A sanding method used for the treatment of scarring

Dermis — The second layer of skin

Desquamation — Peeling

Dilate — To expand, enlarge

Diuretic — A "water pill." A diuretic will pull water out of body tissues and expel it in the urine

DP agent — Drying-peeling agent. This refers to any of the five chemicals: benzoyl peroxide, sulfur, resorcinol, salicylic acid and vitamin A acid, as well as acne products that contain one or more of those chemicals

Eccentric — Lopsided or odd
Edema — Swelling
Encapsulated — Surrounded
Engulf — To swallow
Epidermal turnover time — The time it takes for the epidermis to replace itself; about 27 days
Epidermis — The surface or outer layer of the skin
Epithelium — Any lining of either external or internal surfaces of the body; the epidermis is a type of epithelium
Erythema — Redness
Erythromycin — An antibiotic used in the treatment of acne
Estrogen — Female sex hormone
Eunuch — A castrated man
Exfoliation — Peeling

Fatty acids — A breakdown product of sebum
Follicle — Pore; where all acne lesions begin

Genes — Determiners of hereditary characteristics; found on chromosomes
Genetics — The science of heredity

Hormone — A chemical secreted by a gland

Hydrate — To add water to

Hyperkeratosis — A thickening of the dead cell layer of the skin

Hyperpigmentation — A darkening of the skin color

Hypoallergenic — Less allergenic; less likely to cause allergy

Hypopigmentation — A lightening of the skin color

Hypothalamus — A portion of the brain that influences the pituitary gland

Incision — A cut

Inflammation — Tissue response to illness, injury or infection; characterized by redness, swelling, pain and heat

Ingest — To absorb or swallow

Intralesional — (Injected) into a lesion

Intramuscular — (Injected) into a muscle

Iodide — A chemical thought by some to cause acne

Keloid — A protruding scar

Lesion — Any blemish (comedones, papules, pustules, cysts, etc.)

Lincomycin — An antibiotic helpful in acne but that may be dangerous when taken internally

Lipid — A fat

Macule — A flat red spot

Melanin — Normal skin pigment responsible for skin color

Microcomedo — A beginning plug in a follicle, microscopic in size

Microscopic — So small as to require a microscope to see it

Minocycline — An antibiotic used to treat acne

Moisturizer — An oily or greasy substance designed to hold water in the skin

Nodule — A large red bump

Occlude — To seal or cover

Over-the-counter (OTC) — Available without a prescription

Papule — A small red bump

Pituitary gland — The master hormone-producing gland of the body, it controls all the other hormone-producing glands

Placebo — A "sugar pill"; a "placebo response" refers to a beneficial response not related to active treatment; improvement in a disease just because the patient expects to get better; improvement due only to the mental attitude of the patient

Polyporous comedo — A comedo with more than one opening to the surface

Pomade — An ointment used to groom the hair

Pustule — A small red bump with a central yellowish-white cap

Resorcinol — A drying-peeling chemical

Retinoic acid — A drying-peeling chemical available only by prescription. Also called vitamin A acid or tretinoin

Ringing — Applying a caustic chemical to the edges of an acne scar

Salicylic acid — A drying-peeling chemical

Sebaceous glands — The oil glands of the skin

Sebum — The oily or greasy substance produced by the skin's sebaceous or oil glands

Secondary comedo — A comedo that ruptured but became reencapsulated

Sinus tract — A serious, chronic acne lesion

Stress — Anxiety, worry, tension, pressure, psychological trauma; being uptight

Sulfur — A drying-peeling chemical

Systemic — Medication taken internally (shots or pills); to be distinguished from medication applied topically

Tetracycline — The most common antibiotic used to treat acne

Time bomb — A closed comedo

Topical — Applied to the top or surface of the skin

Tretinoin — A drying-peeling chemical available only by prescription. Also called vitamin A acid or retinoic acid

Ultraviolet light — Artificial sunlight; a sunlamp

Vaginitis — A vaginal infection usually with an accompanying vaginal discharge

Vitamin A acid — A drying-peeling chemical available only by prescription. Also called retinoic acid or tretinoin

Whitehead — A confusing term for closed comedones, not used in the text

Index